THE REBEL KING AND THE RIDER

"Are you sure you are all right?" she felt the need to ask. She reached over and gently stroked the marks still on his neck from the torc.

"I'm fine. Because I'm breathing. And that's thanks to you."

Kachka folded her arms across her chest. "That is thanks to me. And yet I still do not have your kingdom."

"You have my everlasting loyalty."

"The loyalty of a one-eyed rebel king who is allied with two mad queens?" She shrugged. "I could definitely do worse."

They smiled at each other just as the bedroom door swung open. Kachka, her hand on the hilt of her sword, turned at her waist and stared at Celyn. "What?" she asked when he just stared at her.

"Everything all right?" he asked, dark eyes moving back and forth between Kachka and the king.

"Well," the king replied, "she is being rather difficult."

Kachka faced Gaius. "I am difficult?"

"I have needs and you're not fulfilling them."

Other titles in the Dragon Kin series by G.A. Aiken

Published by Kensington Publishing Corporation

FEEL THE BURN

G.A. AIKEN

ZEBRA BOOKS
KENSINGTON PUBLISHING CORP.
http://www.kensingtonbooks.com

ZEBRA BOOKS are published by

Kensington Publishing Corp.
119 West 40th Street
New York, NY 10018

All Kensington titles, imprints, and distributed lines are available at special quantity discounts for bulk purchases for sales
promotion, premiums, fund-raising, educational, or institu-
tional use.

Special book excerpts or customized printings can also be created to fit specific needs. For details, write or phone the office
of the Kensington Sales Manager: Attn.: Sales Department.
Kensington Publishing Corp., 119 West 40th Street, New York,
NY 10018. Phone: 1-800-221-2647.

First Printing: December 2015
ISBN-13: 978-1-4201-3161-1
ISBN-10: 1-4201-3161-3

eISBN-13: 978-1-4201-3162-8
eISBN-10: 1-4201-3162-1

10 9 8 7 6 5 4 3 2 1

Printed in the United States of America

Prologue

The Mad Queen of Garbhán Isle's scream of rage echoed out over the silent valley, sending birds from trees and small animals deeper into their burrows.

Her rage was a horrifying wonder to behold because it was always so raw. So unmistakably vicious. Truly, there was nothing more terrifying than to see that rage directed at an individual or full army. But, at the moment, there was no individual or army for the queen to direct her rage at. They were long gone.

Thankfully, the queen did not redirect her anger toward those closest to her. That was why they all willingly fought by her side. Because as mad as the queen might be, she was never wantonly cruel.

One of the few beings willing to try to reason with the queen when she was in a rage moved her mare closer. The female wasn't human, although she was currently in her exquisite human form. No. She was a She-dragon. Her long white hair draped over the entire backside of her horse, her sharp blue eyes aware of everything around her. Yet if you didn't know the truth about her, you wouldn't guess that under that slim bit of human flesh rested a large white dragon that could render a man in pieces with one swipe of her claw.

"Annwyl?" she called out. "Annwyl?" she tried again.

But the queen couldn't hear her or anyone. She was too busy beating the trunk of a tree with one of her swords. It wasn't helping, though. The action wasn't wearing her out. If anything, it was just making her more pissed off.

The She-dragon glanced back at the squad of soldiers. She seemed embarrassed. Her pale cheeks turning red. But they were the Queen's Personal Guard. They understood Annwyl the Bloody better than anyone. They saw her in battle. They saw her in quiet times. They saw her at her worst and best. The only one who knew her better than her personal guard? Her mate, the black dragon, Fearghus the Destroyer.

"Annwyl, this isn't helping."

The queen slammed her blade into the ground and rested her hands on her hips, her head down, her breath coming out in hard pants.

"I know that," the queen finally barked at the white She-dragon. "Don't you think I know that?"

"I think they were looking for something," their general announced as he walked away from the remains of the temple.

General Brastias was a hero of many wars and in charge of Annwyl's armies. He could, like many generals before him, send men out to do this sort of thing while enjoying the comfort and safety of Garbhán Isle, the seat of power of the Southlands. But his continuing loyalty to Annwyl and the She-dragon, Morfyd the White, was so very strong that he still rode with them on missions like this.

Morfyd—one of the Dragon Queen's offspring, so actually a princess—looked down at her mate, her hand brushing her horse's neck to soothe its tension. "Looking for what?" she asked Brastias.

"I have no idea, but the interior has been torn apart."

"Perhaps they were just leaving a message."

"No." Annwyl shook her head. "They want something."

"Annwyl, they've been destroying temples for months now. Let's not make this into some kind of crazy conspiracy when they're simply trying to damage your reputation among your people."

"It's more than that. I know it is." Annwyl yanked her blade out of the ground and slammed it back into the empty sheath she had strapped to her back. "None of this is working," she complained, stomping toward her battle horse, Bloodletting. "They're always ahead of us because we have no idea what they plan to do next."

"So what do you suggest? We already have spies—"

Annwyl grunted. Not because she was mounting that vicious stallion of hers, but because she didn't want to hear anything else from anyone.

"I don't want to hear about Dagmar's and Keita's legions of spies. This isn't about politics, Morfyd. This isn't about propaganda. This is something else."

She looked over the remains of the burned temple, green-grey eyes glaring out from under thick light brown hair. "I'm tired of this, Morfyd."

"Annwyl—"

"I'm tired of this."

"Don't do anything stupid."

Another grunt as Annwyl turned her horse around. "Give them proper death rites," she ordered, motioning to the temple priests, who'd been tortured before they'd been killed. The cult that did this torture and murder called it "purifying." It was reserved for those who refused to join them in their devotion to the god called The Eyeless One, Chramnesind. "Then burn the bodies."

"What are you going to—?"

But Annwyl and her horse had already charged off. Brastias nodded at a few of the men, those who'd ridden longest with Annwyl and were already well-acquainted with her bouts of rage, silently ordering them to follow their queen. Not to keep her safe . . . but to protect anyone unfortunate enough to cross her path. Especially since the queen didn't look or act like a royal. In this state, it was easy for her to misinterpret a small argument between farmers as some kind of rebel attack.

"What if she's right?" Brastias asked his mate while the rest of the men dismounted and went to work. "What if this isn't about simply making her look bad?"

The She-dragon shrugged deceptively slim shoulders. "Then the gods help us all if they find whatever they're looking for before we do."

PART ONE

Chapter One

Kachka Shestakova, formerly of the Black Bear Riders of the Midnight Mountains of Despair in the Far Reaches of the Steppes of the Outerplains, gazed blindly over the beautiful lands she'd been living in for near on six months now. Lots of grass and trees and fresh water lakes. Ample food supplies and happy people ruled by a benevolent ruler.

Horse gods of Ramsfor! It was like hell on earth!

And Kachka had no one to blame but herself. She'd given up her painful, harsh life as a Daughter of the Steppes when she'd saved her sister from their mother. It was still a decision she'd make again if she had to, but she'd never thought that her life would end like this. She'd assumed that their mother would have tracked them down and killed them both. Kachka had been wrong. Her mother never had the chance because she'd come face to face with Annwyl the Bloody, Queen of the Southlands.

The royal had killed Glebovicha Shestakova, cut off her head, and ripped the eyes from the skull. All in front of the Anne Atli, leader of the Outerplains Tribes. It had been a bold move on the queen's part. Or, as those closest to the queen had said more than once, "a completely insane move." Kachka didn't know. She didn't talk to the queen. Or really anyone unless she absolutely had to.

All of Garbhán Isle was littered with dragons in human form. She couldn't tell one from another without her sister's help. Kachka didn't hate the dragons. She just didn't understand why a human would mate with one as they would a man. True, men were mostly useless, but they served their purpose: trash removal, child rearing, and breeding.

Although in the past few decades, the breeding part had changed where dragons and humans were concerned. The queen herself had a set of twins who were half human and half dragon. And it was because of them—and the other offspring that came after—that the humans' gods had turned on their worshippers. Leaving them to fight the followers of Chramnesind by themselves.

It was shaping up to be quite the long-lasting war from what Kachka could tell. The Southlanders and the inhabitants of the Quintilian Sovereigns Empire were unwilling to give up their multitude of gods. And those who did choose to follow Chramnesind were unwilling to let the others worship anyone else. Armies were being built. Battle plans arranged.

And Kachka wasn't involved in any of it.

That didn't really surprise her, though. She wasn't of these lands. She was a Rider, and her people's fighting style and reasons for fighting were vastly different. The Anne Atli and the Daughters of the Steppes did have an alliance with Queen Annwyl and the Southlanders, but it was less about fighting by the Southlanders side and more about not stopping the Southlanders and their other allies from traipsing through Outerplains territory when necessary.

What dug into Kachka's soul more than anything, though, was that before her sister had returned home with that request to speak to the Anne Atli—the title given to all their leaders since the first Anne Atli wrestled power away from the useless men—on Queen Annwyl's behalf, Kachka had been moving up through the ranks at a nice, steady pace. She would never have been the Anne Atli, but she could have led her own troops into battle. Perhaps sat in on the all-tribes meetings when large decisions were made.

In other words . . . she'd have had a purpose.

Kachka needed a purpose. She needed a goal. She needed to make a name for herself. Their mother had never liked Kachka or her sister, but Kachka's skill and willingness to throw herself into battle couldn't be denied.

Where did that leave her here?

Of course, she could join the Queen's Army, but marching in formation and taking orders from mostly men . . . no. Never!

She was a Daughter of the Steppes, not some sheep blinded to the decadent life offered in these Southland territories.

Which left Kachka . . . where? Exactly?

"Um . . . excuse me? My lady?"

Kachka cringed at the ridiculous moniker these Southlanders insisted on using. She'd gotten tired of correcting them, so she let out a breath and snapped, "What?"

"Margo"—the leader of the kitchen staff—"was wondering if you could perhaps, if you're not too busy, round up some meat for us? Some of the Cadwaladrs will be attending dinner tonight and the butchers don't have enough to feed them all. You know what hearty eaters dragons are. So she was just—"

As the sheep went on—begging—and Kachka stared her in the face, she raised her bow, an arrow already nocked and ready, and shot the first thing she saw from the corner of her eye. The bison cried out once before dropping to its knees and bleeding out from the wound on its neck.

"Anything else?" Kachka asked.

The woman was pale now, her head shaking in answer.

Disgusted—hunting was not a challenge for a Daughter of the Steppes; it was more like breathing—Kachka turned away and started walking.

"Kachka?" She stopped and looked over her shoulder to see her sister.

"Fuck," Kachka muttered as her sister walked over to her.

"You can't be nice?" Elina asked in their native tongue.

Kachka's sister wore a bright purple eye patch where her left eye should be. It had been the last thing their mother had taken from Elina. Over time, she'd grown accustomed to the loss, her skills at using her bow improving day after day. But the eye patches . . . this ridiculous purple one could have only come from that idiotic She-dragon, Keita. Her obsession with what Elina wore bordered on the disturbing. Wasn't it bad enough the Shestakova sisters had already become decadent and lazy? Must they also become pathetic as well?

"I was nice," Kachka replied, but when Elina pursed her lips, Kachka threw up her hands. "What more do you want from me, sister?"

"How about not terrifying the staff?"

"You mean the sheep?"

"And stop calling them that! You know they hate it!"

Gaius Lucius Domitus, Iron dragon and the one-eyed Rebel King from the west, rolled that one eye and continued out of the back halls of the Senate and toward the royal palace. He had important plans to make and he didn't have time for yet another discussion about his poor kingly skills.

"I think you're a fool to do this."

"Thank you, Auntie. I appreciate your confidence."

"Don't get that tone with me."

"What tone?"

Lætitia Clydia Domitus grabbed Gaius's arm and yanked him around. She was a small She-dragon and ridiculously tiny in her human form, but there was a power to her. There had to be in order for her to have survived as long as she had. There were few who had survived Overlord Thracius's reign while openly loathing him, but Lætitia had managed. Somehow.

"First off—" she began.

"Gods," Gaius groaned. "There's a first off."

"—you shouldn't be walking around these streets alone. You're the king now. That makes you a clear target. Second, you're *king* now. You can't run off on stupid errands every time you get a bug up your ass. You have an empire to rule."

"An empire that will no longer exist if I don't get control of my cousins and, more importantly, squash the rise of Chramnesind cults."

"I don't disagree with you, but I don't know why you need to go yourself. You have dragons and men at your disposal. Why do you not use them?"

"Why? Because I trust no one. Except my sister." When his aunt groaned and rolled her eyes at the mention of Agrippina, Gaius gently pulled his arm out of her grasp and walked away.

"Wait! I didn't mean it like that."

"Yes, you did."

"No. I didn't. I love your sister—" Gaius snorted at that, and Lætitia gripped his arm again and yanked him around to face her with even more strength than he'd given her credit for. "Do not, *boy*, question my loyalty to you or your sister. Ever. You two are the only thing left of the one sibling I adored, and that means something. But your sister went through hell. Absolute hell. And she hasn't recovered from it, no matter how much both of you want to pretend that she has. So leaving the throne in her claws while you go off to be the hero king seems a . . . risky decision at best."

"Well then . . . I guess . . ." Gaius glanced off, pretended to think a minute. "You'll just have to give her your guidance while I'm gone."

From the corner of his one eye, he saw his aunt desperately try to hide a smile. It wasn't an evil smile. She, unlike most of his kin, was not evil. But, for the first time, she felt she'd be allowed to use her knowledge and skills directly rather than behind the scenes, which was usually where one could find her. Her machinations had been legendary, but they were often attributed to one of her other siblings. Of course, it was her willingness not to be openly involved that had kept her alive this long.

"Your sister," Lætitia finally said, "won't like that."

"Of course she will," Gaius lied. "She respects you, Auntie."

"Good gods, Gaius Lucius Domitus!" she cried out. "You're just like your father—such a liar!"

Bickering, the sisters began to head back to the queen's castle, but Kachka realized that the kitchen staff person was struggling to drag the bison back with her. Annoyed—at everyone!—Kachka grabbed one leg of the dead animal and her sister grabbed the other. Together, they yanked the bison back to the house, arguing all the way, while the girl was forced to run in order to keep up.

"I just don't understand why you're so unhappy," Elina said, yanking the bison over a ridge. "There's plenty of food and water and soft beds to sleep in."

"You don't have to remind me of how pathetic we've become, sister."

"How is enjoying a few amenities pathetic?"

"The fact that you have to ask that upsets me more than you'll ever know."

"Then find something to do, Kachka, rather than sitting around glaring at everyone."

"What can I do here?" Kachka demanded. "What is there for me to do? Farm?" She stopped, glared at her sister. "Is that what you want me to be? A farmer? Like some . . . man? Is that what you think of me? That I'm a worthless *man*?"

"Of course not! I'd never say that. But perhaps you can talk to the Northlander, Dagmar Reinholdt. She is always up to something."

"She hates me," Kachka reminded her sister.

"Well, maybe if you hadn't fucked her nephew . . ."

"*He was there!*"

They began dragging the bison carcass again.

"There has to be something *constructive* you can do," her sister went on. "I'm sure General Brastias would be more than happy to have you—"

Kachka stopped again, now only a few feet from the queen's home. "Take orders from a *man*? Have you lost your mind?" she yelled. "*Has everyone lost their mind?*"

As if in answer, the queen herself rode up to the steps of the castle, dismounted from her oversized black steed—honestly, who needed that much horse?—walked up a couple of steps, then abruptly stopped.

That's when the queen suddenly screamed. And screamed. And screamed some more.

Everyone who had been going about their day ran when they heard that scream. Soldiers. Merchants. Nursing mothers. Everyone. They ran and hid.

"That answers my question," Kachka muttered.

"Shut up."

The queen disappeared into her home, and Kachka and Elina finished dragging the bison all the way to the kitchens.

Once they dropped it off, they returned to the deserted Main
Hall.

Kachka stood there a moment before announcing, "See?
There's *nothing* to do!"

Gaius walked into the palace that now belonged to him
and his twin. The original palace, the one his cousin Vateria
and her father, Overlord Thracius, had ruled from, had been
torn down. It had been partially destroyed during his sister
Aggie's rescue; then Gaius and a few chosen dragon friends
had ripped apart the rest of it. He would never let that palace
stand, no matter how many of his kin had lived and ruled
there. Not after his sister had been held captive in that place
by the bitch Vateria. They had been raised with their cousin
Vateria, but from the beginning they'd never been close with
her. Never trusted her. Definitely never liked her. And then,
when their father was murdered by his own brother, Gaius
had made it his goal to one day challenge Thracius for the
throne. But, when he was old enough—and strong enough—
to make that challenge, that's when Vateria, always so very
smart, had captured Aggie and held her hostage in the old
palace. She knew it was the one way to control Gaius. To
"keep him in his place," as she liked to say. It had worked,
too. And Aggie had been in a tolerable situation, as she was
still royal born and niece of Thracius. But then Thracius
went to war with the Southlanders, taking on the Dragon
Queen, leaving his bitch daughter alone with Aggie. For five
long, painful years.

Aggie refused to talk about what had happened, but some
nights she woke up screaming. Some nights she didn't sleep
at all.

And yes, Gaius blamed himself, although he knew Aggie

never did. But how could he not blame himself? His poor, weak, defenseless sister trapped in the web of that evil—

"You!" Aggie gripped Gaius's throat, causing him to gag before yanking him into another room. "Excuse us, Lætitia," she told their aunt before slamming the door in Lætitia's stunned face.

"What have you done?" his sister demanded.

"That's vague."

"There are Mì-runach in our throne room. Why?"

"Mì-runach?" Warriors who answered to absolutely no one but the Dragon Queen herself? "Are you sure?"

"Of course I'm sure. Now why are they here?"

"I don't . . . oh." Gaius cringed. "Oh."

"What have you done?"

"I had your best interests at heart."

"You idiot," Aggie sighed out just as Lætitia knocked on the door and quickly entered.

She closed the door, turned to her niece and nephew, and announced, "There are peasants in your throne room. Southland peasants!"

"They're Mì-runach," Aggie told her and gestured to Gaius. "That this idiot requested."

"Gaius!"

"I did *not* request them."

"Then what did you do?" his sister demanded.

"I requested help from the Dragon Queen, but . . ."

"But?"

"But I thought she'd send Cadwaladrs." The Cadwaladrs were a Southland clan of Low Born dragons trained from hatching in the ways of war and defense of the Dragon Queen's territories. They might not be respected, but they were greatly feared. And with reason.

"Why would you want those pit dogs here any more than you'd want the Mì-runach?"

"You need protection."

Aggie suddenly stood tall, her spine straight, her long steel-colored hair reaching down her back in intricate braids and curls. She looked amazingly regal, which was how she always looked when she was getting defensive. "Why would I need protection?"

"Because he's going off on a fool's errand, that's why."

Gaius briefly closed his eyes. "Lætitia," he sighed.

"What? I'm not lying. Tell me I'm lying," she ordered. "Tell me."

If Lætitia hoped to get Aggie on her side, she'd just failed because now the twins were giggling. Like they used to when they were hatchlings.

"The two of you! I swear by the gods."

Aggie cleared her throat. "Aunt Lætitia, could you excuse us?"

"You're sending me back out there? With those plebeians?"

"Or you could just go to your room. But you need to go . . . you know . . . *away*."

Lætitia snatched the door open, gazed back at her niece and nephew. "Hmmph!" she snapped before walking out, making sure she slammed the door in the process.

"Mind telling me what's going on?" Aggie asked. "You know I hate when Lætitia knows more than me. It gives her way too much enjoyment. And we both know that I can't allow that."

Dagmar Reinholdt was deep in paperwork, scrolls and parchments littering her desk. Ink covering her hands. And six of her best-trained dogs surrounding her. It had been that way since the last attempt on her life nearly seven months ago. Her mate, Gwenvael the Handsome, had insisted. She still had an assistant, but he'd been chosen by Morfyd, who used her magicks to ensure the Northland male sent by her brothers and approved by Dagmar's father had no loyalty except to reason.

The only problem, though . . . he loathed dogs. And, in turn, her dogs loathed him.

So he had his own space in the towers, along with Bram the Merciful, Dagmar's nephew Frederik Reinholdt—who was currently in the Northlands working with the local warlords to ensure they were ready for any attacks from Duke Salebiri and the Chramnesind cult—and Dagmar's only son, Unnvar.

That tower. That ridiculous tower the queen had built had become a hub of thoughtful reason and decisive warplanning. Hard to believe since, for months, Dagmar had assumed the queen had been creating a killing factory for her enemies.

Dagmar's dogs began to growl seconds before the door swung open. Three of them went to leap at the intruder, ready to tear face from body, but Dagmar's calm "No" stopped them. They grudgingly pulled back, still snarling, while the queen strode into the room. Oblivious as always.

"They did it again," the queen growled, patting the dogs that had, moments ago, been ready to tear her into pieces. Unlike Dagmar's assistant, Annwyl loved dogs. All kinds. Even the useless ones.

"Who did what again?" Dagmar asked, not looking up from her work.

"That stupid cult destroyed another one of my temples."

"It's not your temple. You don't even like the gods. And you refuse to worship them."

"It was *my* temple because it was on *my* lands."

Dagmar leaned back in her chair, placing her quill down on the desk and massaging her tired fingers. "So what do you want to do, my queen?"

"What?" Annwyl glared at her. "I'm asking *you*!"

Dagmar shrugged. "I have no opinion. I'd hate to get in the way of your big decision making."

Annwyl frowned in confusion. "What the battle-fuck are you talking about? I don't understand you lately. For months, you've been acting like a total dick!"

"I know my place, Annwyl. I wouldn't want to step on any toes."

Leaning down, Annwyl looked into Dagmar's face through all that hair she insisted on not combing off her face. "What is *wrong* with you?" she asked.

"Nothing, my liege. Do *you* find something wrong with me?" Dagmar blinked a few times. "Perhaps with my eyes?"

Annwyl reared back. "What? What's wrong with your . . . ? What are you going on about?"

Dagmar began to say something, but Annwyl cut her off. "Forget it! I'll figure it out myself!"

She turned on her heel and stormed out, slamming the door behind her.

"Why do you torture her, Mum?"

Dagmar glanced behind her. The youngest five of her seven children were sitting on the floor behind her. No. Dagmar hadn't missed their presence in the room. Instead, her daughters had come through the wall. They, Dagmar had discovered, could do that easily.

One second they weren't there . . . and the next second they were.

Something that was getting harder and harder to hide from the rest of the family.

"I'm not torturing your aunt Annwyl."

"You are," insisted the eldest of Gwenvael's Five, as they were now called by their own ridiculous father. "Ever since she threatened to rip your eyes out. But she didn't mean it the way you think she did."

"These are adult issues that I am *not* discussing with you."

"Except that Grandmum would say you're not acting like an adult."

"Well, your Grandmum can suck my . . . wait." Dagmar turned in the chair at the mention of their grandmother, the Dragon Queen Rhiannon the White, so she could see her daughters clearly. "How often are you talking to your Grandmum when I'm not around?"

The youngest of the five began to speak, but three different hands slapped over her mouth to silence her and, without another word, the girls were gone.

Dagmar faced forward again, placing her hands on her desk and softly noted, "That simply does not bode well, now does it?"

Elina's suggestion that they play a game was not helping Kachka's current emotional state. If anything, it just made her feel even more useless.

Elina studied the game board with her one good eye, debating her next move.

This was the life of the Shestakova sisters now.

Decadent. Lazy. Spoiled. Sitting around. Playing board games like children.

It amazed Kachka that adults played these games. Daughters of the Steppes had their three-year-olds playing these games to help them understand the concept of "divide, conquer, and destroy so that the next city or town over just gives us what we ask for."

So for the two sisters to be playing these games again appalled Kachka on a visceral level. How far she'd fallen back. Would it never get better?

Finally, after much thought, Elina went to make her

move . . . and her hand missed the piece by a few inches. Although, based on Elina's reaction, it might as well have been a mile.

Kachka's sister growled, then she swiped her hand at the board . . . which she also missed.

That's when the entire board went flying, her sister's bellow of rage startling the weak, delusional servants who worked for these rich, decadent royals.

Kachka sighed. "You were winning."

"Shut up!"

Kachka leaned back in her chair. "Such whining. Like baby, you whine!"

"I am still weak!"

"You took down bear last week."

"Took me three shots!"

"That's not eye. That's this life we now live." She pointed at one of the dragons walking by. "Decadent! Like that dragon."

The dragon stopped, placed a hand on his chest. "Me? Kachka, you love me!"

"I love your beauty. I have no use for you personally. You represent all that we hate."

"Why do you talk to him so?" Elina asked. "He cannot help that he is beautiful but worthless."

"I am *not* worthless! I am Gwenvael the—"

"We do not care, lizard!" Kachka barked.

"Do not yell at him!"

"Do not be so pathetic! So you miss eye! Get over it!"

That's when Elina kicked Kachka under the table. So Kachka kicked her back.

"Ow!"

"Whine!"

Elina reached and grabbed Kachka by her leather buckskin shirt. *That* Elina could grip with no problem.

Kachka punched her sister's arm, but that only made Elina drag Kachka out of the chair.

Kachka gripped Elina by her shoulders, shoving her back against the table.

"Stop it! Both of you!" the dragon called out. "I have enough beauty to share with everyone!"

Ignoring the beautiful but useless dragon, Kachka drew back her arm to punch her sister, but it was caught and held.

She assumed it was the dragon, but when she looked, it was the queen who held her. What worried her, though, was the look on the queen's face. She stared at Kachka as if she'd never seen her before.

"You," the queen said.

"What about me?"

She didn't answer at first. Simply stared. Then, suddenly, she yanked Kachka off her sister. "Come with me," she ordered.

"No!" Elina cried out, grabbing Kachka's other arm. "Do not kill her!"

The queen blinked. "What?"

"It is all right, sister," Kachka soothed. "I am ready for death."

"What are you two—?"

"Don't worry," the beautiful dragon tossed in. "I'll make sure you have a gorgeous funeral."

"*Gwenvael!*" Annwyl roared.

"Why are you yelling at me? I didn't do anything. It was the outsider!"

Annwyl yanked Kachka from her sister's grip. "She'll be fine," she snapped before Elina could complain further.

"Do not worry, sister," Kachka said as the queen dragged her off. "I will go to my death bravely!"

* * *

"It could be a trap," Aggie warned.

"I know. But I have to chance it."

Aggie nodded and continued to pace. She appeared worried, and he was sure that, to a degree, she was. But Gaius also knew his sister always appeared worried when she was thinking. Analyzing. She was very good at analyzing.

"Are you going to bring him back here?"

"That's not my plan, sister."

She stopped pacing, her grey eyes locking with his. "Good." She began pacing again. "And what about Vateria?"

"No word on her. None. She could be dead."

"That bitch isn't dead, and we both know it."

"I do know that she was wounded."

Aggie slowed to a stop again and turned toward her brother. "Wounded?"

He shrugged. "According to General Iseabail. She wounded her spine. She could walk but never fly again."

Aggie shook her head. "How long ago was this?"

"It's been a few years."

"And you never told me?"

"I don't like to mention her to you. It upsets you."

"No, brother. It upsets *you*."

"I let her get you."

Aggie laughed. "You didn't *let* her get me. If anything *I* let her get me."

"No—"

"She wanted me. She wouldn't have stopped until she'd gotten me. But that was a long time ago, Gaius. I refuse to live in that nightmare anymore. I refuse to let the past rule me the way it once did."

"Until Vateria's dead, I won't rest," Gaius promised his sister. Again. "But until then . . . killing the rest of our cousins, loyal to *her,* will have to do."

"Are you taking an army with you?"

"No. Just a few of my loyal soldiers. And I will go as a centurion, not as king."

"Good."

"I'll find him. I'll kill him. And I'll put his head on a spike outside our palace walls."

Aggie's mouth curled in disgust. "What are we now? Southlanders?"

They ended up in the stables with the queen's giant horses. Elina called them all "travel cows," which always made Kachka laugh.

The queen dismissed her stable hands and proceeded to brush the hair on the black stallion she referred to as "Blood-letting." A rather disturbing name, even by Rider standards.

Once the queen began brushing the long black hair that swept across the horse's large head, her entire being seemed to calm down. The constant swirl of insanity that always surrounded the queen appeared to drift away.

The fact that the horse was so calm around the queen, trusted her so much, told Kachka more than any words or actions of humans and dragons. There was only honesty from horses.

"So you drag me here, Southlander queen. Why?"

Annwyl glanced at Kachka and gave a small smile. One of the first Kachka could remember seeing from the woman. "You're bored, aren't you, Kachka?"

"Bored? No. Becoming weak and pathetic? Definitely."

"Weak and pathetic? You? Really?" Annwyl nuzzled the horse's snout and the horse nuzzled her back. He'd die for her, Kachka knew from just watching them. Then again,

Kachka was also sure that Annwyl felt the same way. She seemed better with animals. Horses. Dogs. Dragons.

"You gave up a lot when you came here with your sister, didn't you?"

Kachka had given up everything, but she didn't want that to get back to her sister. So, instead, she said, "We all make choices. Then we must live with them."

"You know your sister is safe here. With us. The dragons love her. Even Rhiannon, and she used to eat humans as a treat."

"She sniffs my hair sometimes. It makes me uncomfortable."

"Yeah, don't let her do that too long." Annwyl walked to the stall gate, rested her foot on one slat and her arms on the top, the brush still in her hand. "How would you like a job, Kachka Shestakova?"

"I already hunt your food."

"No, no. A real job."

"I will not join your army, Annwyl the Bloody. I will not take orders from men."

"Yeah, I sensed that when you told the captain of my guards that if he didn't get away from you, you were going to tear off his penis and fuck him with it."

"He is lucky I did not go through with it."

"You need a job. I have one for you."

"What job, if not hunter? Getting dragons their daily meat."

"The Chramnesind cult has been attacking temples all across my lands. Killing the priests and priestesses. Or, as they call it, purifying them. They must be working in small groups because they're in and out in a few hours, leaving nothing but death in their wake. By the time my troops arrive, it's all over."

"Groups?"

"There is more than one because they've been known to attack temples that are leagues apart in a single night."

"And what do you want *me* to do about your cults?"

"Find them. Kill them all. Make sure to leave a nice, bloody message that Duke Salebiri and his Chramnesind cult will know is from me. From what I've seen of you . . . I think that's something you can do."

"You think I am what the world says? A barbarian Rider preferring to kill rather than talk?"

"Yes," the queen immediately replied.

Kachka nodded. "You are right. I am. Now tell me more about your Chramnesind cult, Southland queen."

"I understand all of this except one thing, brother."

"What?"

"Why are the Mì-runach here?"

"Well—"

"No, Gaius. No politics. No centaur shit. Just tell me."

Gaius let out a sigh. "I wanted you to be protected by someone outside the empire. So I sent word to Rhiannon. Asking her to send someone to protect you. I thought that she would send a Cadwaladr. They may not be smart, but they're effective."

"And the crazy bitch sent her Mì-runach instead? That's lovely."

"Well, if anything, they can be trusted. Their loyalty is to their queen, and our alliance with the Southland dragons and the human queen is ironclad."

"So you say."

"One queen is insane and obsessed with proving her honor. The other likes me. You can guess which is which.

The bottom line is . . . I trust them both, and they wouldn't send anyone they couldn't trust themselves. That would embarrass them. Nothing they hate more than being embarrassed." He put his arms around his sister's shoulders, pulled her into his chest, hugged her tight. "But if you don't want me to go—"

"Don't even finish that statement," his sister warned, her voice nearly angry. "I am not a hatchling, Gaius. I'm as strong as you, just different."

"And we rule this empire together."

"Aunt Lætitia won't like that. She thinks it should just be you."

"Lætitia is just a nosey old biddy." Gaius looked at the door and called out, "Who should mind her own business!"

"I'm only trying to help!" Lætitia yelled back. "And stop giggling! You're not hatchlings anymore! You're rulers!"

Kachka tied off her travel pack, slung it, her bow, and a quiver of arrows over her shoulder, and walked out into the hallway. She made her way down to the Great Hall and found her sister sitting on one of the tables, in deep conversation with her mate, the black dragon Celyn. When she saw Kachka, she let out a relieved breath.

"Death found you well this day," she nearly cheered.

"Yes. Now I must go."

"Go? Go where?"

"To find honor or death."

"Morfyd said the queen was upset about the temples on her land. So she is sending you to stop the ones raiding those temples," Elina guessed.

"Yes."

The dragon's back straightened. "Wait . . . what? What are you doing?"

Kachka ignored him, because he was male and this was an important discussion about battle plans. A discussion only women could truly understand.

"Will you bring some of her weak soldiers with you?"

"No, no. She offered them. But what could they do except clomp around and make too much noise, letting all enemies know we are coming. They would be useless. Instead, I return to homeland. Find strong woman to fight by my side."

"Good."

"But it will be dangerous. So if I do not return in the next year or two, and you get no message, assume my death," Kachka stated flatly, "and make sure to perform sacred rites so that I can meet our ancestors in next world."

"I will," Elina promised. "And I will cut my face deep in honor of your death."

"Thank you, sister."

They gripped each other's forearms and nodded, knowing this might be the last time they saw the other alive.

With nothing else to say, Kachka headed toward the big doors.

But she'd only moved a few feet before Celyn barked, "*Is that it?*"

"Is what it?" Elina asked.

"A promise of self-mutilation and a nod? Is that all you have to say when you may never see each other again?"

Elina frowned. "As opposed to what, dolt?"

"I don't know. A hug? A kiss good-bye? Something!"

With a shake of her head, Elina let out a long, pained sigh. "Go, sister. You have important work to do and no time for . . ." She waved her hand at the aghast dragon standing beside her, mouth open in confusion. ". . . whatever *this* is."

"Take good care of your dragon," Kachka said as she

moved on. "He will need your protection, being so weak and pathetic."

"Weak? I am a mighty dragon of the Southland—"

The sisters' combined laughter drowned out the rest of *that* ridiculous statement and sent Kachka off on a better note than she could have ever asked for.

Chapter Two

Egnatius Domitus couldn't sleep. He had too much to do. He'd been promised so much and he planned to get everything he'd been promised. Even if that meant worshipping a god he couldn't give a fat cock about.

These religious types with their bullshit rules and beliefs. It meant nothing to Egnatius. Really. He could not possibly care less about any god. What was important to him, the *only* thing important to him, was being overlord of the Quintilian Sovereigns. The throne was his by right. By hatching. And, most importantly, because he fucking *wanted* it.

His idiot cousin now ruled. Not as overlord, though. No, no. He was too "good" to be an overlord. He was *King* Gaius. Who wanted to be king when they could be overlord? When they could rule the *world* instead of just a small portion of it?

But his cousin had always tried too hard to be evenhanded. What, exactly, had that gotten him? A temporary spot as king.

What was funny, though . . . Egnatius's cousin was far from "evenhanded." He clearly remembered those dark days after Gaius's twin sister had been taken by Vateria. The damage that had been done. The blood that had been splattered across good chunks of the Empire. Gaius hadn't been able to go after Vateria directly. No. That would have only guaranteed to get his sister killed quicker. So he'd taken his rage out on everyone else.

It was, perhaps, the first and only time that Egnatius had ever respected his cousin. Seeing the damage he'd done. Smirking at the bodies that had been piled up out of frustration. It had earned Gaius the title Rebel King.

A lot of people thought Gaius had lost his eye during those dark times, but he hadn't. It had been Thracius who'd ripped the eye from Gaius's head when he'd still been a hatchling. Thracius hadn't even blinked when Gaius had screamed in pain, his twin using her own body and wings in an attempt to shield her brother. But it had been too late. While they watched, Thracius had toasted that eye with his flame before gulping it down . . . and smiling. Then he'd gone on with his day.

That was Thracius's style back then, and it would be Egnatius's style when he became overlord. He'd lead as his father had. With fear and hatred and a touch of rage.

But first he had work to do. First he had to—

The blade didn't go all the way through. . . . It just slammed into his spine, severing nerves, so his legs went out from under him as they lost the ability to feel. But Egnatius didn't hit the ground; his cousin's human arm was around him, holding him up.

"Hello, cousin," Gaius whispered into his ear as his Praetorian Guard attacked Egnatius's. "It's been so very long."

Kachka stared at the four Riders that the Anne Atli had allowed her to have.

After several minutes, while other tribe leaders watched,

she finally said to the Anne Atli's second in command, "You must be joking."

"I do not know what you mean," Magdalina Fyodorov replied.

Making sure to sound particularly disappointed—she had a lot to pull off in a short amount of time. She had to handle this just right—Kachka asked, "These are the best you can spare?"

"Watch what you say, Kachka Shestakova," a voice murmured. "At least my sister wasn't run out of here by our own mother."

Kachka didn't even look to see who spoke. Instead, she kept her focus on Magdalina. For many reasons she did this, but mostly because it was dangerous to turn one's back on Magdalina.

"My list clearly requested—"

"Your list?" Magdalina asked. "The list where you requested some of our best warriors to go off with you on a suicide mission for some imperialist queen? Did you really think the Anne Atli would give up her best people for something so ridiculous? No. Instead, we give you these. You'll be happy with them . . . for the short time you will all live."

"You do know we're right here?" a male voice asked. "We can *hear* you."

"Take what you've been given, Kachka Shestakova, and be glad for it."

Kachka gave a heavy, dramatic sigh, "Fine. If there is nothing else."

"There isn't."

Kachka began to walk away when another of the tribe leaders exited the Anne Atli's tent and whispered in Magdalina's ear.

Kachka watched Magdalina's eyes widen. For Southlanders, it would be a "look of concern." But for a Daughter of the Steppes, it was more a look of horror.

"Wait . . . wait here," Magdalina ordered Kachka before returning to the Anne Atli's tent.

Kachka did wait, unable to hear much beyond the sound of Magdalina's voice debating something with a much quieter Anne Atli. Because when one ruled the Steppes, there was no need to yell.

As she waited, Kachka looked over at the four warriors she'd been given to work with.

Marina Aleksandrovna. A truly solid fighter who had one major flaw. She questioned the way the Riders lived their lives. Not roughing it on the harsh Steppes. That wasn't her issue. But the way they treated the males they took, and the harsh way they dealt with the towns and cities outside the Steppes. This particular flaw made her a real pain in the ass to work with.

Then there were the Khoruzhaya siblings. Both excellent trackers and hunters. Better than even Kachka, which she knew was saying much. But they weren't sisters. They were a brother and sister, born only a year apart, and the boy . . . he thought being born into the tribe made him equal to the women. It didn't. Even worse, his foolish sister followed along with that thinking, allowing her brother to speak out at tribal events rather than punching him in the mouth to shut him up as Kachka had been known to do to her own brothers and male cousins. She did it to help them. To keep them safe until they were chosen to be husbands. But Yelena Khoruzhaya's indulgence just made Ivan feel still more empowered. Even worse, she protected him from her sisters and female cousins. In the end, Yelena and Ivan had only each other to rely on.

And, finally—and not surprisingly—one of Kachka's own: Tatyana Shestakova. A cousin loathed because of her love of Southland ways. She'd taught herself the common tongue of the Southlander so well, even perfecting the accent, that no one from those territories could tell that she wasn't local. She even went so far as to favor the clothes of the Southlander and the decadent lifestyle, often wishing—out loud—that she had a "proper bed to sleep in."

"What is happening here?" a voice boomed. "What am I missing?"

Ivan Khoruzhaya let out a bone-deep sigh. "Horse gods of Ramsfor, not her."

Kachka had to agree. She'd hoped to be gone long before . . . *this*.

"What is all this?" the voice continued to ask as a very large body pushed its way through the crowd. It was only seconds before Zoya Kolesova stood before Elina. Towering over Kachka, Zoya gazed down at her from her lofty height. "Kachka Shestakova of the Black Bear Riders of the Midnight Mountains of Despair in the Far Reaches of the Steppes of the Outerplains?" she asked. "Whatever are you doing here? I thought you were tragically banished to the decadent world of the Southlands, never to be seen again!"

Kachka gazed up at the much larger woman. Even larger than her mother Glebovicha had been. Large and, like all of the Kolesovas, strong. Not strong like most of the Riders who had to live in the harsh Outerplains, but . . . *strong*. It was rumored that one of the earliest Kolesovas, determined to fight by the first Anne Atli's side, had sacrificed her favorite husband to the horse gods in hopes of being "as strong as the man I've just killed."

The gods must have liked the sacrifice because they did more than that. They'd not only made that Kolesova bigger and stronger than *any* man, but they'd done the same with the female offspring she had later in life. Now that strength and size was passed down from mother to daughter, again and again.

It seemed strange to outsiders that none of the Kolesovas,

with all their physical strength, had ever once been the Anne Atli. But that was because they all shared a truly fatal flaw. . . .

Zoya threw open her arms and swept Kachka up in a big bear hug, lifting her off her feet and nearly crushing her ribs in the process.

"I am so glad to see you, old friend!" Although they'd never been friends. Old or otherwise. "I thought for sure you were dead! I'm so glad you're not! I'm so very happy!"

Yes. *That* was the problem. The gods-damn good nature of the Kolesovas. There wasn't one of that tribe who didn't find *something* to smile about. Laugh about. Rejoice about. Every day. All the time.

But, outsiders often asked, despite their good nature, with their strength and size and the number in their tribe, still at least *one* of them could have become the Anne Atli. So, why had they not?

Simply put . . . because they had no desire to be. They were just happy to battle occasionally. Drink a lot. And fuck their many husbands. On a battlefield, they were a blessing. Any other time . . . a complete cheery pain in the ass.

Kachka fought her way out of Zoya's smothering embrace and lied. "Glad to see you as well, old friend."

Again, they had never been friends. But Kachka didn't want Zoya to feel she had to *prove* how close friends they once were. That could be painful. Very, very painful.

"Why are you here?" Zoya asked, her voice still booming. "Returning to the Tribes, are you?"

"No, no. Just need a small team to help me on a—"

"I'll come!" Zoya volunteered.

"No!" all five of them yelled.

"Ha-ha! You all make me laugh so! This will be such fun!"

That was another thing about the Kolesovas. They were never insulted. In more than a thousand years, they never once had a blood feud with anyone. Kachka didn't know how that was possible. Even Glebovicha, who had had blood feuds with pretty much everyone, never had a blood feud with the Kolesovas. Because every insult she passed their way, they'd laughed about, slapping her on the back—and nearly shattering her spine in the process—and going on their merry way.

"What about your children, Zoya?" Kachka asked, desperate to keep her here.

"All one hundred and forty-seven of them," Tatyana softly announced, eyebrows raised at Kachka.

"Yes," Kachka said, trying not to show her shock at that number. Even for a Daughter of the Steppes who might easily live over a thousand years . . . that was gods-damn excessive! "What about *all* of them?"

"That's what my husbands are for! They raise the girls while I am gone and the older girls will protect them all!"

"This is pretty much a suicide mission," Ivan offered.

"Quiet, boy," Zoya coldly snapped at Ivan. "No one speaks to you."

And that's what kept the Kolesovas in good standing with the other tribes despite their good-natured attitudes: their complete and utter lack of respect for anything with a penis.

Magdalina finally returned, her face . . . pale. And she suddenly refused to meet Kachka's eyes.

"If you want what we have offered you here, there is . . . one other you *must* take."

Must? Gods, what ineffectual loser were they trying to force on her?

"Really?" Kachka asked. "Who?"

* * *

Gaius forced his cousin to watch while his soldiers were slaughtered. It wasn't a short fight—Egnatius's soldiers were good—but it was still a battle they would not win.

As his soldiers finished off the last few, Gaius pushed the blade still rammed into Egnatius's back deeper, and said against his cousin's ear, "If you want me to end this quick, cousin, you'll have to tell me what I want to know."

"Know?"

"Where's Vateria? I want Vateria. Your sister will *never* escape paying for what she did to Agrippina."

"I'll tell you nothing," Egnatius shot back.

Gaius wasn't shocked by this. Egnatius was one of the stronger of Thracius's offspring. He would not go down easy.

Something he quickly proved when he rammed his elbow into Gaius's face, forcing him back. Briefly free, Egnatius dropped to the ground, but quickly shifted from human to dragon. His legs might be dead, but not his wings.

He lifted himself up, hovering off the ground, and yanking his sword from its sheath.

"Come, cousin!" he ordered Gaius. "Let us see the good king fight."

Gaius nodded. "As you wish."

Kachka found the one to be forced upon her in one of the only wooden huts in tribal territory.

Wooden huts were not usually built because they took additional time to breakdown when the tribes went on the move. More important, they weren't nearly as warm as the yurts.

But, every once in a while, there was a call for a wood hut. For it was to these dwellings that those who had wronged their own were sent. The Southlanders would call it a prison.

The Riders called it, "The place for those who cannot be killed."

This hut wasn't filled with criminals the way the South-landers' prisons were. Instead, there was only one inhabitant. A woman. On her knees, her arms bound in chains. The chains were secured to the ceiling so that her arms were raised above her head and stretched wide apart. This was to keep her from using her hands for anything.

More chains were wrapped around her ankles, and the chains stretched across the floor and were staked to the ground by thick metal spikes.

There was no light in the hut. No fire to warm. Just the prisoner.

Nina Chechneva, the Unclaimed.

Unclaimed because no tribe would have her. The tribe she'd been born to had disowned her nearly two hundred years before. And no other would take her in. So she was nothing more than Nina Chechneva.

As soon as Kachka walked into the hut, she knew that Nina sensed her.

Without lifting her bowed head, she said, "Kachka Shes-takova. I knew you were coming."

"Did your dark gods tell you that, Nina Chechneva?" Kachka asked as she carefully moved closer.

"No. Just the damned souls who roam these lands. Lost and desperate and so ripe for my use."

She said that last bit on a hissing little whisper. Over her three hundred and thirty-six years, Nina had terrified many with that hissing whisper. She'd been using it to her advan-tage since before she could walk, terrifying even her birth mother, who had given her up to the shamans of the tribe not long afterward. But after a time, even their shamans had wanted nothing to do with Nina Chechneva. No one had.

So they'd tried to kill her. Many times. Her own mother

had attempted to bury the first blade in Nina's chest. But, instead, she'd buried it into a mighty oak that had abruptly appeared where the child had been standing, the blade breaking on impact. Then, suddenly, Nina Chechneva had been standing behind her mother, and the five-year-old had slammed her mother head-first into that tree.

Was all that true? Kachka didn't know. Every Rider child was fed stories like these from birth. But true or not, Nina Chechneva was feared by all. Not because she'd embraced the magicks of these lands. Riders appreciated magicks as much as anyone and those who were gifted by the gods were looked upon with slight envy and great respect.

But Nina Chechneva hadn't been blessed by the gods. Her dark soul had been tainted by something else. And the longer she'd managed to live, the more she'd been hated.

So now, the Anne Atli was using Kachka to get rid of that which she could not get rid of herself.

Steadying her nerves, Kachka went down on one knee in front of Nina. She placed two fingers under the woman's chin and lifted until their eyes met. Those dark, soulless eyes, filled with hate. Not the casual hate of someone hated by her own people. But the hate of everyone she encountered. Nina, it was said, absorbed that hate to use when she cast spells. Now that hatred swirled through her body like blood.

"You have so few choices, Nina Chechneva. You can stay here, an outsider among your own—"

"Just like your sister. Does she miss her eye terribly? Does she cry for it at night, tears only dripping from her *one* remaining eye?"

Unwilling to ask how she'd known about that—no one talked to Nina Chechneva if they could help it, not even to gossip—Kachka went on as if she hadn't heard her. "—or you can join me."

"What makes you think you can trust me any more than anyone else, Kachka Shestakova, no longer of the Black Bear Riders of the Midnight Mountains of Despair in the Far Reaches of the Steppes of the Outerplains?"

"The Tribes are giving you a chance to live. Outside of this hut that they've built specifically for you. To allow you to breathe fresh air. To be free of these chains. But they offer you nothing more. The Cult of Chramnesind, however? They won't even give you that. When they take over, even your dark gods will not protect you. But join us and you'll have a chance to stop them. Then, when this is all done, you can go to your dark gods. You can become one with them and do whatever you and your dark gods do. Free from tyranny."

Kachka gripped Nina's chin tight until the woman couldn't help but wince from the pain. "I promise you, Nina Chechneva, the Unclaimed. You will get no better offer than this. From anyone."

"But?"

"But you will swear to your dark gods at the risk of your unholy soul that your loyalty will be to me and to our team. No one else."

"And what of your mad Southland queen? She thinks her tormented soul is too good for the likes of me. She won't be happy."

"My loyalty is to the Mad Queen of Garbhán Isle. Your loyalty will be to *us*. But you must swear it, Daughter of Darkness. You must swear it."

Nina's eyes cut across the room. She took in a deep breath and slowly let it out. When she was done, "Fine."

"*Swear it.*"

Her eyes ripped back to Kachka's face. Kachka saw all that hate there. More than usual, actually. But it didn't surprise her. She'd never seen Nina Chechneva look any other way.

"I swear it. On my soul and to the dark gods of pain and suffering and despair."

Kachka studied Nina Chechneva's face a little longer. She saw resignation in those hate-filled eyes, so she released her grip.

"Zoya Kolesova. Unleash her."

The massive woman gawked at Kachka from the safety of the hut door. She'd come in just far enough that she could watch the proceedings but was still able to flee if necessary.

"Have you lost your wits, Kachka Shestakova?"

"Do as I tell you. Release her. She is one of us now."

"Foolish," Zoya muttered as she began the process of pulling the spikes from the ground and tearing the chains from the ceiling using her bare hands.

Once the chains fell to the ground, so did Nina.

"Remove the chains . . . from my . . . arms," she gasped into the ground. "They are . . . bewitched."

That made sense. Nina Chechneva would definitely need something extra to keep her under control.

Together, Zoya and Kachka removed the chains that controlled Nina while the others stood by the exit and waited. They were clearly concerned, but they said nothing.

Once the chains were off and tossed across the room, Nina Chechneva pulled herself up until she was once again on her weak knees. Her fists against the ground, she panted hard, her head still bowed, her frail, thin body—most likely weakened by starvation—shaking.

Then she was gone.

"Ready?" Nina Chechneva asked from outside the hut, her voice strong again, her body filled out and healthy.

Sadly, that one question sent all of them jumping, but it

was Kachka's own cousin Tatyana who screamed—like some weak male!—and ran into the hut for protection.

"Some pride, Tatyana Shestakova," Kachka barked in disgust. "Any, to show me that you are part of the tribe I still love."

"She's a witch, cousin," Tatyana accused. "Everyone knows that!"

"If only that were the simple truth of it," Zoya muttered as she walked by Kachka. For once, her voice shockingly soft.

Maris watched his leader take on one of his own blood. Poor King Gaius. There was so much hatred between him and his own kin. But the thought of one of those bastards or bitches becoming ruler of the Sovereigns did nothing but fill him with dread.

With all the enemy soldiers now dead, they could all work together to take Lord Egnatius down, but the King wouldn't allow it. He wanted to be the one to finish his cousin without any help from his Praetorian Guards.

Maris approved of that, but he also knew that, even without his legs, Lord Egnatius was a strong fighter. His sword skills were unparalleled, which was one of the reasons they'd crept up on him and his men so carefully. They'd taken days to move up on them, making sure not to alert any of them to Gaius and his guards.

The wind from dragon wings brought up swirling fountains of dirt. Some of the humans were forced to grab hold of nearby trees so as not to be swept away.

Swords clashed, glinting in the early morning light, and, at first, everything was very proper. One royal fighting another.

Then Lord Egnatius disarmed Gaius, the king's sword

flipping end over end until it landed in the ground many feet away.

Maris gasped, worried his king was about to find his honorable death much earlier than any of them had believed.

But as Lord Egnatius's sword came down for a hard blow against the other dragon's shoulder, King Gaius moved in and caught the base of the blade with his claw. The cut it made was deep, blood spurting, hitting a few of the soldiers, but Gaius didn't even cry out. He didn't feel pain the way most of them did. Of course, none of them had been raised around Overlord Thracius, who, many of the old soldiers said, was one of the cruelest bastards to have ever drawn breath.

So with one claw, King Gaius held that sword. And, with the other, he caught hold of his cousin's throat. Using his wings, he spun them around, slamming his cousin into the closest tree. The two snarled, their jaws snapping, trying to tear scales from each other. But there seemed to be a pause, as if King Gaius could not take his cousin down. As if he could not finish him off.

"Is that the best you can do, cousin?" Lord Egnatius mocked.

"I was just waiting," Gaius growled softly. "Until I connected with my sister. So that she can feel every moment of me *killing you!*" Gaius finished on a bellow. Then he yanked his cousin away from that tree and slammed him into the ground, the land around them shaking from the power of it.

King Gaius pinned his cousin down, pressing his knees against his forearms to keep him in place. Then he gripped his cousin by the snout and began pulling his jaws apart.

Lord Egnatius tried to knock the king off, but he was dead below the waist and, with his arms pinned down, he was helpless.

And he knew it.

Lord Egnatius's screams tore through the land, sending birds from the safety of the trees in wild, panicked flocks.

Yet Gaius didn't stop. He just kept pulling—his fangs gritted, his dragon face a mask of rage and hate—until a sickening sound of bone cracking made Maris jump, and Gaius suddenly held up the lower half of Egnatius's jaw.

The royal wasn't dead yet. No. He was still quite alive.

"How does that feel, cousin?" King Gaius asked as he stepped off his kin. "Aggie is laughing. She's loving every second of this. Your pain. She adores your pain. And I love when she's happy. I love hearing her laugh." He stared down at his cousin. "Let's make her laugh some more, shall we?"

Gaius held out his claw and one of the dragon soldiers handed him his own gladius. A short sword, but an effective fighting weapon, as many enemy armies had learned over the centuries.

With his back foot against Lord Egnatius's chest, Gaius started with the claws. Cutting off each one as his cousin gurgled and wept beneath him. Then he cut off the forearms. Sliced the shoulders. Then the legs but, as he reminded his cousin, "You really can't feel that, huh?"

King Gaius stopped for a brief moment. Nodded. "My sister, she's not like me. She can only tolerate so much of someone's suffering. She wants it done. And I want her happy."

King Gaius raised the blade and brought it down, taking what was left of his cousin's dragon head.

With that done, King Gaius shifted back to his human form and took the Praetorian armor and helm handed to him by one of his soldiers. He put them on, not bothering to wipe off the blood. Once dressed, he cracked his neck and began to give orders that would have them out of this valley by suns-set.

Maris let out a sigh, silently glad it was all over. Now they could return home and—

Maris blinked and looked down, saw the arrow head that had come through his armor into his back and straight through his body. He dropped to his knees, unable to really breathe, as he saw his brother Praetorians taken out with arrows from the trees.

Gaius spun around, sword raised, eyes wide in shock. No arrows hit him, though.

"King Gaius," a human woman said from behind him.

Gaius turned, his sword ready, but he didn't strike. She was beautiful despite her missing eyes, sensuous, and clearly human in her white gown. She suddenly leaned forward and placed a gold torc around the king's neck and he, like Maris, dropped to his knees, the power drained out of him immediately. The gladius fell from his hand and he desperately pawed at the torc he now wore, trying to yank it off.

Blindly, the woman stared down at the king, head tilting to one side as if she could still see him without her eyes. Perhaps she could. "She said you wouldn't strike down an unarmed human woman," she said softly. "She was right."

Another arrow tore through Maris's chest, this time hitting his heart, and he fell forward, never knowing whether the king ever said anything to the beautiful eyeless woman or whether he died in that moment.

But it no longer mattered. . . . Maris's ancestors were waiting for him, waving him forward. . . .

Chapter Three

They traveled for days in silence. Even the normally chatty Zoya didn't speak.

By the fifth evening, as they waited for Ivan to finish cooking the boar Kachka had taken down earlier in the day, they sat on boulders and stumps, in a circle, in a thickly wooded forest deep in Annaig Valley. It was a risk to travel through this area, but as Daughters of the Steppes, they could slip through easily enough. Duke Salebiri's men often gave them a wide berth. At least for now. Perhaps, the more power Salebiri obtained, the more difficult it would become. But, so far, no one had bothered them.

Silently, they watched the boar turn on the spit as Ivan cleaned potatoes. His sister had started to help him, but when they all stared at her, wondering what she could possibly be thinking, she stopped.

Then, suddenly, Nina Chechneva closed her eyes and took in a deep breath. At first, Kachka assumed she was scenting the boar. Ivan had seasoned it nicely. But then the strange female slowly got to her feet and her body began to . . . undulate in a manner that made Kachka entirely uncomfortable.

Nina lifted her head, sniffing the air like one of Dagmar Reinholdt's dogs.

"I smell," she whispered, "fresh, untainted souls. Tortured. In pain. And oh-so-*ripe*," she panted out. "Ripe for the taking."

Marina Aleksandrovna leaned over and muttered to Kachka, "Are we going to have to put up with this sort of thing all the time? Because that does not work for me."

Kachka gave a wave of her hand. "Don't worry, comrade. I will handle this." She focused on Nina Chechneva and, after a brief moment, punched the air-grinding female in the leg.

"Ow!" the witch screeched, turning on Kachka, black eyes flashing. "You vicious goat!"

"Whatever you're doing, fiend, stop it. You're making everyone uncomfortable!"

"Not me," Zoya happily argued. "Let the demoness dance to her dark gods! Everyone should do what they love!"

Marina glared at Zoya for a moment, green eyes twitching, until she snarled, "Shut *up*."

Nina sat back on her tree stump. "I was just telling you that there are people over there."

"In the future, find a better way to do that."

"She is right," Zoya Kolesova said, her stomach grumbling like an angry bear. "I can hear them. There are people, maybe a mile or so, over there. I hear weapons."

"You hear weapons a mile away?"

"I am Kolesova. We always know when there are men around . . . fresh for the plucking."

Ivan snapped his fingers, and he and his sister switched places so that Yelena sat closer to Zoya.

"Why did you say they were in pain?" Tatyana asked. Always inquisitive, that one. She simply couldn't leave well enough alone.

"Because they are," Nina replied. "I feel their despair. Their misery. They cry out to be . . . helped." She shrugged. "My guess . . . probably slaves being taken to market."

"Slaves?" Zoya asked. She abruptly stood to her mighty, towering height. "Then we must go!"

"We don't need to go anywhere," Kachka replied.

"There might be a boy or two who would be good for my daughters."

"We don't have time to buy slaves."

"Not buy, Kachka Shestakova. Rescue."

"We don't have time to *rescue* slaves either. Do you not understand what we're doing?"

"Actually," Marina cut in, "none of us understands what we're doing. You haven't told us."

Kachka frowned. "I haven't?"

"No."

She gave a small wave of her hand. "Eh."

Zoya walked off, shooting over her giant shoulder, "With so many daughters, you must understand that I have to find quality men wherever I can."

"We should follow her, shouldn't we?" Tatyana asked.

"Should we?" Kachka glanced around. "I'm quite comfortable."

"And it's not like we asked her here," Marina tossed in. "She invited herself."

"Cousin . . ."

"Fine!" Kachka stood. "We will follow the great beast."

And they did. It wasn't as if they had to try hard. Zoya moved through the trees like a herd of elephants.

"Excellent!" Zoya cheered when they reached the other party. "Slavers! With boys!"

"We really don't have time for this, Zoya," Kachka called out to her.

"Oh, come now!" Zoya cheered, making the slavers wince

at the sound. They'd probably heard little but the sobs of the newer slaves for many days. "There are a few here who could be quite worthy of my daughters."

"Doesn't your human queen have problems with slavers?" Marina asked.

"Large problems."

Ivan stood beside Kachka, looking over the slavers.

"You're not going to let that boar burn, are you?" She was starving.

"No, no. It's fine." He seemed to be studying the group.

"What?" Kachka asked him.

"Seems an awful lot of armed protection for such weak-looking slaves, Kachka Shestakova."

Putting her ravenous hunger aside, Kachka now studied the group herself.

And Ivan was right.

"You and your sister circle around," she told Ivan softly while Zoya examined the wares and commented on them . . . loudly.

The Khoruzhaya siblings eased back into the surrounding trees as the rest of them moved closer to the slavers. Kachka just wanted to make sure there was nothing to worry about. She didn't want to wake up in the middle of the night, fighting for her life against slavers who thought the small group could be added to their purchases.

What Kachka noticed right away was that the slavers became more tense, hands straying to the hilts of their weapons, as her group approached.

"And look at this one!" Zoya went on in the common tongue, oblivious as always. "Why did you have to beat him so?"

Zoya was right. The boy was young and could easily be managed without beating him to a pulp, but men . . . they weren't really thinkers, were they? Always basing their actions on emotion and their own delicate egos.

"Cousin?" Tatyana said softly as she pointed out some random slave that Kachka knew for a fact her cousin would have no interest in.

"Yes?"

"The slave wearing the full cloak, to the far left?"

Kachka glanced over, then away, but saw nothing of interest. "What about him?"

"The boots he wears. Those are the boots of the Praetorian Guard."

"So?"

"The Praetorian Guard provides personal protection for the royal family of the Quintilian Provinces. If my information is correct," and they both knew it was, "your Southlander queen has a very strong and fruitful alliance with the king of that region. I'm sure it would not hurt if you looked into the capture of one of the king's personal guards."

"Look into the capture of a guard so weak he is captured by slavers?"

Ignoring Marina's smirk and soft laugh, Tatyana moved closer and said, "Do you really think a king's personal guard would be so easy to capture?"

Kachka finally looked at her cousin and Tatyana lifted her brows.

"Watch my back," Kachka told Marina, not really trusting her cousin to be able to do it, and slowly made her way down the line of slaves.

"Do not try to overcharge me, worthless male," Zoya argued, her big hands on the shoulders of two boys who looked like they wanted anyone else in the world but this woman to take them.

Kachka moved toward the hooded man with the Praetorian Guard boots. He was sitting now, his hands shackled in front of him, his head bowed so that he was completely covered by the cloak he wore.

The guards near him grew tense, though none tried to stop her. But their grips did tighten on the hilt of their weapons.

She moved past them casually, her hands near none of her own weapons. Finally she stood in front of the male and, slowly, dropped to a crouch in front of him.

"How much for this one?" she asked.

"Sorry, Rider. That one has already been sold."

"Ahh. I see. Can I look at him?"

"If you'd like, but we can't sell him to you."

"I might have a better offer," Kachka said as she reached over and gently pulled the hood back.

"There is no offer you can make, Rider. But we greatly apologize."

"You're right, there is no offer I can make," Kachka agreed upon seeing the face of the "slave" for the first time.

The man looked at her through the single steel-colored eye in his head and with a voice exhausted and raw, he said, "Kachka Shestakova. I see death has found you well."

"Can't say the same for you though, lizard."

"No," he replied with a weak but relieved smile, steel-colored hair falling into his face. "I guess you can't."

Kachka, sensing movement behind her, reached for the sword at her side, but it was too late. The man moving up behind her was now in the grip of Zoya Kolesova. An *angry* Zoya Kolesova.

"What is this?" Zoya demanded. "You strike at our back? Deceitful male!"

Another male came toward Zoya from her right, but she backhanded that one away, crushing his cheek and jaw in the process.

"*None of you are to be trusted!*" she bellowed. "*None of you!*"

Kachka watched Zoya batter the slaver's face in with her fist. While, from the safety of the trees, the siblings killed more of the slavers with their arrows and Marina finished off two more slavers charging at her.

Tatyana, sadly, was still fussing with the blade at her side, so Kachka grabbed her arm and yanked her down beside her.

"My cousin," she said to the dragon in human form. "Tatyana Shestakova of the Black Bear Riders of the Midnight Mountains of—"

"Yes," he cut in. "I remember well."

"This, cousin, is Gaius Lucius Domitus."

Tatyana gasped. "The king himself."

Kachka snorted as more slavers behind her died at the hands and arrows of her companions. "So impressed by rank is she, lizard. You two should get along well."

He was still smiling, but then, slowly, it began to fade, as his eye moved from Kachka to whatever was behind her.

On instinct, she stood and turned, facing an eyeless woman in a simple white dress. Those eyes had been removed purposely, she'd guess, since there were no ugly scars. Her eyelids were simply sewn shut, so that the woman's beauty was not lost.

With arms raised at her sides, the woman grinned at Kachka.

"Greetings, my—"

Kachka rammed her blade into the woman's belly, not letting her finish whatever she'd been planning to say.

The woman's mouth dropped open in shock and she discovered the blade and the blood pouring onto the ground.

"But . . ." she panted. "But . . . I am unarmed."

"I am Rider," Kachka said in return, yanking her blade from the woman, pulling it back and slashing it forward, removing the woman's head in one swipe. "So I do not *care* that you are unarmed."

Tatyana stood, eyes wide. "Cousin! What did you do?"

"She was enemy. I killed her. That is what we do." It galled her she had to remind her cousin of that.

"Look at her," Zoya said as she tossed away a man whose spine she'd snapped. "She has no eyes. She was suffering. Your cousin did what she must."

Tatyana, always so sensitive, growled and crouched by the woman's body. She pulled her dress down in the front until she revealed a mark burned into the woman's flesh.

"Horse gods," Tatyana whispered. "She is Chramnesind."

"What?" Marina asked. "She is what?"

"She is a priestess of the Chramnesind cult."

"Is that a real thing?" Marina shrugged. "I thought that was made up."

"It is not made up." Tatyana stood. "We need to go."

"But we have boar," Zoya argued.

"We must release these slaves and we must go," Tatyana said as she walked toward the weak ones who'd allowed themselves to be captured.

"I get to keep the boys, though, yes?"

"No!" Tatyana shot back. "You do not get to keep slaves!"

"Not slaves! Future husbands for my daughters!"

"Och!" Tatyana snarled with a wave of her hand before she began removing the slaves' chains, Ivan at her side helping.

"And who is that one?" Marina asked, pointing at the Sovereign with her blood-wet sword.

"That," Kachka said, "is Gaius Lucius Domitus. The One-Eyed Rebel King of the Quintilian Empire—"

"And Iron dragon," Nina Chechneva finished, although

to be honest, Kachka had forgotten all about the witch in the last ten minutes.

"He cannot be dragon," Zoya argued. "A dragon would burn all these slavers to embers. Not sit around shackled like weak human male."

"It is not the shackles that stop him from being dragon." Nina crouched beside him and pulled the fur cape from his body, revealing the gold torc around his neck. "It is this thing." She nodded at the headless corpse. "She placed this on him and now he cannot be dragon. He cannot fight. He can do nothing but wait."

"Then take it off," Kachka snapped. She desperately wanted to get back to that boar.

"I cannot."

"I thought you were witch. With all your dark magicks and hip undulating."

"This is dragon magicks, Kachka Shestakova. I have no gods in the dragon pantheon."

"I do not know what that means, but I do know that you have disappointed me, Nina Chechneva."

"That will keep me up nights," she shot back.

Kachka was about to go to Nina and slap her, just to make a point, but her cousin pulled her back.

"We have to get this off him. I mean . . . unless he always looks like he is . . ."

"Dying." Zoya shrugged. "He looks like he is dying."

"He is dying," Nina confirmed. "But a Dragonwitch will need to remove this. A powerful one."

"Fine," Kachka said. "Then we will take him back to the Dragon Queen. She is Dragonwitch."

"He will never reach Southlands," Nina said. "He will be dead by time we get there."

Now they all looked down at him and stared. After a

moment, the Dragon King looked up and his weak eye widened a bit. "What?" he asked.

"We should kill him here," Zoya said. "Put him out of his misery."

"I'd prefer you not," he said simply.

"Quiet, penis-haver."

He smirked. "You say that like it's a bad thing."

"We cannot kill him," Tatyana immediately argued.

"So we should let him die in agony?"

"He is weak, but I would not say he is in agony," Ivan noted.

"No one speaks to you," Zoya snapped. "Useless boy."

"We are not killing him," Kachka cut in. "I know where we can take him for help."

"It must be someplace close. We have maybe . . ." She glanced down at the dragon. ". . . two days. Possibly three. But that is stretch."

Kachka looked up at the sky, studied the stars. "Two days . . . we can do. But we need to leave now."

Zoya rolled her eyes. "What about boar?" she demanded.

"We will eat on way! *Do not irritate me, Zoya Kolesova!*"

Zoya grinned and patted Kachka on the back, nearly breaking the bone where her neck and spine met. "Do not worry, little Kachka Shestakova! I will help you take dying dragon to his final resting place! And everyone will say you at least tried!"

Marina stood next to Kachka, rubbing her forehead and watching as Zoya took the time to gather whatever gold and silver the now-dead slavers had on them. "I am so very glad she volunteered for this job."

Kachka, unable to deal with this anymore, crouched beside the dragon again.

"Because you helped my sister when she needed it most, lizard, I will try to help you now."

"You've already helped so much, Kachka. Because trust me," he said, glancing at the priestess Kachka had killed, "wherever she was taking me . . . I was going to be in for a very long, very *bad* time."

Chapter Four

They rode for two more days as Kachka used the suns and her own memory to guide her. For a Rider, two days on horseback was nothing, but watching the Iron King waste away before her eyes made the trip seem interminable.

He could barely even sit on the horse they got him, and was sometimes forced to lie facedown across the beast. A few times, she feared the dragon had stopped breathing.

The evening before they arrived at their destination, they had stopped for a few hours' rest before the suns rose. Zoya had carried the dragon in human form to a spot near the fire they built, unceremoniously dumping him onto the ground.

Tatyana had hissed at her before surrounding him with everyone's travel furs and using her own pack to support his back. Kachka hadn't been able to tell if Tatyana truly felt bad for him, however, or if she was just dazzled by his rank.

Once he'd been settled, Kachka had sat down beside him and given him some of her water, putting the flask to his lips.

"I need you to do something for me, Kachka Shestakova," he'd said once he'd gotten his fill.

"And what is that, lizard?"

He'd smirked, seeming to appreciate that she wasn't treating him like he would surely die.

"Because of the power of this torc, I cannot reach my sister."

"Yes. That thing you dragons do with your mind."

"Right. So when I die, I want you to tell my sister. No one else."

"Zoya Kolesova may already be treating you like a corpse, lizard, but I have not given up hope on you yet. You royals have a way of surviving when everyone thinks you should have died off long ago."

"I know. But my father always taught me to prepare for the worst. And I don't want Annwyl or, even worse, Rhiannon telling my sister about my passing. I am almost positive that the alliance we have between our people would not last."

"And you think sending *me* will help?"

He'd reached out then and looped one of her curls around his index finger, studying it.

"Help?" he'd asked. "No. Keep Annwyl and Rhiannon away from my sister? Yes. But you have to give me your word, Rider."

"I swear on my honor. But I am surprised you have so little faith in me, lizard."

He'd managed a small smile. "Oh?"

"That you think I would just let you die so easily. You know my sister. She does like to whine. Like big baby. But you helped her adjust to her missing eye, and now she has loyalty to you. So unless I want to hear that whine . . . and I do not . . . then I must at least *attempt* to keep your disgusting scales healthy."

"You've never even seen my scales. They're quite beautiful."

Kachka had curled her lip. "I bet they are slimy. Like snake."

"Snakes are *not* slimy and I am *definitely* not slimy."

"I did not say you. I said your scales."

"I *am* my scales."

"You should stay human all the time. You look much better as human."

"Now you're trying to make me angry."

She'd smiled at that. "Whatever gave you that idea?"

That had been last night, though. When she'd had more hope. Now . . . now he wheezed as he sat upon the horse Kachka had chosen for him. His body was so weak in the saddle, the only thing keeping him up was Zoya riding beside him, one hand gripping her own reins, the other gripping his shoulder.

They stopped outside the back entrance to the cave that Kachka sometimes saw in her nightmares and stared at it.

"You want us to go in there?" Tatyana had asked. *Questioning*, she called it. *Always afraid*, Kachka called it.

"Yes. We're going in here."

They dismounted and lit torches, making their way into the vast darkness.

They traveled for quite a bit in silence. Kachka could hear the sounds of small animals moving around in the dark but nothing else.

So it wasn't a sound that alerted her to another's presence. It was the way the air around them abruptly changed.

Kachka had always been fast with a weapon, but she didn't even have it pulled from her scabbard when she felt a blade press the flesh under her chin.

"Ah-ah-ahhh. Let's not be hasty," a voice ordered.

Kachka released the hilt of her weapon and lifted her hand.

"What are Riders doing in this cave?"

"I am here to see—"

"She's fine," a male voice called out from the darkness.

A word she did not recognize was whispered and torches

lining both sides of the cave walls burst to life, revealing that their small group was surrounded. And probably had been for quite some time.

Something that was not lost on her fellow tribeswomen.

Moving around a boulder, sliding his blade back into its sheath, a male walked to Kachka and smiled at her.

"Kachka Shestakova." Bold eyes moved over her. "I have to admit, I never really thought I'd see you again."

"Abomination," she replied, recognizing the only son of Annwyl the Bloody, Talan. "I see death has found you quite well."

"Why are you here? And stop calling me Abomination."

"Apologies, Abomination. I do not mean to upset. I need help."

"For the dragon?" he asked, nodding at the lizard slumped over his saddle.

"Yes."

The Abomination moved closer. "You do not seem like the kind of Rider who would have many dragon friends, no matter who your sister is fucking. So who is this one?" he asked, gesturing with a gloved hand.

"Gauis Lucius Domitus. Friend of your mother, I—"

"Gods!" The boy immediately stepped to the dragon's side. He reached for him, touching his shoulder and pulling him up. That's when he saw the torc around the dragon's neck and stepped back as quickly as he'd originally stepped forward.

"What the battle-fuck is that thing?"

"Some kind of evil dragon magick."

"Dragon magick is neither good nor evil. It just is," the boy murmured as he studied the torc.

"Whatever it is, Abomination, it kills him. He needs help. Help only—"

"Yes. You'll need to carry him, though."

"I will carry," Zoya volunteered.

Tossing the now unnecessary torch aside, Zoya walked over to the dragon and lifted his human body up and over her shoulder.

"Show me way, freaks of nature!" Zoya happily bellowed.

The other Abominations looked to their leader and, with a sigh, Talan motioned them forward. "Show her. Quickly."

There was a nod and three of the soldiers moved off with Zoya.

"You have giantess friends, too, I see," the Abomination noted.

"No. She is not giant. Just one of the Kolesova Tribe. Is that not right, Zoya?"

Zoya laughed as she walked away. "Giant? My older sisters give me nickname Pee-Wee."

Eyes wide, the Abomination stared at Kachka.

With a shrug, she replied. "She tells truth. They do call her Pee-Wee. And Tiny Toy. And Baby Bear."

The Abomination shook his head. "That's . . . terrifying."

Kachka followed behind Zoya and the others. "Only to the weak and small."

"Well, I'm not weak. . . ."

Princess Talwyn, only daughter of Annwyl the Bloody, sucked the marrow out of the cold ribs left from last night's meal and thought about how bloody bored she was.

Gods, she was bored!

How long was she supposed to stay here in this cave? Bored.

So very bored!

There was a whole world out there, and Talwyn was chomping at the bit to meet that world head-on with her blade out and her fists ready. But instead, she stayed here with most of the other offspring of human and dragon pairings and Brigida the Most Foul.

"Stop it."

Talwyn looked over at her cousin by doing no more than moving her eyes. "What?" she asked around the rib still in her mouth.

"Stop complaining."

"I didn't say anything."

Talwyn's cousin, Princess Rhianwen—Rhi to her dragon kin—sighed rather dramatically, as she liked to do, and said, "It's all over your face. And everyone senses your unhappiness. Just stop it."

Talwyn dropped the now-meatless bone and reached for another. She heard the returning footsteps of her brother, but he was no longer alone.

She glanced over her shoulder to see a motley crew of barbarians standing behind her twin. One had a corpse slung over her shoulder.

"Why is the giant holding that body?" Talwyn asked, confused. "Is that some sort of offering to us?"

Talan's eye twitched the slightest bit, something that gave Talwyn more satisfaction than it should have. But her twin was always so hard to rattle that she took perverse pleasure in doing so.

"That is *not* a body. That's Gaius Lucius Domitus."

Rhi gasped, small hands covering her beautiful mouth. But Talwyn simply asked, "Who?"

Both her cousin and brother gawked at her. "Gaius Lucius Domitus?" her brother pushed, as if saying the dragon's name several times would change anything. "Iron dragon and the one-eyed Rebel King from the west?"

Talwyn shrugged. "Still unclear."

"Just like her mother," the corpse suddenly announced.

"It's not necessary to be nasty, foreign trash," Talwyn snapped back.

With a rare growl, Talan pushed her out of the way and motioned to the giant. "Here. Put him on this table."

As the giant made her way to the table, Talan shoved plates, chalices, and utensils onto the floor to give them a free spot. That included the half-empty plate of ribs.

"I was eating those!"

"Would you shut up?" Rhi snarled.

The barbarian giant dumped the dragon in human form on their table, and even Talwyn had to admit . . . he looked awful.

"What is that around his neck?" she asked, reaching for the bit of gold that sparkled.

Rhi slapped her hand away. "Don't."

Annoyed, Talwyn slapped her hand back.

"Owwww! What was that for?" her cousin whined.

"You hit me first!"

"I was helping!"

"For the love of death and despair," Talan growled, "both of you *shut up*!"

"As entertaining as this is," one of the barbarians said calmly, "can you help him or not?"

Talwyn remembered this female. Kachka . . . something. The Rider who'd come here a few months ago with her wounded sister. That one had lost her eye to their mother, something even Talwyn had never done to her own mum. Of course, that was mostly down to her brother. Talan had always thrown off Talwyn's aim anytime she had her mum in her sights. And then he'd growled at her like it was wrong for a four-year-old to shoot a crossbow at their mother's knees.

Such a Goody Two-claws, her brother.

"Well . . . what is that?" Talwyn asked again about the torc around the Iron dragon's neck.

"Ancient, powerful magicks." Rhi gave a small shake of her head and took several steps away from the royal, her hands lifted as if in surrender.

Talwyn gave the smallest eye roll so that her brother wouldn't see. Rhi was always so dramatic. *How bad could the magicks on this be*? Talwyn wondered, reaching out to touch the item that currently bled the royal dry of life.

As she did, another barbarian moved behind Rhi. This one looked different from the others. All her clothes were dark. So dark they were purple, like the darkest Lightning dragon. She wore dark kohl around her black eyes and her black hair was in several large braids with black gems weaved throughout.

She simply stood behind Rhi, without saying a word. But, suddenly, Rhi took in a breath, her eyes widening. She sensed the woman behind her. And, without a word, Rhi spun on her heel and swung her fist, ramming it right into the woman's jaw and knocking her to the ground.

The torc forgotten, Talwyn burst into shocked laughter. "Holy shit!"

"Rhi!" Talan barked, stunned at Rhi's sudden act of violence. "What the hells is wrong with you?"

Rhi stood over the barbarian, one damning finger pointed at her. "Cause one problem here, woman. Just one—and I will rip that thing you call a soul from your body and eat it whole."

Talan grabbed Rhi around the waist and pulled her to the other side of the table as a loud angry voice blasted from another cavern, "What's all this then! *I was trying to sleep!*"

Talwyn leaned over and whispered to Kachka, "Probably sleeping upside down from the rafters like a bloody bat."

"Something to say to me, demon child?" Brigida the Foul asked . . . from *behind* Talwyn. Her voice had been coming from the cavern in *front* of Talwyn seconds ago. Gods! She hated when the witch did that. And hated even more that she wouldn't show her how to do it.

"Well," Talwyn began, "since you asked . . ."

"We don't have time for this!" Talan cut in. "You have to help the king, Brigida."

The She-dragon in her human form raised a brow. "Help? An Iron? Why would I do that, boy?"

"He's an ally to my mother."

Beneath her black cloak, Brigida's shoulders sort of twitched. "And?"

"Just. Fucking. Fix. Him."

Brigida the Foul debated removing the skin from the insolent boy, but he had a higher purpose in this world than ending up on the wrong side of her anger.

She studied the torc around the Iron's neck. She entertained the idea of leaving it there. Letting him die. He was only a few breaths from death as it was.

She had no good memories of the Irons. She'd been around when that lot had separated themselves from the Fire dragons of the Southlands. Always thought they were so above it all. Calling on the gods to make them all that iron color, twisting their horns around so they looped toward their jaws instead of sitting high on their heads like any proper dragon. Why? Because they truly thought they were better than the rest.

The whole thing had pissed her off so much that Brigida had actually involved herself in that war. Had been knees deep in blood and death and the cries of the innocent, as she often liked to be, but instead of just drinking all that in and taking what she needed from the slain and dying for her spells, she'd actually fought *beside* the Dragon Queen of the time. Together, they'd pushed the Irons back into the west, past the Western Mountains. Brigida had thought that would be the last they heard of them, assuming they'd die out.

That hadn't happened. Instead, they'd grown stronger, working with the humans of the west until they were strong enough to make those humans friend or slave. Once they'd established the Quintilian Provinces, they'd spread out, keeping the Western Mountains at their back while they took over the towns and cities that surrounded them.

Now, they were the Quintilian Sovereigns Empire.

An empire once ruled by another tyrant, Overlord Thracius. But he'd been taken down by one of the new Dragon Queen's prince-lings. The youngest. A Blue, just like his grandfather. And since then, the Provinces had been taken over by some nephew of Thracius's. A young buck not even three hundred, and his twin sister.

It was rumored, and Brigida knew it to be true, that the mother of the twins had been so concerned about them surviving past their first century with that family of theirs that she'd called powerful witches—dragon and human— from all over the west to bless her offspring.

The fact that they still breathed proved the magick must have had some effect.

And this boy was one of those twins. She recognized that face. Not because she knew him, but because she'd known his great-grandfather and, as human, he looked just like him.

"Are you going to save him, old woman, or just stare at him?"

Slowly, Brigida looked up at the Rider standing across from her. She remembered her, too. One of Glebovicha Shestakova's offspring. The one who *hadn't* had her eye torn from her head by her own mother.

She didn't flinch when Brigida stared at her. Surprising when even the Kolesova female turned from Brigida. Most did, if they had any sense.

The Rider pointed at the Iron. "Save him."

"Or what?"

"Or you will have Annwyl the Bloody to deal with. I waste time with dragon only for her."

Brigida knew this human wasn't telling the complete truth, but she didn't care. This dragon would serve his purpose, like everyone else.

Tucking her walking stick against her shoulder and leaning against it, Brigida raised both her hands and centered them over the torc. She was not fool enough to touch the thing, but she had no need to.

She closed her eyes and chanted words filled with ancient magicks while her fingers drew powerful runes in the air. After a few moments, the torc shook until it broke into three pieces and fell away from the Iron's neck.

"He does not breathe," another Rider accused.

"He will." Brigida pulled her hands back and grabbed hold of her walking stick. She was exhausted now, so she used it to keep her upright.

"If I were you," she warned the Riders, "I'd move back a step . . . or eighty."

The small group took a step back just as the Iron's eyes popped open. He took in a large, shuddering breath, and Brigida watched as color flooded his human cheeks and his human body began to grow stronger before their eyes.

After a few seconds, he rolled to the side and off the table, stumbling across the floor.

The boy started after him. Weak like his mother, that one. Always trying to help. Some things you just couldn't help.

Brigida used her staff to block the boy from moving and watched as the Iron made his way to the middle of the room.

With his arms around his waist and his body bent over, he suddenly roared. Flames burst to life around him and he went from frail human to powerful dragon in seconds.

Powerful, *hungry* dragon.

His lone eye searched around the chamber, finally locking on the barbarians.

Brigida lifted her staff and slammed it to the ground once, the sound echoing for miles, the floor shuddering beneath. It was enough to get the Iron's attention.

"Outside," Brigida ordered. "There's a whole herd of—"

The Iron turned, unleashed his wings, and, in seconds, was gone.

Silence followed the Iron's exit until the Kolesova woman suddenly asked, "Herd of what . . . exactly? For we are hungry too."

Chapter Five

Gaius decimated most of the herd of elk and devoured them in less time than he was comfortable with. But his need could not be contained.

Even though he'd been fed by his captors, it had been as if the food did not nourish him in any way. So he'd starved while eating. A nightmare if there ever was one.

That torc had not been designed merely to keep a dragon captive in his human form. It had been designed to torture. But why? He was clearly worth more alive than dead. It wasn't arrogance that brought him to that belief either. It was politics.

And yet the longer they'd taken to travel to wherever his captives had been leading him, the more he'd known he was moments from dying. He was sure of it.

Gaius realized he must have finally sated his hunger if he was sitting around, analyzing his current situation. He could only manage that when he was fed and happy or paranoid and desperate.

Now that he could think clearly again, he finally did what he'd been unable to do since this had all started.

Gaius called out to his sister.

A long, painful moment of silence greeted him and then . . . nothing but yelling.

He winced as his sister called him every derogatory name she could think of—and there were many; she had a mouth just like their plebian mother—while at the same time sobbing with relief.

Gaius let her vent as long as she needed. It was the least he could do. And the gods knew, he wouldn't have been much better if the tables had been turned. As it was, he knew what it was like to live for too long without his twin. But he honestly wasn't sure which was worse—not knowing what happened to his twin or knowing all too well.

Vateria, cunt of the ages, had made sure he'd received detailed reports of what his sister had endured at their cousin's claws. She'd always been that perverse. That cruel. And between Vateria's reports and his own imagination, Gaius had soon grown as cruel as she, his anger leading the way.

When Queen Annwyl had finally tracked him down, he'd been one step away from being no better than his Uncle Thracius. In fact, to this day, he had no idea what had held him back from slaying the human female outright. He'd hated Annwyl on sight, so it should have been easy. But something had stayed his claw. Something had kept him from killing her and her small party of dragons and one human girl.

Whatever the reason, the universe would never know how grateful he truly was for that decision. Because it was Annwyl and her party who had eventually managed to rescue his sister. Killing Thracius and destroying his army had just been a bonus gift.

When Gaius had returned to his cave, he'd found his sister there. Alive and well and waiting for him. In front of their troops, their greeting to each other had been sweet but aloof. They were still royals after all, rebels or not.

But, once they were alone, Gaius had held his sister while she'd sobbed against his chest. Her sobs had been filled with pain and rage and relief that it was all over.

They hadn't discussed it again after that, but they didn't have to. Just like now. Aggie didn't need to *tell* Gaius how worried she'd been about him. He could just feel it. In his bones.

You're safe now, though? she finally asked, slowly getting hold of herself.

I am.

Good. Then I'll touch base with you later.

All right. I'll be here.

You better. Or I swear to all the gods . . .

She didn't need to finish that threat. And it was a threat.

The communication between them abruptly ended and Gaius took in a deep breath. One that he would let out slowly. A technique he'd learned to control his weaker elements. But before he could do anything, an arrow shot past him and lodged into the neck of a bear that had been gnawing on the bones Gaius had littered over the ground during his feasting.

The bear gave a strangled roar before falling flat on its back. A few seconds later, Kachka Shestakova walked past Gaius to retrieve her prize.

"Excellent shooting," he noted, very glad to be distracted from his sister's pain and fear.

"I do not allow for any other kind."

"Of course you don't."

Gaius watched the Rider carefully place aside her bow and quiver before pulling out a short sword and dragging it across the bear's throat. She wiped that blade clean with a cloth and returned it to its scabbard before taking a rope and tying one end to the legs of the bear. She threw the other end of the rope over a nearby sturdy tree and proceeded to haul the carcass up so that the blood would drain and she could remove the fur and butcher the animal.

Gaius didn't offer to help her because he knew better. Rider females didn't need the help of anyone but another Rider. And they definitely didn't need the help of some imperialist male.

Grateful as Gaius was to Kachka Shestakova, he wasn't about to insult her. So he sat there and watched while he ground an elk leg down until the end was a point, then proceeded to use that to pick his fangs clean of flesh and hide.

"So," he finally asked when the sound of her butchering that carcass became too much for him, "what does Annwyl the Bloody have the Riders doing for her that has you sneaking around your own territory, Kachka Shestakova?"

Kachka stopped in the middle of what she was doing to that bear to slowly face Gaius. And, in that three-second time span, Gaius knew . . .

She was debating whether to kill him or not.

Kachka was searching out weak points on the dragon's body when he said, "You do know that killing *me* really should be your last option . . . don't you?"

"Is that because you are royal and think you are important to entire world?"

"Mostly . . . yes. But what's significant is that your queen thinks I'm important."

"You ask too many questions, and she is not my queen. Daughters of Steppes have no queen. No king. We live and die for each other."

"I do not ask too many questions. I ask one. And if you have no queen, then why are you out here? Obviously helping her. Trying to get me, a useless royal, to safety? Willing to face"—his lip curled in distaste—"whatever that She-dragon was that removed that cursed torc from my neck? Why do all that if Annwyl is not your queen?"

Kachka didn't answer, but the dragon thought he could guess.

"Yes. Of course. Your sister. She offered protection for your sister if you do her bidding."

"I know that my sister is safe with the Mad Queen and the giant lizards. They actually like her. And, surprisingly, do not find her weak and pathetic."

"That is big of them." He stared at her a moment. "So you're not in fear for your sister. You're definitely not in fear for yourself. Then what are you doing?"

"Why do you ask, dragon? Why do you need to know?"

"I'm curious."

"You should just be glad to be alive. If Zoya Kolesova had her way, we would have put you down days ago."

"True. And she's very—"

"Loud. Yes. We all know. I did not invite her. She invited herself."

"I see." Gaius studied the Rider a moment. "Kachka Shestakova . . . I owe you much."

"Yes," she replied. "You do."

"How can I ever repay you?"

She faced him, her blade and arms covered in blood. "Give me your kingdom!"

Gaius smiled. "You're adorable."

"See? The royals. They say all this and they say all that . . . but they do nothing but lie."

"We don't lie *all* the time."

"You owe me nothing, royal. But we are even for my sister, yes?"

"I never thought you owed me for that. Your sister needed

help and I understood her problem better than most. That doesn't lead to a tit-for-tat situation, in my humble opinion."

She snorted. "There is nothing humble about you, royal."

"That's true."

Gaius eased around the Rider, watching her as she cut the fur on the bear so that, with one good yank, she could remove it whole.

And, before he knew it, he was snuggled up beside her and on his back.

Although he had no idea why.

Kachka placed the fur aside and was about to cut down the bear when she felt something warm blowing against her bare arm.

She looked down and found giant dragon nostrils right by her. Leaning back a bit, she realized that the dragon's long body circled her and he was on his back, exposing his belly.

"What . . . are you doing?"

"Proving I'm not slimy."

"What?"

"You said dragon scales were slimy. As a matter of honor, I have to show you that's not true. You'll need to touch me, though."

Kachka sucked her tongue against her teeth. "Men are disgusting."

"I'm not a man. And I don't mean that. Just touch my scales."

"Touch them yourself."

"I do. Every day. And they are fabulous. Now it's your turn."

"Go. Away."

"You're afraid to be proven wrong."

"I do not care!"

"Then prove it."

"Fine!" Kachka slapped her hand against his snout.

"Ow!"

"It's sticky."

"That's blood. I just ate. Go down lower."

"Disgusting."

"I don't mean *that* low."

With a heavy sigh, Kachka walked around the dragon. His scales were the color of steel. His horns curled down and the tips pointed in toward the middle of his snout. His wings were tucked under his body. And his hair wasn't nearly as long as the Southlanders, reaching only to his shoulders. It was also steel-colored.

She went under his forearm and pressed her hand against the scales.

That's when Gaius Domitus giggled and turned away from her.

Kachka reared back. "*What are you doing?*"

"I'm ticklish there!"

"You are a king!"

"And ticklish!"

She made the rather long walk back to his snout and her bear. "Pathetic," she tossed at him before she cut her bear down.

He rolled onto his belly, grinning at her, all those fangs flashing in the suns. "Now you sound like my aunt."

He went up on all fours, shook himself like a dog, wings flapping against him, making a small whirlwind around them.

Kachka waited for him to stop before dropping the fur on top of the bear.

"How long would it take for me to get back to Garbhán Isle from here?" he asked.

"Days." Kachka tied more ropes around the bear's skinless ankles. "But old bitch can get you there faster."

"The Dragonwitch?"

"Yes."

"How fast?"

"Seconds. Just make sure you do not drink before you leave."

"Drink what?"

"Anything worth drinking," which Kachka felt was explanatory enough.

She finished tying the rope strategically around the bear carcass. As she did, she felt flames near her, but paid them no mind since they didn't actually touch her.

She wound the rope around her arms to make hauling the animal easier, and turned, which was when she came face-to-bloody-chest with the dragon.

"I still haven't thanked you for saving me," said the dragon, now in his human form.

Kachka looked up into his handsome face. Horse gods in the field! How unfair that a dragon, of all beings, should be so handsome when human. She could overlook his ridiculous political leanings—as she did with most men—but she could never overlook the fact that underneath all that flesh he had scales.

Scales!

"Again with that?"

He took a step closer and soothing heat came off him in waves. "Yes. Again with that. If it had not been for you and your friends, I would have surely died. Or ended up in a worse situation than I was already in."

"Oh. I see." She thought a moment. "True. You should thank me. But we can fix now, yes?" She dropped the rope from her right hand, reached up, catching the back of the dragon's neck, and yanked him down, taking his mouth hard, sliding her tongue past his lips and teeth. His entire body stiffened in surprise, and as soon as she felt him respond in kind, Kachka pulled back and pushed him away with a shove against his blood-covered chest.

"There," she said, grabbing hold of the rope again. "Now you have thanked me, dragon."

She walked off, pulling the bear behind her. As she moved, she did add, "I must admit . . . I thought tongue would be forked."

She heard him growl behind her. "I am *not* a snake."

"So you say," she countered, grinning. "So you say."

Gaius watched Kachka Shestakova drag that bear away, leaving a trail of blood as she did.

For a moment, a brief one, he was nothing but angry and annoyed. And then, suddenly, he was smiling. Still tasting her on his lips. Still feeling where her hand, sticky with bear blood, had pressed against the back of his neck.

Gaius took in a deep, wonderful breath.

The suns were shining. His sister was safe. He was alive.

And Kachka Shestakova had the most delightful tongue he'd ever had in his mouth. . . .

Chapter Six

Brigida stared down at the table in the far corner of her private cavern. It was filled with books on all kinds of magicks and potions and rituals.

She stared and waited until she knew she was no longer alone.

"Nina Chechneva, the Unclaimed," she sneered, slowly turning to face the dark-souled witch creeping around the stone wall into her cavern.

The witch smiled, trying to hide beauty under all that hair and black stuff around her eyes. Trying to make herself look more terrifying.

"And you are Brigida the Foul. My dark gods have told me much about you."

"Have they?"

"They have." She moved closer, easing her way around Brigida. Like a jungle cat easing its way around its prey.

"They say you have great power," the witch smilingly hissed, easing closer and closer. "Power that I must have!"

The witch spun and, using the power of that spin, rammed a blade up to the hilt into Brigida's chest.

Brigida sighed, looked down at the blade, then back at the witch. "Really? That the best you can do?"

The witch stepped back, eyes wide. "I . . . I . . ."

Brigida snorted and flicked the fingers of her free hand, sending the witch flipping across the room and slamming into the wall—where Brigida left her hanging.

"I knew from the way me grandniece reacted to you that you were one of the Dark Soul witches. With your hell gods and soul stealing." Brigida laughed. "I mean, that girl loves everybody. Even me. But not you."

Brigida yanked the blade from her chest and made her slow way across the cavern. "I've been alive for a very long time," she told the witch as she struggled in vain to free herself. "And I done that by being one of the meanest bitches on the planet. And no little Rider girl, not even four hundred years yet, is going to fuck with me."

Standing in front of the witch, Brigida smiled up at her. "But I want to make sure you understand what I'm telling you."

Brigida rammed the blade into the witch's thigh, quickly silencing her screams with a thought.

"Now, see . . . could've put that blade right back in *your* chest. Could have cut your throat too. Didn't, though. Maybe you think I just like torturing ya. And true. I do a bit. Because I am an evil bitch, yeah? An' evil bitches like to torture. But that's not why I'm keeping you alive, little Rider."

Brigida shook her head. "I know what you're planning. Get far from the Outerplains. Get them other Riders on their own. Kill them while they sleep and take their souls. I know you're planning this . . . 'cause I would have done the same thing—a few hundred years back. But you're not going to do that this time."

She waved her hand, releasing the witch, letting her drop hard to the ground.

"Get up," she sneered. "You gonna be an evil bitch, you've got to be ready to suffer for the privilege."

The witch yanked the blade from her leg and snarled, "What do you want from me, old cunt?"

"You want to keep worshipping your dark gods and stealing your souls, little Rider? Want to be as powerful as me one day? Then your job is working with these Riders."

"We do not even know what we are doing. How do you?"

"Don't ask me stupid questions. Just do what I tell you."

"And if I don't?"

Brigida yanked the blade out of the witch's hand and rammed it into her other thigh.

"*Motherfucker!*"

Brigida smiled. "That's what."

"What is your name, little boy?"

Talan glanced over at the giantess next to him. She was leering at him in a way he was entirely uncomfortable with!

"Talan. *Prince* Talan. Beloved son of Annwyl the Bloody."

I can't believe you're using Mum, his sister laughed in his head.

Do you see the size of this woman? She could twist me into a braided loaf of bread.

Have some dignity!

If you're not going to help—fuck off.

"Has she already promised you to another?"

Talan blinked. "Pardon?"

"Polite. My girls will like that."

Rhi, who'd been pacing in front of them and wringing her hands, snapped, "Why did Kachka bring that witch woman here? What was she thinking?"

"When did you and Kachka Shestakova become such good friends?" Talwyn asked, uncaring about her brother's current plight—as always! "If memory serves, she called you either the Brown One or the Weeper. Neither of which sounded like compliments to me."

Rhi stopped pacing and faced Talan. "The woman is evil. We need to kill her."

"The first time you dislike someone," Talwyn asked, "and you want to kill her? When did you turn into my mother?"

"Your mother is a saint!"

Talwyn glanced at Talan, widened her eyes a bit, and mouthed, *Wow.*

"I think we all need to calm down," Talan soothed before he turned to the giant next to him and barked, "And stop petting my hair!"

"It is so pretty. My daughters will like your pretty hair."

"Look, I don't know how things are run in the Outer-plains, but I'm a Southlander and we choose our own mates."

"Who would be foolish enough to let such a pretty boy choose his own wife?"

Yeah? his sister asked in his head. *Who?*

"You need Zoya to get sturdy woman for you. One of my younger girls would be happy to make you first husband."

"Leave the pretty boy alone, Zoya," one of the other Riders admonished.

"I promised my daughters I would bring them strong boys to make their husbands. He is good start, yes?"

Do something!

Rolling her eyes, Talwyn finally came over.

"Back away from him, female," she said.

"And who are you?" the giant demanded. "No one! I am Zoya Kolesova of the Mountain Movers of the Lands of Pain in the Far Reaches of the Steppes of the Outerplains! You are no one but some Southlander bitch who dresses like Kyvich witch."

Talwyn's head tilted to the side. "Mountain Movers? Seriously?"

"Is this you helping me?" Talan wanted to know.

"But come on, Talan! Don't you want to know if they actually *moved* mountains?"

"No!"

"*Is no one else concerned about that woman?*" Rhi screeched.

The twins shook their heads. "No."

"How can you not be concerned?"

"We live with Brigida the *Foul*," Talwyn reminded her. "That She-dragon is the epitome of pure evil. You don't mind her."

"Because she's loyal to family. *This* family."

"I think you're being ridiculous."

"You never listen to me."

"I listen to you constantly. I just think that, at the moment, you're being an emotional nutter."

Rhi stomped her small foot. "For once, just once, I wish you'd side with *me*. Would that be so bloody hard?"

"What are you talking about?" Talwyn demanded. "I always side with you."

"No. You constantly *argue* with me. You argue everything with me!"

"It's healthy debate."

"I don't want a healthy debate. Sometimes I just want you to accept the fact that some bitch is pure evil!"

Then Talwyn did that thing she did that really pissed Rhi off. She blew out a breath and gave a dismissive wave of her hand. Their mother often did the same thing when anyone started talking about anything regarding her kingdom that had nothing to do with battle and war.

But Talwyn wasn't their mother and Rhi was definitely

not their aunt Dagmar. Which was quite evident when she suddenly punched Talwyn in the nose.

"*You cow!*" Talwyn yelled with her hand over her bleeding nose.

Talan tried to get off the table to get between his sister and cousin, but the giant yanked him back and, to his growing horror, put both her big arms around his chest, pulling him close.

"No, no, pretty boy," she said close to his ear. "You should never get between two strong women fighting. That is not your place. Your place is just to be pretty and satisfy one of my daughters."

"Woman," Talan warned, "get your hands off me."

The giant laughed. "Look, comrades! He is so very saucy! I love saucy boys!"

By the dark gods, what is happening?

Kachka was nearing the main cavern when she felt her burden lessen a bit. She looked over her shoulder to see that the Iron dragon, in his naked human form, had picked up the bear and carried it over his shoulder.

"Trying to impress?" she asked.

"Of course! That's what kings do. We either want to impress or terrify."

"I like that you are honest."

As they came around a corner, the old She-dragon limped her way into the tunnel. And moving slowly behind her was Nina Chechneva.

Kachka frowned, wondering what was wrong with her.

"Ahh, Lady Brigida," the king said.

"I ain't no lady, Iron scum. So say your piece."

"Still haven't let that first war go, have you, Brigida?"

"No," the witch replied flatly. "So what do ya want?"

"I was told you can get me to the Southlands . . . quickly. Is that true?"

"Yeah. But what do I get out of it? I do nothin' for free, Iron scum."

"Can anyone just use my name?" the dragon asked . . . the air.

Kachka fell back to walk beside Nina. She sniffed the air. "Are you bleeding?"

"I do not want to talk of it."

"Well, comrade, if it is your monthly, stuff something up there. These dragons and Abominations will have you half-eaten before you can hope to beg for your useless life."

"It is not my . . . forget it."

"Already done."

They entered the main cavern and all of them stopped. And stared.

What else could they do?

In the middle of the cavern, by the big dining table, two of the girl Abominations fought. It was kind of like the wrestling the Daughters of the Steppes taught their little girls when they were still learning to walk. Only the toddlers were better at it.

On the dining table was Zoya Kolesova. She held on to the boy Abomination while he tried to get away from her without using a weapon.

He needed a weapon.

On the other side of that table was the rest of Kachka's team. They were telling Zoya to let the boy go, which Kachka truly appreciated.

With a sigh, Kachka began to move forward, hoping to restore some semblance of order, but the old Dragonwitch yanked her back and moved with a sure-footedness that Kachka found rather shocking considering the female's usual limping gait.

Raising her walking stick, the old witch slammed it into the ground, shaking the cave walls and shocking everyone into silence. The two girls jumped apart as if on fire, panting from . . . what exactly? Exertion? Exertion from that?

"*That is enough!*" the She-dragon bellowed. "I'm tired of this centaur shit!"

"She started it!" the cousins screamed in unison while the boy yelled, "Get this beast off me!"

"You want to go to the Southlands, Iron scum?" Brigida abruptly asked the king.

"Uh . . ."

"Then go you shall."

Brigida lifted her arms, her walking staff held high, the black crystal on the head suddenly glowing.

"Shit," Nina murmured, her hand falling on Kachka's shoulder.

Kachka glanced at her, wondering why the bitch was touching her. But the look of fear on her face . . .

"*All of you,*" the Dragonwitch bellowed, "*get the fuck out of my house!*"

Kachka watched as a spot beyond the dining table turned dark, the air around it swirling, lightning striking the ground beneath.

"What is she doing?" Gaius demanded.

Kachka shrugged. "Cleaning house."

Brigida watched the last pain in her ass go through the doorway. Then she shut it and let out a relieved sigh.

Silence. Wonderful, amazing silence. No arguing. No complaining. No whining. No Riders. Just silence.

Now she could focus on the oncoming war and the Abominations littering the territories around her mountain home. There was training to do. Plans to organize. Sacrifices to make.

And she knew, without doubt, that her three young kin would make their way back here. But for now . . . she would do nothing but enjoy the quiet.

Exhausted, Brigida slowly lowered her arms and rested against her walking staff.

After thinking for a moment, she realized she had made one mistake in her anger.

"Should have kept that blasted bear . . ."

Chapter Seven

Briec the Mighty, second oldest in the House of Gwalchmai fab Gwyar, fourth in line to the throne of the White Dragon Queen, Shield Hero of the Dragon Wars, Gold Shield Hero of the War of the Provinces, Former Lord Defender of the Dragon Queen's Throne, Patient Overlord of the beautiful Talaith's heart, and proud father of the two most perfect, *perfect* daughters in the world merely because they were *his* daughters, which—no matter how much their mother might squawk about it—Talaith had little to do with, placed his legs up on the dining table and sighed happily as he sipped his wine.

Everyone was out at the moment and the Great Hall was wonderfully silent. He loved times like these. Even those vile dogs Lady Dagmar insisted on having around didn't bother Briec when he was this relaxed.

He glanced down at the one currently sniffing around his chair, searching for scraps to feed the never-ending hunger these mammoth beasts never seemed to satisfy.

Briec sniffed a little himself. Gods. It had been ages since he'd had dog. A quick, lovely delicacy. Like finding beef jerky buried in one's travel pouch. He hadn't had dog in ages, not since Dagmar found him feeding on one a few years back. Gods! The drama! And the cursing! Who knew such a polite, well-taught woman had a mouth like a nasty sewer?

Briec glanced around. He was definitely alone. And this dog was not one of Dagmar's favorites. If it was, it would be right by her side. Not trying to get its giant body under Briec's chair to grab a scrap of bread. If Briec didn't know better, he'd think the dog hadn't eaten in days. But Briec did know better. Dagmar's dogs ate better than any of them. The finest meats butchered and braised for the dogs' consumption as if they were royals coming to visit and not four-legged beasts that were so very yummy.

After another quick glance around, Briec smirked and leaned down a bit toward the dog. "Hello, my little tasty niblet. Wouldn't you like to be a delicious treat for Briec the Mighty? Of course you would. Yes, you would! Now come here and—" A sound, like the tearing of a wall from its foundation filled the room and all Briec had time to say was, "*How does she always know?*"

But instead of Dagmar charging in to order him to "get the battle-fuck away from my gods-damn dog, you viper!" a mystical doorway opened in the middle of the Great Hall and he watched in horror as a skinless bear came right at his head—

Gaius hit the ground, his human flesh tearing as he skidded across the hard stone floor. When he finally stopped, he was face-first in a dragon's human crotch.

Yes. This day was getting better and better.

"Why is there a bear on me? What is happening?" a pompous-sounding voice demanded.

Gaius heard something wet hit the ground and assumed it was that poor bear.

"And what the battle-fuck are you doing?"

Gaius slowly raised his head—and smiled. "Hello, Prince Briec," he said, keeping his voice low. "You're looking handsome today."

That's when Gaius took a boot to the face when the prince scrambled to get out from under him. If it hadn't hurt, he'd be laughing more.

"*What is happening?*" Briec snarled as he got to his feet.

"Daddy?"

Briec started. "Is that . . . is that my perfect, *perfect* daughter?"

"Daddy, stop calling me that."

"Yes," Gaius heard Talwyn complain. "Stop calling her that."

"And what's that supposed to mean?" Rhi asked.

"What do you *think* it means?"

"Would you two shut it?" Talan barked. "I can't hear another one of these bloody arguments! *And someone get this crazed female off me!*"

Arms stretched over Gaius's shoulders, Kachka, who'd landed on top of him, rested her head against his cheek. "Be glad we never had chance to drink before that She-dragon threw us out of her lair. This would have been . . . less good."

"I'll keep that in mind for future reference."

Prince Briec pushed his niece out of the way, ignored his struggling nephew, and lifted his daughter by her waist, turning in a circle as if she were still a small child rather than a grown woman.

"There she is!" he announced to the room. "My beautiful, *perfect* daughter."

"Daddy! Stop!"

"You shouldn't be telling me to stop. You should be thanking me for giving you such beauty and perfection."

"Wow," Gaius muttered to Kachka. "That is an amazing amount of arrogance standing there."

"So this is the Southlands," Marina Aleksandrovna said as she stood, turning in her own circle to look at the hall.

"This," Tatyana Shestakova announced with awe, "is the seat of power of Queen Annwyl."

"I bet," Kachka whispered in his ear, "that she wishes she'd landed in the queen's lap, the way you landed in the arrogant dragon's."

Gaius dropped his head and chuckled just as Zoya Kolesova demanded, "Where is your mother, boy? I will barter with her for you."

Briec quickly placed his daughter safely behind him. "Why is there a giantess in this house?"

"Why are you looking at *me*?" Talan asked.

"Because she's holding on to you like she owns you."

"That is plan!" Zoya cheerfully announced. Then, she suddenly looked at Briec. "I will take you as well, pretty one. I have older daughters who will like you, too."

"Older? What does *that* mean?"

Rhi jumped in front of her father, both arms out to block Zoya. "No. This is Prince Briec and he has been Claimed by my mother. An incredibly powerful witch." When the giant smirked, Rhi added, "She can turn your blood to glass."

Actually, from what Gaius had seen of Talaith's magicks, no, she couldn't. But he understood Rhi's need to protect her father from Zoya. He would need that protection.

Zoya stared at Briec, apparently debating the pros and cons of all this when Talwyn suddenly pried the woman's arms off her brother and said, "You need to see our mother before any decisions are made."

In panic, Gaius quickly glanced at Kachka, but she only smirked.

"I do?" Zoya asked.

"Oh, yes. She's the queen and Talan is her favorite. You need to go to her before you do anything else. Right now.

Right this second. And make sure you are bold and pushy. And make sure you're *in her face* about taking her son. The queen likes confidence."

"Thank you, evil Abomination!" Zoya cheered, arms thrown wide. "Your help is truly appreciated!"

"Tal—" Rhi began, but Briec placed his hand over her mouth to silence her.

"I believe the females are down by the big lake." He glanced over. Saw one of the squires walking by. "You there. Boy. Take this extremely large female down to your queen. Immediately."

The boy stared up at Zoya, his mouth open, before he finally nodded his head and started walking. Quickly.

Zoya followed, the Khoruzhaya siblings, Tatyana, and Marina going with her while Nina toddled off in the opposite direction so she could deal with whatever wounds she had. Gaius had smelled the blood earlier, but thankfully he'd already eaten.

"Aren't you going to warn Zoya about Annwyl?" Gaius asked Kachka.

"I didn't invite her here, so . . . no."

Kachka tracked her sister down. Took a bit. She started off outside, assuming Elina was hunting. But she was in bed. Kachka was ready to be disgusted, but when she found her sister on top of that dragon, she understood more. When one had to fuck, one had to fuck.

Without knocking, Kachka walked into the room her sister shared with no one but the dragon. Such a big room. Could get a whole tribe in here.

"When you're done," Kachka said to her sister, "find me."

"Get out!" Celyn ordered, his body covered in sweat, his big hands around Elina's waist, but the sisters ignored him.

"Why are you back so soon?" Elina asked. She, too, was covered in sweat, her white-blond hair stretched down to her hips in drenched ringlets, her back straight, small tits out proud, nipples hard because of excitement. Yes. She'd been giving the dragon quite a ride. "You were to go off and face death after rounding up team."

"Woman!" the dragon snarled. "*Get out of this room!*"

"Team I got," Kachka replied to her sister, "but was sidetracked by your Iron friend. The one missing eye."

"The Rebel King?"

"So many titles with these royals."

"Kachka," her sister pushed.

"Yes. Your precious Rebel King. He had been captured. We rescued him and I beheaded priestess."

"Good. I owe him."

"Well, your debt has been paid. Death almost had him, but he is healthy again."

"*Get out!*" the dragon roared.

"Whine you do," Kachka accused the dragon. "Like little boy." She looked at her sister. "When you are done. Come. Meet team."

"I will."

Kachka began to close door and she heard the dragon sigh in relief, so she pushed the door back open. "One more thing—"

"*I will kill you!*"

"What?" Elina asked.

"Zoya Kolesova invited self on trip."

"Gods, why?"

"Because she is annoying. I wanted to warn you before she got you in hug. But we may not have to worry long."

"*I am going to tear the walls of this castle down!*"

Elina covered her dragon's face with her hand. "Why no worry?" she asked.

"We came back with Annwyl's boy. The pretty one."

"He *is* pretty."

"That's my cousin," the dragon complained behind Elina's hand.

"Well, Zoya has set her sights."

"She cannot be foolish enough to—"

"She is foolish enough. Even now she goes down to lake to tell queen to give the boy to Zoya for one of her precious, oversized daughters."

"And you let her?"

"I do not really like her."

"Kachka!" her sister chastised, pulling herself off the dragon's cock, to his great anger.

"*Where the battle-fuck do you think you're going?*"

"Zoya Kolesova is favored among her tribe, Kachka. If Annwyl takes Zoya's head, the Kolesovas of the Mountain Movers of the Lands of Pain in the Far Reaches of the Steppes of the Outerplains will start war."

"We have alliance with the Anne Atli," Kachka reminded her sister, and the look that Elina gave her was pointed and rude.

Grabbing clothes off the floor, Elina said, "You are not stupid, sister. Who will stop the Mountain Movers? You? *Me*? Even the Anne Atli will not stop them. She will allow them to rain giant stones upon this ridiculous house!"

"Then perhaps you will learn to live like you were meant to. Instead of whiling away hours in soft bed with this lizard."

"Hey!"

"I was *not* whiling. I was fucking. I had needs!"

"Och! You and your needs! Were you going to take a bath after?" Kachka taunted. "In your *tub*?"

"Again with the tub!"

"You look like decadent Southlander when you use it!"

"I like it!"

"Your weakness sickens me!"

"Hey!" the dragon bellowed. "One of you needs to fix this!" he ordered, pointing at his hard cock, which was directed straight at the ceiling.

Since Elina was just pulling on her boots, Kachka shrugged and began to walk toward him, but the dragon quickly held up a hand. "Not you! Her!"

"But you said—"

"Shut up!"

Kachka studied the dragon's human cock for a moment. "It is quite large, sister."

"I know." She grinned. "It is almost too much for me. Almost."

The sisters laughed and now headed toward the door.

"Are you really leaving?" the dragon demanded.

"I must save Zoya Kolesova of the Mountain Movers of the Lands of the—"

"*Do not bore me with that ridiculous name, woman!*"

"Then why do you insist on asking me questions!" she shot back before walking out the door.

Kachka winked at the incensed dragon and followed her sister into the hall.

As they walked down the stairs, Kachka noted, "You torture that dragon greatly."

Her sister sniffed and glanced at Kachka. "*I* do?"

Chapter Eight

"Aren't you freezing?"

Annwyl glanced back at Morfyd, standing on the lake edge, her human form wrapped from head to toe in a white fur. Her human body always had a hard time adjusting to cold weather, even though spring was coming and the ice on the lake had already melted.

But Annwyl was trying something new. She needed a bolt of fresh ideas. She thought sitting naked in this cold water would help her. That's what Elina said the Riders believed.

She was beginning to think the Riders were very, *very* wrong.

"I'm fine," Annwyl lied, wondering how much longer she should keep up this charade.

Think of something new? She could barely think about anything but stopping her teeth from chattering together until they broke into little pieces.

"Annwyl, get your big ass out of that water this instant!" Talaith ordered. The fur around her shoulders was brown to match her fur boots and thick leggings.

"But I'm—"

"No! This instant!"

With a sigh that was meant to sound put-upon but really was deep gratitude, she stood. She wanted to run back to shore, but she was going to walk. Like a proper royal who put herself in freezing water like an idiot. Especially with Dagmar also standing there watching. While the other two were bundled up, Dagmar didn't have a fur on. "You call this cold?" the Northlander had asked. "Seriously?"

Dagmar watched her with a smirk. She knew how miserable Annwyl was, but she was doing this thing lately. This thing where she just let Annwyl do whatever she wanted and then, when it blew up in her face, Dagmar smirked and, without saying a word, clearly stated with the expression on her face, *Told you so, my queen.*

The cow.

Annwyl was near the shore when she heard a voice call out, "*You* are Annwyl the Bloody?"

She looked over and blinked in surprise before glancing back at Dagmar. "Thought you said the giants lived beyond the Ice Lands and wouldn't help us."

Dagmar let out a small, annoyed sigh. "She's *not* a giant."

Annwyl looked over again, took a moment to study the woman, then asked Dagmar, "Are you sure?"

"She's not a giant!" the Northlander snapped. She'd been getting real snappy lately, too.

"Look," one of the women with the giant pointed out, "she wears the mark of the beast on her arms and between her thighs."

Confused, Annwyl looked down at her thighs. She'd had Fearghus's brands there for so long, she'd forgotten about them. They were just part of her now. Like her limbs. Like Fearghus. Not that he ever let her forget his presence. Ever.

"She's definitely the one."

"Oh, all right," the giant said, appearing disappointed, but Annwyl had no idea why. She hadn't done anything yet. She usually only disappointed people after she'd done something.

"Is there something you want?" Annwyl asked.

"Yes." The woman nodded, her grin wide. "The boy."

"What boy?"

"The boy they say belongs to you."

Annwyl sighed. "There are no slaves in the Southlands."

"No, no. Not a slave. Your son. I want your son. I will give you . . . six oxen for him. Good stock. My tribe breeds the best oxen in all the Outerplains."

"My . . ." Annwyl cleared her throat. "My . . . son? Talan? You've seen him?"

"He is here! With his sister and cousin," the giant said with an alarming amount of cheer. "Sent back with us Daughters of the Steppes by the old She-beast Brigida through some magickal portal."

"The children are here?" Talaith asked. And, without waiting for an answer, she started to run off, toward the house, but Morfyd grabbed her arm and pulled her back, holding her in place.

"Yes, they are here. And you can keep the girl. I have no sons for her. They are already promised to others. But once I am done with your son, teach him all he needs to know—in bed and out"—she and the other Riders laughed at that—"I will make sure to marry him to one of my strongest daughters or nieces. He will be well taken care of. Especially if he is good breeder."

Annwyl still stood in the freezing water, but she could no longer feel it. She was naked and it was frighteningly cold, but she couldn't feel that either. She knew that Morfyd had rushed into the water, her hands on Annwyl's shoulders, her beautiful face with the scar down one side permanently marking her as a witch now loomed in front of her, but Annwyl couldn't see her.

No. She couldn't see anything around her—except that dark red haze. . . .

Kachka realized her sister had stopped walking after the last thing she'd said, and Kachka turned to face her. "What?"

"You brought Nina Chechneva here?" she asked in their own language.

"I had no choice."

"But you brought her *here*?"

"I had no choice. I would have left her with the old bitch, but she sent the lot of us here. Brigida was pissed."

"It was dangerous to bring her, sister."

"Bringing her was not up to me. Besides, she's the least of our problems right now."

Elina nodded, suddenly remembering why they were heading to one of the largest lakes on Garbhán Isle, and began walking again.

As they neared the lake, they could hear a repeated thudding sound coming at them from a distance. They glanced at each other, then ran.

They came through the trees just as a naked Annwyl picked up all of a bloody, mangled Zoya Kolesova, lifted her over her head, and slammed her back into the ground. Then Annwyl screamed. That insane scream that Kachka had heard more than once in her nightmares.

Zoya wasn't out completely, but she was close, her eyes crossing as she stared up at Annwyl.

Reaching over, Annwyl yanked the blade from the scabbard Marina Aleksandrovna had at her side and raised it over her head.

Kachka and Elina ran down to the lake shore, throwing

themselves between Annwyl and Zoya just as Morfyd the White caught hold of Annwyl's raised hand and attempted to yank the blade from her while Talaith tried to drag the woman back from behind.

And there, standing serenely by the lake, not moving—not doing anything—was Dagmar Reinholdt. The Beast, she was called by her own Northland kin.

Those cold, grey eyes locked with Kachka's and she knew the cow would not intervene.

"Honestly," Kachka said to her sister in their own language, "you fuck one warlord's nephew and she *never* gets over it!"

Desperate, because Annwyl seemed really intent on cutting off Zoya's head, Kachka grabbed Annwyl by the face and yelled, "Annwyl! The Iron Dragon King is here! He is here at Garbhán Isle! You must go talk to him!"

That's when they finally had Dagmar Reinholdt's attention. "Gaius Domitus is here?" she asked, still dry on the lake's edge.

"Yes," Kachka replied, her hand continuing to grip Annwyl's face, afraid to let her go. "He was being held captive by a priestess of Chramnesind's cult."

Dagmar stepped closer to the water, her eyes now wide behind those little bits of glass she wore. "What? Are you sure she was a Chramnesind priestess?"

Kachka glanced at the Northlander. "She was until I took her head and released the king." She looked back at Annwyl. "Now he needs a royal to talk to, Blood Queen. That is you. You need to go see him."

Annwyl's eyes narrowed, finally locking on Kachka's face. "Are you lying to me?"

"When have I ever given enough shit to lie? To you or to anyone?"

Annwyl took in a deep, long breath, let it out, and nodded. She pulled away from the women trying to control her, tossing the sword back to Marina. While the women moved back to the lakeshore to wait for her, Annwyl washed Zoya's blood off her face, arms, and hands. When she was done, she came back to shore and grabbed her clothes.

As she pulled them on, she stared down at a still-bleeding Zoya. When she had her boots and leggings on and her shirt tossed over her shoulder, she informed Zoya that, "If you talk about my son again like he's a horse to be auctioned off, I'll cut you open from pussy to chin. Understand me?"

Zoya made an unsettling gagging sound and nodded her head, but it seemed enough for Annwyl. Without another word, she disappeared into the trees.

Dagmar walked over to Kachka and asked, "Tell me, Kachka Shestakova, why are there so many Riders now in this territory?"

"Ask your queen."

"I'm asking you."

"I tell you nothing."

"Are you sure that's wise?"

Kachka reached for her own sword, but Elina caught her arm and stopped her.

"Let it go, Dagmar," Morfyd implored. She was crouching down by Zoya, examining her wounds. "I'll need your help—and, Talaith, don't go."

"My daughter—"

"Can wait.

"Fine. What do you need?"

While Morfyd rattled off a list of herbs and things that she needed the Nolwenn witch to retrieve for her, Zoya reached out a bloodied hand to Kachka.

Kachka grabbed it and knelt down beside her fellow

Rider. She really didn't know what she'd expected Zoya Kolesova to say, but it definitely wasn't, "The Southland Queen . . . is . . . *magnificent*."

Kachka's head briefly dropped, then she looked back at the rest of her team. They all knew, in that moment, that they would *never* get rid of Zoya Kolesova. They were stuck with her.

Chapter Nine

Gaius found a kind servant who got him some clothes that actually fit his human frame and then offered him some food. All that meat he'd eaten earlier had worn off and someone had taken the bear away, so he'd happily sat down at the table to enjoy some Southland stew.

As he dug in, Queen Annwyl entered the Great Hall. Her hair was wet and, in theory, she should be freezing to death in this weather, but she didn't appear to be. Since she'd *stalked* into the Great Hall, Gaius knew immediately the human queen was livid. Zoya must have made her demands about the boy. But Gaius wasn't surprised to see Annwyl alive and well and seemingly unharmed. The woman could and *would* fight anything. She used her rage the way the rest of them used their dragon flame—as a lethal weapon that cleared everything out of her way.

Gaius didn't bother to call out to the queen. He'd see her in due time. Perhaps after he'd spoken to Dagmar Reinholdt or Bram the Merciful first. Besides, in the years he'd known Annwyl the Bloody, worked with her, fought beside her, she had *never* remembered him. Each occasion she saw him, it was as if she were meeting him for the very first time.

In the beginning, that had insulted him greatly. But

eventually it had become so ridiculous, he didn't bother to get upset anymore. Aggie, however . . . she always got upset. Greatly.

"Talan!" the queen barked once she was in the middle of the hall.

"Mum!" her son called back. Then he appeared at the back of the hall and ran to her, lifting her up in a big hug and swinging her around. "I'm so glad to see you!"

Annwyl showered her son's face with kisses before getting him to put her down and checking him over as if he'd just come from war.

"Mum, I'm fine."

She finally stepped back. "They wanted to buy you, you know. Like cattle. She won't be doing that again, though."

"Mum . . . what did you do?"

"What any mother would do to protect her son."

"Is she still living?"

The queen shrugged. "Probably. I didn't take her head if that's what you're asking."

"Did you try?"

"Why do you question me so?"

"Mum!"

Annwyl sucked her tongue between her teeth and waved a dismissive hand. "Where's that sister of yours?"

"You mean your daughter?"

"That has yet to be proven."

Talan chuckled. "She went off to find the old bastard."

She punched her son's shoulder. "Be nice to your father!"

"Be nice to my sister."

"I am nice. I haven't killed her yet, have I? And the gods know that I've been tempted."

The boy laughed again until he saw something behind his mother.

Enjoying his delightful stew, Gaius glanced toward the

front of the hall to find out what the boy was looking at and Gaius's mouth dropped open for a moment.

"Oh . . . *Mum*."

Annwyl barely glanced back at a nearly destroyed Zoya Kolesova. Even Gaius, who had been watching gladiator games since before he could fly, still had to stop eating. Yes. It was *that* bad.

"She talked about you like cattle," Annwyl said again. "I didn't like it."

"But this . . . this wasn't necessary."

"She started it. She challenged me."

Poor Zoya was being helped by Kachka and her sister. She had one arm around each sister and her face was bloody, bruised, and battered. The other Riders followed behind them, not even bothering to assist.

"She will not let your witches help her," Kachka explained as they stopped in front of the queen.

"Let her die then."

"*Mum!*"

"*What?*"

"You're better than this," her son argued.

"She is not," Kachka pointed out.

"Truly. She is not," Elina confirmed

They were so direct, Gaius couldn't help but laugh, and that's when the queen's gaze suddenly locked on him, those mad green eyes staring at him through all that hair.

"Gaius. There you are. I'll be with you in a minute."

Shocked, Gaius looked around the hall, expecting to see someone else—anyone else—who might be named Gaius.

When he found no one, he looked back at the queen and pointed at his chest with his spoon. "Are you . . . are you talking to me?"

"Yes, you!" she snapped. "Who else would I be . . . ? What other Gaius is . . . ? What is *wrong* with everyone?"

That's when the queen spotted Dagmar Reinholdt as she suddenly floated into the room with Lady Talaith and Princess Morfyd. Dagmar had always looked so out of place here at Garbhán Isle. An elegant Northland female among the brawny Southlanders. Quiet. Intelligent. And dangerously plotting. She always seemed to belong somewhere less . . . full of yelling.

Dagmar Reinholdt placed her small hand against her chest. "Me? What have I done, my queen?"

The queen snarled and took a step, but her son quickly pulled her back. "Hello, Auntie Dagmar."

The Battle Lord went up on her toes and kissed her nephew-by-mating on the cheek. "Talan. How are you doing?"

"I'm fine. We brought visitors back with us." He gestured toward Gaius with a tilt of his head.

"King Gaius." She moved past the others and over to Gaius's side. He stood, took her outstretched hand, and kissed the back of it.

"My Lady Dagmar. Always good to see you again."

"And you, of course. Although I have to say I am a bit surprised you're here."

"Had a spot of trouble. Nothing to worry about."

A snort from Kachka had Gaius glancing over, an eyebrow raised. "Something you'd like to say, *Lady* Kachka?"

Now Dagmar laughed, and Kachka, snarling a little, pulled away from poor Zoya, her sister almost crumbling under the weight of the much bigger woman.

"Cousin!" Tatyana exclaimed, quickly moving in to help Elina before she was lost under the massiveness of Zoya.

"Something you want to say to me, tiny Northlander, with tiny head I can crush between hands?"

Dagmar, never one to back away from much of anything, stepped directly into Kachka's space, quiet demeanor still in place.

"I'd like to see you try, Outerplains *slut*."

"Fucking your nephew once does not make me slut. It makes your nephew *very* lucky."

They had their hands around each other's throats by the time Gaius and Lady Talaith reached them. Talaith handled Dagmar, yanking her back one way, while Gaius yanked Kachka the other.

"Stay away from my nephew!" Dagmar yelled as Talaith dragged her from the hall.

"I already fucked him, Northlander! I promise I am done with him!"

Dagmar screeched and managed to pull herself out of Talaith's grasp, but the former assassin—a Southlander secret Gaius had known about for years—lifted her up and carried her out the front doors.

"Dagmar Reinholdt's nephew?" he softly asked Kachka. "A little young for you, isn't he?"

"He had to learn from someone. And a boy that pretty to have me . . . ? It was honor for him."

Before Gaius could respond to that, Annwyl took hold of Gaius's forearm. It surprised him. He didn't think Annwyl had ever touched him before. He wasn't sure why she was touching him now. He felt the need to duck . . . or simply prepare for death.

Thankfully, however, none of that was necessary. The queen simply said, "Come on. Let's talk."

Gaius nodded, ready to follow.

"Wait," a *still* bleeding Zoya called out.

The queen looked over to the Rider, waited until her Outerplains sisters had helped her to Annwyl's side. Then the poor, battered woman went down on one knee, all of them cringing a bit at the sounds of bones grinding together.

Annwyl watched silently, the hand holding Gaius's forearm tightening a bit in confusion.

"I apologize, Annwyl the Bloody, for what I said earlier. And for doubting you. Your strength is great. And I, Zoya Kolesova of the Mountain Movers of the Lands of Pain in the Far Reaches of the Steppes of the Outerplains, will fight for you and your queendom as long as I have breath."

Annwyl gazed down at Zoya, then glanced around at everyone else, then back at Zoya. After a long pause, she finally said, "Uh . . . all right then."

After another pause, Annwyl started to walk off, leading Gaius behind her, but she did toss over her shoulder, "Let Morfyd and Talaith take care of your wounds, Zoya . . . whatever whatever."

Gaius silently followed until they reached a large room. There were chairs scattered around and a large table with maps strewn across it. Once the door was closed securely behind them, the pair stared at each for several long seconds, until they both started laughing.

"Mountain Movers?" the queen asked, her laughter light and completely sane.

"I have to say, Queen Annwyl," Gaius said around his own laughter, "although my sister would never agree, *I* always have the most entertaining time when I come here."

Chapter Ten

"Any idea why you were taken?"

Gaius sipped his wine before replying, "I truly don't know. But the torc that priestess put on me . . . it didn't just keep me human. It drained me. Sucked me dry." He shook his head. "That seemed particularly cruel. Even for them."

"Not really. Have you heard about their"—Annwyl pursed her lips as if she tasted something vile—"*purifications*? These are people who enjoy being cruel for cruelty's sake."

"Perhaps, but . . ."

"But?"

"It was clearly killing me. Slowly, but killing me. Yet they were taking me somewhere."

"So if you didn't reach your destination, you would definitely die."

"Right. Which sounds like they wanted to make sure that happened no matter what."

"They must have wanted *something* from you, though, otherwise they would have killed you immediately."

"Yes. But I have no idea what that was. What they were looking for. What they think I have."

Annwyl studied him a moment before asking, "When

Kachka found you, did she tell you anything about why she was back in the Outerplains?"

"No. But she did debate killing me when I asked her about it."

Annwyl laughed, her smile wide and relaxed. Pretty. It reminded him that Annwyl hadn't started out as a royal. She'd been plucked from her town by the warlord father she'd never known and forced to live with him and his evil son as the new rulers of the Southlands.

No one had been sure why her father had bothered. Many human royals left bastard children everywhere they went; they rarely acknowledged them, much less dragged them back to their homes. Then, he'd died and his son had taken over, eventually trying to use his hated sister to secure an alliance with another important royal. Annwyl hadn't taken to that very well, and she'd ended up fighting her brother for the Garbhán Isle throne.

She was a strong warlord, but things could have gone either way since her brother had many allies. Then Annwyl had met Fearghus, and he and his siblings had ridden into one last battle against her brother. Annwyl had won the day and the throne . . . and her own dragon mate.

It had been the talk of the Provinces all those years ago. That the eldest son and heir to his mother's throne had mated for life with a human. Little did any of them know what their bond would really lead to.

The Abominations.

Although Gaius didn't really think of them like that. They were just the offspring of dragons and humans, which didn't automatically make them evil.

"The Chramnesind cult has sent these slaughter groups to temples and monasteries all across my lands," Annwyl said. "And they've been going in and"—she sighed, deeply— "*purifying* the worshippers and destroying the temples."

"But you don't think that's simply in the name of their god."

"No. Everyone else does, but I can't help but think they're after something. Now they've taken you . . . thinking you had something." She leaned forward a bit, stared into his eyes. "Whatever they're trying to find, Gaius, we need to find the bloody thing first."

And he knew, in his bones, that she was absolutely right.

With his arm slung around his daughter's shoulders, Fearghus the Destroyer walked into the Great Hall of the place he lived in with his mate. It wasn't his home. That was his cave in Dark Plains. There, he could be his true self. A happy, relaxed black dragon with a mate and daughter he adored and a male offspring he greatly tolerated.

But when he was here, when he was in Garbhán Isle, he was Prince Fearghus, First Born Son of the Dragonwitch Queen Rhiannon and Direct Heir to her throne.

A position he could honestly not care less about. Annwyl was the true leader. She loved her people. Risked everything for their care, for their protection. And because of her loyalty to her people—and his undying love of her willingness to cut off the head of anyone who threatened those she protected—Fearghus put up with living among so many bloody people . . . and kin. Gods . . . so damn many of his kin.

It was a never-ending nightmare. They never seemed to leave. And even if they did . . . more came to replace them. The Cadwaladrs, his father's side of the family . . . an endless supply of annoying dragon kin to pluck his last black dragon nerve.

"Father!" his male heir greeted him, arms thrown wide. Instinctually, Fearghus reared back.

"No hugs?" his son asked, appearing as annoying as

Fearghus's brother Gwenvael, who watched from the stairs, one of his six daughters planted on his shoulders, her small hands resting on her father's head, the pair smiling together as they viewed the family reunion before them.

"Why do you torture me so?" Fearghus asked. "I let you live. Wasn't that enough?"

"Fine. No hug. How about a kiss?"

When Fearghus sighed, his daughter stepped in.

"Leave off."

"Is it wrong for a son to want some affection from his own father?"

"You don't want affection. You probably made some bet with that one." She pointed at Gwenvael, who gasped in horror, pressing his hand against his chest.

"But, niece! How can you say such a thing to a beloved uncle? Do you not adore me?"

Talwyn let out a sigh, glanced off, and muttered, "I am so afraid I'm truly about to hurt your feelings, Uncle Gwenvael."

Aye. This was *his* girl! Fearghus couldn't be prouder.

"Be nice to Uncle Gwenvael," the boy chastised. "He's the only male of the family who didn't assume I was replaced at birth with someone else's more annoying offspring."

"I'm still not sure," Talwyn snarled, and her brother's eyes narrowed.

Fearghus took a step back once they had each other in a headlock and quickly moved over to his niece Rhi. She stood by her father, Briec, tall and regal and astoundingly beautiful.

Fearghus hugged her. "Welcome home, little one," he said, kissing the top of her head.

Her arms were tight around him, her hugs always as strong as her nature was soft. His sweet niece didn't like fights. Didn't like anger. She wanted everyone to love everyone else.

Unfortunately, she had been born into the wrong family for that sort of life outlook.

"I'm so glad to be back, Uncle Fearghus. But I don't know how long we can stay."

"Why are you here now? I thought you were trapped with that old bit—"

"Uncle Fearghus," she cut in, one silver eyebrow raised. "She's not that bad."

"Oh, sweet child . . ." He hugged her again. Because only his sweet niece could see the best in the evilest of She-dragons, Brigida the Foul. That took some deep understanding, which the rest of them were incapable of.

"By the by, brother," Gwenvael suddenly stated as he swung his giggling daughter off his shoulders and tossed her casually in the air. "The good King Gaius is here as well. Came with the Riders."

Fearghus stated the obvious. "I don't care."

The days of war with the Irons was over, so what did he care if that one-eyed prick came to—

"He's with Annwyl. In the war room. Alone."

Again, Fearghus shrugged. So the prick lost his head to Annwyl's blade. He wouldn't be the first nor the—

"She remembered his name."

Fearghus blinked, surprised by that. "What?"

His brother shrugged, trying to appear innocent. "She remembered his name. And . . . what did you say, little one?" he asked his daughter. But she'd disappeared. While the twins continued to fight, the rest of them glanced around, trying to find the child.

Then, smoke swirled around Gwenvael and his daughter was back on his shoulders.

He squinted up at her. "I thought I told you only to do that when we're alone."

"Sorry, Daddy. I forgot."

Fearghus glanced at Briec. The brothers had noticed the growing powers of Gwenvael's Five, and they didn't know what to say about it. It wasn't like either of them could judge. Not after Fearghus's twins had shown a willingness to kill from a few days after their birth and Briec's sweet Rhi had been able to throw grown adults out of a room with a mere wave of her hand.

But what was missing from Gwenvael's Five was something that had meant so much to Fearghus when his twins were growing up. The balance that Rhi provided them. The three together were powerful, but their energies combined kept them from being something he would eventually have to destroy.

The Five . . . they didn't balance each other out. Instead, they seemed to work as one, and that created a power that concerned both Fearghus and Briec. Two dragons who rarely agreed on much of anything.

"Auntie Annwyl took the Rebel King *gently* by the hand and led him down the hall to her private chambers . . . while knowing his name," Gwenvael's daughter said.

Talwyn abruptly pulled away from her brother and glared down at Gwenvael as Rhi "tsk-tsk'd."

"I don't know why you're looking at me like that. Her mother taught her to be so observant."

"But Auntie Dagmar uses her knowledge for the right reasons," Talwyn argued. "Not just to fuck with family members."

"Oooooh," the little girl chastised. "I'm telling Mummy you said a bad word."

Talwyn took a step forward, tossing her hair off her face with a rough shake of her head.

"Do you know who I am?" Talwyn asked the child.

"Yes," the little girl replied. "You're the one my sister Arlais is going to kill one day so she can take your throne."

Rhi and Talan exploded into laughter, but they also quickly turned away from Talwyn's withering glare.

Talwyn swung back toward her young cousin, her roar shaking the castle walls.

The little girl squealed at whatever she saw in her cousin's face or heard in that terrifying roar and disappeared in a flash of smoke.

Grinning, Gwenvael leaned forward and kissed Talwyn on the forehead. "Welcome home, little niece."

Gaius stood beside the queen, both gazing down at one of the world maps she had spread across the thick wood table, in deep discussion about who might or might not be aligning themselves—and their armies—with Duke Salebiri.

He was just leaning over, pointing out a little-known kingdom behind Salebiri's territory, when the door was thrown open.

Annwyl's hand was on her sword before Gaius could blink—he hadn't realized exactly how fast she was, especially for a human—but she quickly relaxed when she saw her mate standing there.

"Oh. Fearghus," she said, before refocusing her attention on the map.

The black dragon's dark eyes locked on Gaius, and that's when Gaius noticed Fearghus's two idiot brothers standing behind him.

Instigators.

True, it had only been Gaius and his sister when he was growing up, and they'd worked with each other, not against. But he'd had enough cousins who'd wanted him dead or, at the very least, truly annoyed, to immediately know what was going on here.

He could have been the bigger dragon. His sister would

expect that of him. She was very big on etiquette, his Aggie, which explained why she was so annoyed by Annwyl and her queendom. Annwyl the Bloody had absolutely *no* etiquette outside the battlefield. She'd be the first to rattle off the rules of war. No killing of the innocent. No rape. No unnecessary destruction. How she had gone on and on before their first and only battle against his Uncle Thracius. But etiquette here? In her home? That was more limited and, to Gaius's secret delight, much more flexible.

So he leaned into her a bit—she didn't even notice, so focused on the map in front of her—placing his arm on the other side of her so that he had her caged in next to him.

The black dragon's head lowered, a fang flashed, and smoke eased from his nostrils while, behind him, his brothers grinned. Even the cranky Silver who never seemed to smile about anything except his daughters.

"*Annwyl!*" the dragon snapped and, again, Annwyl moved so very fast, pulling her swords from the sheaths strapped to her back and assuming a combat-ready pose before Gaius had a chance to take his next breath.

"What?" she demanded, eyes searching the room. "What is it?"

With his brothers watching him, the Black searched for a response. "Uh . . ." He found one. "Aren't you going to introduce us?"

"Introduce you? To who?"

The prince's eyes narrowed and he gestured at Gaius. Annwyl glanced back and shrugged. "Don't you already know him? We took down Overlord Thracius together and he's stayed here several times." She blinked, glanced down at the floor, then asked Gaius, "Right?"

Gaius nodded. "Right."

"Oh, good. Thought I was confusing you with someone else."

"No, no. That was me," Gaius replied before gently putting an arm around her shoulders. So very casual. So very comfortable. He could never explain how he knew he had nothing to fear. At least nothing from Annwyl. Perhaps because when it came to off-the-battlefield etiquette, she truly didn't care. They had an enemy to squelch and as long as Gaius wasn't grabbing a breast, Annwyl just didn't notice. Already she'd let her gaze drift back to the map, in search of more information on the kingdom Gaius had just mentioned to her.

But the black dragon prince . . . ? Ah, that was another story altogether.

It was as if he planned to shift right there, in the middle of the human castle, into his full dragon form just so he could tear Gaius limb from limb. But before he did any of that, Prince Gwenvael's head was snatched back, his yelp startling his silver-haired brother beside him.

"What was that for?" Gwenvael whined seconds before Dagmar Reinholdt marched into the room.

"King Gaius," she greeted, "I wanted to make sure you had everything you need."

"I'm more than . . . satisfied, my lady."

Gwenvael and Briec snorted at that, but before Fearghus could direct his anger at them, The Beast did. She locked eyes with both—such cold eyes behind boring round pieces of glass—and pointed.

"Go," she ordered.

"But—"

"*Now*."

Gwenvael immediately skulked off, but Briec attempted to resist.

"I don't take orders from—" he began and Dagmar's cold eyes narrowed behind those pieces of glass and her head tilted to the side. It was a small gesture, but apparently enough for the arrogant bastard.

Throwing his hands up, he said, "No need to get hysterical." Then he, too, was gone.

"Now," she said, turning to Gaius and Annwyl, "what are we discussing?" With a casual air and extremely gentle hands, she grabbed Gaius's forefinger and removed his arm from Annwyl's shoulders. Then she stepped between them and stared at the map as well.

With a snarl, Fearghus turned on his heel and left.

While Annwyl leaned in to study the map, amazingly oblivious to everything going on around her, Dagmar gently whispered, "Stop that."

"Stop what?" Gaius asked.

She briefly glared at him. "You know what. And I can only protect you from that one for so long. He's not like his brothers. He's much smarter and meaner than they are." She jerked her head toward Annwyl—who was *still* oblivious. "That's why he likes her so much. They're mean together."

"But the males of that clan make it *so* easy."

Dagmar sighed. "Don't you think I already know that?"

Chapter Eleven

Kachka sat on the front steps that led into the Great Hall and watched her sister speak with her husband, Celyn.

Her walking out on him with his cock still hard and unsatisfied seemed to have been forgotten and now they talked softly to each other, Elina grinning at some joke he'd made.

Something large dropped down next to Kachka on the stairs and she glanced over to see the Rebel King casually sitting beside her.

"It's too easy, you know," he said.

"What is?"

"Toying with the Southlander dragons. At least the males. It's simply too easy."

"I have noticed that as well. Like cat toying with mouse."

"Exactly."

Kachka motioned to her sister across the courtyard. "She seems happy, yes?"

The king studied Elina for a moment, then nodded. "Very."

"Good. I always wanted her to be happy. She never was, you know? When she lived with our tribe."

"It was my understanding your mother didn't make it easy for either of you."

"Glebovicha Shestakova made it easy for no one. Though she tolerated me well enough."

"Because you're not afraid to kill."

"Do not be fooled. Elina is not afraid to kill. But she is just more . . . defense fighter. When you come at her, she will do what she has to in order to survive. But me . . ." She smiled at the dragon. "I am *offensive*. I need little reason to do what I feel is necessary."

"Yes. I've noticed that about you."

"You, peasant," a young voice said from the bottom of the stairs. "Remove yourself from my way."

Kachka and the king smirked at each other before Kachka turned and stared down at Dagmar Reinholdt's eldest daughter, Princess Arlais. She wished she could say Arlais treated her this way because she sensed her mother's intense dislike of Kachka, but no. Arlais treated anyone she deemed beneath her this way—which was pretty much everyone.

The nine-year-old waved at Kachka. "Move!"

"You have plenty of space. Go around, demon child."

"Isn't it bad enough we have you barbarians here? My aunt allows it, but you don't need to be sitting there in front of our home, making the rest of us look bad."

"And one day," Kachka replied, "the peasants here will rise up . . . and destroy you. And I will laugh."

"Damn, Kachka," Gaius laughed.

"What? Should I lie?"

"She's a child!"

"She is spoiled brat who is lucky no one has put pillow over head while she sleeps."

"Do you think you frighten *me*?" the girl demanded. "Have you *met* my mother?"

"I *quote* your mother."

A large shadow fell over the girl and wide gold eyes stared up at a battered and bruised—but somehow still smiling—Zoya Kolesova.

"So they managed to keep you alive, Zoya Kolesova," Kachka noted, but the disappointment in her voice had the dragon tapping her thigh.

"Be nice," he muttered to her.

After rolling her eyes, Kachka lifted her hands, wiggled her fingers, and cheered, "Yay, you are better! We are all so happy you are not dead."

Zoya nodded, pleased with that ridiculous display.

"You are *huge!*" the little princess exclaimed after making her way up the stairs. Now she walked around Zoya like a side of beef. "Look at her," she said to Gaius, who she probably felt was on her level. "She is peasant perfection!"

"Princess Arlais," the Iron dragon gently chastised. "It is never polite to—"

"You will be my bodyguard," Arlais ordered a grinning Zoya. "You will do my bidding and protect me from all dangers."

Zoya stared down at the little girl until she finally exclaimed, "Look at her, Kachka Shestakova! Look at this tiny person." She leaned down so that she could look the girl in her face. "How old is she? Three? Four?"

"I am nine."

"Nine?" Zoya gasped. "How tiny you are! My girls at nine are ten times your size!" That's when Zoya, who had never understood the word "boundaries," suddenly grasped the child around the waist and lifted her up. "She is like toy! I shall take her back to one of my young granddaughters. She will be her tiny playmate!"

"Put me down, you oaf! You vicious beast! Unhand me!"

Gaius bumped Kachka's leg with the back of his fist and

jerked his head at the tiny Southland royal struggling with Kachka's giant comrade.

Kachka sighed. Loudly. "Must I?"

"*Yes.*"

"Zoya, put her down."

"But my granddaughters will love her!"

"She is princess here and although I am sure her mother will happily give her over to you—"

"Oy!"

"—her father, a dragon, will definitely not. He seems to like her, though none of us can understand why."

"Vicious cow," the little girl hissed at Kachka.

"Keep that up and I will let Zoya's granddaughters chain you like stray dog in street. Now, Zoya, *put her down!*"

Zoya dropped the girl to the ground and they all watched her tumble down the stairs, rolling head over ass.

"So," Zoya asked, forgetting the child since she could no longer have her as a pet, "where are others?"

"At some pub in town. Head north . . . that way." Kachka pointed.

"A pub, eh? They must be celebrating my amazing recovery!"

"Are you going to join them, Zoya?" the dragon asked.

"No. I have something else to do first." She patted the travel bag strapped across her shoulders. "But do not worry, Kachka Shestakova. When you are ready to leave, I will be by your side."

"Oh . . . yay."

Zoya walked off and Kachka crossed her eyes at the dragon. "How can anyone be that . . ."

"Oblivious?"

"You didn't even *try* to help me!" the little girl snapped

as she got to her feet. "And look at my dress. It's filthy! *I will have you executed!*"

"Go!" Kachka ordered her. "Before I have you skinned and gutted like that bear we will have for dinner."

The child screeched and stormed off, up the stairs and into the Great Hall.

"It seems . . . unwise to make that one an enemy," the king noted in that sensible tone of his.

"She is child."

"Child today. The beast that rules these halls tomorrow. If she has her way."

"I would kill her myself before I let that happen. Now come." She studied his face. "You need rest."

"Are you taking care of me, Kachka Shestakova?"

"Someone has to. The male dragons here will ignore you. Dagmar Reinholdt will try to use you. And Annwyl the Bloody will try to take your head. So come," she said again, grabbing his arm and helping him to his feet. "Let's get you some sleep. Just few hours."

Kachka led him into the Great Hall even as Gaius protested, "I think they made a room for me in the building where they put visitors."

"The rooms here are giant. I could put most of Zoya's big-legged and big-armed sisters in the queen's chamber and I doubt the queen would lose her giant bed. Why these Southlanders waste so much space I will never know. Now come."

Kachka led Gaius to her way-too-big bedroom. With a yawn, he sat down, rubbing his hands across his face and neck.

"Are you sure you are all right?" she felt the need to ask. She reached over and gently stroked the marks still on his neck from the torc.

"I'm fine. Because I'm breathing. And that's thanks to you."

Kachka folded her arms across her chest. "That is thanks to me. And yet I still do not have your kingdom."

"You have my everlasting loyalty."

"The loyalty of a one-eyed rebel king who is allied with two mad queens?" She shrugged. "I could definitely do worse."

They smiled at each other just as the bedroom door swung open. Kachka, her hand on the hilt of her sword, turned at her waist and looked at Celyn. "What?" she asked when he just stared at her.

"Everything all right?" he asked, dark eyes moving back and forth between Kachka and the king.

"Well," the king replied, "she is being rather difficult."

Kachka faced Gaius. "I am difficult?"

"I have needs and you're not fulfilling them."

"Why aren't you fulfilling them?" Celyn wanted to know. He was new to his job as . . . something or other for the Dragon Queen. Kachka didn't know or care. But, like her, he had much to prove.

Which made him easy prey for the Iron dragon . . . and for Kachka.

"You want me to help him?" Kachka asked the young dragon, Celyn. The only thing Gaius knew about him was that he was a Cadwaladr and that his father was the wonderful Bram the Merciful. Unfortunately, Celyn's mother was Ghleanna the Decimator. A true Cadwaladr was that one.

"Would it kill you to do *something* for our queens?"

"So I should fuck him?" Kachka asked, forcing Gaius to quickly look away before he started laughing.

"Wait . . . what?"

"That is why royal dragon complains. Because I will not fuck him to sleep. Are you saying I should fuck him to sleep?"

Now this would be where Bram the Merciful would smoothly extricate himself from the situation, probably removing Kachka with him. But the dragon was young and untrained.

"You couldn't help him out a little?" the young dragon asked.

Gaius quickly dropped his head lower.

"He has hand."

And now Kachka was not helping!

"But did you have to make him angry when you rejected him?"

"No. But it amused me to do so."

"He is an ally of the queens."

"So?"

"Does that matter to you?"

"No."

"Can't you just be nice to him?"

"You want me to fuck him for you?"

"No! That's not what I mean, Kachka. I mean, just be *nice* to him. Polite. Try not to piss him off, yeah?"

"So you want me to use mouth?"

That's when Gaius couldn't keep it in anymore. He fell back on the bed laughing, and Kachka laughed with him.

"Really?" Celyn demanded. "I'm trying to help and you're tormenting me?"

A slightly smaller, prettier version of Celyn sauntered into the room. Gaius knew her immediately. Branwen. He'd known her when she was still Branwen the Black. A young She-dragon with dreams of being a great warrior like her mother. Now, years later, after helping the queen and

Iseabail rescue Gaius's sister, she'd become Branwen the Awful. A name he'd heard she was quite proud of.

A well-respected captain in the Dragon Queen's Army, Branwen was dressed from neck to toes in chain mail and leather, with a sword and several daggers on her belt, and a shield at her back. And from what Gaius had heard over the years, no matter the day or time, Branwen the Awful was *always* ready for battle.

"Ho, ho!" Branwen laughed as she stared at her annoyed brother. "Is the great Celyn the Charming trying to be in charge?"

Gaius had also heard that Branwen had not taken her brother's promotion to the rank of sergeant major in the Queen's Army well at all. He outranked her, although he was more a guard to the queen than a hardened battle warrior.

"I am in charge," Celyn snarled at his sister. "At least of you, *Captain*."

"What does his lordship want you to do, Kachka?" Branwen asked, ignoring her brother.

"Suck the cock of a king for the queens' benefit."

Branwen gasped, feigning horror, her free hand pressed dramatically against her chest. "Celyn!"

"I asked you to do no such thing, Kachka!"

Kachka shrugged. "They all think if there is available hole, they must fuck it."

"That is not what I said!" Celyn argued.

Branwen shook her head. "Mum would be disgusted."

"Don't you have something to do, Captain?"

Branwen grinned. "Not at the moment."

After another withering glare at his sister, Celyn again focused on Kachka. "I was just saying that King Gaius is our ally, and I need you to remember that."

"I remember. I just do not care."

Branwen giggled like a child while her brother tried his best to ignore her.

"I do not care if you care," he snapped at Kachka. Everyone seemed to have forgotten that Gaius was right there. Right in front of them. Gods, he hadn't been this entertained in ages. "I just need you to remember and treat him as befitting an allied royal."

"By burning down his home, destroying his lands, and making his sons one of my many husbands? Because that's how Daughters of the Steppes treat royals."

"*Allied* royals?"

"If they piss us off." Kachka shrugged. "Maybe he pissed me off."

"Well, do me a favor," Celyn said, staring Kachka in the eyes while he reached over and slapped his hand over his sister's laughing face, "and pretend he *didn't* piss you off."

"Pretend? What is pretend?"

"Fake it. Just do that for me, Kachka. Please."

"Fine. But only because my sister is forced to choose you as husband because she is weak and has no other options."

Branwen laughed loudly behind his hand and repeated, "No other options! She has no other options!"

That's when Celyn shoved his sister out of the room, her startled squeak surprising them all. She was a feared captain of the Dragon Queen's Army after all.

"Please, Kachka," Celyn pleaded.

"Yessss," she hissed. "I will be nice to him."

"Thank—" was all he got out before his sister grabbed him from behind, yanked him out of the room, and tossed him head first over the banister.

Gaius cringed when he heard the dragon hit the hard stone floor of the Great Hall.

"Crazed female!" Celyn yelled at his sister.

"King Gaius," Branwen went on with a large smile. "It's good to see you, as always."

"You, too, dear Branwen."

"Now if you'll excuse me. I'm going to beat my brother to death."

Kachka watched Branwen walk out and head toward the stairs.

"She will not really beat him to death," Kachka felt the need to explain.

"You sound disappointed."

Kachka shrugged. "I do not know if disappointed is right word, but it is close. . . ." She stared at him. "Did I give you enough entertainment before you go to bed?"

"Yes. You did. And it was amazing."

"Now sleep. No one will bother you in this room. The sheep never come to this room."

"Sheep? You call the servants sheep?"

"What would you have me call them?"

"People?"

Kachka waved that suggestion away and walked to the door. "Sleep well, royal."

"No kiss good-night?"

She walked into the hallway, shaking her head. "Males. All of you are pathetic."

"But you can't blame us for trying."

She smirked. "I blame males for all things. You deserve no less. Now sleep, dragon. And try not to burn house down with flame-y snores."

Kachka closed the door, and Gaius stretched back out on the bed, arms above his head.

He was just starting to drift off when he realized

something—Kachka Shestakova was really adorable when she was torturing others.

Zoya Kolesova finished writing her note on the parchment. Once done, she opened the top of her leather travel bag and smiled down at the white crow staring up at her.

"Hello, my lovely," she cooed to the bird. She reached in and carefully removed it. While she held it in one hand, she used her other hand to wrap the note around its leg and secured it.

She then kissed the bird on its head for luck and set it free. It headed north and Zoya watched it until it disappeared.

Pleased, she set off back to that giant house that the royals lived in. Such fanciness the Southlanders needed to survive.

Zoya made it past the trees and that's when she saw Kachka and Elina Shestakova. It seemed life in the Southlands had been good for poor little Elina. A solid hunter, that one, but worthless in battle.

"Ho, comrades!" Zoya called out, waving when they slowly turned to face her. "Off to the pub?"

When Kachka didn't reply, Elina bumped her with her shoulder. "Yes. We are going to pub to meet with others."

"Good! I will join you! I could use drink!"

Kachka made a strange noise, but she was always making strange noises. Zoya ignored it. It was probably a defect of some kind, but no reason her mother should have gotten rid of her at birth or anything.

Zoya stepped between the sisters and threw her arms around their shoulders.

"The witches here are great. I feel better already from the skills of that white-haired one."

"Really?" Kachka Shestakova sighed out. "That is so wonderful."

"Is it not?" Zoya asked, hugging the women tighter. Nothing meant more to Zoya than the bond of her tribeswomen. Why, though, Kachka had brought along that useless boy and the evil witch, she didn't know. But she wouldn't argue with her. Not when drinking was about to begin!

Chapter Twelve

They found the others in a pub not far from the main house. Kachka wanted to ease in and sit down at the table with the others without being noticed, but that was impossible with Zoya by their side. Not simply because of her size, which was daunting enough, but because as soon as she walked in, she announced, "Hello to the sheep of the Southlands! Zoya is here!"

Kachka was just spinning around, about to tell the big oaf to shut her mouth and go the hells back to the Outerplains, when Elina caught her shoulder and shoved her toward the table.

With a sigh, Kachka sat down and, in their native tongue, said, "As you can see, Zoya feels better."

"Yay," they all weakly said, though Ivan didn't even bother.

"I know you are all glad to see me! And I am glad to see all of you, my comrades!"

Zoya dropped into a chair, the wood creaking.

Once they were settled, Ivan Khoruzhaya leaned in and asked, "Why are we here, Kachka Shestakova?"

Zoya slammed her fist on the table, startling everyone in the room but the Riders. "Do not question her, useless boy!"

Ivan began to say something, but Kachka cut him off. "Wait." She couldn't afford to lose Ivan, and Zoya would twist him until he was nothing but flesh and shattered bones.

"Zoya," Kachka patiently explained in their native tongue, "while Ivan is with us, he will have a say in our decisions and be able to ask questions."

"A man? You'd trust a man to ask smart questions? Why?"

"Because our group is small, we need all the help we can get. Plus, this is the Southlands. Here, the women and men work together. The men are just not for breeding and trash removal."

Stunned, Zoya sat back, strange noises coming from the back of her throat.

"It's all right, Zoya," Elina tried, resting her hand on Zoya's arm. "My mate and I make decisions together all the time."

"Your mate is a *dragon* male. And you are weak and only alive because your sister saved your ass." She gave a small shrug. "No offense."

Elina's eye narrowed dangerously and she growled out between clenched teeth, "No offense taken."

"Just get used to it," Kachka told Zoya. "We all have to work together. We have to have each other's back. None of this tribe bullshit."

"What do you need from us, Kachka Shestakova?" Nina Chechneva asked. She was pale and kept rubbing her legs, but Kachka didn't bother to ask how she was feeling. She assumed if there was a problem, the witch would be smart enough to tell her.

"The Chramnesind cult has sent out assassins to kill worshippers of other gods and destroy their temples. They've been doing it all over the Southlands. But we are going to get to them first."

"And do what?" Marina asked.

"Kill them all."

"Oh." She nodded. "All right."

"The ones we kill," Nina interjected, "I can have their souls, yes?"

"For what?" Tatyana asked.

"You do not ask me questions, I won't ask you questions."

"You just asked a question."

"That's my business."

"Take what you want from them, Nina Chechneva. Who knows," Kachka sighed, "perhaps we can find way to terrify them with your presence before we send them off to their god."

Smiling, Nina sat back in her chair.

"But," Kachka quickly reminded her, "you are not to do that to *us*."

"Never." She began rubbing her legs again. "My loyalty is to all of you. I've promised."

"Who?" Marina asked.

"Don't worry about it."

"You keep saying that . . ." Ivan muttered.

Finally, a serving girl brought over several pints of ale. Kachka and Elina didn't bother to drink theirs, and the others spit theirs out as soon as they took a sip.

"What is this? Water?" Marina Aleksandrovna demanded.

"This is . . . tepid," Tatyana delicately admitted.

"We know." Elina stood and waved at the pub owner. He nodded and, a few minutes later, brought over a case of drink that the sisters paid him to keep just for them. They made it themselves, letting it ferment in the ground before asking several pub owners to keep some on hand for them.

"Thank the horse gods," Marina sighed before taking a large swig from her own bottle.

After they drank a bit, they all slammed their hands on the table and snarled in satisfaction.

"It will be good night, my fellow comrades . . . and the boy!" Zoya added, vaguely waving at Ivan.

But he was smart and simply rolled his eyes before getting on with his own drinking.

And, as they all drank . . . they planned.

Duke Roland Salebiri finished his morning prayers, lifting his face to the suns. A true blessing from his god.

Once done, he slowly got to his feet. He no longer felt the need to rush. To always be going, going, going. That was how he used to live. Before.

Before he'd been shown the true light. Given the true sight. For what you see with your eyes is all a lie. It is an untruth created by evil to blind one to the realities of this world.

To blind one to the darkness that was covering the world in its filth.

Roland faced his second in command, General Falke de Vitis. He was a strong, *clean* human. A powerful knight of the realm, untouched by the darkness of this world. Roland had complete faith in de Vitis because de Vitis had complete loyalty to their god. He would never betray Roland because Roland would never betray Chramnesind.

The great, the mighty Chramnesind.

"May your sight shine bright, my king."

Roland smiled. "I am not king yet, de Vitis. But when the blood-soaked whore hangs from my battlements . . . I will be. Now, what news do you have to tell me?"

"The agreement has been signed by all parties. We're done here."

"Excellent. And? Anything else?"

"Our men lost their grip on the Quintilian King."

"Ah. I see. That's unfortunate. Did he get away on his own?"

"The men were all slaughtered, the slaves released, but not by dragons. By human hands. They were in the Outerplains at the time."

"Riders. The Whore Queen's new allies." He sighed, sad for the barbarians. "Foolish women. To trust such a . . ." He shook his head. "Nothing we can do about it now. They've lost their souls, which is not our problem."

"Should we keep looking for Gaius Domitus?"

"No. He'll be back in the Provinces soon enough to be with his sister. Have our spies keep an eye on him once he's there."

"As you wish, my lord. And Lady Ageltrude is looking for you."

"Yes, of course. My wife is ready to return to our home, I think."

"I'm sure she is, my lord."

Together, they left the suns-soaked battlements and headed down to the first floor. As soon as they walked into the main hall, Roland's oldest boy ran to him.

"Daddy!"

Roland lifted his son in his arms, held him tight. "There's my boy. Ready to go home?"

"Yes. I'm very bored."

His son was smart like Roland's beautiful wife and would one day make a great king. He'd brought his son on this peacekeeping mission because Roland wanted to be the one to teach him not only the ways of their god, but the ways of politics.

"Where's your mama?"

"Outside. Waiting for you."

"Then we'd best go to her."

Still holding his son, Roland walked out the large double doors and onto the stairs, with de Vitis behind him.

Roland's beautiful wife, Ageltrude, stood waiting with her orphaned nephew and niece. They were the children of Ageltrude's brother who'd died many years ago. Armed and ready, they protected their aunt without question. Something Roland appreciated.

The early morning suns beamed down on his wife's regal head. She was everything Roland could ask for in a woman. Intelligent. Beautiful. Royal. *Pure*.

In their ten years together, she'd given Roland four beautiful sons and a wealth of excellent advice. She was also dedicated to his god and, Roland truly believed, a gift from Chramnesind himself for loyal service.

"Ready, my love?" he asked.

"Of course." She tightened the fur cape around her shoulders and walked down the stairs, leading the way for the rest of them.

Roland happily followed, watching his wife as she moved. Laughing, she looked over her shoulder at him, and said, "A beautiful sacrifice to our god."

He had to agree, for the screams of dying heretics were music to the ears of Chramnesind.

Roland glanced around at the field of those who would not submit to Chramnesind. In order to save their wretched souls, each heretic was held or tied down and molten silver poured into their eyes. It was an excruciating death, but it purified them. Brought them closer to Chramnesind. A gift, really.

So the screams and cries of those not already dead . . . ? Nothing but hymns of praise to the one true god.

When they reached their carriage, de Vitis took Roland's son from his arms and placed him inside. Ageltrude turned to him, smiled in that beautiful way she had.

"Anything I need to know?" she asked quietly.

"They lost the Quintilian King."

Her beautiful eyes darkened and Roland knew that she was angry. Not with him, but with incompetence. His wife had no patience for incompetence. "That is unfortunate."

"Do not worry. We'll get him—and if he does truly know anything, we will cut it out of him."

She let out a breath, smiled. "I don't worry when you're in charge." She pressed her hand to his cheek and kissed him softly on the lips. "Now . . . let's go home before that smell of burned flesh invades all my clothes."

Chapter Thirteen

Gaius slowly woke up. He felt warm and safe and very comfortable. The Southlanders had the best beds. So good, in fact, he let himself luxuriate in that warm, comfortable feeling until he heard snoring. Deep, loud snoring.

Male snoring.

Gaius forced his eyes open and immediately noticed that his arms were around tiny Tatyana Shestakova. But she wasn't the one snoring. That was Ivan Khoruzhaya behind her.

Even more horrifying, Yelena Khoruzhaya was pressed up against Gaius's back.

What the hell had happened last night? What the hell was happening right now?

Gaius sat up and barked, "By Iovis's cock, what is happening here?"

Marina Aleksandrovna, who slept by Gaius's feet, lifted her head, stared at him a moment, then turned over and seemingly went back to sleep.

So Gaius dropped his head back and unleashed flame, burning the ceiling above and rousing every Rider near him as they reached for and brandished their closest weapons.

That's when Kachka Shestakova slowly sat up. She was

on the far side of the bed, her eyes bleary from drink. She yawned and scratched her head as she gazed at him. "What?"

"*Why are all these people in my bed?*"

"*My* bed, royal. This is *my* bed. Not yours. I allow you to sleep here. And I allowed them to sleep here. I do not see what problem is."

The door to the bedroom slammed open. Dagmar Reinholdt stood in the doorway with her mate. She took one look and her hand covered her open mouth, her eyes widened in shock and despair.

Her mate, however, began to laugh—until Dagmar brought her fist down very close to his balls.

"Ow! What was that for?"

"King Gaius," Dagmar began, "I am *so* sorry about this."

"Sorry for what?" Kachka demanded. "We do nothing wrong. It is not like we fucked him while he slept." She abruptly looked at Ivan Khoruzhaya. "Did we?"

"Why are you looking at *me*?"

"Because you are male. And if there is hole, you must fill it."

"Well, I did not fill any of *his* holes."

Unable to listen to another second, Gaius roared, "*Get the fuck out of my bed!*"

"Not your bed. My bed."

"Shut up!"

"I saved your life!" Kachka shot back.

"You should have left me to die!"

"Next time I will!"

"I do not understand," Dagmar snarled, "why you did not just take him to one of the *many* rooms we have available."

"You all waste space. I do not understand why you waste so much space! And it is *not* like he is so important."

Fed up, Gaius took in a breath, ready to unleash flame that would destroy every Rider . . . and most likely the entire room. He didn't care. He cared about nothing at the moment. Because this was ridiculous!

But before he could burn them all to ashes that he would roll around in like a pig rolled in its shit, Dagmar's mate joked, "Maybe you should fuck him, Kachka. It might loosen him up a bit."

When Gaius's head snapped around, Dagmar squeaked a little, then dropped into a crouch, her arms over her head. He appreciated that. Because he unleashed a ball of flame that sent the gold dragon flying out of the room and over the banister outside.

"Owwwww!" the Gold cried out when he hit the hard stone floor below. Gods, that poor floor took a lot of abuse.

"Feel better now that you hurt another?" Kachka asked.

"Shut up."

"King Gaius," Dagmar said, standing. "Please. Allow me to show you to another room. Your own room."

"Yes. Horse gods forbid some royal should be forced to share anything with another."

"Shut *up*," Dagmar snarled at Kachka. Then she took in a deep breath, let it out, and stretched out her arm. She motioned to Gaius with a twitch of her fingers. "Please, my lord. This way."

Gaius stood, trying to pull the fur covering around his bare ass. But none of the Riders would move. So, he yanked, sending them all flipping to the floor.

Feeling sadly triumphant over that, he wrapped the covering around his waist and allowed Lady Dagmar to show him from this room and these ridiculous people!

Dagmar placed him in a room beside Annwyl's.

"King Gaius, I am so sorry—"

"No, no," he said, sitting on the edge of the bed. "No need to apologize, Lady Dagmar. This was not your fault."

And it wasn't! Gaius wasn't lying or trying to ease her discomfort. It really wasn't Dagmar's fault.

It was *Kachka's!*

"Would you like me to order water for your bath?" Dagmar asked.

"Actually, I think I'll go out to one of the lakes." He needed to shift to his natural form. He needed to feel water against his scales. He needed to be away from here!

Dagmar nodded. She'd lived with dragons long enough now to understand. She stepped out into the hallway and peered in both directions. She finally raised her hand. "You. Boy. Come here."

A young boy ran over and Dagmar gestured to Gaius. "Please escort the king to the lake that Prince Fearghus likes to use."

"Aye, my lady."

"And make sure to stop by the gates and get some clothes for his majesty as well. He'll need them when he's done bathing."

"Aye, my lady."

Gaius moved into the hallway, stopping by Dagmar's side long enough to nod down at her. "Thank you."

"Of course. Anything you need, King Gaius."

Normally, Gaius would never need so much use of his title, but at the moment . . .

Gods! That woman!

Kachka was pissing in the chamber pot, sighing loudly from the pleasure of it. She'd drunk much the evening before and was glad she hadn't pissed the bed.

Honestly, she didn't remember getting in bed with the dragon. Or bringing the others with her, but she truly did not see the big deal of it all. Riders shared beds. The winters on the Outerplains were brutally cold and sharing beds for warmth was typical. Yet these Southlanders acted like it was the most outrageous thing one could do.

Whatever. Let the dragon be pissed at her. She didn't care. Life was too short for such bullshit!

Deciding she wouldn't worry about it for one more second, Kachka was about to stand when the door slammed open again.

"*What is wrong with you?*" the tiny Northland female bellowed from the doorway, her pale face red with rage, her entire body shaking like a small dog's.

Kachka glanced around. "Nothing," she replied honestly. "Why?"

"Why would you *all* get in bed with him?"

"Because we were tired."

"And drunk," Zoya Kolesova volunteered as she got to her incredibly large feet. She'd tried to sleep in the bed with them, but there just hadn't been enough room for her, so they'd rolled her off and onto the floor. Like a thousand-year-old oak chopped at its roots, she'd gone over, and never woke. Not even for a second. She slept like the dead.

Nina Chechneva rubbed the sides of her head. "Very drunk."

"I don't give a battle-fuck!" the Northlander raged. "He is a royal and an ally of this court and every last gods-damn one of you will treat him with respect!"

"I do not think—"

"*Do I make myself clear!*" Dagmar Reinholdt briefly closed her eyes behind those small round pieces of glass. "Because I swear," she finally said, her voice low, but oddly more terrifying than when she was yelling, "by all reason, that if you don't, I will personally hunt down each and every one of your kinswomen and kill them, starting from youngest to oldest until I've wiped out your entire fucking bloodlines. Do I make myself clear?"

Zoya sauntered up to the Northlander. "Look, little person, I—"

"Do I make myself," and the Northlander's head tipped to the side a bit before she finished with, "*clear?*"

Zoya and the Beast locked eyes for a very long time before Zoya finally looked away and nodded. "You make yourself clear."

The Beast looked at the others and they all nodded in agreement.

She stepped out of the room, slamming the door behind her.

Zoya spun around, raised her hands, and, in their language, demanded, "*Where the fuck did you bring us, Kachka Shestakova?*"

Gaius was very pleased with the lake the boy led him to before leaving a pile of clean clothes carefully placed on a rock nearby.

Of course, the Southlands were known for their lakes. And the dragons here loved them, even though they were made of fire.

The Irons had fewer lakes to choose from, so they built their own inside the Quintilian Provinces, allowing for communal bathing, where political ideas and decisions could easily flow. Many deals were struck among those easing sore muscles in the communal baths.

Dropping the fur around his hips, Gaius dove into the water. When he pulled himself up, he was dragon again. Just that alone made him feel better.

Gaius dove under the water again. The lake was much deeper than he'd thought it would be, and he wondered if dragons had dug it out over time.

When he swam back up, breaking the surface, he launched himself up and out, unleashing his wings and taking to the skies. As he flew toward the two suns, he realized that he hadn't flown simply for the feel of it since his capture. He'd flown out of the cave the day before, but that had been in a desperate search for food.

Gods, how he'd missed it.

Gaius turned over so that the suns warmed his belly, his wings keeping him aloft. A trick he and his sister had taught themselves at a very young age.

He put his claws behind his head, closed his eyes, and let out a long, relieved sigh.

Gaius didn't know how long he flew like that. He'd heard the cheers and laughter for a bit, but he just assumed it was other Southland dragons. Something that didn't worry him. He knew he was as safe as he was ever going to be among the Southlanders as long as he had his alliance with the two queens.

Still, he never expected anyone to crash on top of him in mid-flight and then immediately flip off.

His eyes snapped open and he stared at the large round shield that bore Annwyl's coat of arms—two black dragons with two crossed steel swords between them and a shock of red that represented the "blood" in "Annwyl the Bloody."

As he gazed at the shield, he heard the screamed, "Shit!" and flipped over in time to see a human warrior falling toward the lake below.

"Fuck," Gaius growled before diving down, his front forearms out. He caught the human seconds before the warrior hit the water, turning his body and pulling the human in tight.

He crashed hard, his body going deep down, but he couldn't stay. The human in his arms would never last as long as he would under the fresh water, so Gaius quickly swam back to the top. As soon as he broke the surface, he held the human up.

Gaius shook his head to get the hair and water out of his eyes and to see whom he held in his claws, sputtering and cursing.

When he could finally see again, he still blinked several times before asking, "Iseabail?"

The high-ranking general in Annwyl's army coughed a few more times before replying, "Hello, Gaius. Long time."

"Not really. Just saw you a few months ago."

"Oh. Right. Forgot."

"What were you doing?"

"Don't tell Mum."

That didn't really answer his question. "What?"

"I was just doing a bit of run and jump."

"Run and jump?"

"Where I . . . run and jump from dragon to dragon."

"While they're *flying*?"

"No need for that tone!" she shot back.

There was a soft throat-clear from the banks of the lake and they both looked over to see a stoic but drenched Annwyl standing there, arms crossed over her chest, green eyes glaring. The power of the splash when Gaius had hit the surface of the lake had been so strong that Annwyl's hair was blown off her face, revealing how annoyed she was at the moment.

Even worse than the overall wetness of the queen was that her daughter had been several feet behind Annwyl. Only Talwyn's booted feet were wet. The rest of her was dry, and she was laughing hysterically at her mother.

This was not a good situation.

"My liege—" Izzy began.

"Shut up!"

"Are you all right?" Gaius asked the queen in order to

stop himself from laughing. Because, gods! Did he want to laugh.

"I'm fine," she growled between gritted teeth. She cast an angry glare at her daughter, who was now doubled over at the waist, tears streaming down her face. Although they could no longer hear her laughter . . . because she'd begun to wheeze.

"Talwyn!" Izzy hissed at her cousin. "Stop it!"

"I . . . I can't!"

The queen didn't seem to particularly like this response, so she reached back and slapped her daughter on the back of the head.

The laughter stopped immediately, and Talwyn shot up, crazed black eyes burrowing into crazed green ones.

"No, no, no!" Izzy begged. She hit at Gaius's arms. "Get me over there. Get me over there!"

With a shrug, Gaius tossed her halfway across the lake and onto the shore.

"I meant *swim* me over here, you git!" she yelled when she'd landed and rolled several feet.

True, if he was back in the Provinces, his sister would have a general's tongue removed if one dared speak to him in such a manner, but Gaius and Izzy had quite the long history. Besides, he was enjoying himself, which was nice, considering the morning he'd already had.

Izzy got to her feet and stepped between glowering mother and daughter.

"Why don't we focus on something else besides each other?" she asked the two women, but if they heard Izzy . . .

Instead, the pair tried to look around Izzy's wide shoulders so that they could keep eye contact. Like two pit dogs ready to fight, they would not be distracted from the rage they seemed to feel toward each other.

Gaius took the quiet moment before what he felt certain would become a full-out brawl to swim to the other side of the lake. He pulled himself onto the shore, shifting at the same moment. Human and naked, he walked to the clothes that the squire had left and grabbed hold of a piece of thick white material, which he used to dry himself off.

After several minutes of hearing nothing from the women, he looked at them over his shoulder. They'd stopped fighting long enough to stare at him as he dried his human body.

"Problem?" he asked.

"Damn, Gaius," Izzy muttered, one side of her mouth quirked up in a surprised smile.

Gaius was about to smile back when he heard a sound he dreaded *every* time he was forced to come to the Southlands.

"Yoooo-hooooo!"

"Fuck," he growled, his head dropping as she came out of the trees by the lake. She was stunning, as always. In her human form, wearing a dress made entirely of Eastland silk. Her red hair reached to the back of her knees and she, as always, wore no shoes.

She was Keita the Viper, one of the Dragon Queen's daughters. Known worldwide for her beauty and her ability to successfully poison anyone who put the Dragon Queen's throne at risk or got in the Princess's way.

"King Gaius!" she greeted. She was, without a doubt, the most beautiful creature to walk these lands, whether in her natural form or as human.

But beauty was not enough. Not for anyone *this* annoying.

"Princess."

"I was so happy to hear you were back! And guess what I have for you," she teased, liquid brown eyes gazing up at him.

Gaius briefly closed his one eye. "An eye patch?"

"Yes! This time I went with a steel grey. To match your hair!" She held out the silk eye patch.

"I really don't need—"

"Put it on," she ordered, a threat implied in her flat tone. Then, just as quickly, the brilliant smile returned, the coquettish act back in place. "It will look so wonderful on you."

Gaius didn't understand the She-dragon's obsession over eye patches and one-eyed dragons and humans, but he didn't want to spend the rest of his time in the Southlands worrying about what he ate. It was never a good idea to piss off a well-known poisoner.

So, grudgingly, Gaius took the patch from her small hand and tied it around his head.

"Happy?" he asked.

She went up on tiptoes, stretching her arms out so that she could adjust the stupid thing accordingly. "There. Perfect. Just like me!"

She giggled and twirled away from him. He wanted to hit her.

"You know, King Gaius, with you visiting, an outside dignitary and all, we really should have a dinner in your honor with—"

"Dancing!" Izzy cheered. "There must be dancing!"

"Of course!"

Her queen and cousin quickly forgotten, Izzy ran back toward the castle. "I'll get everything started!" she called out.

"I don't need dancing," Gaius informed Princess Keita.

"I know," she replied coolly, her hand patting his bare chest. "I know."

He watched her walk off. How the Northland chieftain, Ragnar of the Olgeirsson Horde, tolerated that wench as a mate, Gaius would never know.

Deciding not to worry about it, Gaius began to get dressed. He was pulling on his chain-mail shirt when he realized that the queen and her daughter were still standing there, staring at each other. They hadn't said a word in all that time, so he'd forgotten about them completely.

But, with a nod to each other, they suddenly walked away together.

"Where are you two off to?" he asked.

"Training rink," they replied as one.

"Huh," Gaius said, before he shrugged it off and finished getting dressed.

Kachka caught the wood bow that her sister tossed to her as she made her way into the Great Hall.

"What's this for?" Kachka asked.

"They are having dinner tonight in honor of your Iron."

"He is not my Iron, Elina."

"Whatever. The Cadwaladrs will be attending."

"So they need more meat."

"Exactly. Up for a hunt?"

Kachka was always "up for a hunt" so she didn't bother to say as much and instead replied, "Need to eat first."

Her sister nodded and they walked to the table. They'd barely gotten their seats before the other Riders arrived and began eating. The kitchen staff rushed to get more food on the table, especially once the other dragons came in.

They were mostly eating in silence until the gold dragon walked to the table. He seemed fine now, after his morning getting tossed around by the Iron King. "Greetings, my kin!" he happily announced, his Northland mate following behind him. "How are we all doing this beautiful morning?"

There were grunts from his sisters and abject silence

from his brothers. But that had never stopped the Gold before.

"It *is* a beautiful day, isn't it?" He stood behind Marina Aleksandrovna and reached over her to grab one of the warm loaves of bread from the table. Marina, as any Rider would expect, yanked the dagger from her belt and slammed it into the table, only missing the Gold's human hand because dragons were quite fast.

The Gold held his hand against his chest and stared at Marina. "Woman, have you lost your mind?"

"Get own food," Marina warned.

Tatyana rolled her eyes. "We discussed this," she reminded them all. "In the Southlands you do not have to defend your food like a wolf defending its carcass."

"He was still too close."

Dagmar Reinholdt sat down at the table with a sigh. "It's like eating with my brothers again."

"At least your brothers have some manners!" Gwenvael walked around the table to find another seat and easier access to the food while Marina yanked her blade from the table and slid it back into her belt. The entire time, she never stopped eating.

Once seated, Gwenvael eyed Tatyana. "You dress like the other Riders, but your accent . . ."

"I've been trained in the ways of the Southlanders," Tatyana explained. "I know many languages and the etiquette of many cultures. There are a few of us among the Riders. We relay information from the Anne Atli to those we—"

"Conquer?" Dagmar asked.

Tatyana smiled. "Of course not. We prefer the term—"

"Destroy," Zoya volunteered.

Tatyana gritted her teeth before snapping, "Why are you here, Zoya Kolesova?"

"Because you need me!" she cheerfully replied.

"Like wolf needs fleas," Nina Chechneva muttered.

Gaius walked into the hall. His hair was soaked and he wore a chain-mail shirt to go along with his grey leggings and brown boots. As human, he looked . . . exceptional. Why couldn't he be human? Why a lizard? It was unfair.

"Ladies," he greeted. Elina smiled up at him and Kachka kept eating.

Exceptional or not, he was still a spoiled royal who couldn't have a few extra people in his bed.

"We have to go hunting because of you, royal," Kachka accused.

The dragon snorted. "You don't need a reason to go hunting, Rider. So don't put that on me."

He reached between two of the Southland royals, ignoring the glares as he did so, and grabbed a loaf of bread. "Before you two go, though, you may want to check out the training ring."

"Are you suggesting my sister needs training?"

Elina's head popped up. "Do not come at me. He did not say me."

"Not you two. But Annwyl is in there with Talwyn, and I'm guessing that will be quite entertaining."

The room had become horrifyingly silent, and the three of them froze, fingers moving toward their weapons, waiting for an attack at any time. When they finally looked at the others, the Southlanders were staring at them, mouths agape, eyes wide.

"What is happening?" Kachka asked her sister.

"I do not—" was all Elina got out before the Southlanders moved with such speed that all she, Elina, and Gaius could do was stand there and hope not to get knocked down in the stampede as the others charged for the door.

When all that was left were her sister, Gaius, and Dagmar Reinholdt, Dagmar sighed, pushed back her chair, and stood.

"Come on," she barked at her dogs, which followed obediently behind her as she left the hall.

Gaius went back to eating his bread. "Well . . . that was interesting."

Chapter Fourteen

Talan didn't know how he'd ended up in the stables. The last thing he remembered was going to the local pub with his cousins and meeting up with some of the Riders. . . .

Thankfully, he woke up fully dressed and none of the horses appeared traumatized. So he decided to assume that even drunk, he'd managed not to end up in a situation where he'd become one of the "husbands" of Zoya Kolesova's—most likely—big-boned daughters.

Talan stood, paused, threw up in some hay, then stumbled out of the stable after patting a horse on his head.

He really shouldn't try to keep up with his dragon cousins and the Riders. There were few who could outdrink that lot.

Making it past the stable doors, Talan immediately shielded his eyes from the bright light of the two suns and leaned up against the stable wall.

"Are you all right?" sweet Rhi asked, her arm slipping around his waist.

"Too much drink."

"You must know better by now."

"Apparently not." He glanced at her. "What are you doing here?"

"I spent the night at Izzy's house. You should have come with me."

He was guessing Rhi was right.

"Come on," she coaxed. "We'll get you back to the main house. I'm sure Mum has something to help."

Talan put his arm around Rhi's shoulders and did his best not to put too much of his weight on her. Together, they headed toward the house until several of the Cadwaladrs ran past them.

"What's going on?" Talan asked one of his younger cousins. He wasn't armed at the moment, and if he needed to get Rhi to safety—

"Your sister and mum are in the training ring together!" his cousin replied before charging off after the others.

Mouth open, Talan and Rhi turned to each other. Then, hangover forgotten, the two ran toward the training ring. They pushed their way past their kin so that they were right up against the fence.

Loaves of crusty, fresh bread were passed around while their kin all silently watched in fascination. None of them doing anything to stop this. Not even his father.

"Are you just going to stand there?" Talan demanded of Fearghus.

"I learned long ago not to get between your mother and her prey."

"Talwyn isn't her prey! She's her *daughter*! She's *your* daughter!"

Fearghus shook his head. "Not when she's in the training ring, she's not."

Disgusted with everyone, Talan started to go over the fence to put a stop to all this, but Briec and Gwenvael grabbed him and yanked him back.

"Oh, no, you don't," Briec said.

"Daddy!" Rhi quickly chastised.

"Sorry, love, but we have been waiting since that child's birth to see this moment. Just let it play out."

"Plus we already have gold on this," Gwenvael stated. "You can't stop it now."

"You're all horrible!"

"Shhhhh."

Eyes wide, Talan focused on one of his favorite kin, shocked and disgusted all at the same time. "Auntie Morfyd?"

"Don't hate me," she pleaded in her sweet way. "But even you have to admit this has been a long time coming."

Realizing that unless he wanted to fight all his kin—he didn't—he'd have to wait this out, Talan turned back to the battle already raging inside the ring.

Talwyn was going after their mother with a shocking amount of power. An unnecessary amount, as far as Talan was concerned. Although she trained every day with two Kyvich witches and many of their fellow Abominations, Talwyn always held her true skill back.

Until now. Until she faced their very human mother.

Annwyl had a round shield that she held up as her daughter repeatedly brought down a sword and axe, hacking away at the wood with such brutality that Talan couldn't believe that no one—absolutely *no one*—was stepping in to stop it.

Why? Why wasn't anyone helping?

Even more frightening, where was his mother's rage? If she ever needed it before in her life, it was right now, with her full-of-herself daughter!

But his mother seemed cool and calm under that badly damaged shield.

Why? What the hells was happening?

"Such easy money," Gwenvael laughed.

Talan yanked his arm away from Gwenvael, ready to tell him where he had every intention of sticking that money when Gwenvael got it, when Annwyl finally raised one of her blades, blocking Talwyn's sword.

Mother and daughter locked eyes and, in that moment, Annwyl used what was left of her shield to slam it into her daughter's leg.

With a scream, Talwyn dropped to the ground and Annwyl got to her feet. She tossed the shield away and walked around her daughter, gazing down at her. Still no rage. No anger. But there was definitely something there, something Talan didn't actually recognize.

As Annwyl blankly gazed at her daughter, she suddenly raised her leg, and brought it down hard.

Hard enough to crush Talwyn's chest. But Talwyn blocked her mother with her arm and rolled away. She stood on one leg, the other unable to bear any weight. Talwyn still had her sword, though. And even on one leg, she was ready to fight.

She struck first, swinging her sword at Annwyl's head, but Annwyl slipped out of the way with such speed that for a moment, Talwyn could do nothing but stare at the spot their mother had been standing in.

It wasn't simply that Annwyl moved so quickly. She'd never been slow. But there was an . . . elegance to it that Talan had never seen in his mother. An elegance of movement.

He loved her, but even he had to admit she was a bit of a lumberer.

"Like elephants marching across the plains," Morfyd had muttered more than once when Talan was growing up.

Annwyl ended up behind Talwyn, but Talwyn sensed her immediately and moved quickly to block the oncoming blow. Their blades clashed under the morning suns and held for a moment. The power of each female halting the other was palpable.

Until Annwyl kicked Talwyn, sending her only daughter flying halfway across the ring. She hit the fence near Talan, cracking the wood as her body made contact.

While his mother casually returned her sword to its sheath, Talan rushed to his sister's side, crouching near her right. Rhi on her left.

"Good job," he whispered to his twin. "Let her think she's winning."

That's when Talwyn looked at him, dark eyes crazed behind all that black hair, bruises blossoming on her cheeks.

"You are letting her win . . . right? I mean, I know the blow to your leg was a lucky punch, but . . ."

With a roar of rage he hadn't heard from his sibling in more than a decade, his sister pushed herself up until she was standing again on her one good leg.

Talan grabbed her sleeveless chain-mail shirt, but she batted him off and went after their mother.

"This is going to be awful," Rhi said, almost in tears.

She was, as always, right.

Without weapons, Annwyl outmaneuvered every attempted attack by her daughter. She used her steel gauntlets and speed to block Talwyn's blade, quickly disarming her after a few seconds. When Talwyn then struck at Annwyl with her fists, the queen blocked those blows too, and she didn't even lose her breath.

Talwyn began to use Kyvich hand-to-hand techniques on their mother, but, again, the queen blocked them easily until she had both of Talwyn's arms gripped in her hands. Then, by shifting her weight, she sent Talan's twin flying into the far wall of the barracks adjoining the training ring.

Annwyl dusted off her hands and leggings, and said, "I expected you to be more advanced, Talwyn. We've got a war coming up. And you're not ready."

Talwyn lifted her hands and drew runes of fire in the air,

chanting words that allowed her to craft a spell against her own mother.

"Talwyn, no!" Rhi cried out.

Talan leaped over the fence and ran until he stood in front of his mother. He raised his hands and created a shield, but the power of Talwyn's unleashed spell rammed into it, pushing Talan back into Annwyl. Her hands braced against his spine, keeping him upright and trapped in one space.

That alone shocked him beyond words. His mother shouldn't be strong enough to keep him in place. No one should be strong enough to do that, considering the rage behind Talwyn's rune spell.

Talan and Talwyn, of equal power, pushed against each other, their spells fighting for dominance.

"Stop it! Both of you!" Talan heard Rhi screaming. She didn't want to unleash her power. Not with her cousins' powers in combat. The combination of the three together . . .

But just when Talan was afraid nothing would control his sister's wrath, the wind around them whipped up, sending dirt and stones from the ground into his eyes. Talan turned his head but kept his shield up.

"*That is enough!*" a voice bellowed before a line of flame lashed out, splitting at the end to tear into the spells of both Talan and Talwyn, until they were both forced to stop. Talan, because he was sent flipping back several feet. Talwyn because she simply didn't have the strength to fight the onslaught.

When everything had stopped and Talan could see again, his eyes watering from the dirt still irritating him, it was his mother who held her position. Standing tall.

But it was the Dragon Queen who had stopped the whole thing.

"Have you all lost your minds?" Rhiannon the White demanded of her grand-offspring, standing regal in the clearing on the opposite side of the training ring. Her white scales fairly glowed under the sunlight and her wings flickered angrily as she glowered down at them.

Their grandfather, Bercelak, had landed on top of one of the barracks, overseeing all, but saying nothing. As a Cadwaladr, he'd never stop a fight. His main concern was the safety of Rhiannon.

The queen's head turned toward Talan's mother. "Are you all right, Annwyl?"

"Is *she* all right?" Talwyn exploded.

"*Silence!*"

Annwyl didn't answer Rhiannon; instead, she walked over to Talwyn, who was still trapped on the ground because of her damaged leg.

With cold indifference, she gazed down at her daughter.

"Come after *me*, little girl," their mother warned, "and you'd best be ready."

"Annwyl," Fearghus said, softly. But Annwyl raised her hand, keeping him quiet.

"Understand me, Talwyn?"

Breathing hard, her rage a palpable thing surrounding her, Talwyn spat out between gritted teeth, "Oh, I understand."

"Good."

Annwyl turned and walked across the training ring. As she passed Talan, she stopped to get him back to his feet and patted his shoulder. Then she went over the fence and headed toward the stables.

No one stopped her. No one tried to speak to her. They all just watched her until she disappeared.

Rhi was the first to move, rushing over to Talwyn's side along with her mother and Morfyd. Together, they examined the damage to his sister's leg.

His grandmother shifted to human and accepted a robe

from her mate while Bercelak quickly put on human clothes and followed her into the house so that she could, most likely, meet with King Gaius.

Talan went to his sister's side. He crouched beside her, putting his arms under her, careful of her damaged leg, and lifted her.

"Let's get her in a room so we can fix this leg," Morfyd suggested.

Talan had started to follow his aunts and cousin, when Talwyn grabbed the scruff of his shirt.

"Why did you stop me?" she demanded, the pain of her leg making her voice deeper, sweat rolling down her face from the recent battle.

"Because," Talan replied, gazing deeply into his sister's dark eyes, "she's our *mother*."

Talwyn blinked, as if she'd forgotten that very important fact. "Oh . . . yeah. Right."

Gods in the heavens, she *had* forgotten!

Chapter Fifteen

"King Gaius!" a voice trilled.

Gaius cringed. He hadn't bothered to go outside to watch the battle between mother and daughter, mostly because he hadn't cared. Plus, he'd thought he'd have some time alone to eat.

Sadly . . . that was not to be.

Gaius stood and faced the Dragon Queen of the Southlands.

"Queen Rhiannon."

She held out her hand, apparently a new bit of etiquette she'd borrowed from the humans.

Gaius grasped that hand and kissed the back of it, which got him a lovely growl from Rhiannon's mate.

Exasperated, Gaius snapped, "She offered it to me!"

"Oh, stop it, Bercelak!" She crinkled up her nose in an adorable manner that Gaius found annoying, and said, "He gets so testy around other males. But nothing to worry about."

Yeah . . . Gaius wasn't so sure about that. Not with black smoke pouring out of the dragon's human nostrils.

"You should have come to see, Gaius Domitus," Zoya Kolesova stated as she and the other Riders returned to the hall. "Mother and daughter battling for dominance. It was beautiful sight to behold."

The Dragon Queen's eyes grew wide at the sight of Zoya as she exclaimed, "Good gods! When did we start letting giants in? Bercelak, I thought we had them banished!"

"Queen Rhiannon," Gaius quickly stepped in, "please let me introduce you to the *Riders* of the Outerplains, brought here by Kachka Shestakova. First, this is Zoya Kolesova of the Mountain Movers of the Lands of Pain in the Far Reaches of—"

"*No!*" the queen snarled, hands up and swiping through the air. "Absolutely not! I will not sit here and listen to those ridiculous names! No!"

She turned on her heel and stormed toward the back of the castle. "Come, Iron. We have much to discuss!"

Gaius glanced at Kachka and she mouthed, *Thank you,* at him.

He gave a small smile and began to follow, but he'd barely gotten a step before the queen yelled through the doors at the back of the hall, "Are you coming or do you need an engraved invitation, Iron?"

Letting out a pained sigh, Gaius mouthed back, *You owe me, female*, which only made Kachka laugh.

Kachka watched Gaius make the walk to the back of the hall, his feet dragging like a little boy sent to be reprimanded by his mother.

When she turned back around, Elina was staring at her.

"What?" she asked in their language.

"What's wrong with you?"

"Nothing. Why?"

"You're smiling. It's disturbing."

"Do you want to go hunting or not?"

"All right. I was just letting you know."

After the extremely long meeting with Rhiannon and Bercelak—discussing what he'd already discussed with Annwyl—Gaius had barely been able to get back to his room to change clothes for dinner before he heard the knock on his bedroom door and opened it to find Izzy standing there. She'd changed out of her chain mail and was in a dark blue dress that hugged every curve. She had small blue flowers weaved throughout her hair, but she still kept several of her warrior braids and had two decorative—but quite functional—swords strapped to her back.

"You look beautiful," he noted.

Her smile was wide. There was something about her that still reminded Gaius of the young woman he'd met all those years ago. A cheerful innocence that belied the brutal warrior she'd become, who was feared throughout the realms.

Many warlords and generals called her "The Blood Queen's Pit Dog."

A rather dismissive name for a warrior who had personally destroyed the orc kingdom of the west and laid waste to the Three Kingdoms of Ice right outside the Ice Land territories.

And that same terrifying general was now outside his door . . . blushing.

"Thank you," she gushed, giving an awkward little curtsy. Awkward because Izzy, like Annwyl, had not been raised in the court as most of the lords and ladies of this land had.

"Are you here to escort me to the dinner?"

"I am. Celyn was supposed to come get you. As you

know, he's sergeant major of the Dragon Queen's Army now
and he thought it was his duty to escort you."

"Why?"

"I don't know. But his sister, Brannie, she wanted to
escort you because she's also a captain *and* she thinks you're
quite cute." Gaius laughed as Izzy went on. "But Celyn
wasn't having it. And Brannie . . . she's never been one to
back down about anything. So the pair of them are in a right
brawl now . . . that's when I decided to come get you myself.
I'm hungry and, as soon as we're done eating, we can
dance!"

She reached in and took his arm, pulling him out into the
hall.

"Are you happy with your room?" she asked as they
made their way toward the stairs.

"Much happier now."

She winced. "Heard about that."

"I'm sure *everyone* has heard about that."

"You have to understand the Riders live differently than
we do. I'm sure they didn't see anything wrong with it."

"I'm sure the Riders who arrived with me didn't see anything wrong with sleeping in my bed. But I'm sure that
Kachka Shestakova knew *exactly* what she was doing. She
did it on purpose."

"I doubt that. Kachka doesn't seem to care about anyone
enough to torment them."

"You could say the same thing about a diseased jungle
cat, and yet they still love to torment the large rats that live
in burrows beneath them."

Izzy laughed. "I guess you're right."

They reached the first floor and walked toward the head
table, taking a moment to easily leap over the bodies of
Celyn the Charming and Branwen the Awful as they rolled
by, fists and curses flying.

"How many legions do you command now, General?" he asked her.

"Three. The Fifteenth, the Twenty-Third, and the Thirty-Ninth. All good, strong soldiers I'm proud to lead. I'll be heading off to the base camps in a few days for inspections. Making sure everything is prepared for whenever Annwyl is ready to move."

"We're doing the same. But quietly."

"Why quietly?"

"The Senate hasn't approved our armies joining this war."

Izzy stopped and faced him. "But don't they understand—"

"Oh, they understand perfectly. But this is Sovereigns' politics, which is a breed unto itself. I wouldn't worry, though, Iseabail. Politics is what the House of Domitus is known for. Between me and my sister, they'll give us what we want."

"But it's not about what you want. It's about what's right. If you've seen what the cult has done to some of the temples . . ." She briefly glanced off before snarling, "The orcs were kinder to their victims than the Cult of Chramnesind."

Gaius grasped both the general's hands, looked directly into her eyes. "Izzy, you and I . . . we have a very long history. And I owe you much."

"Gaius—"

"No. Let me finish. I owe you much. But even my debt to you does not match the loyalty I have to my people. I will do whatever is necessary to protect them. I play the game now, with the Senate, because it's in my best interest. But when the time comes, when it is *necessary,* nothing will stop me and my sister from doing what is right. Don't forget who I am, General Iseabail. Who I've become at the talons of Overlord Thracius himself."

Izzy—*General* Izzy—studied Gaius coldly. "Those were

days past, Rebel King. With your sister back, many say you've . . . lost your edge."

"And what do you think?" he asked her. "Do you think I've lost my edge?"

Her smile small, Izzy again took Gaius's arm and continued toward the main table. "I think Duke Salebiri had best pray that you have."

Talan pushed open the door to his sister's room and walked in. Sitting up in the bed, she was in complete darkness. Even the pitfire was not lit, nor any candles or wall torches.

And, in that darkness, she gazed forlornly out the open window.

"Could you possibly look more pathetic?" he asked, in no mood for one of his sister's dark episodes.

"Get out."

Talan lifted his hand and, with a wave, lit all the candles and torches and the pitfire.

"Do stop feeling sorry for yourself," he ordered her.

"I want to feel sorry for myself. I want to sit in the dark and be miserable." Talwyn snapped her fingers and everything went out again.

Becoming truly annoyed, Talan flicked a finger and brought the light back. Snarling a little, Talwyn snapped. Growling back, Talan flicked. And it went on like that for so long that when Rhi walked in carrying a tray of food for Talwyn, the siblings were about to start lobbing the giant fireballs they held at each other.

"Stop that!" Rhi slammed the tray down on a nearby table. "Right now!" She clapped her hands together and the fireballs fizzled out. "Are you trying to set the whole house on fire?"

"She's being a prat."

"You're being a right bastard!"

Talan geared up to start lobbing things at his sister again, Talwyn more than happy to fight back, her fingers twitching.

Rhi stomped across the room and pressed her hand against Talwyn's wounded leg. The pain she was feeling as the bone quickly knitted itself together with the help of Morfyd's magicks slashed through Talan's system. Rhi was allowing him to feel what his sister was feeling but, in Talwyn's usual way, refused to show anyone.

Talan dropped to one knee, unable to support his weight on that wounded leg.

Looking up at his sister, he asked, "Why didn't you tell me?"

"Tell you what?"

"That you were in so much pain?"

"Pain is a part of life."

"See?" he told her, again lighting everything with a flick of his finger. "This is why I want to throw fireballs at you. Pain *is* a part of life, but that doesn't mean you have to suffer in silence. Or, even worse, wallow in that pain."

"It does when you've been an idiot."

Rhi winced for Talwyn and asked, "Because you tried to kill your mother?"

Talwyn looked down at her hands, shrugged. "She made me mad," she admitted.

"The big thing is," Talan noted, moving over to the bed and sitting next to his sister as the pain he'd felt eased away, "is that she never got mad."

"What?"

"Our mother *is* rage. Especially in a fight. But with you . . . she was calm, controlled . . . precise. Plus, I've never seen her fight like that before. Those new skills she has, combined with this newfound control of hers, just made her attacks on you more devastating. You need to find out what she did to get like that. Who she's been training with, learning from. And then you need to start learning too. Learn everything you can."

"He's right," Rhi agreed, placing the tray of food on Talwyn's lap. "I'm sure if you talk to Auntie Annwyl—"

"How can I talk to her?" Talwyn asked, clearly ashamed. "I tried to kill her."

"Oh, come on! You act like you're the first in the family to try. You, sister, are not the first and, honestly, I doubt you'll be the last."

Rhi gave a sad little nod. "He's right."

"You'll sit here. By Annwyl," Izzy said, tapping the chair.

Gaius cringed. "Do I have to?"

"Of course. She's the queen and you're a king. Grandmum will be up here with you as well." She leaned in and whispered, "But don't worry. Annwyl mostly reads at these things. And Grandmum is too busy sniping with Ghleanna about . . . well . . . everything to bother paying any attention to you at all."

"Excellent." He took Izzy's hand and kissed the back of it. "As always, General Iseabail, it's been a delight. You'll have to save me a dance tonight."

She giggled. "I will!"

"Izzy?"

Izzy cringed before plastering on a big smile and spinning around to face her mate, Éibhear the Contemptible. He stood behind her, his untrusting gaze locked on Gaius, his small team of Mì-runach warriors behind him. The lot of them were covered in travel dirt, wearing the heavy fur coverings of the Northlander.

"Éibhear!" Izzy cheered. "You're home!"

The youngest offspring of Queen Rhiannon nodded at his mate, but kept his angry gaze right on Gaius.

"Prince Éibhear," Gaius greeted.

"Iron scum."

One of the Mì-runach, the one they called Aidan the Divine, quickly pulled his overly large friend back. "Isn't this nice?" Aidan asked. "We've come just in time for a feast in honor of your mother's *ally*."

"I don't give a battle-fuck who he is."

Aidan gave Éibhear a shove and said to Izzy, "Why don't you take your mate upstairs, General, and get him cleaned up for the evening."

The blue-haired dragon snarled at his friend. "But I'm not done here."

Izzy grabbed her mate by the collar of his chain-mail shirt. "Oh, yes, you are." She pulled him away with that strength she was known for, and Aidan gave Gaius a smile he could only call "perfectly royal" in its attempt to soothe the situation. But before he could add words to that smile, one of the other Mì-runach next to him complained, "I'm hungry."

Aidan glared at his friend. "Then get food."

The Mì-runach thought on that for a rather long moment before nodding. "Yeah. All right."

"That was Caswyn," Aidan said. "And this is Uther." He pointed to the last Mì-runach standing next to him. "Who's going to walk away now."

"I am?"

"Yes."

Uther shrugged. "Yeah, all right."

Once his friends were gone, Aidan let out a breath and greeted Gaius with, "My lord."

"Aidan."

The Mì-runach turned toward the stairs just as a seething Brannie stormed past him, gesturing with two fingers at her equally seething brother Celyn.

"Hello, Brannie," Aidan happily greeted.

"Shut up!"

Aidan watched her stomp away before Gaius heard him sarcastically mutter to himself, "I'm just so glad to be back."

Kachka glanced at her sister, then turned back to the female holding up the exceedingly bright pink gown.

"Get away from me," she told the female.

"If you would just—"

"Get awayyyyy from me, She-demon!"

Keita the Viper stamped her bare foot. "Why won't you at least try it on? This color would look divine on you!"

Kachka nearly had her blade pulled from her scabbard, but Elina caught her hand and held it in place.

With her free hand, Elina reached over and took a bright red patch from Keita's hand. "Here. I will wear this. Happy? Yes?"

"At least one of you has some style!" the royal snarled before storming out of the room.

"What does that even *mean*?" Kachka demanded.

"I do not know. I stopped asking." Elina removed her simple—but completely useful!—black eye patch and replaced it with the ridiculous-looking red one.

"You are actually going to wear that?" Kachka asked, unable to hide her disgust.

"Do you want her to go on and on about that dress, sister? Because she will. Trust me. She *will*."

Slamming her sword back into the scabbard, Kachka walked out of the room and down the stairs, her sister right behind her.

Most of the tables were already filled and the food was being passed around. Big platters of ribs and sliced roast boar and roasted potatoes. All of it smelled good.

So Kachka reached over and took a rib from a plate, before heading to a free chair beside Gaius. Deciding she wasn't done annoying him, she sat down, tossing the now-clean rib bone behind her.

"Barbarian!" she heard roared at her, and Kachka looked over her shoulder to see the Dragon Queen.

"What?" Kachka asked when the queen continued to glare at her.

"You hit me with that rib bone."

"Then you should move quicker."

Gaius snorted. "You lot are killing me."

"That's my seat," the queen announced. Then she . . . waited? Kachka didn't know.

Pointing at an empty seat at another table, Kachka said, "Go over there."

"That is not my seat, peasant. You're in my seat."

"I am sure your large royal ass can fit just as fine in that chair as it can fit in this one."

The queen took in a deep breath and Kachka went for her sword, but the queen's mate quickly slapped his hand over Rhiannon's mouth, dragging her away while Gaius quickly caught Kachka's hand and held it in place to prevent her from pulling her sword. How many times would that happen in one evening?

"I wouldn't do that if I were you," Gaius gently chided.

"Bitchy royals do not scare me."

"Oh, *she* should. Not only can she tear you to ribbons with her claws, she can also turn you into ash where you sit, using only her whip-like flame, or turn your blood to molten lava with her magicks. So, if I were you, I'd be glad that Bercelak didn't want her sitting anywhere near me."

Kachka released her sword and took several handfuls of ribs from a plate offered by one of the servants.

"Why does Bercelak not want you sitting next to big-assed queen?" she asked.

"I'm not really clear why any of them act like that. It's not like I've *tried* to fuck any of their Southland females."

"Are you sure?" Kachka asked.

Gaius glanced over at Annwyl, who sat on the other side of him. She had her legs raised, her knees pressed against the table, her heels pressed against the seat, and a book balanced on her kneecaps. While she read the book and turned pages with one hand, she held a half-eaten turkey leg in the other. She had part of it in her mouth, noisily sucking the marrow from it.

When Gaius looked back at Kachka, he replied, "Oh . . . I'm so very sure."

Once the dinner was done, tables were pulled back and musicians began to play. Izzy and Gwenvael the Slag were the first out on the floor, something no one seemed surprised at.

The Riders went into a small huddle over in a corner before Zoya Kolesova marched out. When she returned about a half hour later, she held several bottles covered in dirt.

"Whatever you do," Talan suddenly whispered to Gaius, "don't drink that. You'll regret it forever."

Zoya dropped the bottles on an empty table, then grabbed two. She walked over to Briec, for some unknown reason, and yanked away the cup of wine he'd been drinking, tossing it to the floor.

The dragon gawked at her—shocked she'd dare touch

anything of his and clearly ready to blast her through the wall
with his flame—before she shoved a bottle into his hand.

"Here, beautiful one," Zoya told him. "Drink this. Beauty
such as yours only deserves best."

Then Zoya squeezed his ass and Briec's eyes grew wide
in panic.

"Come!" Zoya ordered the room. "Everyone drink! Especially all these pretty boys!"

"Yeahhhh," Talan said on a harsh breath. "I'm out of
here."

Gaius watched Prince Talan quickly cut through to the
back and disappear out the door. When Gaius turned around
again, Kachka stood in front of him, a bottle in her hand.

"Are you brave enough, royal?" she asked, holding up
the bottle.

"Brave enough? Or *stupid* enough?"

"Sometimes," she said, pulling the cork out, "there is
truly no difference."

Kachka began to pour some of her people's ale into Talaith's chalice. But she'd barely put in a splash before Briec
the Mighty physically lifted his mate and moved her away.

"Hey!"

"No. Just . . . no," he insisted, carrying her off.

"What's that look for?" Annwyl asked, waving off the ale
when Kachka offered it.

"She allows male to tell her what she can and cannot
drink? My mother cut one of her husband's throats once because he suggested she had 'had enough.' She did not kill
him, but he never questioned her choice of drink again."

"Your mother was . . . unpleasant."

Kachka didn't bother to argue that point.

"And Talaith can't hold her drink," Annwyl went on.

"He's just saving himself the bother of having to carry her to bed tonight while she miscounts absolutely everything. Loudly. The drunker she gets, the worse her math gets."

The queen's dragon mate passed them. He signaled to Annwyl with a slight jerk of his head toward the door at the back of the hall.

Suddenly smiling, the queen put down her chalice of whatever weak Southland wine she'd been drinking.

"See ya," she said.

"Wait."

The queen stopped. "What?"

"You go to fuck him?"

"Unless he's calling me back there to yell at me about Talwyn . . . most likely."

"Do you not mind that he is not human?"

Annwyl put her hands on her hips. "Is this an Abomination question? Because those just make me angry."

"No. I do not care about you and your unholy children."

"I would never call my son or Rhi un—"

"But Fearghus has scales. That does not bother you?"

"Oh." Annwyl grinned, chuckled. "That." She shrugged her big shoulders. "I find his scales beautiful. Human or dragon, he's always been beautiful to me. Why do you ask?"

"Just curious. Watching my sister, she seems very happy."

Annwyl frowned, head tilting to the side. "Does she? Really?"

"For Daughter of Steppes . . . she is happy."

"Well . . . if you say so."

The queen followed after her mate, disappearing through the back door. Kachka stared after her for a long time, wondering if she was being a little too . . . harsh about dragons. Unlike her mother, she was willing to change her opinion when it was truly warranted. She just didn't know if it was.

Once she became bored staring at the empty doorway,

she studied the room. Everyone seemed to be having a good time. Even the Rebel King, laughing at whatever Gwenvael the Handsome was saying to him.

Kachka lost track of how long she stared at him, but he seemed to sense her, glancing at her across the room. He raised a brow, silently asking if all was right. She gave a small head shake to let him know she was fine. Then he nodded toward Zoya, who had some poor young soldier practically pinned against the wall, her big arms caging him in from either side as she talked to him. About what, Kachka didn't dare to guess.

If only the woman hadn't healed so damn quickly. Or, you know . . . at all . . .

Celyn eased up behind his mate and kissed her neck.

"Your sister done slapping you around?" Elina asked.

"She's so drunk now, I'm sure she's done slapping everyone around. And she didn't slap me around," he argued. "We had what my father calls a Cadwaladr Disagreement."

"Southlander way of saying she slapped you around."

"Thanks for that." Celyn leaned his butt against a nearby table and pulled Elina close, her back against his chest. "Your sister seems quiet tonight."

"There is much on her mind. No time for dancing, I think. She will hunt later. She works out much when she hunts."

"You two look for any excuse to hunt things down."

"We are good at it."

Celyn rested his chin on Elina's shoulder, his arms loose around her body, and he asked the question that had been plaguing him for a few weeks now.

"You wish you were going with your sister, don't you? To make a name for yourself." He'd understand if that's what Elina wanted to do. She'd be no different from nearly every one of his kin.

So, when she turned her head to look at him, Celyn readied himself for her answer.

"Truth?"

"Of course."

"I would rather set myself on fire than go with my sister in this task she undertakes for Annwyl."

Celyn reared back a bit. "I . . . uh . . ."

"You are disappointed in me."

"No. No, not at all. I'm actually relieved. But, I thought—"

"My sister and I are close. As close as you and Brannie. But we are vastly different from each other. There are some things I just cannot do."

Celyn kissed the side of her head and hugged her closer. "And to be quite honest with you, Elina Shestakova, I'll be forever grateful for that fact."

Gaius stood back and watched the Riders show Izzy and Branwen the dances of their people. As drunk as Izzy and Branwen now were, it was so much more than simply entertaining.

"Why do you not drink or dance, foreign king?"

Gaius glanced down at Kachka. She stood next to him, her pert ass resting against the thick wood table. "Because I am a foreign king not in his homeland."

"But you are safe here."

"I am safe from my enemies. But I don't think anyone's really safe from Annwyl."

"Good point."

He studied the group dancing and clapping. "Where is Tatyana?"

Kachka looked up at him. "You noticed?"

"I may have one eye, but I notice lots of things. You live longer that way."

"She has gone to town. Talk to people in pubs. That is what she does. She talks to people. She gets information. She is very good."

"When you're done here, you know, she won't want to go back."

"I know." Kachka sighed. "She hugs, you know."

Gaius laughed. "What?"

"She hugs. Who hugs?"

"I don't know. . . . *Everyone*?"

"Not Riders. What is there to hug about? You hug your children, of course. When they are young and needy. You hug your horse, if it lets you. You do not hug each other. It is so weak."

"It's not weak. It's affectionate."

"Which is weak. Affectionate is for the weak. The strong do not need."

They silently watched Zoya Kolesova dance by, a very large soldier in her arms. Since he didn't seem to want to dance, she hugged him off the ground as she moved by.

"Zoya seems to like to hug."

"The Kolesovas—"

"Have a use if you would just look beyond how annoying their good humor may be."

"Is this kingly advice?" she asked.

"It is. The first thing my father taught me was how to use what you have access to. Nothing is worse than trying to force others into roles that do not fit them."

"What role would you fit me in?"

Gaius didn't hesitate. "Lord Executioner."

Kachka nodded. "You *are* good."

* * *

Leaning against one of the open front doors of the Great Hall, Gaius watched a weaving Éibhear carry his human mate up the stairs to their rooms. The big Blue had tossed a passed-out Izzy over his shoulder, but he wasn't holding on much better. Gaius thought about helping the young prince, then thought . . . "Eh."

The party had been quite . . . raucous. A little more low-brow than what Gaius was used to. Of course, in the Provinces, parties involved actors, storytellers, dancers, musicians, poets . . . and the entertainment and feasting went on for days. Then, of course, there were the gladiator games. He'd changed them a bit, though, since he'd become king. They no longer involved slaves. They were no longer used for punishment or torture. Many—mostly his aunt—thought this meant that they would run out of gladiators. They were wrong. With a healthy purse to win and a chance to become a beloved champion, they had more than enough men, and some women, willing to battle to the death without chaining them in their off time.

Still, this had been . . . fun.

Gaius watched a few servants come in to start cleaning up now that almost everyone had either gone to bed or was passed out on the floor. While they worked, Gaius silently watched as Prince Fearghus and the queen walked into the hall together. They held hands but said nothing, smiling at each other like two youngsters in love.

It was a little embarrassing, considering who they were. The names and reputations they'd built for themselves over the years. But Annwyl stopped at the bottom of the stairs and did something extraordinary. She ordered the servants to bed.

"You can clean it up tomorrow," she told them when they began to argue. "Trust me. You don't want to clean around these big oafs passed out on the floor. Wait until they get up, throw up, and go to bed."

Agreeing with that logic, the servants went off and Annwyl the Bloody, like a much younger woman, jumped up so that she was on Fearghus the Destroyer's back, her legs around his waist. Her arms loose around his shoulders.

Laughing, they walked up the stairs, Fearghus—most likely purposely—stepping on the head of one of the Mìrunach who'd passed out on the steps.

And for some unknown reason, Gaius had the strangest feeling. Of regret?

No. No, no. That was impossible. He hadn't fallen that far, had he?

Deciding it was best to go to bed since he was getting a little maudlin, Gaius walked to the stairs and carefully stepped over those who'd passed out on the steps. As he neared the bedroom he'd been given by Lady Dagmar, he heard noises that he assumed were coming from the queen's bed chamber. But when he pushed open his door, he realized he was wrong.

Tragically, disgustingly, appallingly wrong.

Slamming the door closed, Gaius went to Kachka's room but only found the Khoruzhaya siblings and Marina Aleksandrovna passed out on the bed. He slammed that door, too, and went to Elina's room. He pushed the door open without knocking and ignored the roar of the dragon getting his cock sucked.

"Where's your sister?" he demanded.

"*Get out!*"

"Quiet, boy, before I *burn this house down!*"

Celyn's cock popped out of Elina's mouth and she calmly replied, "She went hunting."

"It's pitch black out."

"She is Daughter of Steppes. We do not let darkness stop us from—"

"Oh, shut up. Where did she go?"

"Go east from front doors." She waved Gaius away. "Now go. I must finish sucking his cock or he gets very cranky."

"I'm past cranky!"

"See?" Elina asked flatly.

Gaius slammed the door shut and stomped down the stairs, out the doors, and headed east. He stalked for a while until he heard something charging at him in the darkness. He turned just in time to see the eyes of a boar shining at him.

In a rage, Gaius blasted it with his flame, turning it to ash in seconds.

"That was mine," Kachka complained as she moved out of the darkness, where the moon above made her easier to see.

"You," he snarled.

"What did I do?"

"You brought Zoya Kolesova here. And now she's in *my* room, fucking some poor soldier who, I have to say, appeared quite terrified by the entire experience."

Kachka stared at Gaius for a moment, and then she burst into laughter. So hard that she was bent over at the waist, dropping her bow and quiver to the ground at her feet.

"What is so gods-damn funny?"

Arms around her middle, Kachka stood up, but she was laughing so hard, she couldn't speak.

"It's not funny! I am a king. Kings get their own room, heartless female! But what they don't get is forced to share a bed with Zoya Kolesova and her obvious victim!"

Kachka stepped over her weapon and went to Gaius. She placed her hands on his chest and looked up at him. She opened her mouth and Gaius thought she was about to apologize. She didn't.

She did, however, keep laughing!

Only now she was leaning against him. Laughing.

"I'm the One-eyed Rebel King," Gaius complained. "People, everywhere, fear me. Fear my wrath. But then I come to the Southlands and it all falls apart."

Kachka stepped back and grasped Gaius's hand, pulling him.

"Where are we going?" he asked, but she didn't answer. Because she was still laughing!

Kachka led Gaius to her favorite tree here in these Southland woods. She'd taught herself every inch of this territory since coming here with her sister. That way she could maneuver in the day or night.

When she reached her spot, she stopped and faced the king.

"There was so much grunting," he complained about finding Zoya in his bed. "*So* much grunting."

"Stop it," she ordered him around more of the laughter that seemed to annoy him so. "If you want me to stop laughing, you must stop it."

"I'm trying to wipe it from my mind. I'm hoping talking about it helps. But I fear nothing will help."

He looked so despondent; she felt nothing but humor at his misery.

Not that she blamed him. She couldn't imagine how horrified she'd have been to find Zoya Kolesova in her tent . . . grunting.

"Look," she said, patting his chest, "I understand. I, too, would be filled with horror if I saw what you have seen. But you must let it go. Or you will never sleep again."

"I walked in on your sister sucking Celyn's cock. He was not happy."

"Did you torture poor Celyn?"

Gaius shrugged. "But the Southland males make it so very easy." He finally glanced around. "What are we doing here?"

"We will stay here tonight. You and I."

"So you're not going to get Zoya out of my room?"

Kachka stared at him. "Do you really want to sleep in bed that Zoya Kolesova just fucked in?"

"Excellent point," he conceded.

"Besides, we can fuck here under stars."

Gaius blinked. "We can?"

"Why would we not?"

"Well . . ." he began. Then he finally said, "I have no argument."

"Good." She slid her hand behind the back of his neck and pulled his head down. "Now kiss me, complaining dragon."

"You tell me to kiss you *and* you insult me. Romantic." He brought his hands up, slid his fingers into her hair, all while he gazed down into her face.

"This could be a very bad idea, you know?"

"You worry too much."

"I'm king. I was born to worry." Gaius tilted her head back, his eyes locked on her mouth. "But, as king, I can also worry later."

Kachka slipped her hands around his waist, pulled him close. "That is good, dragon. That is very good."

Gaius kissed Kachka's smiling mouth, easing his tongue past her lips and taking his time tasting her.

He had no desire to rush this. He wanted to savor. Something told him this would be the only chance he ever had with her, so he wouldn't waste it by rushing. Instead, he took his time and just kissed her.

Kachka's hands tightened around his waist, pulling him against her before sliding under his shirt, easing across his back. She traced scars she found there with the tips of her fingers, and the simple action drove him nearly mad.

He released her long enough so that Kachka could pull his shirt off. She tossed it aside and then removed her own. Once she'd dropped it, she was back in his arms, kissing his neck, her hands moving over his shoulders.

At that point, they sort of dragged each other to the ground. Somehow, as they rolled across the grass, leggings were pulled off and boots went flying. Gaius lowered his head and wrapped his mouth around a nipple, his tongue teasing the tip, Kachka's back arching. He moved to the other breast, and slid his hand between her thighs. As he eased two of his fingers inside her, Kachka tightened her legs around his waist and flipped him onto his back.

Shocked, he stared up at her. "Gods, you're strong."

"I know." She moved until she straddled his waist. Gripping his now hard cock, she pressed it against her pussy and slid down onto it until she completely enveloped him.

She placed her hands against his chest and without moving her hips, tightened her muscles around his cock.

"Wait, wait," Gaius gasped out, gripping Kachka around the waist.

"Too much?" she asked, deservedly looking smug.

"No, no," he panted out. "Too perfect."

She chuckled and pressed her chest against his, her tongue easing across the muscles of his neck while her pussy squeezed and released his cock, over and over again.

Gaius's eyes crossed and his toes curled.

It had to be all the gods-damn horse riding. Either that or

the gods had blessed her pussy, because he didn't think he'd
ever felt something so strong and yet so absolutely wonderful.

She teased his nipples while she continued to squeeze his
cock.

And the little viper knew exactly what she was doing.
Torturing him! Keeping him under her control!

Gaius couldn't even think straight. He couldn't do anything but let her keep going, praying that she didn't stop.

She didn't.

She squeezed his cock until he came, hard, his arms
wrapped tight around her and holding her against him until
she'd wrung him dry.

The big arms wrapped tight around her finally loosened
and dropped to the ground. He panted beneath her, eyes
closed, sweat on his brow even though it was a very cool
evening by Southlander standards.

Kachka placed her elbow on his chest and rested her chin
in the palm of her hand.

"Poor dragon," she said, smirking down at him.

"Huh?"

"You sleep while I wait here."

"I'm not sleeping. Just getting my breath back."

Kachka tapped the fingers of her free hand against his
stomach. She was teasing him, but only because it was
Gaius. She had patience. She could wait until he was ready
again.

"You're a smart ass," he said, his lips curled into a smile.

"I said nothing. I am just waiting."

His eyes opened and he stared at her.

"What?" she finally asked.

But he didn't answer. Not with words anyway. Instead,

he quickly pulled out of her, and flipped her around until she was on her knees and he was behind her.

She was about to ask what he thought he was doing, but her words were cut off when he was suddenly inside her once more.

He was hard again. Already!

She'd never had a man come that hard for her and then be ready to go again that quickly. But then she remembered Gaius Domitus was not a man. He was dragon. And now the sounds from her sister's room late at night made sense. Actually . . . the sounds from all the females in that blasted castle late at night suddenly made complete sense.

Gripping her hips tight, Gaius powered into her with as much vigor as if this were their first time. It was so hard and fast and delicious that all Kachka could do was plant her hands hard in the ground and take it. Something she was not used to doing. But he wasn't giving her much of a chance to take back control.

Then he slid one hand down around her waist and between her thighs. His fingers gripped her clit and began to squeeze and toy with it.

That felt so damn good, her arms gave out, and she was resting on her elbows, her forehead pressed against the backs of her hands while Gaius stroked her clit again and again. Then he circled it. Then he squeezed the gods-damn thing and that's when everything exploded around her.

She heard herself scream out into the night, surprising herself more than the birds in the trees.

Then, to either her dismay or her sheer happiness, he didn't stop. He'd already come once, so apparently he was ready to keep going. And he did, taking Kachka over the edge two more times before he pulled out of her and placed her on her back.

Gaius entered her again, going slow now, staring down into her face until he kissed her.

His kisses, like his fucking now, were slow and sweet, taking his time with both while his fingers played with her nipples or stroked her hair or simply touched her bare skin.

When he finally came this time, she came with him. They gripped each other, groaning and panting into each other's mouth, their hips grinding against the other until they were both so spent that they were too weak to push their partner away.

Kachka couldn't even get up and leave, something she would normally do since they were outside. If they had been in her room, she would have thrown him out. But he'd worn her down and she could do nothing but fall asleep in his arms.

The dragon bastard!

Gaius woke up when he felt something balanced on his nose.

It was a loaf of bread.

"What's happening?" he asked the naked woman who was sitting there, watching him silently.

"Thought you might be hungry."

"I'm a dragon. I'm always hungry."

He took the loaf of bread off his face and sat up, his back pressed against the tree they'd happily fucked under.

Gauis tore the bread and handed one half to Kachka. They ate in silence at first until Gaius asked, "Why have you never chosen a husband, Kachka Shestakova?"

She smirked at him. "In love with me already, Rebel King?"

"We both know you'd be lucky if I were. I am a king and," he teased, "pretty damn benevolent."

Kachka laughed. "So you say. In answer to your question,

I chose no husband because husband and children would lock me into life in Outerplains. I always felt I was . . . destined for more."

"To be Anne Atli one day?"

"No," she said, shaking her head. "That is not life for me. Nor the life I desire. What about you? Is this life you want?"

"This is life I have. In the Sovereigns, you're born into your life."

"You were not born into your life. You took it from the hide of your uncle."

"Only because he made me."

"So you think you would have been happy being just a royal? A title with no power?"

Gaius let out a breath. "I honestly don't know. When Vateria took my sister . . . all bets were off, as they say."

"Meaning?"

"They gave me no choice but to kill them. Each and every one of them. There are, of course, a few of my kin still roaming free. But I'll find them, too. If I have my way, I'll find them all."

Kachka suddenly smiled.

"What?" he asked.

"I was just thinking . . . if you were woman, you would make good Daughter of Steppes."

"I would?"

"You have strong sense of vengeance. Daughters of Steppes were born of vengeance. The first Anne Atli, it was need for revenge that sent her to take control of the tribes. Once she started, she never looked back." Kachka studied him closely. "Will you look back, Rebel King? Will you have regrets?"

"The only regret I will ever have . . . is that I let Vateria get my sister. And as long as she still breathes, that account will never be settled."

Kachka reached into the darkness and brought back a bottle of that damn ale. She pulled the cork with her teeth and took a long swig before handing it to Gaius. Wincing, he drank a bit . . . then worked hard not to immediately spit it back out as it burned its way down his throat. A throat that could spew out fire at a mere thought.

Fire didn't bother him, but Rider ale did. Interesting.

"Awake now, dragon?" Kachka asked, her smile almost warm.

He handed the ale back to her. "Well, if I wasn't before . . ."

With their knees raised and Gaius's back still resting against that tree, Kachka sat on Gaius's lap, his cock buried deep inside her. Neither moving. It felt good just to sit like this. Enjoying the calm Southland night. Their hands roaming without specific intent.

Gaius seemed to like stroking his fingers against her scars.

"Where did you get this?" he asked, his index finger easing down the raised flesh of her left side.

She glanced at it, tried to remember. "Fell off a horse and onto a spike buried in ground. Which was why my horse reared in first place. Some city, trying to keep us out. It did not work. Nor did it kill me."

Kachka ran her thumb down the scar on Gaius's face. It cut across his forehead, past where his eye had once been, and part way down his cheek. "You do not want to tell me about this," she guessed. "Do you?"

"Not at the moment. It brings up bad memories. Maybe I'll tell you one day, when I don't have a beautiful woman sitting on my cock, bringing me extreme pleasure."

"I am not even squeezing." She smiled. "Yet."

"You don't need to squeeze. Sometimes the pleasure is in the waiting."

Gaius reached up and pushed Kachka's hair from her face. "Tell me . . . why did you choose me?"

"Choose you?"

"To fuck. You had an array of dragons to choose from, if you just wanted to try a dragon. . . . Why me?"

Kachka ran her hands across Gaius's square jaw. "Honestly? You irritate me less than most males do. That makes you very desirable to me."

Gaius leaned forward, pressed his lips against her throat, easing up to her jaw.

"Rebel King?"

"Yes?"

She pressed her mouth against his ear and whispered, "I feel like squeezing now."

He smiled against her flesh. "Then please . . . don't let me stop you."

Chapter Sixteen

Gaius awoke under that tree, his arms around Kachka, and looked up into the faces of the Riders surrounding him.

He tapped Kachka's shoulder.

"What?"

"We are not alone."

She opened her eyes, focused on her fellow tribeswomen. "What?"

"Tatyana has something," Marina announced. "A temple. About three to four days' ride from here. It might be at risk."

Kachka was out of his arms. She grabbed the clothes they'd tossed aside the night before and, naked, started to walk off with her team.

Before she could get anywhere, though, Gaius reached out and caught hold of her ankle.

Zoya grinned. "He is going to beg!"

Gaius smirked. "I'm a king, Zoya Kolesova—ruler of an empire. I don't beg. Now piss off."

Zoya and Marina looked to Kachka, and she jerked her head to the side. With a nod, the women walked away, leaving the pair alone.

"Did you think I was just going to let you walk away?" he asked.

"Did you think that because you are king, I would stay?"

Gaius slowly ran his hand up the back of Kachka's bare leg. "I thought you'd stay because you're madly in love with me."

Kachka crouched down in front of Gaius and, grinning, he slid his hand between her thighs, which Kachka quickly caught and held.

"I have to go."

"You don't *have* to go. You choose to go."

"I have name to make. Honor to obtain. I do not have time to let a man get in my way."

"I'm not a man. I'm a dragon. And I want what I want." He let out a truly regretful sigh, pulling his hand back so he could take hold of her hand. "But I also understand your need to earn a name." He kissed the back of her knuckles. "So go. Get your name."

"And you will wait for me like loyal puppy?"

"That I can't promise. But if death finds you well, Kachka Shestakova, I'm sure I'll be around. Somewhere."

She smiled. It stunned him how . . . sweet it was. Her true smile.

Kachka leaned in and kissed him, one hand pressed against his cheek, the other digging into his hair.

When she finally pulled back, she gave him one more soft kiss on his nose. Then she picked up her clothes again and walked off. Never once looking back.

Gaius stood and pulled on his clothes. He returned to the Great Hall, finding that a few, who had avoided the drink of the Riders, had managed to make it downstairs to get something to eat. But many servants were carrying tea and very dry bread up the stairs to those who couldn't handle more.

Dagmar, sitting at the table surrounded by missives and

parchments filled with figures, smiled at him as he entered. "King Gaius."

"Lady Dagmar. I'm heading home," he told her flatly.

Dagmar's eyes narrowed the slightest bit behind those spectacles she wore. "Is everything all right?"

"Everything's fine," he promised, since it was. He and Kachka had no commitment beyond what they'd done the night before. In fact, he doubted that woman would make a commitment to any male if she could avoid it. "But it's going to be a long flight, and I need to go. I just didn't want to disappear without saying anything to you or Queen Annwyl."

Dagmar stood from the table and walked to his side. Her voice low, she said, "Is it Kachka Shestakova? Rumor has spread that you were with her last night, and although I am greatly concerned about your taste in females, I can have her killed if she's displeased you in some way. Do you need me to have her killed?"

Shocked and also trying not to laugh, Gaius shook his head. "That's not really . . . necessary."

"Are you sure? It would be my *extreme* pleasure."

"No . . . no. Really . . . no."

"Then why the rush to leave if she hasn't yet again destroyed some male's good name?"

"Because I have an empire to run?"

"Something I know your sister can handle in your absence, but I understand your not wanting to be here unless necessary. In case that evil heifer returns."

"Or I just want to go home. But whatever."

"Understood," she said, straightening her back, regal as always. "But, of course, you'll still need to have an escort."

"That's not really necess—"

"*Brannie!*" the tiny woman bellowed, causing Gaius to jump a bit.

"I'm up!" Branwen the Awful announced as she bounced to her feet from behind the banister at the top of the stairs. Her shoulder-length hair was . . . everywhere. Her pretty brown eyes red rimmed. Her human skin alarmingly pale. "I'm up. No need to scream so."

"King Gaius is returning home today. You'll need to accompany him. Bring a few Mì-runach with you to ensure his safety."

Branwen nodded. "Of course." She turned and began kicking something that started grunting and cursing. "Get up, you sorry lot! We have to move."

After she did that, she came down the stairs, and stopped in front of Gaius.

"King Gaius, I will be happy to . . . happy to . . ." She covered her mouth with one hand and held up a finger with the other.

Gaius took a step back and let her dart past him so that she could throw up outside. A few seconds later, most of the Mì-runach quickly followed her out.

"Don't worry," Dagmar said. "From what I've heard of Rider wine, they should be fine in a day or two."

"That does give me great ease, Lady Dagmar."

She patted his shoulder before returning to her papers. "Don't think for a second I don't hear that mocking tone, m'lord."

An accusation that just made him laugh, because how could he not laugh at the Southlanders?

Chapter Seventeen

Gaius shifted to human and took the clothes handed to him by a servant before stalking down the palace halls to his throne room. The guards protecting the doors saw him coming and immediately shoved the thick wood open.

With Brannie the Awful and several Mì-runach behind him, he walked into the throne room. Aggie jumped up and ran over to him, throwing herself into his arms. He held his twin tight and swung her in a circle.

"Out!" he ordered those waiting to meet with his sister.

The humans and dragons in human form quickly walked out.

But Brannie and the Mì-runach still stood there, peering around the large throne room, completely oblivious. Gaius knew for a fact that, in battle, Brannie was amazing. Yet when it came to the more social graces . . . yeah, well . . . huh.

Brannie focused on Aggie, brown eyes blinking.

"Do be kind," Gaius told his sister. "That Cadwaladr saved your life once." Then, to the captain, he said gently, "Could you excuse us, Branwen?"

"Oh! Of course!" She motioned to the Mì-runach. "Come on, you lot. Let's give them some privacy."

The Mì-runach who'd traveled with Brannie and Gaius exited the room, but those who'd been guarding Aggie did not move.

Brannie glared. "Move your asses," she ordered.

"We don't report to you, *Captain*."

Uh-oh, Gaius silently told his sister. *She's going to blow.*

Brannie had her hand around the offending dragon's throat, her blade nearly out of its sheath when Aidan the Divine, who'd also escorted him here with his Mì-runach brethren Uther and Caswyn, came back into the throne room and quickly separated the pair.

Calmly, without the obvious intensity of the other Mì-runach, Aidan pushed Brannie back and said to the others, "Come, brothers. Let's leave kin to speak alone."

"But we're supposed to protect her ladyship."

"Of course you are. From outside the door."

"Yes, but—"

"Now."

Snarling and muttering, the rest of the Mì-runach walked out, the royal-born Aidan winking at Gaius before he closed the doors behind them.

"So," he finally asked his sister, "how's it been going while I was gone?"

Before Aggie could answer, Lætitia walked into the throne room. "It's about time you returned," she announced. "You have an empire to run and you can't be—"

Aggie's face turned red and she snarled at their aunt, "Get. *Out*."

Lætitia spun on her heel and headed back to the door. "I'm leaving of my own volition, *but this discussion isn't over!*"

Gaius smiled down at his sister. "So . . . did you miss me?"

"Oh, shut up."

* * *

The Riders reached their destination four days later, and it seemed that Tatyana's information had been correct. In another day or so, these men they watched from the safety of the trees would be attacking a nearby temple.

Now would be the real test of her team, a team she'd actually planned from the beginning.

Kachka knew the Anne Atli well enough to know that she would never allow Kachka to take any of the favored warriors. But Kachka had never wanted the favored warriors. They would be difficult and untrustworthy. At least to her. Their loyalty, unto death, would be to the Anne Atli.

So, Kachka needed more . . . unusual choices. Marina. The Khoruzhaya siblings. Tatyana. They all had skills and, Kachka was sure, their dreams were of a life outside the Outerplains.

Now, this moment, would prove whether she'd been right.

All that game playing was how one got what one needed from the Riders. Ask for what you wanted directly and the Anne Atli would fall all over herself denying it to you. So Kachka had feigned annoyance, regret, disappointment. But when Zoya and Nina had been forced on her—she'd no longer had to fake anything.

They could be her ultimate downfall.

She could only hope that she could make this work *despite* those two. Right now, she had to focus on what was in front of her.

Brutal men, brought in for one singular purpose. Killing a group of women bent on doing nothing more than worshipping a goddess of their choice in solitude.

They needed nightfall and to regroup before they did anything else, so Kachka signaled for them to back up and silently leave the area until they could figure out their next—

"Oy! What are you doing?"

The man had quietly come up behind them and Kachka turned, her sword pulled, but an arrow went through his open mouth. He dropped back and Kachka looked at her cousin.

Tatyana cringed as she lowered her bow. "Sorry. I panicked."

In order to keep their privacy, Gaius and Aggie went to their favorite private garden deep within the palace.

The servants brought them fresh fruits and wine before silently leaving. Once the door was closed, and they were left alone, Aggie hugged Gaius again.

"If you had died," she explained, "I would have been really pissed at you."

Gaius stretched out on a lounge chair before popping a grape into his mouth. "Me, too. I do like living. And I'm so good at it."

Aggie dropped onto his stomach—hard—and while ignoring his yelp of pain, she reached over and grabbed her own bunch of grapes.

"So," she asked around the fruit, "did you have a good time with the crazy queen?"

"She wasn't that bad. At least not this time. She actually remembered me!"

"She's only met you two thousand times."

"Don't exaggerate, Aggie. More like one thousand."

"Still." His sister sized him up. "It must have gone well. You seem . . . unnaturally relaxed. For you, I mean."

Gaius grinned. "What can I say? I met a very nice girl."

"You? You met a nice girl?"

"She's lovely. Sweet. Charming. Royal born perhaps."

Aggie's eyes narrowed. "I'm sure Auntie Lætitia will like that."

"Oh, when it comes to prospective mates for her favorite nephew, this girl is *just* what Auntie Lætitia has been hoping for. . . ."

No longer unseen, Zoya moved first, charging into the middle of the camp and swinging her axe, randomly chopping off heads and body parts.

Kachka motioned to the Khoruzhaya siblings. "Go around!" she yelled in their language, not quite sure if these men could understand her or not.

The siblings ran and Kachka pushed her cousin back to the trees. "Protect us from above." Tatyana was prone to panic and she was not good in battle. Kachka would rather have her watching their backs than trying to attack from the front.

Some male swung at her, and Kachka blocked the sword with the metal gauntlet on her forearm before slashing at his gut with her blade.

"Marina!"

Marina came in after Kachka, ducking a pike to the belly and barely avoiding a sword to the leg. But once she'd cleared all that, she struck, ramming her blade into the first male who crossed her. Behind her, two men went down, taken out by the siblings.

Kachka dispatched another man with a sword to the throat. Another with a stab to the back. He went down and that's when she sensed someone coming up behind her. She turned in time to see a warrior running toward her. Kachka raised her blade, but Nina Chechneva jumped from the trees, landing on the man's shoulders. She didn't have a sword, but a long blade dagger that she stabbed with both hands into the top of the man's head.

Perhaps bringing Nina Chechneva hadn't been such a big mistake after all. . . . .

"So what's on your mind, sister?" Gaius asked as he now reached for the cheese.

"What makes you think there's something on my—?"

"Aggie, please," he begged. "Not with me, sister."

"What happened to you . . . it bothers me."

"Because I was stupid?"

"You weren't stupid. You were eager. We both were. And those who captured you knew we would be."

"Everyone knows we want our cousins. They're traitors to the empire. To us."

Aggie pursed her lips and Gaius studied her for a long moment before he asked, "What are you thinking?"

"I'm just thinking that instead of waiting for them to come to us . . . to bring our cousins to us—whether it's that ridiculous cult or someone else working with them—we go find them ourselves. Hunt our kin down and wipe them out."

"All right. And who do you think would take on such a task?"

Aggie shrugged. "You."

"Me? After I almost got myself killed?"

"That only happened because they had something to lure you with. Lure *us* with. We were *re*acting, not acting. I say no more of that bullshit. If we kill our cousins first . . . the rest of the world has nothing left to bargain with."

Gaius grabbed Aggie around the waist and sat up, plopping his sister beside him on the lounge.

"You take the best and most trusted of your soldiers," Aggie said, leaning in close, her voice low. "Dragons only, so they can fly when needed. *You* get the information. *You* hunt our cousins down. *You* kill them all. Then we'll be done with it."

"The Senate—and especially Aunt Lætitia—will not like me going off again." Gaius smirked at his sister. "And some will think you're purposely sending me off to my death."

"And that will work until you get back. At least for me and my still tenuous reputation among our own. But don't worry." She patted his knee. "If I wanted you dead, I'd do it myself to ensure it was done properly. You know how picky I am."

"Very true. Sadly, though, all my most trusted warriors were just killed during my last excursion."

"But you forget the ones you traveled here with. A Cadwaladr and some Mì-runach. If nothing else, you know those Low Borns don't want our throne and they'll happily kill anything you tell them to."

"Do you think they'll fight for me?"

Aggie flicked her hands up. "Couldn't hurt to ask."

With the knife buried to the hilt in the top of his head, the man stumbled and dropped, while Nina rolled away, coming immediately to her feet. She then rammed another dagger into a different male, but she didn't kill this one instantly. Instead, she just incapacitated him.

And, while he struggled to breathe, eyes wide in fear, she pressed a bloody hand against his chest, chanted a few words, and then yanked the man's screaming soul from his body. She made a fist, silencing the screams and taking the soul as her own.

Panting, exuberant, she faced Kachka, raising her brows.

A silent question. Kachka knew Nina would only ask it once.

Kachka looked around at what they'd already done. And remembered what Annwyl wanted. For the Chramnesind cult to start feeling some fear. To know that they were fucking with the wrong queen.

The man that Nina had attacked looked . . . wrong. Mouth twisted open, eyes bulging wildly from their sockets. Muscles strained and locked in pain so the whole body was contorted in death.

Sure. They could chop all these men to bits, but that could happen in any war. This . . . this display would send a message that would not soon be forgotten.

Kachka waited no longer. She nodded once and Nina, smiling wide, turned and found a few more victims. Her body trembled in ecstasy with each soul she ripped away from the screaming men.

While Nina did that, everyone else pursued their own forms of mayhem. Zoya twisted men until they broke for her. Marina cut men down quickly, without fuss or pleasure. It was just a job. The siblings killed like they were on the Outerplains hunting boar. Tatyana watched from a distance, her bow ready, if it was needed. But she'd done her job. She'd brought them here. She'd provided good, solid information. Kachka would not now make her fight.

Kachka herself tracked down the one she was sure was the leader. He had an arrow to the back, but his armor had stopped it from going all the way to his heart. He was dragging himself off into the trees when Kachka caught up with him. She grabbed his leg and dragged him back to the middle of the carnage. She flipped him over and held him down with a foot against his chest.

"Why did your cult send you here?" she asked him.

"You, *whore*, will burn in the pits of hell for what you have done here."

"Was it just to cause fear in the Southlanders? Or do you look for something? Tell me and we make quick work of your death."

"My god will find you. He will destroy you. He will destroy all you love. For his power is great!"

Kachka stopped listening and stepped away from the man, motioning to a joyful Zoya Kolesova.

The larger woman slammed her foot on the man's chest, forcing him to the ground, the arrow in his back pushed until it broke. Then she stepped back, hefted her battle axe high above her head, and brought it down six times. The man was nothing but big chunks when she was finished.

Panting, she faced Kachka. "I *like* this, Kachka Shestakova."

And, for the first time ever, Kachka grinned at Zoya Kolesova. "I can tell, comrade. I can tell."

"Do we clean this up?" Marina asked.

"No," Kachka said, walking back to the oversized Southlander horses they had been forced to take because they'd left their Outerplains mounts back in Brigida the Foul's cave. "We leave them for the crows to dine on."

"And us?"

"Us? We go find more to kill."

"Yay!" Zoya Kolesova cheered. "I was hoping she'd say that!"

Kachka stopped, faced the others. "But first, we need to get better."

Zoya looked around at the carnage. "You don't think we did well here?"

"We were lucky. Caught them off guard. They weren't expecting us. But word will spread and we'll need to find a better way to fight."

"She's right," Marina agreed. "There's only seven of us. We'll need to learn to be quieter. Faster. They should never know we're coming."

Yelena Khoruzhaya nodded. "Faster. Quieter. And maybe different weapons." She nodded at her brother. "Bows are good. Javelins and spears also."

Kachka re-sheathed her sword. "And we will only attack at night. We were *very* lucky today. We won't be again."

She looked over those who'd fought with her. Yes. She could make this work. She could make this team work. She just had to be smarter than their enemies. For the first time, Kachka was in charge. Out here, roaming these lands, there was no one above her, no one to report to, no one to watch her back except the six tribesmen she was looking at.

"Come," Kachka ordered, again heading to the horses. "We have much to do, comrades."

Servants led them to a large dining table covered in fresh fruits and vegetables, warm bread, and succulent meats.

Brannie only had a moment to think, *My, that looks good* . . . before she realized that the Mì-runach had already hunkered down so they could feed.

"Like wild animals," she muttered as she took the only open seat, by Aidan the Divine.

He grinned at her around a mouthful of turkey leg, which caused Brannie to reply, "Shut up."

"I didn't say anything!" he said on a laugh.

"You were *thinking* at me."

The Rebel King and his sister entered the dining hall from the back. As they approached the table, Brannie quickly realized that they were staring at her. She just didn't know why.

The pair grabbed two chairs and pulled them up beside

Brannie. The king at the head of the table, his sister on her other side, almost between her and Aidan.

When neither said anything, Brannie asked, "Is there something you . . . need, King Gaius?"

"Loaded question," Aidan leaned over to whisper. So she punched him in the thigh to shut him up.

"Ow! Vicious harpy!"

"Is there a chance," the king's sister began, "that you and your"—she glanced at the dragons eating heartily of her people's food—"friends can stay at my brother's side for a bit longer?"

"Here? Don't you have guards for that?"

"Not as guards. Protection, yes, but he'll be going out to . . ." The king's sister glanced up, thinking, before finishing with, "*handle* something. Important to the Empire. And it would be wonderful if you lot could go with him."

Brannie looked back and forth between the king and his sister. The king smiled, but she didn't trust that smile. Then again, his sister wasn't much better. She raised her eyebrows, which appeared just as untrustworthy, so Brannie returned her gaze to the king.

That's when he offered, "You'll get to kill things."

"Ooooh," Aidan said near her ear. "Now doesn't that sound lovely? Let's do it."

Brannie brought her fist back and popped the chatty bastard in the face.

"Owwww! Heartless wench!"

"We were just supposed to bring King Gaius here," Brannie reminded the twins. "Nothing about helping either one of you. I'll have to get special permission for that."

"We're tight on time," the king's sister said. "Do you know how long this will—"

Brannie, closing her eyes, cut the Iron royal off with one raised finger.

Mum?

Yeah?

It's Brannie. King Gaius wants me and the Mì-runach idiots to stay and kill stuff for him. I said I had to check in with you first, though.

Yeah. All right. Just be careful.

Yeah. Will do. Brannie opened her eyes and nodded at the Rebel King. "Me Mum says, 'Yeah, all right.'"

"Oh," the king said, glancing at his sister. "Well then . . . excellent. We'll get started in a day or two. But, for now, relax and enjoy your time here."

The twins left after that and servants returned with more food and what Brannie would guess was the better wine.

"That was smoothly handled." Aidan nodded.

"Shut *up*."

Laughing, "I was giving you a compliment!"

"Shut up anyway."

As soon as the suns rose in the sky, Annwyl slid out of bed, leaving her mate asleep. She quickly dressed, grabbed her weapons, and headed out to get some training in. The Rebel King was gone. Kachka and her Riders were gone. Rhi was off with Izzy somewhere. Her son had gone to Bram's castle to meet with his Uncle Bram and cousin Var.

Everything was now back to normal, which meant she had to get back to work.

As she crossed the courtyard, she knew someone was walking behind her.

Annwyl had her swords pulled and pressed against the follower's throat before she realized it was her daughter.

"Do *not*," she snarled, "sneak up on me, Talwyn!"

"I wasn't. I was *walking*."

"Behind me. You know I hate that." Annwyl lowered her weapons. "What is it? What do you want?"

Talwyn shrugged her shoulders, glanced off, shuffled her feet.

Annwyl had never seen her daughter appear awkward before. It was disconcerting. "What the hell's wrong with you?"

"Well, I just thought . . . ya know."

"That is not a full and complete sentence," Annwyl informed her daughter. "I know we taught you better."

Talwyn took in a breath and Annwyl debated backing away from her. Was she planning to attack her again? Annwyl didn't know.

"Talwyn, just spit it out. You're irritating me."

"I thought . . . instead of going back to Brigida's with Talan and Rhi in a few days . . . I'd stay here for a bit."

Now Annwyl did step back, her eyes narrowing on her daughter. "Why?"

"I thought perhaps I could train with you."

Annwyl's eyes narrowed more, her every nerve on high alert at what her daughter might be planning. "Why?" she asked again.

"Look, you're the first to say war's coming."

"Of course war's coming."

"And while Talan and Rhi have their magicks to manage during battle, *I* will be the one leading the troops. You know it. And I know it. And the best one to learn that skill from, shockingly . . . is you. And, of course, Daddy."

"Of course."

"But he's dragon and I'm not. Not fully. Not like Auntie Ghleanna or Branwen. I'll be on the ground, fighting with other Abominations, to stop Salebiri and the Chramnesind cult. And I think I'd best learn how to do that from you."

Annwyl snorted. She couldn't help it. "You expect me

to believe that you—*you*—will take orders from *me*? Really?"

"You forget. I spent years with the Kyvich witches. And I followed orders. Quite well, actually. Never got lashed once for disobedience."

"How did you manage that?" Annwyl asked. And even she knew her tone was taunting.

"Just give me a chance, Mum."

"I kicked your ass and now you want me to teach you how to not let it happen again? Is that it?"

Talwyn had the good sense to cringe a bit. "Kind of."

Stepping close to her daughter, Annwyl slapped her hand against the side of Talwyn's neck and yanked her close.

"Good," Annwyl told her. "Because everything I've done—and everything I plan to do—I've only ever done for you and your brother. To keep you alive. To keep you strong." Annwyl moved her hand to the back of Talwyn's neck and rested her forehead against her daughter's. "No matter what you think, you spoiled brat, you and your brother mean *everything* to me. Everything. Never forget that."

Talwyn swallowed, her eyes blinking quickly, as if she fought back tears. She finally gave a small nod and Annwyl stepped back.

"Now come," she said, turning away from her child. "War's coming fast, and we have a lot of work to do to get you ready."

Annwyl led her daughter to a place a good distance from the castle and out of sight of most. As they cleared a few boulders, Talwyn stopped, reaching out to grab Annwyl's arm, her face pale, her eyes wide in shock and panic.

"Mum . . . Mum . . . Mum . . ." she kept muttering as she stared.

"Stop that," she ordered her daughter. "You sound like an idiot."

"But . . ."

Annwyl gestured with a wave of her hand. "Talwyn, this is Mingxia. Eastland goddess of war and love."

The goddess smiled, her mouth revealing row after row of fangs. "You can't have one without the other, I'm afraid."

"My daughter wants to train with me."

The goddess's tiger-shaped dragon's head turned and she studied them for a moment.

"Hhhmm," she said, dark eyes unreadable.

The goddess's long dragon body rose up without benefit of wings, impossibly long whiskers floating around her. The winds rose, surrounded Mingxia, and when they were gone, she stood before them as a human Eastland woman in leather armor with many weapons on her person.

She walked around a still-stunned Talwyn, sizing her up as she'd once done to Annwyl.

Mingxia circled her once, and when she stood in front of her again, she pulled her sword from its scabbard and held the scabbard up before Talwyn's face, letting her eyes settle on the intricately embossed steel.

It took seconds for Talwyn to throw her arms up to block her eyes and fall to the ground, trying to shield herself from what she'd seen. It had taken Annwyl far longer to see what Mingxia had wanted her to see: a full battle come alive in that scabbard. A full battle that she was suddenly a part of, on a magnificent steed, slashing and killing as she rode into the fight.

In fact, the only reason Annwyl's vision had ended was that Mingxia had grown bored and pulled Annwyl out of it.

Talwyn, however, had panicked.

"It seems we have much work to do with this one,"

Mingxia noted. She held out her hand, and Talwyn seemed to force herself to take it. The goddess helped her to her feet.

"She's powerful, your daughter. She saw me in seconds, even though I didn't reveal myself to her. So, once we get this one up to speed, you two together will be a mighty thing to be feared among the enemies of your world."

"Good," Annwyl said, cracking her neck and pushing her stunned daughter out of the way. "Then let's get started."

Lady Ageltrude sat in a thick wooden chair, staring out over the night sky. This was her own private place. Her husband had made it for her. This place on top of the keep. He knew how much she loved heights and how important her privacy was to her.

Sadly, only her husband and his soldiers understood the importance of privacy to her.

"Auntie?"

She sighed. "What?"

Her niece came through the door, closing it tightly behind her. She plopped on the ground in front of Ageltrude the way a man would, her back against the short wall, her long legs stretched out in front of her.

"What is it?" Ageltrude asked when her niece didn't speak.

"What are we going to do?"

"Do about what?"

"They lost him, didn't they? But he's not dead. And you said—"

"Don't remind me," she quickly cut in, "of what I said and what I didn't say. My memory is perfect."

"But you said losing Egnatius would be worth it if he brought us—"

"Again, I know what I said."

"But we don't have him."

"Yes. And my favorite priestess is also dead." Ageltrude glanced off and muttered mostly to herself, "She had such a high tolerance for pain."

"How are we supposed to find it, if we don't have him? You said he was the key. You said if we didn't have him, we at least had to be sure he was dead. You said—"

She let one of the appendages her god had given her slide out of her back, across the ground, and around her niece's neck, choking her until she stopped talking. Ageltrude also may have waited longer than necessary, until the youngster's face turned blue, but she really wanted to get her point across.

When her niece was moments from passing out, Ageltrude released her.

"Are you done?" she asked.

Hands around her throat, her niece nodded, eyes wide in panic.

"Good. Now listen well." She stood and walked to the wall, standing beside her niece, and staring down at the valley before her. "If there's one thing I know well, it's how Gaius Lucius Domitus thinks. He's weak. Like his worthless sister. But determined." The wind picked up and she knew a storm was rolling in. "And if there's one thing he wants more than anything . . . one thing he'll never stop until he gets . . ." She turned and looked down at her niece, the wind pulling the hood off her head, her iron-colored hair spilling out around her shoulders.

Ageltrude, once called Vateria, pressed her hand to her chest. "It's me."

PART TWO

Chapter Eighteen

Eight months later . . .

They locked themselves away behind their thickest doors deep inside their temple. And they stayed inside even after the cries of battle started. They stayed inside when someone banged on the door, begging for help. They stayed inside when blood began to seep beneath the door. They stayed inside even when a cold, brutal silence abruptly descended.

It wasn't until they knew the suns had come up that they finally unlocked and opened those thick, protective doors.

Their most priceless items remained. Gold statues of their chosen goddess. Silver chalices they used for rituals. Jewel-encrusted clothes they wore during ceremonies remained untouched.

But there was that long line of blood leading from the protective doors, through the temple, and ending up outside.

Together they followed that line until they reached the stairs. That's where they stopped. Some of the acolytes looked away. Others vomited. Even more dropped to their knees, arms raised, thanking their goddess for protecting them through the night.

But their priestess . . . she knew. It hadn't been a goddess who'd come to her early in the day to warn her to hide behind those thick doors before suns-down.

It had, however, been a woman. Made of muscle and sinew and a few scars. There was no pity in those eyes that the priestess could see. At first, the priestess thought the whole thing a trick. A trick to get her to leave their temple's precious treasures untended for anyone to take them. Sell them. Make more than a few pieces of gold.

Now, as she stared out over the organized carnage left behind, she realized that the coldness in those eyes had not been for her or her goddess. But for the men who had come here, the mark of Chramnesind branded into their chests.

It was through those marks that spears had been rammed, pinning the men to the ground, on their knees, lifeless heads lifted toward the suns.

The priestess's second in command ordered the others to release these men from their vile ends, but the priestess stopped that order.

"You want us to leave them here? Like this? Defiling our temple?"

"They're not defiling our temple. They're outside our temple. Have the blood inside cleaned up now, but we'll burn the bodies later."

"Why would we do that?" she asked.

"So the world can see that in the Southlands whom one worships is still a protected choice."

"They did steal," one of the acolytes pointed out. "The ones who did this."

"I saw nothing missing."

"That barrel of apples we just picked . . ."

The priestess, who was very tall, moved in close to the acolyte and glared down at her. "Really? They saved our lives and our temple and you're bitching about gods-damn apples?"

"I'm just saying," she replied, "they could have asked."

"I swear," the priestess sighed out, heading back inside. "You people."

Kachka tossed another apple core to Zoya—she liked apple cores, which Kachka thought was disgusting, but to each her own—while Kachka pulled two more apples from her travel pack. She gave one to her horse and ate the other.

They still used the Southland horses that had been given to them eight months ago. They managed pretty well considering their size. Although they had to take frequent breaks or the horses became bitchy.

"So where are we off to now, Kachka Shestakova?" Zoya asked.

They were very close to the Western Mountains that separated the Southland territories from the Quintilian Provinces. Kachka chuckled to herself thinking about just showing up at the fancy palace of the Rebel King. What would his royal family think?

"I don't know," Kachka finally replied in their language. "We'll have a better idea once Tatyana gets back from that town we passed."

"We should have gone with her," Ivan complained. He complained a lot now that Zoya had stopped hitting him when he did so. "Stayed at a pub for the night."

They all stopped and looked back at him.

"I can't be the only one who likes a nice soft bed. I can't be!"

"I hate the beds here," Zoya replied, walking off with her horse right behind her. It was the biggest horse the queen's stables had and was feared by almost all her soldiers, but he had immediately adored Zoya. Of course, she always treated horses and other animals much better than she treated men. "They are too short for me unless the pub caters to the dragons."

"Everything's too short for you, Zoya," Marina pointed out.

"I know!" she replied gleefully. "I never have to go up on my toes. I see all just from here!"

Yelena pointed. "Tatyana's returning."

Kachka's cousin rode up to them, reining in her horse when she reached the Riders. "I tracked a group of travelers to a nearby town. Their boots and scabbards were in that fancy style of Annaig Valley. I'm guessing they're Chramnesind followers."

"That's rather blatant," Marina noted.

"What worried me," Tatyana went on, "was that they disappeared without a trace into the surrounding forest right by the base of the mountains. Their tracks just ended." She pulled out her water flask. "I know of at least three monasteries on the other sides of those mountains." She took a long drink before adding, "But that's no longer your queen's territory, Kachka. It belongs to the Rebel King."

"So?" Kachka tossed her apple core to Zoya before mounting her horse. "Take me to where the tracks end. We'll decide what to do from there."

"What is there to decide, comrade?" Zoya asked. "We hunt them down and kill them."

"It's not the queen's territory," Tatyana said again.

"And it could be a trap, Zoya," Marina added.

"So? I am tired of this sneaking around. Let's confront them head-on. I am ready!"

"But you're so good at being stealthy."

Zoya mounted her horse, the animal grunting a bit as she settled into her saddle. "Unlike my sisters, I'm very delicate and small. That gives me an edge."

Nina Chechneva, who hadn't spoken a word in two days

for no other reason than she simply hadn't felt like it, shook her head. "No," she said to no one in particular before riding off. "I can't with you, Zoya Kolesova. I just . . . I can't!"

Zoya watched the witch ride off before asking the others, "She can't what? She says that around me a lot, and I have no idea what it means. What can she *not* do, Kachka Shestakova?"

Didacus Domitus scrambled up the hill, pushing himself to run fast. As fast as his human legs would take him.

He knew who these dragons were. Why they were here. What they wanted. He knew. He'd heard the rumors. The tales coming from all over the Empire.

That his cousin Gaius Lucius Domitus had been hunting his "treacherous" kin down like dogs. And even more horrifying, he'd been using the vilest of the Southland dragons to help him. The Mì-runach. The most hated and feared of the Dragon Queen's soldiers.

And then there was that female. He knew that female from reputation alone. The dreaded Branwen the Awful, a captain in the Dragon Queen's Army. It was said her cackle had rung out as Didacus's cousins were put to the spear, the sword, or the cross.

It was that heartless female chasing him up the hill right now, while the Mì-runach took down the soldiers who had once been loyal not only to Didacus but to the mighty Overlord Thracius, rightful ruler of the Empire and Didacus's beloved uncle.

He'd sworn on his uncle's bones that he would destroy his treacherous twin cousins himself, but even he had to admit he'd underestimated not only the Rebel King but that sister of his. His cousin Vateria should have killed the little bitch when she had the chance, but they hadn't foreseen what a force the pair of them together would be.

Didacus reached the top of the hill, ready to shift to his natural form so that he could fly to safety, but just as he made it over, something slammed into him, tackling him to the ground.

Big hands pinned his shoulders down and Didacus looked up into the only eye Thracius had left the Rebel King.

"Hello, cousin," Gaius said to him, grinning.

"Bastard!"

"Now, now. Tone."

Panting, Branwen the Awful reached the top of the hill, her blood-covered blade out and ready.

"Want me to take his head?" she asked like she was asking if the king wanted tea.

"No," Gaius said . . . much to Didacus's horror. "I have a few questions for my cousin." Gaius leaned in, leering. "Let's get reacquainted, dear Didacus. We have so much to catch up on, don't we?"

Then, the big bastard reared his head back while lifting Didacus up and—

After head butting his cousin until he passed out, Gaius released Didacus's leather jerkin and let him drop to the ground.

"What do you think this one will tell us that the others didn't?"

Gaius stood, rubbed his nose. "Didacus was a favorite of Thracius. Loyal to him unto death. If anyone knows where to find Vateria . . . he will."

"You really hate her."

"Can you blame me?"

Brannie shook her head. "Not really. I just want to make

sure you're not becoming what me mum calls 'obsessive.' She says obsession is the one thing that will weaken any warrior."

"She's right. But I promised my sister. I owe her Vateria's head on a platter."

Gaius kicked his cousin, watching him roll down the hill toward the Mì-runach, who were busy finishing off the few soldiers who'd been traveling with him.

It had been a good decision he and his sister had made. Sending Gaius out with the Mì-runach and Branwen the Awful. Brutal warriors, all, there was never a fight they backed away from. Nor did they question where they were going or why. The most Gaius got was Brannie asking him his logic behind certain tactical choices, but she was always up for the ride. He really liked that about her.

Before they'd left the Provinces, Gaius had had the royal blacksmiths fit them all with special armor. It vaguely re- sembled that worn by his centurions but not enough to make them stand out. They looked like soldiers for hire who made decent coin from their exploits. And, more important, their armor, like their weapons, grew with them. If they shifted to human, their armor shifted with them. And when they shifted back to dragon, it went with them also. That way, they never had to worry about losing their armor if they suddenly had to go from human to dragon.

"We're hungry," Caswyn complained once Gaius and Brannie were in earshot. Of course, they were always hungry.

Rolling her eyes, the temper-growing-shorter-by-the-day captain snarled, "Then get something to eat."

"Don't have to snap," the Mì-runach snarled back.

She nearly had her sword out when Aidan stepped between the pair. "There's some sheep over that hill. Over there. Go get some, brother."

Growling—or perhaps that was their collective stomachs—Caswyn and Uther wandered off.

"And bring us something back." Aidan smiled down at Brannie. "I'm sure you're hungry, too."

"Shut up." She reached down and grabbed Didacus by his jerkin, dragging him off toward the horses.

Aidan smirked at the king. "She adores me, you know."

"So that's how the Southlanders get by." Aidan frowned at that, so Gaius added, "Delusion."

Aidan laughed. "Well, it works for our queens. . . ." He motioned to Didacus and Brannie. "Are we going to question this one?"

"Yes."

"We'll have to wait until Caswyn gets back from eating. He's the one who's been trained in the art of torture."

"My Uncle Thracius had whole detachments trained in torture. I never saw it as an art form, though."

"It is. If you want to keep them alive long enough to get the information." He motioned to Brannie and Didacus. "I'd best go with her. If he wakes up and gets a bit mouthy . . ."

Gaius chuckled and nodded.

Feeling a little worn down these days, Gaius made his way over to a large tree stump. He sat down and stopped to dig his hands into his hair, resting his elbows on his knees.

He honestly didn't know how much more of this he could do. He missed his home. He missed his sister. He even missed Aunt Lætitia. And while Brannie and Aidan were tolerable enough, the other two Mì-runach put Gaius's fangs on edge. The constant bickering. The less-than-intelligent discussions.

As a son of the Sovereign Empire, Gaius had no tolerance for stupid dragons. And by gods, those two Mì-runach were just plain stupid.

Plus, he was growing frustrated. Despite hunting down

so many of his kin and those loyal to them, Gaius was still no closer to finding Vateria. It was as if she'd vanished. He wanted to believe her dead, but no. If she was dead, Gaius was sure that Aggie would sense it through the lines of magick. They had an unholy connection now. One forged in blood and hatred and the need for vengence.

With the tips of his fingers Gaius briefly scratched his scalp in frustration before dropping his hands. He gazed at the ground, already feeling defeated when he hadn't even asked Didacus a question yet.

Knowing he couldn't face his cousin like this, Gaius did the one thing that had helped him get through these months away from home. He thought about Kachka. Just remembering her face always made him feel better. Gods, what he wouldn't give to have had her riding by his side during all this.

"Do not be so weak, lizard. You will be fine."

Shocked to hear her voice, Gaius immediately sat up . . . but . . . it wasn't Kachka. It was some other woman. A woman he'd never seen before.

"Pardon?" he asked, trying to slow down his heart.

"I said, mind if I sit?" She gestured to the stump he was on. He quickly realized this woman did not have the accent of someone from the Outerplains. She also didn't look like anyone from the Outerplains. She was tall, true. And beautiful. But brown skinned like those of the Desert Lands. Dressed for battle and travel, she smiled down at Gaius.

"Of course."

He moved over a bit, blew out a breath. He should *not* have been that excited just to hear Kachka Shestakova's voice—which he guessed had just been his imagination. What the hell was wrong with him?

The woman dropped her travel pack to the ground with a

heavy sigh and moved her shoulders around as she sat down beside Gaius.

"You wouldn't be looking for a sword for hire, would you?" she asked.

"Sorry, no." He had more than enough swords at his disposal at the moment.

"Thought I'd at least ask." She held up a small pouch, offering the jerky within.

Gaius shook his head and stared off, trying to again focus on dealing with Didacus and finding Vateria. How was he ever going to find Vateria?

"What about Annwyl?"

Gaius blinked. "Pardon?"

"Queen Annwyl. Is she looking for a sword for hire?"

"Oh." He gave a little laugh. He was so tired these days, wasn't he? That was the only thing that could explain . . . forget it. "Uh . . . sword for hire? Probably not. Loyal soldier? Yes. Annwyl's always looking for those."

"Does she pay well?"

"Well enough, I'm sure."

The mercenary pulled out the sword she was offering for hire and he cringed at the sight of it.

"Oh, come on," she laughed. "It's not *that* bad."

"It's awful," Gaius disagreed, reaching out and running his hand over it. "The edge is dull and it's rusted. Perhaps you should join Annwyl's army just so you can get a decent weapon."

She studied the blade. "It's served me well, though. Over the years."

"I'm sure it has, but sometimes things that have served us well need to be retired."

"Good point." She studied him for a long moment until she scrunched up her nose and asked, "Not to be rude, but . . . are you all right?"

"I'm fine. Just a lot on my mind."

"Aye. I understand that. World is changing. Not for the better."

"It's not that bad. I have hope all will work out."

"That's rare."

"What is?"

She smiled. "Hope. Not a lot of people have that these days."

"Well . . . that's what their leaders are for. To give them that hope."

She snorted. "You serious? Do you think the leaders of this world give a shit about us?"

"They have to. Their people are their responsibility. A responsibility most have willingly taken on their shoulders in the hopes of making the lives of their people better."

"Not all of them are like that, though."

"No. But then it's up to the rest of those leaders, who do care, to deal with the ones who don't. A leader has to care for the people. The state. The Republic."

"You sound like one of them Sovereigns."

Gaius smirked. "I like their philosophy."

"A reader, are ya?"

"I am. But I never saw that as a flaw."

She laughed as Brannie walked up to them. She nodded at the woman by Gaius's side before she said to Gaius, "Caswyn's back. So whenever you're ready."

"I'll be right there."

Brannie started to leave, but abruptly stopped, glancing at the woman next to Gaius. She gazed at her a moment before shaking her head and walking off.

"Do you know my friend?" he asked the woman.

"I've seen her around. Besides," she teased, "I have a face that's very familiar."

"No, you don't." They both laughed a bit and then Gaius stood. "It was nice meeting you."

"You too."

With a nod, Gaius started to follow Brannie. But he just couldn't. Not until he fixed it. The problem just ate at him!

He walked back to the woman and pulled his gladius from the scabbard at his side. "Here. Take this."

She reared back a bit, staring at the sword. It was of the highest quality. One of the royal blacksmiths had made it exclusively for Gaius. But honestly, he just couldn't let that mercenary go off with that rusted piece-of-shit blade she had.

"I—"

"Don't say you can't. Just take it. I can get another."

"If you're sure."

"Don't test me, woman. Just take it."

With a shrug, she took the blade from his hand. "That's very kind of you."

"Yeah . . . well . . . whatever."

"You know," she said, running her hand over the weapon, "I think I'll just deal with all this head-on."

"Deal with what head-on?"

She shrugged. "Life. I keep searching. Keep looking. Trying to solve old problems. Instead of going for the problem sitting right in front of me. Understand?"

"No."

She chuckled. "Yeah. Guess I'm babbling. It just . . . it seems that sometimes, you're dealing with the old, instead of facing the new. And when you do that, your old enemy comes up right behind ya and leaves you dead in the dust."

"Secure him!" Brannie yelled, and Gaius turned to see if he could make out what was going on a few dozen feet behind him. Sure everything was fine with his team, Gaius turned back to the woman—but she was gone.

Gaius turned in circles trying to find her, expecting to see her walking off somewhere, but . . . no. She was gone.

Perhaps he *should* have hired her. A woman who moved that stealthily would be a definite asset.

Gaius returned to the others to find his cousin awake but finally subdued enough to no longer be fighting his captors.

Once he was standing in front of Didacus, Gaius just stared at him. What was he doing? Why was he wasting any more of his time on this? Eight months and he'd found out nothing about Vateria. And all the while, the curse of Chramnesind continued to spread over his lands.

The problem sitting right in front of him.

Aggie? Gaius called out to her.

Gaius! Is everything all right?

Yes. I have Didacus.

He heard his sister's snort in his head, could imagine her dramatically rolling her eyes. *So?*

Exactly. I fear, sister . . . I fear I will never find Vateria. And I'm thinking maybe we should no longer be bothering.

Aggie was silent for a bit before she replied, *Before you left, brother, I would have punched you in the throat for even suggesting we let her go. That we not find her.*

And I would have let you, he answered.

But I've got the Senate on my ass; Aunt Lætitia going on and on about the Gabinius family and how they're becoming a problem—and they kind of are; the grain imports are low this harvest, which means overpricing from the merchants; and there's something unclean in the water . . . so I must deal with that.

Gaius grinned. *You're enjoying it all, aren't you?*

I am. To be honest, other than worrying about you looking for Vateria, I haven't thought about that slit in ages.

Good.

Besides, we might have a bigger worry.

Which is?

Rumor is that Annwyl has successfully pushed the killer Chramnesind cults out of the Southlands territories . . . and right into ours.

Balls.

Exactly. I have several legions out looking for—

No. Call them back.

But—

Trust me. They tried the same thing with Annwyl. Pulling her army apart. Then they'll strike. So pull our legions back.

All right. But what about the priests and priestesses who reside in our empire? Who expect our protection.

Gaius stood tall, his eyes narrowing. *Where did you send the first legion?*

To the Priests of the God of Suffering.

He knew the location. Knew of the head priest. *All right. And when will you be home?*

Soon.

"Gaius?" Brannie asked. "Everything all right?"

"Everything is fine. Just checking with my sister."

Gaius faced Brannie and pulled the sword she had hanging from her belt and swung it once, cutting Didacus's head in half. He handed the blade back to her.

"Let's go. We head back to Sovereign territories immediately."

She stared at the gore-covered weapon for several seconds before looking up at Gaius.

"What happened to your own sword?"

"Gave it away. But I need a new gladius. These oversized, cumbersome Southlander swords are ridiculous."

"What's wrong with our swords?" Brannie demanded, the pair walking away seconds before Didacus's body returned to its natural dragon form, destroying many trees in the process.

"They're useless."

"Mine seemed to do fine with your cousin's head!"

Brigida had been napping on a pile of books when she snapped awake. For a few seconds, she was panicked. She felt lost. Incoherent. She hadn't felt that way in so long, she was almost positive she'd been a young one again. Still hanging on to her mother's tail.

"If you'd been anyone else," a voice from a dark corner told her, "you'd have woken up screaming."

Brigida spun around, her tail sending magick text flying across the room, the tip raised, ready to strike.

After a moment of silence, the darkness cleared and Brigida let out a breath. "It's just you."

Princess Rhianwen gazed at Brigida in a way that made her feel—for once—surprisingly uncomfortable. No one made her feel uncomfortable. Brigida made *others* feel uncomfortable. She enjoyed it, feeding off their fear.

But this mostly human child . . .

"What do you want, girl?" Brigida snapped.

Only two of The Three had come back a few months after spending some time with them royals and the Cadwaladr clan. That hadn't surprised Brigida, though. Talwyn needed to be near her mother. She needed to learn from her. But the boy and the princess . . . they needed to be *here*. The boy, he'd taken on the other Abominations. Training them.

Organizing them. Just like his father, that one. He didn't like being in charge, but he accepted it when it was necessary. And the girl . . . to be honest, Brigida hadn't paid much attention to her since she'd returned. They spent their time reading books. Doing rituals. But never together. They barely spoke. And when the girl was feeling lonely, she went outside and spent time with the other Abominations and the monk and two Kyvich witches that the twins had brought with them so many months back. Her "friends," she called them.

Witches shouldn't have friends. Not ones that had real work to do. And them three, Talan, Talwyn, and Rhianwen, all had work to do.

But needing friends. *Needing* family . . . that just made the girl weak in Brigida's mind. Weak and useless. Something Brigida had no time for.

"What were you dreaming, Auntie Brigida?"

"Don't you never mind, girl. Just an old She-dragon dreaming of the—"

"Stop lying to me," the girl said, for the first time sounding dangerous. "We don't have time for your lies and we both know it."

"What I know, girl, is that I'm the last one you should think about getting uppity with. I ain't one of them precious aunts of yours. I ain't got no real use for you, so stomping on you until you're nothing but shit on me claw won't mean nothin' to me."

With a slight shake of her head and a deep intake of breath, the girl sighed out, "Fine."

Then the girl slapped her hand against Brigida's forearm, pressing her fingers against the scales. And, in that instant, Brigida knew the girl was in her head! Physically inside her mind. Looking around, examining shit. Being nosey, Brigida's mum used to call it.

Shocked and annoyed, Brigida tossed her out, but when the girl's eyes snapped open, there was nothing there but cold rage.

"You bitch," the brat growled, her voice low. No longer the sweet darling of the Cadwaladr Clan. "You know what they're looking for. What they've been torturing and killing for all these months. *You know!*"

"Don't bellow at me, little bitch! I'll rip that puny soul right out of you and drink it down like wine."

She faced Brigida head-on. "Then do it."

"What?"

"You heard me. Take my soul. Drink it down like wine. *Do it.*"

Brigida reared back a bit. "What is wrong with you?"

"What's wrong with me?" Rhianwen asked. "I'm tired of your shit."

"You've lost your mind, little girl, if you think you can take me on." Brigida flicked her claws. "Get from my sight until you get control of yourself."

Then Brigida turned to go, but she reared back and, for the first time in eons, she gazed in horror around her. For she was no longer in her cave. But in a field of vast green, with trees and lakes and mountains as far as her old eyes could see.

"What the . . . what the fuck have you done?"

"What's going on?"

Brigida looked over her shoulder and saw the twins. They were both here. Physically. Although she knew for a fact that the boy had been far outside her cave with the other Abominations and the girl had been with her mother leagues away at Garbhán Isle.

"What's happening?" Brigida demanded. "Where am I?"

"She knows," Rhianwen told the twins. "She knows and she hasn't said a word."

The boy "tsk-tsk'd" her. "Oh, Auntie Brigida. Still choosing sides?"

"The only side I have is me own. Thought you knew that."

"We're beyond your side," Talwyn told her. "Right now, there's only two. Ours. And his."

She was talking about Chramnesind.

"So if you're not helping us," Talwyn went on, "you're helping him. And we can't have that."

"You lot think you can take me down? *Me?*"

"Take you down?" Rhianwen asked. "No. Leave you here to rot? *That* we can do."

"See over there?" Talwyn asked, pointing. "Those three?" Brigida glanced over and spotted the souls of three shamans. They looked like Riders of the Western Mountains. Unlike the Riders of the Outerplains, these Riders were slave traders and Queen Annwyl had made it her business to destroy them. A war that had come right to Annwyl's door when the children were still very young. "They tried to kill us when we were . . . eight?"

"Nine," Talan corrected.

"We've had their souls here ever since. When I need a little extra oomph, I feed off them. Which Rhi hates."

"It's one thing to keep them here, because what they did was wrong. But to feed off them is tacky." Abruptly those silver eyes locked on Brigida. "But with you, Auntie, we'll do it."

"You see," Talan explained, "our mother gave up her *life* for us. And now she risks her life, every day, not just for us, but for her entire queendom. The least we can do is help her succeed. Not only to keep her reign, but to keep her people safe."

"And if that means," Talwyn went on, "that we need to drink from you like a piglet draining its mum's teat, we will. Leaving nothing but your fucked-up eye and your tail. So whatever you know, bitch—"

"—*you better fucking tell us!*" Rhianwen finished on a bellow.

Brigida studied the three of them and realized that she'd underestimated the little shit stains.

"Yeah," Brigida finally admitted, "I know what they're looking for."

"Tell us and we'll go get it first."

"Do you think if it was that easy, I wouldn't have done it by now? Even just to have that power in me claws. But we can't. No witch or shaman or priest can. It would just absorb our magick, trap us. Kind of like you've done to them over there." She pointed at the shamans, who were reaching out to Brigida, begging for help. Any other time, she'd drain the bastards dry. But this place, with all its beautiful greenery, wasn't a safe place for her. It was a safe place for these three. *Created* by these three.

They were Abominations, all right. Brigida had her own safe place, just as she knew Rhiannon, powerful white Dragonwitch that she was, had as well. But it had taken them centuries to create a sacred space of their own.

But to hold one, to keep it at the ready for any time they had need of it, like a bloody vacation home? To keep souls trapped in it for their own use? Brigida knew that Rhiannon had nothing like that. And it had taken Brigida more than centuries to build that kind of power. It had taken her eons.

Yet these . . . offspring . . . the youngest was not even thirty winters yet.

For the first time. For the first time *ever*, Brigida felt . . . defeated.

"We'll need someone else to track it down. Someone with no magicks at all, who can track it down and destroy it."

"My mother—"

"No. Gods swirl around her. And your father's bloodline is filled with magick, even for them that don't use it much." She let out a breath. "We need a warrior. Because this won't be an easy get. A warrior with no magicks in her blood."

"Her?" Talan asked, understanding immediately whom Brigida had in mind. "Are you sure?"

"Yeah. Her. Because I only know of one that has all them requirements."

Chapter Nineteen

It had become a ritual for them. Cooking a meal, eating heartily, then using the ash from the cooking fire to cover their faces, hands, behind their ears, and their necks so that they blended into the darkness when the suns went down. They even covered the steel of their weapons so that their blades and arrow tips didn't flash in the night.

Then, before they moved, they waited. With no light, they waited for about thirty minutes, until their eyes could see in the darkness. Until they became one with the night.

Once they were ready, they moved with stealth—yes, even Zoya—easing through the trees and brush. Bows strapped to their backs, swords and daggers at their waists, spears in their hands. The Khoruzhaya siblings split off and circled around the temple. Each of the siblings always seemed to know where the other was, so Kachka worried less they'd accidentally kill each other.

Tatyana still remained a safe distance away with her bow nocked and ready while Nina Chechneva lurked in the trees, keeping lookout and using magicks if necessary. When the heat of the battle was over, she would come in and take the souls she deemed worthy. Over the months, she'd become quite . . . choosey.

Zoya came in from the rear while Marina and Kachka went in head-on.

Once they were all in place, Kachka watched and waited.

They hadn't had the chance to warn the temple priests as she often liked to do. But, to be honest, Kachka worried less about what she'd find when walking in on an attack on an all-male religious sect. True, she often walked in on torture and abuse, but with the women . . . there was worse waiting for them and Kachka refused to allow that. She refused. So, when she could, she always warned the all-female sects. She had to.

She watched as these priests were dragged from their religious home and tossed to the ground.

"Tear the place apart," the gang leader ordered. That's how Kachka thought of them now. Not as soldiers, but as gangs of crazed cult members, running around, destroying everything, sometimes searching the temples. Kachka often kept one alive to find out what they were looking for. And every time she got no answer. Some killed themselves. Others allowed Zoya to twist them like bread dough until they died from the agony. But none of them ever talked.

Kachka would be impressed if they weren't such self-righteous bastards who believed their way was the only way. Their god, the only god.

And, again, tonight, she would try to find out what these men could be looking for. And, again, tonight, she'd probably fail.

Glancing at Marina, Kachka nodded, and Marina let out what sounded like a crow caw. As soon as she did, the first javelin shot out from the darkness and slammed into one of the cult members' chest. Then another. And another. The Khoruzhaya siblings had become unbelievably skilled in the javelin and spear. They practiced every day, for hours. And, in battle, all that work paid off.

After the first javelin attack, Kachka, Marina, and Zoya moved, charging into the midst of the confused men, using their spears to quickly kill them. There was no time for torture or fancy moves. They were almost always outnumbered. So they had to move with speed and efficiency.

With their spears, they attacked one of five spots on the body: through the chest to the heart; through the neck to the main artery; through the inner thigh to the main artery; through the back to sever the spine; or under the arm to another main artery.

Whichever was available, they hit it and they hit quick. They didn't bother with disembowelings—as many Riders liked to do during big battles when they had unlimited backup—since it took too long for the victim to die and they were often still able to fight for quite a bit.

The priests, who had been waiting for death, backed up, clinging to each other and praying to their gods, most likely. Kachka was always fascinated how these sects were quick to thank their gods when it had been she and her team who'd saved them. And, last she looked, there were no gods helping. Even the horse gods didn't leave the Outerplains for all this human drama, so she never bothered to call on them for assistance.

A flash of steel came at Kachka and she spun to the left, rammed her spear into the armpit of one man, tore it out, and rammed it into the chest of another.

She'd just turned to go after a different man when Tatyana sent out a call.

Kachka knew that meant more men were coming. It was a trap. She wasn't surprised, and it wasn't the first she'd encountered. The better they got at this, the more pissed off Duke Salebiri became.

However . . . she'd expected a few extra men. A squad.

Maybe two. Even a platoon. The six of them could easily handle fifty fanatics.

But the Duke hadn't sent a platoon of mad fanatics.

He'd sent a battalion of his troops. At least three hundred well-trained, well-armed men. And all of them running right toward Kachka and her team.

Gaius stood on a hill and stared down at the men charging toward the temple and the Riders standing between them and the defenseless priests.

"What do you want us to do?" Brannie asked.

The old rage, the one that had gotten him his reputation during those dark years, roared through his blood. Like Annwyl's insanity, his rage never went away, it just lay dormant, waiting to be roused from its slumber.

Well, it was wide awake now.

Gaius looked at Brannie and growled out, "They're on *my* territory. Uninvited. Kill them all. Leave nothing for even the crows to dine upon."

Brannie's slow grin showed how much of a Cadwaladr she truly was.

Shifting to her true form, her weapons and armor growing with her, she turned to the dragons with her and screamed, "*With me, Mi-runach! With me!*"

The siblings ran out of javelins and turned to their bows. Each arrow hit its mark, taking down their victims instantly. But they would run out of arrows soon, too.

The soldiers climbed the trees to get to Tatyana and Nina, forcing both women into the battle.

They'd all been helping to train Tatyana, making her a

stronger fighter. But this was not only too much for her—it was too much for all of them.

They had to pull back. Kachka took a moment to look around, trying to find an exit. A way out of this.

"Kachka!" Marina bellowed. "To your left!"

Kachka turned, her sword raised to block the oncoming blow, her spear low to strike and kill. The soldiers charged toward her and she readied herself for the onslaught. But as the men came near, the wind around them whipped up and a black dragon in dark steel armor dropped all its weight on the men, stomping them into the ground.

"Down, Kachka!" a female voice ordered.

"Down!" Kachka yelled at her comrades and they all dropped as flame shot out, covering the soldiers near them.

Screams and battle cries rang out, but there were more dragons, their flame tearing across the troops.

Human bodies covered in fire, the men screaming for death, fell around Kachka, but ignoring them, Kachka scrambled to her feet and ordered, "*Strike!*"

Her team moved quickly, ignoring the ones trying to put out the flames on their flesh and focusing on the ones wily enough to avoid the blasts.

Kachka speared the first soldier who ran toward her, but she sensed someone moving up from behind. She yanked out her spear and prepared to turn and use her sword to slash the one behind. But before she could turn, a body slammed into her back, pushing her forward as the edge of a giant blade cut deep across her cheek.

The soldier who'd been impaled rested against Kachka's back, eyes wide in death, mouth forced open by the tip of the blade that had been shoved through it.

Snarling, Kachka jerked her body to the left, avoiding the body hanging from that ridiculous weapon.

"Gods! Kachka! Are you all right?"

Recognizing that voice, Kachka slowly turned and faced the steel-colored dragon behind her. She had to raise her gaze to look him in the eyes, blood from her wounded cheek dripping onto her shoulder and down her chest.

"It's not my fault," he said, yanking the weapon from his victim. "It's the fault of this ridiculous blade I had to borrow from Brannie."

"Me?" Brannie barked, using her tail to pound soldiers into the ground. "You're blaming me because *you* can't handle a bloody long sword?"

"This is a ridiculous weapon!"

Shaking her head, disgusted, Kachka refocused on the battle. Her team doing what it did best.

Those who'd come with the Rebel King, Brannie and her team, used their weapons, their flames, their tails, and one was just stomping on the enemy, the ground beneath Kachka shaking with each pound of its big feet.

A cloth was pressed against her wounded face.

"I'm so sorry," Gaius said softly. He was in his human form now, his armor and weapons having shrunk down with him, so that he appeared to be any other soldier for hire, traveling the roads.

Fingers slid under her chin, turning her face toward him. He lifted the cloth and winced a bit. "You'll have to get that sewn up, I'm afraid."

Kachka continued to look over the continuing battle.

"You won't look at me?" Gaius asked, humor in his voice.

"You are king and used to many protecting your back." She glanced at him. "I am not king."

"I see."

Marina came over. There was much blood on her and some of the fur on her vest was singed from flame. She grabbed Kachka's face, pulling it away from Gaius's grasp.

She yanked off the now blood-soaked cloth and studied the wound.

"You will live," she said. Marina then studied Gaius. "Why are you here, Rebel King?"

"Heard there were enemies on my territory."

"And you do not send troops? Legions you have, and you come yourself?" Marina laughed. "I will never understand you dragons."

"Yes, well . . . since I was nearby . . . why waste the resources?" Gaius pulled another cloth from his belt. Gently gripping Kachka's cheek, he carefully placed the soft material against her face and held it there.

Marina, smirking, quickly turned and walked back in to finish off the rest of the soldiers.

Kachka knew what her comrade was laughing at and she wanted to slap that smirk off her face, but Gaius was so close and she couldn't do it without pulling herself away from him.

For some unknown reason, she didn't want to pull away. At least not at the moment.

"I hope you didn't mind us . . . helping out."

"It was trap set for us. I expected extra troops of more crazed god lovers. Not three hundred trained soldiers."

"More like two hundred soldiers."

"First you cut my face, then you question my counting. You irritate me."

"Yeah, Kachka. I missed you, too."

That's when Kachka jerked away from him, reaching back to snatch the cloth from his hand so she could press it against her face. She walked away, not even bothering to look back at him.

"If you laugh," Aidan warned from behind him, "she will cut your throat."

"I'm well aware. And I'm trying." And Gaius was trying. He didn't want to laugh at her. Well . . . actually, he did, but he knew that would be tacky at best. He had nearly sheared her head off while trying to protect her. Damn Southland swords!

Brannie continued slamming her tail down until the crying of the men stopped. "That was fun!" she said with a grin. For the last eight months she'd been forced to do stealthier work, sneaking up on the Rebel King's kin and taking them down quickly and efficiently. Plus, there were often more than one or two dragons in the mix. And while that was a true challenge, sometimes a Dragonwarrior just wanted to kill. Human men were the best for that. So aggressive and sure they were strong enough to take down dragons, it made proving them wrong quite enjoyable.

Brannie lifted her tail, realized there was a human torso attached to it, which led to her flinging her tail around trying to get it off. She did, and it flew away, slamming into Caswyn's face.

"Oy!" the dragon barked. "Watch it!"

"Oh, stop whining, you with bits of leg hanging out from between your fangs."

"I was hungry!"

"Gaius Lucius Domitus!"

"Oh. Hello, Zoy—" Gaius froze, realizing that not only was Zoya hugging him, she was lifting him off his feet.

Even more annoying was that Kachka and Marina were standing behind her . . . not helping.

Zoya dropped Gaius back to the ground. "It is so good to see you again, my friend!"

"You, too, Zoya." Gaius quickly stepped back in hopes of stopping her from hugging him again.

"You look so much better than first time I saw you. Nearly dead. Nothing but a walking corpse I thought I would be forced to bury."

Marina laughed out loud and walked away, but Kachka merely shook her head, the cloth on her face soaked through.

Worried about that wound, Gaius moved around the Rider and over to Kachka. He motioned to Aidan and the dragon pulled a cloth from his travel pack. Gaius peeled the saturated one off Kachka's face—noting that she didn't even wince, although he was sure it must hurt—and placing the new one on.

"We need to get this tended."

"It will not kill me."

"I'm sure it won't, but that doesn't mean we should ignore a wound like this." Gaius glanced around. "Uther," he called out when he spotted the brown dragon.

Uther shifted back to human and came to Gaius's side.

"Her cheek."

Uther pulled the cloth back and studied the wound. "Yeah. I can sew that up in no time. Let me get me bag."

After he walked away, Kachka muttered, "Uther Giant Head? He will sew me up with those large, orc-like hands? Sew me up like stuffed doll?"

"First, don't mock the dragon's head. He can't help that it's so big. From what I heard from Brannie, he's been cursed with that giant head since hatching. And second, he's sewn up many of our wounds over the last few months, and he's done a fine job."

"Did you give them wounds yourself? With your ridiculous sword?"

"You're not letting that go, are you?"

Kachka didn't answer, simply walked around him and followed after Uther.

"Do not feel bad, Rebel King," Zoya said, patting Gaius

on the back—which actually felt like the time his Uncle Thracius ripped a one-hundred-year-old tree from the ground and slammed it against his spine. "Kachka has no interest in men once she fucks them."

Gaius turned and faced Zoya. "You forget, Zoya Kolesova. I am not a man."

"Oh. You are king! You think that makes you better?"

"No, my friend. I'm better because I'm dragon." He winked at her and walked away as Zoya's loud laugh rang out over the valley.

Chapter Twenty

Uther leaned back and smiled. "There you go! Should heal up real nice. Leave little scarring."

Kachka stared at the dragon. "Why do I care about scars?"

"Well . . . pretty girl like you. Figured you'd want to keep your looks as long as you can. You know, until you can trap a man."

As Kachka debated how to remove Uther's human head from his human body, Brannie pulled him away by grabbing the scruff of his chain-mail shirt and yanking him off the tree stump he'd been sharing with Kachka.

"But—"

"No!" Brannie barked. "Don't speak, Uther. Just go. Go!"

"You females," he muttered.

"Sorry about that," Brannie said, carefully touching Kachka's chin and examining her cheek. "Shame Morfyd's not here. She could have made you completely scar free."

"If true, then why does Annwyl have so many scars?"

"Annwyl likes her scars. Fearghus likes her scars, too. They're a unique couple." She dropped her hand. "So . . . where are you lot off to next?"

"Do not know. We need to figure out how we move from here. Clearly the cult knows about us." Kachka blew out a breath. "Annwyl may order us back. She will be disappointed."

"Are you kidding?" When Kachka just gazed at her, "After the name you lot made for yourselves over the last few months? You've pushed the cult out of her territory"— she leaned in and whispered—"and right into King Gaius's."

"Name?" Kachka had to ask. She'd been out of touch with everyone from Garbhán Isle since she'd left.

"Yes." Brannie dropped her travel pack to the ground, squatted next to it, and began digging through it. "The priests and priestesses you've saved have been calling you Ghost Saviors."

Kachka couldn't hide her disappointment. "Oh."

"But everyone else has been calling you lot—oh! Here it is." She stood, a small jar in her hand. "This will help with healing." She unscrewed the top and dug a large white glob out with her finger. She came at Kachka with whatever that shit was, and Kachka pulled back.

"Come on. Give it a try. It won't hurt."

"The rest have been calling us what . . . exactly?"

Brannie briefly glanced away before admitting, "The Scourge of the Gods."

"What?"

"For their great sins . . . the gods have sent you as punishment."

"I see."

"I wouldn't take it personally, Kachka," she rambled on, taking Kachka's silence to mean she was upset and also that she acquiesced to putting that useless cream on her face. "Annwyl gets mad when they call her Annwyl the Bloody, but I don't know why. A name like that buys one respect.

Strangely, she doesn't mind Mad Bitch of Garbhán Isle, and that one seems a tad rude to me. But," she kept going, continuing to put that stuff on Kachka's throbbing wound, "neither of us likes Whore Mother of the Abominations."

"Because only women can be whores."

"Not with dragons. We are quick to call out our male whores. Like Gwenvael. My grandfather."

"You have many whores in your family."

"I wish I could say we don't . . . but I'd be lying." She stepped back. "There. Now don't you feel better?"

She did, but Kachka wasn't about to admit it. Instead, she just walked away and appreciated that doing so didn't seem to offend the She-dragon.

"The Scourge of the Gods," Gaius said from behind Kachka. "Fancy name you've got there."

"If you knew name, why did *you* not tell me?"

"I'm a royal. I was trained to only reveal so much excitement. But Brannie is still a young dragon. She can happily reveal all to everyone without concern. I thought you deserved that."

"We should camp together!" Brannie suggested. She had a spear in her hands and was moving through the fallen soldiers, finishing off any who still breathed with a quick jab to the back of the neck or to the heart. "It'll be fun! But let's move away from this smell. It's getting a bit over—gods! Caswyn! Stop eating! I can't think with all that bloody crunching!"

"But I'm still hungry!"

After eating her dinner, Annwyl was lounging on her throne, deep into a fascinating book about the wars between the Southland dragons and the Irons, when she saw her daughter walk quickly into the Great Hall. Talwyn leaned down and whispered to Elina. The Rider's eyes grew wide and she abruptly walked out; Celyn and Talwyn went after her.

A minute or so after that, Talwyn returned, quickly moving over to Dagmar. They spoke in whispers until Dagmar stood and together they rushed out, with Morfyd, Briec, and Keita right behind them—leaving a table with fresh food behind.

Dragons didn't leave fresh food unless it was important, and Annwyl briefly debated going outside to see what was happening. If it was important, though, wouldn't someone tell her? Of course they would. So why bother getting up?

But the voices became louder, angrier, ruining the quiet enjoyment of her book. Sighing loudly, Annwyl marked her place, set the book carefully on the floor beside her throne, and stood. She walked over to a far wall and studied her options. With a shrug, she pulled off the battle axes that once belonged to Fearghus's uncle Addolgar. She took a few practice swings, liked the weight. This was a giant steel axe covered in ancient dragon runes that could be used by a dragon in human form. When it was hit at the right angle at the base of the handle, it would extend to a weapon that could easily be used by Addolgar in his true form.

But since one of his nieces had become an amazing blacksmith who created weapons that could go from human-sized to dragon-sized with no more than the thought of its handler, Addolgar and many of the Cadwaladrs had given Annwyl their old weapons to decorate the house walls. She liked how such mighty steel looked on her walls . . . and the very direct message they conveyed.

Now, with this battle axe in hand, she walked outside into what was quickly spiraling into a very ugly fight.

The strangers sat on their almost-too-tiny-for-their-size horses and glared down at Dagmar and Brastias, completely ignoring Elina, who stood three steps up from them. Keita and Briec stood on one side of Brastias. Keita with her arms crossed over her chest, bare toes tapping, and Briec appearing beyond bored, occasionally yawning. But both quite ready to unleash their collective flames, which could take down most of the courtyard and all the humans within it. And on the other side of Dagmar was Morfyd, appearing concerned that everything would get out of control. She hated that. She liked things nice and orderly.

And, behind them all, a getting-angrier-by-the-second Talwyn, who paced the top of the stairs like a caged jungle cat.

"You will not see the queen," Brastias said in his best commander cadence, usually only used before he destroyed an entire village of orcs. "You will do nothing but leave. Now."

"We do not waste time talking to something as useless as man," the tallest of the invaders informed Brastias, dark blond and grey hair a wild riot of curls and braids that reached down her back. "Be gone from my sight before I turn you into my dog's pet."

"Then you will talk to me," Dagmar informed them.

"What is tiny Northwoman doing here? Did your men free you from your bonds? Or did you sneak away like weak female you were born to be?"

"She is away from controlling Northmen for two minutes," said another with short hair that exposed every scar on her face and neck—and wow, were there a lot. Had she purposely walked into every edged weapon she'd ever come upon? "And now she thinks she can talk to women with actual power like she has any of her own. That is funny. Laugh with me, sisters!"

"No laughing," Dagmar ordered, "just go."

"Nika Kolesova—" Elina began, but the lead Rider quickly cut her off.

"Elina Shestakova, we are so glad you are not dead. We were sure when your own mother ripped the eye from your head . . . you were. But your general weakness makes you unworthy of speaking to someone of our glory, so stop talking to me."

"Oy!" Celyn barked.

The woman's blue eyes cut over to him. Annwyl knew immediately the Rider didn't realize that she was talking to dragons as well as humans. So when she looked at Celyn, all she saw was a man, which she made clear when she told him, "And you have penis, so do not make me cut it off."

Talwyn's hands balled into fists at that, and she glanced at Briec, gesturing to the three Riders. "I'm going back inside to finish my meal," she ground out between clenched teeth, reminding Annwyl of Fearghus. "Briec and Keita, kill them all. Don't leave a mess."

"Wait," Annwyl stated before Briec and Keita could— because they would—kill them all. They were both already taking in breaths to unleash their flames.

"Annwyl, let us handle this," Brastias said.

"No need, old friend."

She walked past Dagmar and Brastias, big, long-handled axe still in her hand.

"Annwyl," Dagmar argued, "they're here to kill you."

"No. They're not."

Annwyl walked around the horses of the three Riders to the fourteen men and young boys they had chained behind them. Men and boys whom Annwyl was sure the three Riders had picked up along the way. The way Annwyl might pick up stray puppies while on a campaign.

The males cowered away from her, and Annwyl didn't bother saying anything to calm them down. Sadly, her reputation as a murdering queen always seemed to precede her, so she didn't bother to argue the point these days. That always just seemed to upset people more. Instead, Annwyl gripped Addolgar's old weapon in both hands and swung it over her head. She brought it down on the chains, breaking them.

She pointed toward one of the guard barracks. "You'll find someone in there to remove the rest of the chains and give you fresh clothes and food. Go. Now. We'll find a way to get you home later."

The boys and men ran off, and Annwyl faced the Riders watching her. "First rule in my kingdom, no slaves."

"They were not slaves. They were future husbands for our daughters and granddaughters."

"Your daughters and granddaughters can get their own husbands. Preferably ones mutually chosen by both parties."

"Why would we do that? As queen—if you are—you must know men are too stupid and emotional to make their own decisions."

"No, actually, I don't know that."

Annwyl rested the axe over her shoulder. "Rule number two." She gestured to Dagmar. "This is my Battle Lord, Dagmar Reinholdt." She pointed at Brastias. "And this is my General Commander. They speak for me when I'm not available. And mostly when I'm available and don't want to be bothered—which is kind of right now."

"You give man position of power? And such a tiny, weak-looking woman?"

"Yes."

"Why?"

"Because he earned it. In blood. And Dagmar Reinholdt is the Beast of the Northlands."

The lead Rider shook her head and said to the females with her, "I do not know, sisters. Perhaps our Pee-Wee was wrong. This tiny human queen, who gives honor to worthless men and weak-armed women, cannot give us our glorious deaths on the field of battle while at her side."

"Perhaps not," Annwyl cut in, lifting the axe off her shoulders and slapping the other end of the handle, beneath the blade, into her free hand, "but I can give you your glorious death right here."

"Annwyl." Morfyd raised her eyebrows in warning. "Calm. And rational. Remember?"

Dagmar snorted and Annwyl glared at her friend. "What does that snort mean?"

"Nothing," Dagmar stated with that wide-eyed innocence that made Annwyl want to slap her against the head! She didn't—it would be unseemly—but gods, did she want to!

She refocused on the Riders. "Look, I understand you're all from a different . . ." She struggled to find the right word, and Celyn provided it.

"Culture."

"Yeah. Right. That. But that doesn't mean you lot can come in here and start ordering everyone around like you—gods-damn it, Gwenvael!" Annwyl shouted when she heard the damn dragon climbing the side of her house, his talons crunching into the precious—and extremely expensive!—stone that she did not want to hire yet another stonemason to fix.

Eyes wide, everyone turned and looked at the house, then back to Annwyl. She knew they couldn't see him. As Rhi had once told Annwyl when Rhi was still a young girl, "Uncle Gwenvael is a chameleon. He can blend into anything. He creeps around here all the time. So when you think you hear him and sense him moving around . . . you do. You're absolutely not insane. No matter what Daddy says."

So even though no one else could see him, Annwyl knew

he was there. So she pointed her axe in the general direction she figured he was in, and warned, "Fuck up that stone again, and I will rip the head from your shoulders!"

Annwyl heard a repressed little chuckle and knew she was right, but she didn't bother to explain that to her kin. What was the point? So instead she simply screamed at him, "Stop laughing at me!"

"Mum?" Talwyn asked, the Riders seemingly forgotten.

"*What?*"

Talwyn shook her head at Annwyl's bark. "Nothing."

Annwyl now pointed that axe at the three Riders, briefly wondering why they sort of leaned back in their saddles—and away from her. "Now you three, if you stay, then you follow my rules and you listen to these people when they tell you things. And yes," she said when one of them opened her mouth, "that includes the ones with penises. And if you decide to go . . . then good day to you, it was nice having you."

Annwyl forced a smile—Fearghus always told her she had a pretty smile—but that only seemed to disturb the Riders more, so she dropped the pretense and returned to her throne and her gods-damn book.

Dagmar wasn't sure what the Riders would do after all that. She knew what she would have done if she didn't know Annwyl as she did and hadn't come to Garbhán Isle under the protection of Gwenvael the Handsome. . . . She would have bloody left.

But the lead Rider, the one called Nika, simply smiled at her sisters and announced, "She is quite mad, sisters! Our potential deaths will be glorious!"

"Then let us join the Mad Queen and seal our fate!" cried another.

"I am so happy we listened to our sweet Pee-Wee!" announced the third.

"Pee-Wee?" Dagmar softly asked Celyn.

"Zoya Kolesova," he replied. "They call her Pee-Wee."

And, as they stepped off their poor, beleaguered mounts, Dagmar understood why.

Fearghus came around the corner of the building, his attention focused on one of the scrolls in his hand. He walked between the Riders, but stopped and lifted his head. He looked at the three women before focusing on Dagmar. "When did we start inviting giants to the house?"

"Not giants. Riders. They are the—"

"I can't," he quickly cut in, "listen to those endless names."

Focusing again on the scroll in his hands, he began to walk up the stairs, which was when one of the Riders leaned forward and slapped his ass.

Briec and Keita made a quick and poor attempt at stifling their laughter while Morfyd quickly rushed to her brother's side and led him up the stairs. "Dinner's ready, brother. Come, let's eat."

Fearghus looked back at the Rider and in reply, she winked at him . . . and leered. That's when Morfyd yanked him up the stairs.

Dagmar waited until Fearghus was inside, along with the others, before she told the Riders, "And don't do that unless the man asks you to—and I'm sure some will."

One of the Riders snorted. "I see we will suffer like saints while we are here, sisters. Making us clean for our glorious deaths."

"It is price we will pay for such honor," Nika promised.

She pointed at one of the stables. "Come. Let us trap the horses in that tiny box so they can eat and have water."

Dagmar watched the Riders as they walked their horses to "that tiny box." When they were gone, she finally looked at the stone wall of the house. "Your timing was perfect."

Gwenvael appeared, no longer blending with the stone he gripped his talons to. "I know. Nothing makes dear Annwyl crazier than dealing with that poor stonemason."

He shifted to human and landed nimbly on his big feet. Naked, he walked over to Dagmar and leaned down and kissed her. When he pulled back, he said, "She always worries me more when she's calm and rational but still holding a weapon. She needed a little insanity to distract her from their insults. Do you think more Riders will be coming?"

"No. Zoya Kolesova—from what I heard—only told her three eldest sisters to come and fight for Annwyl. Those three are more than seven hundred years old and have nearly three hundred offspring between them." Dagmar winced. "My womb throbs at the thought."

"Don't worry. I think we have more than enough offspring."

Gwenvael glanced back at the wall and whistled. "Come on, you lot. Time for dinner."

Like their father, The Five appeared. And, like their father, they were hanging from the wall. But they weren't dragons; they were human and fully dressed, which meant they could appear or disappear on a whim rather than simply being able to blend into their surroundings as their father could.

The Five dropped to the ground and ran into the Great Hall. Dagmar glanced around before asking her mate, "Can Arlais do that?"

He shook his head. "No. Why?"

"Why do you think?"

"Oh, come now. I doubt she'd ever try to kill you . . . until she's at least eighteen winters."

"That gives me such comfort," Dagmar growled, pushing past Gwenvael and returning to her rapidly cooling meal.

Chapter Twenty-One

The Khoruzhaya siblings hunted down several boar and, after seasoning the carcasses, Aidan cooked them with his flame.

The meal was hearty and the discussion pleasant. Even when Kachka tried to goad Gaius into a fight about returning the Quintilian Sovereigns Empire to a republic. A concept that Gaius didn't actually hate. Although under Thracius's rule, dragons and men had been crucified for even suggesting such a thing.

Still, no matter how hard she might try, Kachka could not get him upset. How could she when he was happy just to see her?

Especially after spending these last few months with Brannie, who, unless in battle, was inherently sweet; and the Mì-runach who, except for Aidan the Divine, were not exactly scholars.

So while Kachka thought she was annoying him with her talk of politics, Gaius was enjoying every second of it.

"One day," she said, "all those . . . what do you call them?"

"Plebes."

"Yes. All those plebes will rise up and kill all of you slave-owning royals in your beds."

"Perhaps. Although we no longer allow slaves within the Empire."

"So you killed them all?"

"No. Just made them freemen."

"And free dragons?"

"Dragons are always free. We make very poor slaves."

"It's the flames," Brannie piped in while eagerly cleaning a rib.

"All dragons under royal rule are slaves. They are slaves to their kings and queens and gods."

"I see," Gaius said. "I hadn't thought of it that way."

"Because it's the wrong way," Caswyn argued, well into his cups after indulging in the Rider ale. Foolish boy. "Dragons can never be slaves. We are much too powerful and mighty."

"Really?" Kachka asked.

"Aye, Rider female. Really."

Marina, who sat beside Caswyn and was steadily working her way through half the ribs on her own, suddenly brought her greasy fist back. Not too hard. But it did connect with Caswyn's nose and dropped him to the ground like a felled great oak.

"Aye," the Rider females all said in unison, their voices deliciously flat, "*much* too powerful and mighty."

As her comrades taught Brannie and the still-sober Mìrunach old songs of their land, Kachka went into the surrounding forest, far from the priests' temple. She walked for a good ten minutes, finally stopping by a large tree.

She rested her back against it . . . and waited.

It wasn't long before Gaius passed her. She watched him, not moving or making a sound. He abruptly stopped a few feet from her, his head lifting a bit. She realized he was sniffing the air, searching for her scent.

If he were human, she'd say he was a proper tracker. But it was the dragon in him that searched for her. Probably did the same thing when looking for sheep to devour.

"I never go back," she told him.

Gaius faced her. Smirked. "Really?"

"Once I have man . . . I have no need of him again."

"Yes," he said, moving toward her. Stalking really. She kind of liked it. "I learned that about you from the way Dagmar wants you dead. You clearly broke that poor nephew's heart."

"Clearly," she replied, certain she'd done no such thing because his reputation had grown substantially among the unattached females of Annwyl's court.

Gaius stood in front of her now, reaching out and taking a lock of her hair. One of the braids. Twirled it around his index finger.

"I didn't know I'd find you here in my lands, Kachka. But I'm glad I did. I missed you."

"Why?" she asked, curious.

"You're so . . . difficult. It makes me hard."

Kachka laughed. She hadn't expected that, but she liked his honesty.

Gaius had the braid wrapped around his finger until his fist was near her ear. She expected him to grab her by the hair. But he didn't. Instead, he just rubbed his thumb against it and stared at her mouth until she finally demanded, "Are you going to kiss me or not, dragon?"

The grin that spread across his handsome face told her that was what he'd been waiting for.

He pressed his free hand against the tree behind her and leaned down, his lips touching hers.

But in that second, in that split second—everything went . . . weird.

The light went from dark to bright. As if the suns were

out. But when Kachka pulled back from an equally confused
Gaius, she looked up and saw only one sun.

And it was warm. Summer warm.

"What is happening?" she asked.

Gaius released her hair and stepped away, turning in a
circle to see everything around him. The beautiful grass, the
lovely trees, the bright blue sky.

"I have no idea," Gaius finally replied.

Kachka heard a soft cough and walked around the tree
she was now against. "The weepy brown girl."

"I prefer Rhianwen."

"And Brigida the *Most* Foul."

"I kind of like it," the She-dragon shot back.

"We are so sorry," Rhi said. "We didn't mean to interrupt
you two."

"I can't believe a Rider would lower herself to fuck an
Iron," Brigida scoffed.

Gaius nodded at the female. "Brigida. Nice to see you
again, too."

"Liar like your father, I see."

"Auntie Brigida!" Rhi snapped. "Please."

The dragon threw up her claws, and fell silent. But then
neither female spoke.

Kachka glanced between the two, little Rhi and Brigida
in her dragon form, which was as disturbing as her human
one.

The two females continued to stare at Kachka but said
nothing else.

Finally, Kachka couldn't stand it anymore. "Do you
have actual words for me, witches, or do I just walk back to
camp? Because already I grow bored with both of you strange
bitches."

Brigida snorted. "Yeah. She'll do."

* * *

"She'll do for what?"

Brigida's milky white eye turned on its own to stare at Gaius before her head slowly swiveled around in the same direction. He worked hard not to flinch, although he doubted he was fooling her. The witch lived off others' fear. Craved it the way he often craved fresh, unburnt lamb.

Brigida the Foul was still talked about by the old guard. The dragons who, in their youth, had fought during the wars against the Southland dragons. Even now, centuries later, they still feared her. Rarely mentioning her by name and always talking in low tones, as if she could hear them from whatever hells she'd been dropped in. Little did any of them know that the She-bitch still walked this plane, quite alive, and just as unpleasant as ever.

"You're going to let this dragon speak for you, Daughter of the Steppes?" Brigida asked Kachka.

"I am already bored with you, old She-beast. So talk to him or do not. I do not care."

"Well, this is off to a great start," Gaius joked.

Talwyn came out of the beautiful green trees, moving toward them. But when she spotted Gaius, she stopped.

"What's he doing here?"

"And always a pleasure to see you, too, Princess Talwyn."

Talwyn ignored him, instead focusing on Rhi.

"What's happening?"

"I was waiting for you?"

"Why?"

"And *more* bored," Kachka sighed.

"We need you to retrieve something for us, Kachka," Rhi said.

"I am not thief."

"It's not really a stealing situation."

"Then get it yourself, lazy royals. I am not workhorse for you."

"That's it," Brigida growled. "I'm gonna bite the bitch's little tits off."

Unwilling to let that threat possibly come to pass, Gaius immediately stepped between the females, both arms raised. "How about we discuss this calmly? Yes?"

Looking between all the parties, Gaius realized that "calm" was maybe the wrong word. There was little calm here. There were just different levels of dangerous.

Except for Princess Rhi. She may not have been calm, but that was because she didn't want any fighting. She wanted everyone to get along. A born peacemaker.

Gaius focused directly on her. "What do you need, Rhianwen?" he asked.

"The eyes of Chramnesind."

Gaius's arms dropped to his sides. "Pardon?"

"You heard," Brigida sneered.

"You want the eyes of Chramnesind?"

"I thought he had no eyes," Kachka said.

"Apparently, he once did." Talwyn leaned against a nearby tree.

"And what?" Gaius had to ask. "He wants them back now?"

"No. His cult wants them. Salebiri wants them. And they're not going to stop until they get them."

Kachka crossed her arms over her chest. "Is that what they have been doing at all those temples? Trying to find this . . . this . . . artifact?"

"I'm sure that's been one goal. Along with the terror the attacks cause. The message they send." Talwyn took in a breath. "These people have a very . . . large world view. There's little they do that doesn't impact as many lives as possible. If their whole agenda didn't involve destroying me and everyone like me . . . I'd be impressed."

"Will you help us, Kachka?" Rhi asked.

"Yes. I will help."

Gaius faced her. "Wait . . . what? Why would you do that?"

"That has been my job from beginning. To stop this cult from attacking temples on Annwyl's land. And if they are looking for this thing . . . then I will find it."

"But is there a reason none of you are doing it?" Gaius asked the others. He pointed at Talwyn. "She's perky and likes to destroy."

Talwyn smirked. "Do you really want to see *me,* Iron, with the unlimited powers of a god? Is that what you really want?"

"No, Talwyn. You with unlimited power is the last thing I want."

"Kachka has to go," she explained. "She has no magicks in her blood. She can handle the item without fear of it having repercussions except perhaps revulsion. The three of us can't say that. Even Annwyl can't. Not with the way the gods are constantly around her. They must be drawn to something about my mother."

"But you can go with her, King Gaius," Rhi said, an adorable smile on her lips.

"That's sweet, Rhi, but I can't."

"Since I do not need you?" Kachka tossed in.

"*No,*" Gaius replied, glaring at the Rider. "Because I have magicks in my blood."

Brigida leaned her giant, misshapen dragon head close to Gaius, looked him over, sniffed him, then said, "No, you don't."

Shocked, Gaius insisted, "Yes, I do. I don't use them, of course. I leave that to my sister."

Brigida snorted. "You have no magicks, foolish boy, because your twin sister leeched them from you before hatching.

She left you with the brawn and some brains, but that was about it. So go with the Rider or not, no one cares."

"What about team?" Kachka asked.

"They can travel with you, but keep Chechneva and the Mountain Mover away from it."

"Zoya Kolesova? She has magicks? There are no shamans in her tribe."

"Do you think her size comes naturally?" Brigida asked with a laugh.

"And where is this thing?"

"That's the fun part," Talwyn said with a smile. "It's with the Dwarves of the Western Mountains."

Gaius's head dropped back. "Oh, fuck."

"What? I get along fine with dwarves."

"With Outerplains Dwarves, I'm sure you do great, Kachka. But these are the Dwarves of the Western Mountains," Gaius pointed out. "And they are *assholes*."

"Gaiusssssssss!" Brannie called out, quickly beginning to panic. She'd assumed Gaius had snuck off to spend some time fucking Kachka Shestakova, since she'd heard before leaving Garbhán Isle that the king had spent the night with the Rider. So she wasn't being *nosey* necessarily. She had just wanted to make sure everyone was all right.

What? It was her job!

And when she hadn't found the king right away, she still hadn't been too worried. But after a half hour of searching, she was moments from completely freaking out!

Where could they be?

"Brannie?"

Brannie glanced back at Aidan. "What?"

"What are you doing?"

"Looking for Gaius."

"He's probably off fucking the Rider. He could barely keep his eyes off her through the entire meal."

"But where could they be? Would *you* travel that far away from camp to bang a Rider up against a tree?"

"That's quite . . . descriptive, and if she was a screamer, probably."

Brannie snarled at the Mì-runach. "Why are you bothering me?"

"I was making sure you're okay. You wandered off—"

"I didn't wander. I'm not a hatchling."

"No, but you are a tad nosey. Is that what you and Izzy do when you're not destroying nations? Follow young lovers around and gossip about them?"

Brannie was about to answer that with a fist to Aidan's big, giant, stupid, handsome face, but then there they were! Suddenly. Walking and talking. Coming from absolutely nowhere!

"You can't do this," Gaius was telling Kachka, which seemed like a bad idea if he really didn't want Kachka to do something.

"I am over one hundred. I have killed many enemies. And I have never been slave. I can do as I like, lizard."

"Not with the Western Mountain Dwarves." He caught Kachka's arm, pulling her up short. "I know them, Kachka. They will not help you. They won't even see you."

"No," Aidan piped in. "But they'll help me."

Gaius raised a brow. "Really?"

"You forget who my kin are, King Gaius. The House of Foulkes de chuid Fennah are sworn to protect the Western Mountains from the invasion of the awful Irons. That would be *you,* my lord," Aidan finished on a whisper.

"So?"

"That requires a healthy relationship with the Western

Mountain Dwarves. One I'm not above exploiting. If I'm asked nicely," he added, leaning a little too close to Brannie.

"Do it, imperialist dog," Kachka ordered. "We leave in morning."

"This discussion isn't over," Gaius called after her seconds before he realized the Rider was clearly not listening to him.

"That woman is frustrating," he growled, stomping off after her.

Aidan smiled at Brannie, and she snapped, "Shut up."

The dragon threw up his hands. "I didn't say anything!"

Chapter Twenty-Two

Kachka woke up just as the suns began to rise. The others were still asleep, all of them with weapons at hand, ready to be grasped and used.

But she quickly noticed that Gaius was not among them, his bedroll empty.

She stood. Stretched. Then followed his tracks down to a small stream. A stream he was pissing in while yawning.

Kachka bit her lip and eased up behind the dragon, being sure not to make a single sound or—

"Stop that," Gaius said without even turning around.

"Senses like wolf."

"Senses like a dragon."

"Why do dragons need such senses?" she asked, curious. "You are so large and have fire and talons and wings."

"You humans can't help yourselves. You always have something to prove, and killing a sleeping dragon seems to bring you the highest honors."

"Not humans. Men."

He put his cock away, adjusted his chain-mail leggings, and crouched down to wash his hands in the stream.

"You don't have a very high opinion of males, do you?"

"Of course I do. I love them. But they have many flaws.

It is not their fault, though. They are born with weakness. It is the weakness of their sex that makes them so hysterical and egotistical."

"You do understand that none of the races can survive without both genders? We need each other."

"Yes. Of course. Who else would take out our trash? Lift heavy things?" She grinned, and the dragon shook his head, but still laughed.

"I've truly missed you, Kachka."

"You have?"

He ran wet hands through his hair. "Yes. I have. I've thought about you often when I was traveling the last few months. Especially," he sighed out, "when Caswyn and Uther would have . . . debates."

"Debates? About what?"

"Whatever their tiny little brains would deem interesting." He looked up at Kachka. "It's been a long eight months. You helped keep me sane."

"And I was not even there. I never knew I was so gifted."

"Well, you are female."

"Very true."

Gaius stood and took a step, moving close to her. "Did you think about me?" he asked, gazing down into her face.

"Not often," she admitted. "Mostly just when I masturbate."

Gaius closed his eye. "You do that on purpose, don't you?"

"Do what? Tell truth?"

Sliding his hands into her hair, he tilted her face up. "Evil harpy."

"Imperialist dog."

His grip tightened and he leaned down as Kachka went up on her toes, their lips a hairsbreadth awa—

"Morning, my friends!"

Kachka gritted her teeth and growled, "I will kill her."

Gaius massaged Kachka's skull with the tips of his fingers, as if he was trying to soothe a dangerous animal. "Morning, Zoya."

"Such a beautiful day!" she announced.

"Looks like rain, comrade."

Gaius, laughing, kissed Kachka's forehead before releasing her.

"Do you come with us, Rebel King? To retrieve these eyes of god?"

"Yes."

"No."

Gaius shook his head. "Really, Kachka? Really?"

"I am the one who needs to retrieve this thing. You need to return to your kingdom and your royal life."

"My sister reigns with a fair claw and hard heart. She'll be fine without me. This is more important."

"And why do you believe that?"

"Because I'm here. And I don't think that's by accident."

While Zoya used the stream to scrub her face and neck clean, Gaius explained to Kachka, "Two days ago, my only plan, my only goal in the world, was to track down Vateria, with the help of Branwen and the Mì-runach, and cut her throat. That was it. I've hunted down every cousin or blood relative still loyal to my Uncle Thracius in order to find her."

"But now you are here, instead of hunting your cousin."

"Yes."

"Why?"

"I met a sword-for-hire on the road, and what she said . . . resonated with me."

"Resonated?"

"Made sense," he clarified. "Even my sister tires of

thinking about Vateria. Worrying about her. She told me that Chramnesind's cult killers had been pushed out of Annwyl's territory and into ours. I came to the temple closest to me to take them on, and found you. I'm a firm believer in signs, Kachka Shestakova. This was not an accident. We should do this together."

"Just two of us?"

"Well . . . more like you, me, Brannie, your team, the Mì-runach—"

"And Zoya, of course!" Zoya announced, patting them both on the back before walking off. Singing.

"Does she grasp that it hurts when she does that?" Gaius asked.

"No," Kachka said with a shrug. "Not even little bit."

Roland Salebiri kissed his wife's long neck before slipping out of their bed and walking to the large doors. He opened them and stepped out onto the balcony, gazing down at his troops preparing for the upcoming war.

There were many nations who wanted the Whore of Garbhán Isle brought to heel and were ready to join Salebiri, whether they believed in his god or not. Although he didn't worry. They too would take the blood oath and give their souls to the one true god. In time.

But, until then, Salebiri cared for only one thing. The destruction of the Whore Queen and her brood of Abominations. He'd kill them all in the name of his god.

Hands slid around his chest and soft lips pressed against his neck. His wife was as tall as he, but it had never bothered Roland.

"Come back to bed," she purred, tempting him as no one else had ever been able to do before.

"How I'd love to. But I can't. I had a dream."

"A dream? About what?"

"About you, my love. About you traveling from these lands."

"Me?"

He turned and faced her, sliding his hands around her waist. "It's sweet. That you pretend my connection to our god is as strong as yours."

"Roland—"

"No." He kissed her cheek. "I have faith in him and he has faith in you. Take what you need. Leave as soon as you can manage. I will not question."

"Are you sure?"

"I do not deny our god anything. That includes you."

Vateria had just pulled on her boots when her niece walked in.

"You ready?" she asked.

"Yes."

Vateria stood, smoothing down the gown that covered her leggings. "Our people ready?"

"Handpicked by me. They're ready to move when you are."

"Good."

Pulling a fur cape over her shoulders, Vateria walked across the room. As she neared the doors, her niece asked, "Are you sure about this, Auntie? Once Uncle Roland finds out the truth about—"

Vateria stopped by her niece, pressed her middle and index fingers against her lips. "Sh-sh-sh," she whispered. "One must have faith."

"Yes, but—"

Vateria stepped into her niece, quietly enjoying the way

the young She-dragon immediately backed up, her head banging into the door.

"Faith," Vateria said again. "Understand?"

"Yes. Yes, Auntie Vateria. Faith."

"Good." She petted her niece's cheek. "Then let's go. Once we have our prize, all will be well."

Chapter Twenty-Three

Once the two groups had moved out that morning, they'd separated, traveling along different routes to a spot predetermined by Gaius. The suns had already gone down when they met again. But the Riders came with several freshly slaughtered boars, ready for Aidan's flame, and Ivan Khoruzhaya boiled up some potatoes.

While the food was being made, the Riders tended to their horses. Taking them to a nearby lake, getting them fed, and checking them over for any injuries due to the hard ride.

The dinner itself was a surprisingly friendly affair, with stories of Outerplains tribes and dragon clans. The only one who didn't offer anything was Aidan. He listened. He laughed. But considering they were heading toward his family for help, he'd said little about them.

That's when, after spending eight months with the dragon, Gaius realized he knew little about Aidan the Divine. Instead, Aidan was brilliant at getting others to talk. At getting others to reveal much about themselves. Even Gaius, who'd learned early on in his life to keep things to himself or between him and his sister, had told stories about life with Thracius and some of his kin.

Yet Aidan revealed very little. And if his brother Mi-runach knew anything about him, they didn't reveal it either. They talked of their own lives, but never about Aidan's. Nor did they ask questions.

Gaius didn't think Aidan was hiding anything bad about himself, though. His silence made Gaius worry about how difficult it would be to deal with the Southland royals maintaining that area. And about his chances of getting in to see and successfully negotiate with the Western Mountain Dwarves.

But they had at least another day's ride before they even reached that territory. And Gaius didn't want to spend all his time obsessing over what might or might not happen. He preferred to leave the fretting and obsessing to his twin and Aunt Lætitia. They were really good at it and Gaius was pretty certain they sort of enjoyed it.

After the meal was finished and the chatter died down while weapons were checked and sharpened and readied, the Khoruzhaya siblings took first watch. The pair separated and disappeared into the trees like the ghosts the rescued priests and priestesses called these Riders.

Gaius spread out his bedroll and quickly went to sleep until he was lightly kicked in the shoulder.

He might normally have woken up, ready for battle, but he was certain if someone wanted to hurt him, they'd have kicked him somewhere with more potential impact. So Gaius turned over and saw Kachka motion to him before fading into the trees. He quickly got to his feet and followed, already getting hard at the mere thought of Kachka Shestakova. A reaction he hadn't had since he'd first begun to have sex and gone through a time that his father had called "The wind blows and you get hard" phase of male dragon growth.

Gaius stopped when he reached a boulder where Kachka's armor and furs were neatly stacked. Not only did he stop moving, his heart kind of stopped. But it started again at a hard, rapid pace as soon as Kachka moved out into his line of sight. She was completely naked, walking past him and over to another, bigger boulder.

His mouth dried up as he watched her turn and, using only her arms, lift herself onto that boulder and brace her hands behind her. Then, slowly—gods, so very slowly—she opened her legs for him, inviting him into that wet pussy that was practically calling his name.

Attempting to swallow, Gaius walked over to her, gawking while he pulled off his fur cape and chest armor and chain-mail shirt. He tossed his gauntlets away and placed his weapons off to the side. Still within arm's reach, but he really hoped he wouldn't need them for quite a bit.

He left his leggings on for now, needing them to keep himself from immediately burying his cock inside Kachka and coming within seconds. He didn't want to do that. Not yet. He wanted this to last.

Gaius stepped close to the boulder until his thighs pressed against the cold stone. As he stared Kachka in the eyes, he slid his index fingers from the base of her feet, up her calves, and down her thighs. He gently stroked his fingers against her pussy, watching it tremble under his touch and become wetter by the second.

Kachka's breathing got deeper, but she never turned from him. She didn't look away. There was no teasing. No insecurity. No pretending sex was something she needed to be drawn into. That was the way of human women in his Empire and some of the Southlands. But not for the Daughters of the Steppes. When they wanted something or someone, they just made those intentions known.

There didn't need to be games between them, and Gaius couldn't believe how knowing that made him harder still.

He dragged his fingers, now wet from her, back up Kachka's

thighs until he reached her knees. Slowly, he pressed her legs down, making her even wider for him.

Letting out a breath, his mouth no longer dry but watering at the thought of tasting her, he brought his mouth down and pressed it against her, licking her long and deep, using his tongue to explore every bit of her. And the more he enjoyed himself, the wetter she became.

Kachka finally lay back against the boulder, pressing her hands deep into his hair, holding his head against her.

Her hips began to move, making circles as she tried to follow his tongue, her breath now coming out in hard pants, her toes gripping the rock beneath her.

"Yes," she growled beneath him. "Yessss."

Gaius lowered his hands a bit, so they rested on the inside of her thighs and he gripped the strong muscle there, squeezing and releasing. Her buttocks tightened as she raised her hips like he was already inside her.

He finally snaked his way to her clit, circling his tongue around it. When her legs began to shake, he held her down harder and pressed the tip of his tongue right against her clit, moving it while at the same time releasing his hot dragon breath against it.

The sound that came out of her then was a cross between a growl and a stifled cry, her fingers gripping his hair tighter, her legs struggling against his hands to close. To control the strength of the sensations flooding through her.

Gaius didn't stop until he was sure he'd made her come, and her entire body was shaking beneath him, her cries muffled as she pressed her mouth against her shoulder.

When he felt certain he'd wrung her dry and he knew he could no longer wait, he pulled back long enough to shove his leggings down past his knees and yanked her down so that he could push his cock into her while lifting her up into his arms. He heard Kachka scream against his neck, and he wished he could say he was dragon enough to stop and make sure she was okay. . . .

Sadly, at the moment, he was anything but an etiquette-minded dragon.

The dragon's big cock pushed inside her and Kachka let out a scream of satisfaction against his neck. All she'd been thinking about, all day, while riding on her oversized horse, was having this dragon's cock inside her.

And now that she did, she was unbelievably happy about it. It felt good. Right. Like she didn't think it should be anywhere else but inside her.

She pushed against his shoulder. "On your back," she ordered.

Without a word, the dragon complied, taking her place on the boulder, stretching out beneath her.

Kachka placed her knees on either side of the dragon and rode him as she'd ridden her horse. Rocking against him, squeezing his cock each time she did. Gaius reached up, his hands almost around her breasts—exactly where they belonged—when a voice behind Kachka announced, "Hello, my fucking friends! I am on watch now and wanted to make sure you are doing okay!"

Snarling, filled with rage, Kachka reached down and grabbed the small axe that Gaius had placed next to his other weapons. Grasping it, she turned and flung it at Zoya Kolesova.

The large woman ducked, barely missing getting her head split open by the weapon. With that, Zoya spun on her heel and headed back toward camp, tossing over her shoulder, "I see you are both well. Call if you have trouble! See you in the morning!"

Satisfied she wouldn't be coming back, Kachka faced

Gaius again, pressing her hands against his shoulders. Now that she was angry, she fucked him harder, but he didn't seem to mind. Instead he gripped her breasts with his big hands and squeezed them, briefly stopping to play with the nipples before squeezing them again.

Kachka continued to ride, clutching the dragon's cock with her pussy until his back arched and he released her breasts so that he could grab her waist and power into her from beneath.

When he started to come, Kachka went down on his chest and pressed her mouth against his, swallowing his yell and kissing him as if she hadn't kissed a male in eons.

She finally pulled away when she was sure she'd gotten all he had.

Kachka sat up, his cock still inside her, and grinned down at him.

"I don't know why you have that look on your face, Kachka Shestakova," he said as he wrapped his arm around her waist and stood. He pulled her off and turned her, placing her face down over the boulder, and roughly entering her pussy from behind.

"We are not nearly done," he rasped against her ear before he began fucking her again, burying himself deep inside her with each thrust.

"Good," she told him between gasps, "I was . . . about to . . . be . . . disappointed."

Gaius shared his flask of water with Kachka before putting his arm around her shoulders and pulling her naked body in close to his side.

He was afraid that she would try to pull away, but she

didn't. She relaxed into him but didn't cling, which he definitely preferred.

"I thought you never went back," he reminded her.

She dismissed that with a wave of her hand. "You are not even human, so shut up."

"I have to admit, I do enjoy fucking you."

"Thank you. I can promise, the feeling is mutual."

After a few minutes of comfortable silence, Kachka lifted her head and asked, "Did I kill Zoya Shestakova?"

"No. But you did try."

"Yes. I could not quite remember. But she ducked in time. That is good."

"I didn't think she could move so fast."

"The Mountain Movers do not let their size stop them. I am glad I missed her. She has turned out to be good for our group. I would feel . . . bad if I had taken off her giant head."

"That is so big of you."

"It is."

Gaius chuckled. "The suns will be up soon."

"Yes."

"Do you want to go back to the camp? Get some rest before we have to ride?"

"No."

"Okay."

"Why? Do you?"

"Actually no. I'm comfortable here."

She peered up at him. "Do you want to go on being comfortable?"

Gaius took in a deep breath. "Not particularly."

"Good." Then her head was in his lap and her mouth was swallowing his cock whole.

Gaius's eyes crossed and he dropped his head back against the boulder they rested against.

His toes curled and that's when Gaius realized he'd never actually taken his leggings completely off.

Of course, he wasn't about to bother with that now. Not when he could barely put two cohesive words together. Instead, he just stroked the back of Kachka's bobbing head and thanked the gods for taking such excellent care of him the last few years.

Chapter Twenty-Four

Dagmar held up the dried bit of meat and watched her dogs watch her. They sat tall, proud, and drooling in the courtyard. She wasn't a fan of the drooling, but it was the one thing she couldn't get rid of through breeding. And reason knew she'd tried.

Still, they were strong, they lived nearly a decade longer than most dogs their size, and they were loyal until death.

So if Dagmar had to put up with a little drool, that's exactly what she would do.

"Where is she?"

Surprised, Dagmar turned and saw Rhiannon standing there. And she was seething. She didn't think she'd ever seen the Dragon Queen seething. Not like this.

"Where's Bercelak?"

"At home. Where is she?"

Dagmar sighed. "Annwyl? What did she do now?"

"No. Not Annwyl. But take me to her." Rhiannon walked off, barking over her shoulder, *"Now, Northlander!"*

Dagmar tossed treats to her dogs, then followed the angry queen.

Rhiannon was substantially taller than she so her strides

were long. Dagmar had to run to catch up with her, her dogs running alongside her.

By the time she reached the Dragon Queen, she was panting and Dagmar didn't like it one bloody bit.

Rhiannon lifted her robes and charged up the stairs and into the house.

Morfyd and Talaith were chatting on the stairs—probably gossiping—but they stopped when they witnessed Rhiannon storm by.

"Mum?" Morfyd asked her mother's back, brows raised at Dagmar.

Dagmar threw up her hands and continued to follow, while Morfyd and Talaith fell in line behind them.

Rhiannon cut through the entire house, and continued out the back and into the forest. She didn't stop until she reached a small clearing.

Dagmar saw Annwyl and Talwyn sparring with short swords and shields. And watching them were the three giant Riders.

"What are those Riders doing?" Talaith asked.

"They never leave her side," Dagmar pointed out. "They escort her to her room at night . . . which apparently is freaking out poor Fearghus."

"I can't blame him."

"I think Annwyl likes them, though. They're quiet when she reads."

Talaith glared at her. "Are you saying I talk too much?"

"Everyone says you talk too much. You're only outdone by your own daughters."

As the mother and daughter moved around, swords clashing, Rhiannon suddenly stalked between them, separating the pair.

Annwyl looked at Dagmar. "What's happening?" When

Dagmar's only reply was a shrug, Annwyl rolled her eyes. "Are you still playing that game with me?"

"I really don't know what she's doing."

"Where is she?" Rhiannon demanded.

Annwyl faced her fellow queen. "Where's who?"

Rhiannon crossed her arms over her chest. "Mingxia."

Dagmar had no idea who that was until Morfyd asked, "The war god?"

"The Eastland dragon war god."

Talaith made a tsk-tsk sound. "Is there any god you're *not* involved with, Annwyl?"

"She's just been helping. Teaching me new battle skills. I don't see the problem."

"Do you want to tell her the problem, granddaughter?" Rhiannon asked Talwyn.

"Nope."

And that's what Dagmar loved about her niece. She didn't know anyone more straightforward.

"She's been using Talwyn behind your back," Rhiannon accused.

Talwyn let out an annoyed sigh. "No. She hasn't."

"Sending you out to fetch the eyes of Chramnesind? Like one of Dagmar's dogs?"

"My dogs don't fetch."

Rhiannon waved at Dagmar to shut her up.

"That's not even close to what happened," Talwyn replied, putting down her weapons and reaching for a carafe of water. She poured a chalice full and handed it to her mother. Then poured one for herself.

"Then what did happen?"

Talwyn glanced at Annwyl and the queen shrugged. "Might as well tell her now. Before she tears the house apart in one of her tantrums."

"I don't have tantrums. I have fierce rage."

"I didn't find anything out from Mingxia. It was from Brigida."

"Brigida told you?"

"No. We just . . . got it."

"We?" Talaith's eyes narrowed. "You mean you, Talan, and *Rhi*?"

"Things come to us. We hear things. It's not a big deal."

"It is," Rhiannon insisted. "It could change everything."

"How?" Dagmar asked.

"Any talisman from a god is powerful. Especially something stolen. If these things fall into the wrong claws—"

"They won't."

"*You* are the wrong claws, my dear."

"I'm aware, Grandmother," Talwyn shot back and even Dagmar could tell she was a bit hurt. "Which is why the three of us aren't going after it. We sent someone else. Someone with no magicks in her blood."

That's when everyone looked at Dagmar.

"I don't fetch either," Dagmar reminded them all.

"Not Dagmar. We needed a warrior. And although she has a warrior's heart, Auntie Dagmar was panting running after Grandmum."

"She has very long legs!"

"We sent Kachka Shestakova," Talwyn said.

"You sent the Scourge of the Gods after this . . . thing?"

"It seems fitting."

"Dear Kachka Shestakova is *the* Scourge of the Gods?" the Rider called Nika asked. "How impressive for her! If her mother were not dead, killed by you, Mad Queen, she would be so proud!"

Rhiannon's entire body tensed. "Who are *they*?" she asked, pointing a damning finger at the three outsiders.

"They are three Riders who have come to follow me into battle so that they may have an honorable death."

"You have suicidal Riders hanging around you now?"

"There is no honor in suicide!"

"Again, you are talking to me, giant woman! And I thought Bercelak said we forced the giants underground!"

"Mother," Morfyd admonished.

"Can we all just be calm?" Dagmar finally asked.

"You don't understand—"

"Rhiannon, I understand that your three oldest grand offspring are no longer children. They're adults and they're part of the game now." Dagmar walked over to her niece, stared up at her. She was a little taller than Annwyl. But not by much. "I'm sure Talwyn is doing what's best for the family."

"And if this doesn't work?" Morfyd asked, her voice quiet.

"Then we'll have a bigger fight than we were planning on." Annwyl gestured back toward the house. "So if you don't mind . . . my daughter and I have work to do."

With Annwyl effectively ending the conversation, all Rhiannon could do was snarl before stomping off, Morfyd and Talaith following behind her.

Dagmar looked over at the three Riders. "Could you please excuse us?"

"No," Nika replied.

Dagmar's dogs, glaring at the Riders, began to growl even though Dagmar hadn't said a word.

"Get something to eat," Annwyl ordered, and without question, the Riders did as she bade.

"When you go off to battle, they *will* be going with you, yes?" Dagmar asked, nearly pleaded.

Annwyl laughed. "I promise."

"One of them," Talwyn whispered, "took down a male elk with her bare hands. I thought she was hungry . . . but she was just playing with it. The way I like to play with your dogs."

Dagmar looked up at her friend. "Annwyl—"

"I know."

The friends gazed at each other for a long moment until Dagmar finally asked, "What exactly are you thinking?"

Annwyl glanced at Talwyn and her daughter nodded. "I'm thinking . . . we can't wait around for Salebiri to come to us. Not anymore."

"I think you're right. I've been working with Brastias. Quietly. No need to make everyone panic."

Annwyl smirked—knowing that neither was speaking of the common people but their own kin—and reached out, grasping Dagmar's forearm. "You do understand I can't do this without you. Knowing you're keeping my people safe here."

Dagmar swallowed, shocked by the admission. "I'll make sure everything is ready when you are." She cleared her throat. "What about Rhiannon?"

"Let her focus on this Eyes of . . . whatever. Work with Bercelak and Celyn. They'll make sure their troops are ready."

"All right."

"And we're okay?"

"As long as you stop taking baths in the freezing-cold lake water . . . I'm sure we'll be just fine."

Annwyl stomped her foot. "I *knew* that bothered you!"

Chapter Twenty-Five

"The thing to remember," Aidan told them as they neared his childhood home on horseback a few hours before sunset, "is that they are horrible, reprehensible, detestable beings and should be treated carefully. Like poisonous snakes."

Kachka frowned. "We still speak of the dwarves?"

"No," he replied. "My family. The dwarves are a whole other issue."

"You talk about your family that way, handsome dragon?" Zoya asked.

"Well, they're not like, let's say, Brannie's family. Are the Cadwaladrs rude and abrupt with no social etiquette whatsoever? Absolutely. But they are also direct and honest, to the point of absurdity. My kin? They smile and embrace you as one of their own while they stick a dagger in your back and steal the gold from your fangs. Never forget that, any of you, no matter how much they may smile. In fact, the more they smile, the farther you should move away from them. If they all start laughing as if they're having the best time? Find the nearest exit and run for your lives."

"I am just *adoring* this plan," Gaius grumbled.

"I have no plan," Kachka reminded him, enjoying the way he glared at her.

"I am keenly aware of that, and I have to admit, it greatly disappoints me."

"Also," Aidan went on, "if you truly expect any help from them, plan to barter. There's always a price to pay in my father's territories."

"These are the Dragon Queen's territories," Brannie reminded him.

"You keep thinking that and see where it gets you, Captain."

Kachka didn't know what to expect when she arrived at Aidan the Divine's home. She'd never come this far before because Salebiri's fanatics had stayed far away from this area. Now that they neared the lands, she understood why.

The territorial lines that divided Annwyl's lands from that of the Western Horse Riders went from soft grasslands covered in rushing rivers and peaceful lakes to harsh marshlands in the blink of an eye.

No wonder Annwyl didn't try to claim any of this territory as her own. If it weren't for the slaves the Western Riders insisted upon having—and selling—Kachka doubted that the queen would bother with anyone in this region unless she was specifically called upon.

It wasn't that it was ugly land. It wasn't. But it was dark and foreboding. The air thick, the land soft, the vegetation overwhelming.

This would be a harsh place to fight any war.

Their horses, unused to such muddy terrain, were miserable before they'd traveled more than a few hours, but Aidan brought their party to a stable where they could leave their horses until they were ready to return.

Once their horses were tended to, they set off on foot.

But it was difficult going. So difficult, even Zoya stayed silent, focusing on where she stepped and how deep she might sink in.

Aidan was more surefooted, and they followed him, finally forming a single line rather than spreading out.

It was nearing suns-down when Aidan finally said, "Up here."

They followed him up a very small hill and when they reached the top, Kachka had to admit her surprise at what she saw.

They'd reached the very edge of the Western Mountains and jutting from them was a beautiful castle made entirely from mountain rock.

"My great grandfather and a few dragon stonemasons built this right from the mountain. Took them several years but well worth it."

"I can't believe you left," Brannie said.

Aidan chuckled and began his descent down the hill. "When you meet my family, Branwen the Awful, you'll understand that I had very little choice in the matter."

The armor gleamed. The soldiers stood ready. Dragons in human form guarded the front. Dragons in their natural form, but still in full armor, flew around the castle walls.

A swampy moat circled the front of the building, and Gaius was sure that there was something in there ready to eat whatever was thrown in.

The drawbridge was already down, but a line of guards stood ready on both sides.

"Very well protected," Gaius murmured to Aidan.

"My father," he replied, "is very . . . concerned with the safety of his lands."

"Does he fear attack from Sovereigns?"

"From everyone."

They moved through the lines of dragons, each soldier dropping to his knees as Aidan passed.

"They treat you like a king," Brannie noted.

"No. They treat me like a prince. My father they treat like a king."

Gaius knew that would be something that truly bothered Rhiannon. It wasn't just loyalty she relied on, but the respect that went along with being a born queen. She didn't take it for granted, and she wouldn't ignore someone else being treated like the ruler of her lands.

But Gaius would have to figure out how to give her that information at a later date.

They passed through the gateway, over a bridge, and when Gaius glanced over the side, he saw something sliding through the murky water beneath. They moved through the courtyard, filled with still more soldiers, and to the castle proper.

As they entered, even Gaius had to admit he was impressed. He'd thought nothing could parallel the palaces and villas of his home, but this place did manage to rival them. Everything, save for the wood furniture, was cut from the stone mountain. The walls, the floors, the balconies, the rooms, the stairs and banisters. But nothing was plain. No, intricate depictions of battles of old were cut into the stone. And after one passed the large front hall, it was all deep passages and caverns for dragons in their natural form to disappear into.

The whole thing was astounding, and Gaius admired the work that must have gone into it.

"Wait here," Aidan ordered before disappearing deep into the caverns.

While they stood, waiting, Gaius noticed that the only one who had a hand on her weapon was Brannie. He had to admit, he found that odd. The House of Foulkes de chuid Fennah was still part of Rhiannon's queendom, and Aidan's father would risk much by losing that connection. Not only would he have to deal with the Cadwaladrs coming here and crushing his forces in the queen's name, but then he'd have to worry about Gaius and his sister sending a few legions to help out. Even if Gaius and Rhiannon weren't allies, it was still a dangerous game to play because neither of them would allow the Foulkes de chuid Fennahs to keep these lands as their own. It was too important a territory for that.

And yet . . . he didn't mind that Brannie was feeling her most distrustful. That would definitely work in their favor. He was sure that not only did Branwen the Awful have her mother's eyes . . . she had her battle instincts. Especially since she seemed to have gotten very little of Bram the Merciful's peacemaking talents.

"Oh! We have guests. How wonderful!"

The She-dragon came down the stairs in human form, a gown of gold covering her from neck to feet. Her gold hair reached the entire length of her long back until it trailed behind her like a wedding veil.

She was stunning despite her age.

But those eyes. Some things could not be hidden and those eyes revealed all.

"I am Lady Gormlaith of the House of Foulkes de chuid Fennah, and who may all of you be?"

"Lady," Brannie said with a slight head nod. "I am Branwen the Awful, Captain in the Dragon Queen's Army. Daughter of Ghleanna the Decimator and Bram the Merciful."

"Ah, yes, Captain. I am well aware of your name. I've heard much about you over the years. But why are you here?"

"I'm escorting King Gaius Lucius Domitus along with your son Ai—"

"King Gaius!" Hand against her chest, Gormlaith pushed past a startled Brannie and held out her hand. "How delightful to meet you!"

Gaius took the hand offered and kissed the back of it. "And you as well, Lady Gormlaith."

"Oh, please. Just call me Gormlaith. And tell me you're spending the night. I'd hate for you to run away too soon."

"If you can accommodate us all, I'd love to stay."

Those dead, cold eyes flickered over to the others. Her nose lifted the tiniest bit, but Gaius wasn't sure which disgusted the royal more. The Outerplains Riders being in her beautiful home . . . or the Mì-runach. Or maybe it was just having a Cadwaladr here, since the royals had little use for what they'd oh so affectionately termed "the pit dogs of Southland dragons."

"Well, of course. I'm sure we can find them something."

"Wonderful."

"Let me get a few servants to help you and we'll get you settled. Then we'll have to have a feast in your honor and you can meet my offspring and we can talk. Won't that be fun?"

Gaius gave his best lying smile. "Delightful."

Gormlaith clapped her hands, and fast-moving but very put-upon human servants rushed into the main hall.

When they neared the Riders, ready to take their fur capes and weapons, Kachka held up a blocking hand. "No, sheep."

It was rude, but it did get her point across.

Gormlaith's eyes locked on Kachka and she forced her own lying smile. "Hello. And you are?"

Kachka stared at her. "I am what?"

Gaius briefly closed his eye, trying desperately not to laugh. Kachka had been around the Southlanders long enough to know *exactly* what Gormlaith was asking her; she was just being difficult. Because she could.

"This is Kachka Shestakova," Gaius began and he kept going, through each and every long-winded Outerplains name ever invented. If he thought he could get away with it, he'd have added more to their names just to see how long it took his fellow royal to snap.

Unlike Queen Rhiannon and her offspring, Gormlaith held out for the entire length of introductions, never once interrupting or complaining.

To be honest, Gaius was a little disappointed. He honestly preferred Keita the Viper's snarled "shut up with all that shit!" before she flounced away in her flowing dress and bare feet.

When he was finished, Brannie gazed at him, as if she couldn't believe he'd bothered, while the two Mi-runach appeared half asleep.

"Well," the lady said when Gaius was finished, "it's lovely to have representatives of the Outerplains among us."

"Is it not?" Zoya asked. Loudly. "Everyone loves when Zoya comes!"

"Because there is usually grunting," Kachka whispered to him.

Gaius snorted and Gormlaith's eyes locked on him. "Yes, well . . . just follow the servants to your rooms. We'll send up water for baths and something to tide you over until the feast."

"Where's Aidan?" Brannie asked.

"Who?"

"Your son?"

"Oh, I have no idea. In the Northlands, I suppose. Are you a friend of his?"

"He brought us here. He went off that way," she added, pointing toward the caverns.

"Oh. Did he?" There was that lying smile again. "How lovely. It's been too long since he's come home." She gestured to the human servants, prompting them to follow. "Just let them know if you need anything else."

As they walked up the stone stairs, Brannie leaned over to Gaius and whispered, "Don't stray too far away from my side, Gaius."

"Even while I bathe?" Gaius teased, then he immediately cringed. "Some days you really do look like your mother. Especially when you glare at me like that."

Aidan had his second oldest brother on his back and his sword over his head. He had every intention of impaling the bastard right through that thick skull of his, but his mother walked into the cavern before he could.

"You bring the king of the Quintilian Sovereigns Empire here and you don't give me any warning whatsoever?" she snapped.

"And hello to you, too, Mother. Long time, no—"

"Shut up! And, Harkin, get off the floor! What is wrong with you?"

"*Me?*"

She walked back to the cavern entrance and yelled out, "Airmid! Cinnie! Get in here!"

"No Orla?" Aidan asked about the youngest of their kin.

"I don't even know where she is."

"That's good. That's very nice. A concerned mother, as always."

Cinnie came in first. She was in her dragon form, but she

had several gold chains around her neck and rings on her talons. He'd bet anything she'd been rolling around in a pile of gold. She really loved doing that. Kind of like a pig in shit.

"Where's your sister?"

"How would I know?" Cinnie glanced at Aidan and back at her mother. She hadn't seen him in at least two decades, and it was clear she didn't care.

"Well, get into something beautiful. That pink dress you have should work."

"What for?" She again glanced at Aidan. "For *him*?"

"No. King Gaius is here."

"The Rebel King is here? Oh! Is he handsome?"

"Missing an eye, but tolerable. And still unmarked, from what I understand," his mother said eagerly. "We'll toss you and your sister at him and see what happens."

"You'll never be queen," Aidan felt the need to point out. "He rules the Empire with his sister. She's his queen."

"Ewwww."

"Not like that, you idiot. And if I were you, Mother, I wouldn't waste my time throwing any of your offspring at the king."

"Why not? Both my daughters are high-born enough for the usurper of Thracius's throne."

Aidan took a moment to crack his neck, relieving the tension that had been building there since he'd first stepped into the marshes surrounding his parents' territories. "First, you have *three* daughters. Just as you have *three* sons. Let's keep that in mind, shall we? And second, you may not want to refer to Gaius as a usurper to Thracius's throne. At least not in front of him. I'm relatively certain that will insult him and make Rhiannon *extremely* paranoid about you. With good reason. And third, Gaius is only here to get access to the Western Mountain Dwarves. *Not* so that you can throw your daughters at him."

Lips pursed, his mother narrowed her eyes on Aidan. "You call him Gaius? He allows that from some worthless little Mì-runach?"

Aidan slowly nodded his head and replied, "Yes, Mother, I missed you, too."

Chapter Twenty-Six

Gaius didn't know how long he slept on that soft bed in his room, but he felt a hand caressing his bare chest and immediately grabbed it.

He was really relieved when he opened his eyes and saw Kachka grinning down at him.

"Thank the gods it's you," he sighed out.

"I am good fuck."

"That's not what I mean . . . mostly." He raised himself up on his elbows. "Did you see the way Gormlaith was salivating at me? She wants me for her daughters. Something I'd like to avoid."

Kachka sat cross-legged on the bed. "You do not want royal wife?"

"I don't want any wife at the moment. But based solely on Aidan's reaction to his kin, I definitely don't want anything to do with his sisters."

"No one gets along with family."

"There's not getting along, Kachka, and there's warning you to run. That's a big difference."

"Brannie does not like it here either," she admitted. "She paces in her room like chained dog."

"She has her mother's instincts."

"And tits."

Gaius dropped back on the bed, one arm thrown over his eyes until he felt Kachka land on his lap, her thighs on either side of his hips, even though a fur still separated her from his naked body. He lifted his arm enough so he could peek at her.

"Can I help you?"

"Just wanted to be comfortable while we wait to feed."

"Well, if you really want to be comfortable—" he began, placing his hands on her hips. But before he could take even a tiny step farther, Aidan walked into the room, with Brannie right behind him.

The poor dragon dropped face down on Gaius's bed, ignoring the fact that, save for the fur covering, Gaius was naked and Kachka was on his lap.

"I hate these dragons!" Aidan roared into the bedding.

"What happened?" Brannie asked, closing the door behind her and throwing the bolt. Like that would help with dragons.

The walls were made of stone, but not the doors.

Aidan lifted his head to look at Gaius. "Just so you know, you're expected to pick a queen from one of my sisters. But only the two eldest because no one cares about my younger sister or even knows where she is."

"No offense, Aidan, but—"

"You don't even have to say it. I wouldn't wish my two oldest sisters on my worst enemy. Besides, they're already queens. Queens of vapidity."

"I'm sorry we needed to bring you here."

"I offered. I just forgot how hard it is to deal with them." He turned on his side, resting his head on his fist, his elbow on the bed. "Two decades I've been away and they're still intolerable."

"You haven't been home in twenty years?" Brannie asked.

He leveled his gaze at her. "Do you feel comfortable here, Cadwaladr?"

"No," she quietly admitted. "But I thought I was just being paranoid."

"You can't be paranoid enough around my family."

Gaius again raised himself up on his elbows, but he wasn't about to move Kachka. He liked her right where she was, even if there was an audience.

"Are you sure we have to go through your father for this? Can't we just bypass him and the rest of your family?"

"No. In order to get to the dwarves, we have to go through this castle and into their tunnels. My father's soldiers guard those entrances. It'll be a fight if we try to get by them without his permission."

"You keep them busy," Kachka offered, "and I will get by them."

"And then what?" Gaius asked.

"He's right. Without my father providing you with an invitation, with his seal, the dwarves will chop you to pieces. They hate Riders." Aidan shrugged. "They actually hate everyone. But they do tolerate my father. Speaking of which . . ."

Aidan sat up. "I also think I should mention that my father is slightly . . . uh . . . hmmmh . . . insane."

Gaius blinked. "Wait . . . what?"

"Yeah."

"He's insane? Like Annwyl insane?"

"See, I don't view our dear Annwyl as insane so much as quirky. My father, however . . . he's what I would classify as truly insane. Thinks the walls are talking to him. Thinks stray dogs are plotting his death. Thinks his hair is magickal."

"What?"

"Don't ask. Just let me handle him."

"Are you good at handling him?" Gaius had to ask.

"I still have all my limbs and my scales so . . . yes."

"But he sent you to be one of the Mì-runach," Brannie reminded him.

"That was my decision."

"Why would anyone choose to be *that*?"

"I knew working directly for the Dragon Queen could only be good for me."

Flabbergasted, Brannie pointed out, "I've seen you in battle. You could have easily taken the trials and been a Dragonwarrior, and worked directly for the queen. Wouldn't that have been easier?"

"If you think taking the trials under the oh-so-gentle tutelage of your Uncle Bercelak is easier than being thrown in a pit with sixteen drunk Mì-runach attempting to cave my head in with their warhammers . . . then I must point out that you're very wrong."

Once the two dragons left, Kachka was still sitting on Gaius's lap—and she was quite comfortable. She could feel his big cock pressing against the inside of her thigh and she was tempted to suck the whole thing into her mouth. But she knew they'd have to go to dinner soon.

"Are you going to wear that to our meal tonight?" he asked, gazing at her.

Kachka had put on leather leggings and a sleeveless fur vest and fur boots. She still had open wounds on her arms from her last fight with Salebiri's troops, although the cream that Brannie had insisted putting on her cheek each morning as they'd traveled had healed the face wound much more quickly. The stitches were still in, because Uther was not willing to pull them out for another day or two.

But she wasn't about to hide herself away. She was as proud of her scars as any Daughter of the Steppes should be.

"Yes."

He grinned. "Good. Make sure to sit next to me."

"What if they try to make me sit somewhere else?"

"Be your usual, etiquette-minded self. I'm sure it'll be fine."

Kachka leaned in and kissed Gaius's nose. "You are funny for lizard."

"Oh, your compliments. How I do adore them."

Unlike Gaius, Aidan couldn't sleep. He couldn't nap. He couldn't relax.

So he headed deep into the Stone Castle, as the Western Mountain Riders called Aidan's home. He'd spent his early decades exploring every nook and cranny of this place. It was his escape when he felt no escape was possible. And it was while exploring as a young dragon that he'd met the Master of the Guards. A green dragon and distant relation of the Cadwaladrs, the older warrior had taken pity on Aidan. He'd trained him how to fight. First with claws and tail, then flame and fang, then sword and shield—then with everything else. He taught him how to be a warrior dragon while Aidan's grandfather taught him how to think. How to maneuver in a world of politics and royals.

His grandfather thought Aidan would one day take over protecting the Western Mountains for the Dragon Queen. According to him, "One brother is a mouth-breathing idiot. The other is so pliable as to be ineffective. Two sisters who are as vapid as your mother and a baby sister who will be crushed under the weight of so much uselessness. So . . . that leaves you."

It had also been his grandfather who'd sent Aidan away. "Go to the queen," he'd said. "She'll treat you better than your own kin." And, as usual, he'd been right. Going to Queen Rhiannon had been the best thing Aidan had done. As had choosing the Mì-runach. The queen had been downright giddy when he'd told her. She adored her Mì-runach while the rest of the world loathed them. In fact, she'd been the one to give him the name "Divine."

"Not only because you're pretty like my Gwenvael," Rhiannon had said, "but you are just absolutely delightful!"

Gods, he missed the queen. He wished he was back at Devenallt Mountain, the seat of power for the Southland dragons. Nothing more entertaining than sitting around and watching the growling Lord Bercelak snarl and snap at the royals and Elders who made the mistake of breathing near him.

Yet Aidan knew that he belonged here. At this moment. King Gaius, whom Aidan had grown to greatly respect, wanted to help his Rider lover find the artifact before Salebiri's people could. How could Aidan not help?

Aidan was about to turn down another corridor when he knew—*knew*—that he was being watched.

Smiling, he raised his gaze up to the rocky ceiling above. "Hello, sweet Orla."

Wide brown eyes stared down at him, gold hair falling in her face, gold scales glinting in the torch-lit cavern as Orla hung by her talons.

"Hello."

"What are you doing up there?"

"Nothing. Why?"

"Have you been hiding from the family again?"

"I wouldn't call it hiding. . . ."

"Avoiding?"

"Yes. I would call it that."

Aidan wanted to smile and hug his baby sister, but he knew they had a few things to work out first. "You still mad at me, luv?"

"You left me," she reminded him—and accused.

"I had to."

"You left me alone with *them*."

"I know."

"Why?"

"You were a hatchling that couldn't shift yet. I couldn't take you into human territory with me. Not yet."

"So . . . you came back for me?"

Aidan couldn't lie to her, even though he really wanted to.

"I didn't. I came to help a friend. But—"

Orla didn't even let him finish. With a flap of wings and a dangerously long tail, she was gone, nearly taking his head off in the process.

An arm circled Aidan's neck and he wasn't surprised when Brannie's chin rested on his shoulder. He'd bet she couldn't sleep either. Naps were hard when you were waiting for the worst to happen.

"I should point out," Brannie said, "that baby sisters have very long memories. We forget nothing and hold absolutely *everything* against you."

"Thank you for that," he told her flatly.

"But have no fear. We may never forget or forgive, but we always love our big brothers. Despite everything and no matter how much you may owe us emotionally. And, gods, do you owe big!"

Aidan finally laughed. "Cow."

* * *

Gaius and Kachka napped together until the door opened and Lady Gormlaith stuck her head in. She smiled when Gaius opened his eyes, but they quickly narrowed in annoyance when she realized that there was a scarred arm tossed over his chest.

"Food is ready whenever you are, *King* Gaius."

"We'll be right down," he promised, grinning when the door finally closed.

"I hear tone from that female," Kachka noted without moving.

"There was definitely tone when she said 'King' like that. Apparently I'm forgetting my place by bedding such a Low Born human."

Kachka used her free hand to rub her eyes, but she still hadn't moved the arm draped over his chest.

"Who?" she asked.

"That would be you, Kachka Shestakova."

"Me?" She moved her hand away from her eyes, blinked at him. "I am Kachka Shestakova of the Black Bear Riders of the Midnight Mountains of Despair in the Far Reaches of the Steppes of the Outerplains. I am better than any imperialist dog."

Gaius kissed her. "And that's why I am going to have *such* an entertaining night tonight."

He threw the fur wrap off and stood. "Come, beautiful Kachka Shestakova. I have *much* introducing to do this evening!"

"And this, Lady Cinnie, is Nina Chechneva, the Unclaimed."

Bored eyes glazed, the She-dragon called Cinnie nodded.

"Nice to meet *all* of you," she managed to get out without yawning.

Gaius moved down to Aidan's brother Harkin. "Lord Harkin of the Foulkes de chuid Fennah, second son of Lady Gormlaith and Lord Jarlath. And Lord Harkin this is . . ."

Annnnd he introduced all of them again. *All* the Daughters of the Steppes. Full names. Never shortening any of it. For each of them. Even Ivan, who just seemed confused by that since he'd never been introduced by anyone before except out of necessity.

Suddenly, Kachka had a deep understanding of the annoyance the Southlanders felt when her people began to say their names.

"And this, Lord Harkin," Gaius finished, "is Nina Chechneva, the Unclaimed."

Harkin was staring blankly at the stone wall behind Gaius's head, but a shove from Aidan had him barking, "Yes. Right. Nice to meet all of you."

"Oh, look!" Aidan cheered, jumping up from his chair and running to the front of the hall. "My eldest brother, Ainmire, is here!"

His brother stepped back from Aidan. "What are *you* doing here?"

"I am so glad to see you, too, big brother." Aidan yanked the bigger dragon in human form over to Gaius while Ainmire stared at his brother for what seemed like a very long time. As if Aidan had been thought dead and was now suddenly in front of them alive. Perhaps he'd been gone so long that's how it felt to his kin? Kachka didn't know.

"King Gaius Lucius Domitus, this is my eldest brother, Ainmire."

"Ahh. Nice to meet you Lord Ainmire. Please, allow me to introduce you to Kachka Shestakova of the . . ."

Annnnd again off he went! Clearly enjoying every torturous moment of it.

While food was brought out of the kitchens by the servants, Gaius sat down near the head of the table. The big stone chair that resembled a throne a little too much for Gaius's liking—or, at least what he was sure would be Rhiannon's liking—stood empty. He wondered where Lord Jarlath might be. Odd that he hadn't come. If not to meet with Gaius, at least to see his son.

Brannie plopped into the chair on his left. He got the feeling she sat there because she was protecting him.

Lady Cinnie pulled the chair out on the right side of Gaius, but Kachka easily pushed the She-dragon aside.

"I sit by him." Kachka dropped into the chair, one foot resting on the opposite knee. "Go sit elsewhere."

The She-dragon glared down at Kachka with such venom that Gaius was sure he'd have to step in to protect the human. Perhaps kill for her.

When Lady Cinnie didn't move fast enough, Kachka dismissed her with a hand wave that rivaled that of a true royal.

"Go sit *down* over there, Cinnie dear," her mother growled at her through clenched teeth.

Cinnie walked away, her chair scraping ominously as she pulled it back.

Zoya watched the servants carefully place the food in front of the guests and Aidan's family, her gaze moving back and forth the length of the table before she asked, "Is this what you call feast?"

"Yes," Lady Gormlaith replied. "Is there not enough food for your"—she gestured at Zoya—"proportions?"

"Enough food. But where are the musicians? The talk? Everyone is happy and talking at Queen Annwyl's feasts.

Here it is like someone died. Has someone died? Are you mourning? Then we should mourn with you. Nina Chechneva!" Zoya barked, slamming her fist on the table. "Sing the song of death to honor our hosts!"

That's when Nina Chechneva stood and began . . . wailing. It was musical wailing, but it was definitely wailing. A grating, painful wailing with a strange backbeat.

Aidan's grin was a sight to behold. Big and happy. He couldn't be more pleased. Yet his kin . . . not nearly as happy. Not even close.

Nina stopped and the wailing seemed to be over, until she ordered, "Now everyone!"

Then all the Riders began to wail. Musically.

Gaius had to drop his head, especially when he realized that Brannie was shaking next to him. She was so desperately trying not to laugh, but the tears falling into her lap betrayed her failure.

"We do not have a death!" Gormlaith finally yelled out. "There is no reason to sing the song of . . . whatever."

"The song of death—"

"I don't care," Gormlaith cut in. She cleared her throat. "Because no one has died. So . . . no need for any of it. We, here, are just more . . . reserved than the human queen of the Southlands. That's the dragon way."

"Is it?" Zoya asked, clearly surprised. "Brannie, she is dragon. She dances, yes, Brannie? Dances and drinks!"

"Well, Branwen the Awful is . . . is . . ."

"Low Born?" Aidan asked. "Is that what you mean, Mother?"

"Can't we just eat and enjoy our meal? Or must you ruin everything?"

"I don't have to ruin everything . . . but I can—"

"Or," Brannie cut in, desperately wiping tears from her

face, "we could just eat." She chuckled a little more. "This does look good."

"And so does that," Caswyn grumbled under his breath, his eyes looking past the empty throne-like chair.

She was shy, eyes cast down, her long gold hair parted in the middle but managing to hide a good portion of her face, hands laced in front of her, shoulders curved. But no matter how hard she might try, she couldn't hide the beauty of her human body. And, Gaius would guess, in her natural form, she would be stunning.

Aidan immediately stood, placed his hands on the back of Caswyn and Uther's necks and snarled, "That's my baby sister." Then he slammed their heads into the table.

"Understand?" he asked the friends who were now rubbing growing knots on their foreheads.

They nodded, however, even as they winced.

"Excellent!"

The warning given, Aidan rushed to his sister's side, leading her to a chair next to Brannie. Then he forced Caswyn and Uther to move so he could sit on his sister's other side.

"King Gaius," Aidan said, grinning, "this is my baby sister, Orla. Orla, this is King Gaius Lucius Domitus."

"Lady Orla," Gaius said, nodding his head, noting the pride on Aidan's face. "And, please let me introduce you to my friends—"

"*Later!*" Lady Gormlaith barked. But she quickly cleared her throat and forced a smile before again saying more calmly, "Later. Why don't we enjoy our lovely meals first?"

"Of course," Gaius obliged.

Kachka leaned over and softly whispered in his ear, "You are what charming Celyn calls, 'a bit of a dick.'"

"No, no," Gaius corrected. "I'm a *major* dick."

"The food," Zoya announced, "it tastes also like you are mourning. Are you sure no one is dead?"

That's when Nina Chechneva offered, "I can sing song of death again."

"*No!*" most of the Foulkes de chuid Fennahs yelled.

Nina shrugged. "Fine, but let me know if you change mind."

They were halfway through their meal—and Zoya was right, the food at this place was bland, not like the food of Queen Annwyl—when guards marched into the hall. They preceded an older man or, Kachka was guessing, a dragon in human form. His gold hair was streaked with silver, and he moved quickly, glaring as he stomped to his chair. He dropped into it, gold eyes glowering at the entire table. Kin and stranger alike.

"Why are we sitting here, eating like humans?"

"A feast in honor of King Gaius Lucius Domitus, my love," Gormlaith easily replied, most likely used to the moods of her mate. "He brought with him some humans, so it seemed like a good idea to enjoy a meal together."

"A feast?" the dragon asked, eyeing Gaius. "For an Iron?"

"The queen has an alliance with King Gaius now, Jarlath." She briefly glanced at him. "Remember?"

"Why so much food?"

"To celebrate."

"Did anyone taste it yet?"

"It is bland," Zoya said, even while she continued to eat.

"Not for flavor, barbarian. For poison."

The Southlanders immediately spit out their food, but Kachka and her Riders kept eating, as did Gaius.

"You're not worried about poison?" Lord Jarlath pushed, staring at Gaius.

He swallowed before replying, "The first thing every Sovereign's mother does is to protect her hatchlings from poison. Mostly because the best poisoners in the world are from the Quintilian Provinces."

"How do they protect you?" Cinnie asked.

"They poison you. With a whole . . . host of things. You throw up a lot when you're a Sovereigns youth, but eventually . . . it passes. And you're either dead or you have a cast-iron stomach." He smiled. "As it turns out, we have a very healthy population in the Sovereigns Empire."

Jarlath looked at Kachka. "And you?"

"We are Daughter of Steppes," she said with shrug. "You do not survive Outerplains without strength."

"But poison—"

"We had an Anne Atli who was poisoned by enemies once. It took her thirty years to die and she ruled with steel fist entire time." Kachka briefly pursed her lips. "Yet many still saw her as weak for dying at all. Poison is for . . ." Kachka looked over the table of Southlanders. "You people."

Brannie snorted but quickly dropped her head.

Lip curling, Lord Jarlath asked, "Who *are* you?"

Annnnd Gaius introduced all of them again.

"And this, Lord Jarlath, is Nina Chechneva, the Unclaimed," Gaius finished.

But unlike his mate, Lord Jarlath didn't even attempt the basic rules of Southland and Sovereign Empire etiquette. He seemed greatly focused on his eldest son, watching him the entire time Gaius was speaking.

"Why aren't you eating, boy?" Jarlath asked Ainmire.

Blinking slowly, Ainmire looked up from his untouched

food, and glanced around the table as if he'd never seen any of them before. Not even his own kin. "What?"

"What's wrong with you?" Harkin asked.

"Nothing. Why?"

"You seem . . . strange."

"I'm just glad to be back with my family."

"How long were you gone?" Brannie asked.

"Ummm . . . three, four years."

"You were sent off for training? Like Aidan?"

"No," the dragon replied. "I just . . . left."

"I see." Brannie looked back at her plate and whispered to Gaius, "My mum gets upset when she doesn't hear from Celyn in two days."

"Your mother obviously pampers him."

Eyes wide, Brannie adamantly replied, still in whispers, "*I know!* But she doesn't see it. He's just a big, fat baby!"

"Why are *you* back?" Ainmire asked Aidan.

"For the love of my family," he replied and, in response, his family blankly stared at him. "It's been so long, I just had to see you all again."

When there was still nothing, Brannie muttered, "Wow."

The silence stretched on so Gaius turned to Lord Jarlath and said, "Perhaps when we have done eating, Lord Jarlath, you and I can talk for a few minutes."

The Southland royal shook his head while picking at his food. "No."

Brannie suddenly sat up in her seat, the playful, goofy Brannie gone, and Captain Branwen the Awful of Her Majesty's Army now present. And pissed off.

"Lord Jarlath," she admonished, her voice no longer that of an annoyed baby sister. "King Gaius is a very close ally to Queen Rhiannon, which means that all lords of her queendom give him the utmost respect and consideration. That, my lord, includes *you*."

"My dear—"

"Quiet!" Jarlath barked at his wife before focusing on Branwen. "Who are you? Some pet of the queen?"

"I'm Branwen the Awful. Captain of the First and Fifteenth Companies."

"You've heard of them, haven't you, Father?" Aidan asked, his grin wide. "The nicknames for those companies, I believe, are Destroyers and On Pain of Death. And if I also recall correctly, Captain, your Uncle Bercelak was also once Captain of the Destroyers and On Pain of Death, but he never commanded them together. That means you have quite the body count to your name. Oh! And in case you're wondering, Father. That's Bercelak of the Cadwaladrs. Just like his sister and Branwen's *mother,* General Ghleanna the Decimator."

Aidan's mother nervously fussed with the collar of her gold dress before gently suggesting to her mate, "Dearest, it couldn't hurt to spend a little time with King Gaius. He is our guest after all."

"Your guest," Jarlath snapped. "Not mine." He stood and walked off, his guards quickly falling behind him and following him out.

"I'm so sorry, King Gaius," Gormlaith said, her embarrassment evident on her human face. "My mate is—"

"Rude," Brannie boldly stated, but Gaius quickly placed his hand on her knee under the table. She had to let this go. They still needed Jarlath, even if he was incredibly difficult.

Or, as Gaius's sister would say, "An asshole. He's an asshole!"

"It's fine, Lady Gormlaith. Perhaps Lord Jarlath will be more comfortable talking tomorrow. After a good night's sleep."

"Of course, of course."

But one look at Kachka's face told Gaius she wasn't

about to wait for Jarlath or anyone else to help her meet with the dwarves.

Kachka was not about to wait for some ridiculous royal to give her permission to go see the dwarves. She'd been sent here for a reason and she had no time for this sort of thing.

And she was just about to point that out to the entire table, when Gaius suddenly leaned over and kissed her on the side of the head. To those watching, it probably looked like the sweet gesture of one male fucking one female. The She-dragons of Aidan's tribe gawked at Kachka as if she'd abruptly grown another head—because they didn't hear Gaius softly growl against her skin, "If you try to go off and handle Jarlath without me, I will lose my gods-damned mind."

Kachka felt herself smirk but didn't argue the point with Gaius. She'd quickly learned that arguments in front of others brought out the worst stubbornness in the royals. She'd seen it again and again every time Annwyl and Dagmar got into one of their disputes in the Great Hall. So why turn this into a struggle that neither would really win?

They needed each other. At least for now. Besides, Kachka was simply in no mood to fight with him. Not here. In this place. Where she knew damn well they weren't safe.

She watched the royals pretend everything was perfectly fine, which was such a lie. There was nothing perfectly fine here. Absolutely nothing. She'd never disliked a place as much as she disliked the Stone Castle and this tribe. The Foulkes de chuid Fennah. Every one of them—save Aidan, of course—were liars. The kind of royals that Tribes leaders talked about. True imperialist dogs. They were the ones who held back the workers. Who had no respect for the servants, the farmers, the people who dug the soil, hunted the elk, cleaned their mess.

Unlike Annwyl and Rhiannon, these royals didn't get involved with "the little people." Whether those little people were human or dragon.

No. Kachka didn't like these people. And she knew from their silence that neither did her comrades. They wouldn't be searching out a pub tonight as they did when they were in Garbhán Isle. She doubted any of them wanted to be here longer than was absolutely necessary.

She'd give these dragons the night to get Lord Jarlath under control. If they couldn't, he'd be facing her in the morning. Kachka waited for no male.

As she pushed her half-empty plate away—Zoya was right, the food was bland—Kachka noticed Aidan's brother Ainmire suddenly get up and walk out the front doors. None of his family seemed to notice or care, and Kachka just found it odd.

Then again, was there anything about these dragons that was normal?

Gaius had never been so happy to have a meal end. At least not since the Thracius days. And even then his uncle had ensured the food was excellent, the entertainment actually entertaining, and the company interesting.

Sadly, none of these things held true for this dinner at the Stone Castle. Gaius couldn't remember ever being so bored before. Except when he tormented the Foulkes de chuid Fennah, that is, which he only did because it seemed to bring such joy to poor Aidan and his youngest sister, a sweet but painfully shy—and a little sad—dragoness.

Now they stood around in the hall, sipping wine and waiting for this night to mercifully end.

"I don't like him."

Gaius blinked and looked down at a narrowed-eyed Brannie, who studied everyone in the hall as if she expected a massacre at any time.

"Don't like who?"

"Jarlath mostly. But all of them."

"Is that what you told your mother?"

Feigning innocence with those big brown eyes of hers, Brannie asked, "My mother?"

"You said something to your mother, didn't you?"

Unable to keep up any façade, she snapped, "He's bordering on treason."

"I'd say he's more than bordering, but I don't need a herd of angry Cadwaladr storming the gates here to make that point. Not yet."

"I didn't tell her to send anyone. I just told her what happened."

"Do you think she'll tell your Uncle Bercelak?"

"Well . . . uh . . . maybe."

"So how long before your extremely protective and easily pissed-off uncle tracks down one of his brothers or sisters in a nearby town and sends them, along with a bunch of other Cadwaladrs to kick the unholy shit out of Jarlath and his sons?"

Brannie glanced off before finally admitting, "About twenty-four hours."

"Or less."

"Or less, but it's kind of late and they've probably already started drinking."

"Then I guess I'd better get Jarlath to help us in the morning before your kin arrive."

"That's probably a good idea."

* * *

Kachka and her comrades sipped their tepid wine and coldly eyed the royals of the household.

"What do you want to do?" Marina asked in their own language, voice very low.

"Siblings, you take first watch."

"I'll take second," Marina offered. "Tatyana, you'll take third?"

"Yes."

"Good." Kachka glanced over to make sure none of the others were paying them any attention. And like true royals, they weren't. "Everyone stays with weapons close at hand."

"What do you think they will do?" Zoya asked. "These"— she looked them over, lip curling in disgust—"*royals?*"

"I don't know. But I don't trust them and neither does Branwen. She has very good sense of things. So, we will be ready. I will stay with the king tonight to ensure his protection."

Tatyana snorted while the others smirked at Kachka.

"What?" she asked. "What does that mean?"

"Yes, Kachka Shestakova," Nina suddenly said. "Protect the king—with your very strong pussy."

"I like it better when you do not talk, witch."

"If anyone can protect a royal with her pussy, it's Kachka Shestakova," Ivan laughed.

"All of you, shut up."

"It's all right if you like him," Zoya explained. "I've liked several of my husbands."

"I know that was hard for you," Ivan muttered.

"Shut up, hysterical male."

"Are you all done?" Kachka asked.

"At least we don't have to worry about getting drunk from this weak wine," Marina complained. "It's like drinking water with some flavor thrown in."

"You know, Kachka Shestakova," Zoya suddenly said, "I'm thinking of trying a dragon male myself. You seem so happy with the dragon king's cock."

"It is effective."

"And that's all a Daughter of the Steppes wants," she said, sagely. "An effective cock."

Brannie dropped down in a chair next to Aidan's sister, Orla.

"You couldn't look more uncomfortable if you were covered in acid," Brannie noted.

"I only came out to see Aidan."

"I understand. I'm close to my brother Celyn. We're only twenty years apart, so we might as well be twins."

"Did he ever leave you behind?"

"All the time! It drove me crazy. He got to do such fun things and I was left back at the cave. Always with a 'you're only forty, you're too young to go.' It drove me mad. But I always had aunts, uncles, and cousins around that I liked. They taught me how to fight, how to grill my meat properly, and how to destroy an entire village without killing absolutely everyone. Things every She-dragon needs to learn." She patted Orla's hand. "But you can shift now, which will make it easier for you to get around."

"Aidan says it's still not safe for me to go with him. Especially with the war coming. He thinks I'll be safer here."

"He does?" Brannie asked.

"It's hard to destroy the Stone Castle walls. They were built to withstand pretty much everything."

Brannie was forced to shrug. "Well, he's not wrong. . . ."

"But *you* wouldn't leave me here."

"As miserable as you look? No. But brothers focus on how safe their sisters will be. That's all they care about."

"I guess."

"Don't be sad. He does love you. Very much."

"How do you know that?"

"You're the only one here he hasn't purposely tried to destroy emotionally."

Gaius stood by the stairs as Aidan made his way over to him.

"How are you holding up?" Gaius asked.

"Fine. Sorry about my father. I know he's—"

"A prat?"

"Basically."

"I do have to say he didn't seem insane. Paranoid perhaps, but then so am I."

"I'll work on him."

"We don't have tons of time here, Aidan."

"I know."

"And we can only get the Riders to wait for so long before they'll decide to move on their own."

"I'm also aware of that. Just leave it to me."

"And you should also know . . . that Brannie complained to her mum about your father."

Aidan let out a breath. "So we have less than twenty-four hours now?"

"Pretty much."

"Got it."

"King Gaius," Cinnie trilled as Aidan's two sisters walked over to him. "My sister and I have a little dispute we need you to settle."

"Who's going to fuck him first?"

A question that got Aidan backslapped across the face.

Aidan snarled, his hand going to his jaw.

Gaius quickly stepped between the siblings, sure Aidan was about to punch his sister back. Not that he would blame the dragon. The backhanding was a rude, disdainful act, born of obvious contempt.

"I'd love to help, Lady Cinnie," Gaius said in his most royal-soothing tones.

"But he cannot," Kachka announced as she stepped in, her hand gripping his arm. "He must go to bed with me so we can fuck night away. Have good sleep, alone, She-lizards."

Then Kachka dragged him off, Aidan's laughter ringing out over the hall until it turned to, "Owwwww! You bitch!"

Which then led to Brannie's voice begging, "No, no, no, no, no! Everyone just calm down!"

Once they were in Gaius's room, he closed the door, and turned to Kachka, slipping his arms around her waist.

"No," she said, moving away from him. "You must sleep, but I must stay awake and protect you from dangers here."

"You do know I can take care of myself, don't you?"

"You are a very sweet royal," she said while dismissively patting him on the cheek. If she could have reached his head, Gaius was sure she would have patted him there instead.

Gaius watched Kachka pull her sword and stand facing the door.

"You're going to stand there all night?"

"Yes."

"And that seems logical to you?"

"Yes."

Fully dressed, Gaius stretched out on the bed, arms behind his head.

"You could stand there all night, guarding my precious

royal body . . . or you can just lie here. I'm sure both of us will be ready for whatever attempts to come through that door."

She glanced over, and Gaius raised a brow and nodded his head toward the empty side of the bed.

"Come on," he urged. "You know you want to."

"Only because I am tired. Not because I want you."

"You do want me, yet I will allow you to keep lying to yourself because that is the kind of benevolent king I am."

Kachka slammed her sword back into the sheath and removed it from her waist. She settled on the bed beside him, the sheathed sword between them.

Gaius rolled toward her and smiled. "Thank you for rescuing me from Aidan's awful sisters."

Turning on her side to face him, Kachka said, "They were awful. If Elina was like either of those two, I would not have saved her from our mother."

"And I would not have blamed you."

Kachka suddenly looked down until she finally admitted, "My comrades make fun of me. Because of you."

"Because you like me?"

"Yes."

She sounded so dejected, it broke his heart a little. "I'm glad you like me, Kachka Shestakova."

"Of course you are. Because I am a Daughter of the Steppes and this is great honor for imperialist dog."

"That's very true." He leaned in a bit and kissed her forehead. "And I like you *despite* your saying things like that to me."

She laughed. "You are right. That was bitchy. Even for me."

Gaius reached out to put his hand on her waist, but she gripped his index finger and tossed it back to him. "No," she said firmly. "We do not fuck until we are some place safer than this."

Gaius growled but had to grudgingly agree. "All right. But if Aidan doesn't work something out with his father by tomorrow, *no one* will enjoy my attitude."

Chapter Twenty-Seven

Aidan couldn't sleep, so he decided to go and search out his father.

He and Aidan's mother had not shared the same room or cavern in decades, so he knew he'd at least find him alone.

As Aidan eased out of his room and made his way down the hall, he quickly noticed that his eldest brother, Ainmire, sat on the top step of the stairs.

Ainmire had been acting strange all night. He'd always been strange, but now he was managing to be stranger. He'd said nothing at the feast, not even bothering to insult Aidan, which had been the dragon's one true passion for several decades. It was like Aidan wasn't even in the room.

Of course, when Aidan thought about it, it was like none of them had been in the room. Like Ainmire was just floating along . . .

And where had he been for the last three years? None of the rest of his kin seemed to know or care. He was Jarlath's eldest son and heir to the Stone Castle and surrounding territories. Yet his absence didn't seem to mean any more than Aidan's.

That realization made Aidan slow down, his eyes searching for signs of a trap. Perhaps his petty brother wanted revenge for being so ignored. For being treated no better than Aidan.

When Aidan didn't see anything, he carefully eased his way over to his brother.

"What are you doing?" he asked the back of his brother's head.

"Thinking."

"That's new for you, isn't it?"

"Ahhh, yes, Aidan the Gold's sense of humor. How could I forget?"

"It's Aidan the Divine now."

Ainmire snorted. "Given to you by the queen, no doubt. What did you have to do for such an honor, little brother?"

"Watch what you say, Ainmire. Such words are considered treacherous by those of us who protect the queen, which includes Bercelak the Great. Her very protective mate."

"Do you think the Cadwaladrs scare me? That anything scares me anymore?"

"They should. The Cadwaladrs should scare you greatly."

"You were always a fool, brother. Always so eager to please. So eager to be loved by all."

Aidan frowned. "Who *are* you talking about?" Because it couldn't be him. He might be known as divine, but Aidan had never been known as "eager to please."

"They said I wasn't ready to commit. That I wasn't ready to give myself . . . completely. So they sent me back."

"Who sent you back?"

"They sent me back here and I then realized they were right. I couldn't go on like this. Like them. Mother and Harkin and . . . you."

"I'm not that bad."

"So beholden to the whores."

Aidan's hands curled into fists. "If you have any sense, brother, you'll shut up now."

"Or what? You'll kill me for betraying a She-dragon unworthy of your devotion? So very foolish, brother. Now I have made my commitment. Now I am ready to act."

Slowly Ainmire stood and, just as slowly, faced him.

Horrified, Aidan stumbled back. "*Your eyes, brother. Where are your eyes?*" he screamed.

"I do not need eyes to see the evil before me, boy. You come here and bring true evil with you, without once questioning. Without thinking. Because you are beholden to *them*."

Ainmire suddenly lifted the axe he'd held low against his side and swung it at Aidan's head.

His aim, even without his eyes, was true, and the only thing that saved Aidan was his speed. He'd learned to move fast among the Mì-runach.

He dropped to the ground and scrambled back, away from Ainmire. His brother lifted the axe again, his eyeless gaze locked directly on Aidan.

Aidan didn't know if it was because it was his brother or just general fear, but he couldn't move. He couldn't think. All he could do was wait until that axe came down.

And it did. Right for Aidan's head. But a hand reached out of the dark of the hall, grabbing Ainmire's wrist and stopping the axe before it met its target.

Marina Aleksandrovna stood behind Ainmire. She yanked his arm back with one hand and drove her blade into his chest with the other.

Without a word, she shoved the dragon off her blade and over the stone banister to the floor below.

"We move. Now," she ordered, walking away from Aidan and going down the hall to wake up the others.

Forcing himself to get to his feet, Aidan moved to the

banister and looked over. There was blood where his brother had landed, but . . .

Aidan scanned the floor and saw his brother, still in his human form, stumbling toward the front doors. Ainmire had his hand over his chest, and there was a trail of blood behind him.

But, by all rights, Aidan's brother should be dead. A dragon in human form, impaled directly in the heart, does not survive. But giving his soul—and eyes—up to his new god, must have changed everything about him.

For Ainmire was not only surviving . . . he was on the move.

"Out!" Aidan yelled, running down the halls of his kin, and banging on the doors. "Everyone, out!"

His mother yanked her door open. She probably never slept in these rooms, but tonight she'd wanted to be as close to the Rebel King as she could manage.

"What?" she barked at him. "What's happening?"

"We need to go."

"Go? Go where?"

"In." He grabbed her arm, yanking her out of her room. Aidan pointed toward the cave entrance that began at the back of the hall. "Go."

By now, his two eldest sisters and other brother were out in the hall.

"Go," he ordered. "To the caves."

"What for?" Cinnie demanded. "You're home five minutes, and already you're annoying the hells out of me."

Caswyn and Uther, already dressed and ready for battle—they probably had gone to bed clothed and with weapons, if they went to bed at all—stalked toward him.

"Take my mother and sisters," he commanded.

"And your brother?"

Aidan rolled his eyes. "Who cares?" he asked as he moved off in the opposite direction.

"I care!" Harkin complained. "I care very much!"

Aidan saw Brannie coming toward him. "I have to find my sister Orla."

Brannie pushed her door open. "Come on."

He leaned into the room and saw his sister crawl out from under Brannie's bed.

"What—?"

"I was going to sneak her out with us when we were done. Figured she could stay at Devenallt Mountain."

"It looks like that will be happening anyway."

He kissed Orla's forehead before pushing her toward the others.

Brannie began to follow but he caught her arm, held it. "Thank you. For looking out for her."

"It's the little sister club," she replied, giving him a wink. "I'm a founding member."

Aidan released her and watched the Rebel King stride up to him. He was no longer Gaius, dragon searching out and eliminating the rogue elements of his kin. Now he appeared kingly and very royal. A dragon ready for anything.

"What's happening?" the king asked. A cold but prepared Kachka Shestakova stood by his side.

"My brother Ainmire . . . we've been betrayed, King Gaius."

"How badly?"

Aidan glanced at his mother, brother, and sisters as they made their way down the stairs. "His eyes are gone. Torn out of his head since the feast."

"So," he said simply, "very badly."

"I fear he's not alone. I fear he's—"

Aidan froze. He knew that sound. He'd been in enough

battles over the years. Enough attacks. Seen them. Caused them. Been blindsided by them.

"Down!" he commanded, staying by the king and Kachka, instinctively knowing that Brannie would watch out for Orla.

Everyone dropped as the first boulder rammed into the front of Stone Castle.

"What is that?" Gormlaith screamed.

"We're under attack! Everyone go!" Aidan jumped up and motioned for them all to head down the stairs.

As they moved, more boulders hit the front of the castle and Aidan could hear the cries of soldiers coming from outside.

Then it stopped and Aidan turned to see his eyeless brother standing in front of the open doors. The hand pressed over Ainmire's chest was covered in a massive amount of blood, but still he lived.

Zoya stopped by Aidan's side, saw what he was looking at.

"Nina Chechneva! The doors!" she ordered.

The witch spun around, lifted her arms, and brought her hands together. The massive stone doors shut in Ainmire's face, closing him out.

"Come, handsome dragon," Zoya said, tugging on Aidan's arm. "We must go and you must go with us."

Aidan took one more second to stare at the hall he'd been raised in before turning and following after the others.

Chapter Twenty-Eight

They reached the end of the cavern. There were two ways to go from there. East or west.

Gaius stopped when Kachka did. She looked up at him. "My plans have not changed, dragon king."

"We still need to meet with the dwarves," Gaius said to Aidan.

The Gold nodded. "Do we have any idea where Father is?" he asked his kin.

The blank looks on their faces told Gaius all he needed to know. It was as if Aidan were asking about a stranger.

Eyes crossing, Aidan turned to his Mì-runach brothers. "Take Orla out of here," he told them, pointing toward the eastern tunnel. "She knows the way. Follow her down that tunnel and get her to Devenallt Mountain."

"And leave you here to face your mad eyeless brother and his fanatic friends alone?"

"As long as I know my sister is safe—"

"And your mother!" Gormlaith tossed in, her grin wide as her eyes pleaded with her son.

Aidan stared at his mother for several seconds before turning back to his friends. "As long as Orla's safe, nothing else matters."

Uther placed his hand on Aidan's shoulder. "For our queen, for our honor, brother."

"For our queen, for our honor," Caswyn repeated.

Kachka motioned to the Khoruzhaya siblings, Nina Chechneva, and Tatyana. "Go with them, comrades. Make sure to keep the She-dragon and the Mì-runach safe."

"And the rest of Aidan's family!" his mother tried again.

"The rest of us," Kachka went on, ignoring Gormlaith, "will go and get our prize before the idiots do. We will meet back in the Southlands. Yes?"

Aidan hugged Orla and kissed her forehead.

She stepped away from Aidan and turned to Brannie. "You'll go with Aidan, won't you? Keep him safe?"

"You don't think I can take care of myself?" Aidan asked, smiling a little.

"She's a Cadwaladr, brother. And meaner than you."

"She's right," Brannie agreed. "I am meaner than you."

He smiled down at his sister. "Go. I'll see you soon."

She nodded and took Uther's outstretched hand. Together, with Kachka's comrades, they headed down the tunnel, the rest of Aidan's kin following without even bothering to tell Aidan good-bye.

"I like your sister," Zoya noted, "but rest of family I do not like."

"Yeah," he sighed. "Neither do I."

"And what about your father?" Gaius asked.

"My father trusts few, but I doubt he left the mountain."

"So you think he's with the dwarves."

"I do."

"And will his presence still help us or hurt us now?"

"King Gaius . . . I honestly don't know the answer to that."

* * *

Dagmar barely managed to hold on to the pile of books in her arms until she reached her study. Once she was inside, she dropped them on her desk and let out a relieved sigh.

"Didn't think those books or you would make it."

She sat in the back of the room, curled into a chair like a cat. Long black hair, parted in the middle, reaching to the floor, framing a beautiful face. Her armor was made of leather and steel; small blades were threaded through the jerkin and leggings, ready to be used at any moment. Dark brown eyes watched Dagmar impassively, as the pair stared each other down.

Finally, Dagmar admitted, "I hate when your kind insists on dropping by."

"Most beings would be honored by my presence before them."

"Then go find those beings. I have work to do."

She laughed. "I see why Rhydderch Hael has always spoken so highly of you."

"Rhydderch Hael is not a friend of mine," Dagmar practically snarled, the father of dragons having pissed her off all those years ago when Annwyl's twins were born. "But he should have told you, when he spoke so highly of me, that I worship none of you."

"He did mention that. You're a follower of Aoibhell. That great bastion of reason."

"And who are you exactly?"

"Mingxia, goddess of war and love."

"I thought Eirianwen was the goddess of war."

"Goddess of war and death and she is. But I am the East-land god of—"

"By all reason, I don't care!" Dagmar finally snapped. "Why are you here? What do you want? Because if it's just to chat—"

"It's begun."

"What's begun?" The god raised an eyebrow and Dagmar felt air leave her body. "But how? Are they right outside now?"

"I know you think that everything begins and ends in Garbhán Isle, my dear. But it doesn't."

"Really?" Dagmar asked, her arms crossed over her chest. "You're giving me attitude?"

"I think this is a bad idea, Uncle."

Rhys the Hammer, third born to Ailean the Wicked, and one of the few Cadwaladr known for his patience, stopped long enough to let the hammer he favored slam into his nephew's snout.

"Any more questions?" he asked his kin as his brother Addolgar's son rolled on the ground, knocking over trees and holding his cracked snout between two claws. "No? Good! Let's keep moving."

"That was a little harsh, Daddy," Rhys's eldest daughter gently chided.

"If Addolgar's sons weren't so dumb, I wouldn't have to do such things."

"It was a simple question, though."

"A question he *kept* asking."

She laughed, sounding just like her mother. "Sure we shouldn't wait until morning? When cooler heads can prevail?"

"You and your fancy words and ridiculous logic."

"You insisted on my education—I promised to use it when I could. Besides, I know that my dear, sweet cousin Brannie does have a tendency to be very sensitive about dragons who don't show the queen the level of respect she thinks Rhiannon deserves. This is probably nothing."

"It probably is. And once I slap that snobby bastard

around, we'll leave him and his family alone, but with the additional understanding that if he thinks he *rules* any part of the Southlands, he's horribly wrong."

"But an entire *battalion* of dragons? Seems excessive."

"I like excessive. It works for me."

She curled her forearm around his and pulled him close to her side, but her laughter abruptly stopped when one of Rhys's younger sons, who Rhys had sent out to scout ahead, landed in front of them.

Rhys stepped away from his daughter and held up his fist, the battalion coming to a halt behind him.

"What is it?" he asked his son.

"It seems, Father, that we have a bigger problem than moody royals."

Kachka had to admit . . . she felt a little trapped.

The farther down they went, the more the walls seemed to be closing in. The dragons and poor Zoya eventually had to stoop over in order to clear the ceiling. No wonder the dragons here spent a good amount of time in human form. There was no way a dragon in its natural form could maneuver down here.

Kachka had thought Annwyl's castle was too closed in for her, but she was wrong. This was much worse, and she was working hard not to allow herself to panic. As it was, the more they traveled, the more she seemed to have trouble breathing.

As they continued on, Kachka realized she was falling behind the others. She should be the one leading, but her labored breathing held her back until she knew that she couldn't go any further.

She stumbled to a halt, one hand pressing against the

stone wall that was just too close and the other against her chest.

In a moment of pure panic, she actually thought about running back. She'd rather face an entire horde of crazed Chramnesind fanatics than spend another second in this crypt.

But before she could bolt, before she could spend her life in shame, he was there. Gaius was there, standing in front of her, blocking the others' view of her.

"She's fine," he called back to the others. "Just banged her foot. Go and we'll catch up."

The others kept moving forward and Gaius waited until they disappeared around a corner before he crouched in front of Kachka.

Kachka shook her head. "I . . . um . . . uh . . ."

That's when Gaius suddenly gripped her chin tight, and lifted her head up so she was forced to look at him.

"You are the Scourge of the Gods, Kachka Shestakova. And Daughter of the Steppes. Do you want your mother and ancestors laughing at your weakness from the Great Plains of the Skies? Do you want your mother saying it was the wrong sister she tried to kill? Then suck up the pain, ignore the panic, get off your ass, and let's *move*."

Without another word, Gaius stood, yanking Kachka to her feet with him. As soon as she was standing, she shoved him back, and pressed one of her daggers against his throat.

"Speak unkindly of my sister again, lizard," she warned, "and there will be one less royal in the world."

She turned away from him then, setting off after the others. But only a few feet later, she stopped. Her breath came easy now. Her heart no longer racing.

Kachka faced him, went up on her toes, kissed his mouth. Thank you," she said softly, then added, "Bastard."

Gaius grinned, but it soon faded, his head turning, his one eye briefly closing. "They're coming," he finally said.

There had been little doubt that the fanatics would come looking for the royals who resided in the castle, but Kachka had been secretly hoping that they'd follow the tracks of the others. With the siblings, Nina, and the Mì-runach protecting them, Kachka had little doubt that Aidan's sister would be safe.

But whether they'd sent two groups or the one had just happened to follow them, Kachka didn't know. In either case, the fanatics were quickly approaching.

"Move," Kachka ordered the king, pushing him ahead of her so that she could protect them all. "Now."

Rhys stood on the mountain, staring down on the attack taking place at Stone Castle.

He had to admit, the castle itself was holding up quite well. Boulders smashing against it were causing damage, but it was minimal. It seemed strange that the attackers would continue even so.

"What is it?" his son asked.

"They just keep hitting it. Why?"

"Distraction," his daughter said. Even with her fancy education and her upper-crust thinking, she still had one of the best down-and-dirty battle minds he'd known. And he had known *the best*. She outdid them all.

"They're keeping the soldiers distracted," she said, pointing at Lord Jarlath's military force trying to keep the attacking enemy out.

"Distracted from what?"

"The attackers aren't after something in Stone Castle. They're after something in the mountains."

"So we go in?" Rhys asked.

"My suggestion, we wipe this lot out. I'm guessing they already have someone inside."

"Then shouldn't we go in and stop them?" his son asked.

"No. You forget, brother, our Brannie's inside. This is the sort of thing that She-dragon was made for."

"She's on her own."

"Hardly. She's got the Mì-runach with her."

"And King Gaius," he reminded her.

"I fought in that last battle against Thracius." She turned and motioned to the battalion, sending them off in different directions with a flick of her talons. "So trust me . . . the Rebel King can handle himself."

They continued on, but the troops behind them kept getting closer until Gaius realized that Kachka was no longer right behind him.

He turned and went back and found her with Zoya Kolesova.

"What are you doing?" He could hear the zealots and he was now guessing they were dragons.

"There is other way out, yes?" Kachka asked him.

"I'm sure the dwarves have many ways out of—"

"Good." Kachka waved at the tunnel walls. "Go, Zoya."

"What's Zoya going to—"

Zoya began hitting the walls and low ceiling with her fists until she'd gone from one side to the other.

"There," she said.

But Gaius didn't see what she was talking about. There were spots where her fists had damaged the stone—impressive enough—but he didn't see how that helped them.

"Go," Kachka now said to him.

"Go . . . what?"

"Use your flame."

"It needs the extra pressure," Zoya said to him, although that didn't really explain anything.

Needing to get them to move, Gaius decided to play along. He motioned the two women behind him, and unleashed his flame against the wall.

That's when everything began to shake. The walls. The ceiling. The ground beneath his feet.

Gaius stopped and stared until he heard Kachka yell, "I would move if I were you, dragon!"

That's when Gaius realized the women were about fifty feet away from him.

He charged back as the ceiling and walls caved in, blocking the tunnel.

Stunned, Gaius looked at Zoya. "How did you do that?" he asked her.

"What did you expect, Rebel King? I am Zoya Kolesova, am I not? Of the Mountain Movers of the Lands of Pain in the Far Reaches of the Steppes of the Outerplains! Did you think the Daughters of the Steppes just made names up?"

"Yes. Yes, I did." Gaius thought a moment, then asked Kachka, "Your tribe rode bears?"

"We did. Then we changed to the horse because horse may kick your face in, but bears will rip it off completely. I had a great aunt who had no skin on her face whatsoever. And no nose. But she kept both eyes, so she was considered lucky."

Gaius began to respond but ended up shaking his head, closing his mouth, and walking away.

Because, really . . . what was there to say?

Dagmar headed for the stables. There she found mother and daughter grooming their horses. The two mighty black stallions towering over their riders but causing them no fear.

And, for once, the two women weren't fighting. They weren't arguing. Nor were they giving each other the kind of brutal silence only a mother can give to her daughter and vice versa.

Also lurking in the stables were Annwyl's new companions, the Kolesova sisters. They ate apple cores and made everyone nervous but that was about the extent of what they'd seemed to bring to the Southlands. So far. But Annwyl didn't seem to mind them and they had much less to say than their younger sister.

Hands folded primly in front of her, Dagmar asked the three women, "Could you please excuse us?"

The eldest Kolesova, Nika, bit her apple core in half but didn't actually . . . move anywhere. She just stared at Dagmar as did her two sisters.

Cracking her neck, Dagmar faced them, when Talwyn announced, "When my Auntie Dagmar tells you to get out . . . you get out."

"She did not tell us to get out," Nika explained. "She asked us to excuse her. We thought she meant excusing her from being imperialist dog or weak Northland female, neither of which we will excuse."

"No. She meant get the fuck out. So get the fuck out."

"That could have been clearer," Nika complained, walking toward the front of the stables, her sisters following behind.

"And I thought the Shestakova sisters were literal," Talwyn sighed.

Annwyl rested her arms on the stall gate, her horse nuzzling the back of her head. "What is it?" she asked Dagmar.

"I was visited by a god."

"You're always visited by gods."

"Yes. Much to my joy," Dagmar stated sarcastically. "But

this one's a friend of yours. The one Rhiannon was unhappy about."

"Mingxia. What did she want?"

"To tell me the war has begun."

Annwyl frowned. "She told you the war's begun, but she didn't tell us?"

"You'd think she'd tell us," Talwyn complained. "We've been training with her all this time, yeah? So how come she didn't tell us?"

"I don't know. But you really would think she'd tell *us* before she told anyone else."

"I know!"

"By all reason," Dagmar hissed. "Are you two like this with her? When you're training?"

Mother and daughter glanced at each other before Annwyl admitted, "Sometimes."

"Yeah. That's what I thought." She blew out a breath. "It's hard for me to admit this," Dagmar said, placing the palm of her left hand against her forehead. "But I liked it better when you two didn't get along. I had fewer head-aches."

"We've heard that before," Annwyl said.

"From Daddy."

"And Rhiannon."

"And Briec."

"And Talaith and Morfyd . . . where are you going? Don't we have plans to make? Dagmar?"

Aidan suddenly pulled to a halt, raising his hand to stop them all.

The tunnel had grown even smaller and Gaius was glad to see that Kachka was holding on. Not letting the tight space wear on her as it had been.

But now, even he was starting to panic a bit. His cave—which he rarely used these days—might have small tunnels like this, but he never went down them. And many he closed off to prevent humans wanting to make a name for themselves from entering.

So why had they stopped now? Here?

Aidan leaned in to the small opening, with Brannie watching him closely, her body coiled as if ready to yank him back should some crazed dwarf try to take his head.

Yet there was no crazed dwarf. Instead, Aidan unleashed a line of flame into the opening.

And, after a minute or two, there was a, "Yeah?"

"Aidan the Divine," Aidan replied. "Lord Jarlath's third son."

"Yeah," the voice replied. "Come on in."

"Follow me," Aidan told them. "Be calm. Be respectful." He looked right at Zoya. "Keep your pronouncements on men and males to a minimum. Understand?"

"Why do you look at me, pretty dragon?"

Marina reached up and placed her hand on Zoya's shoulder. "Do not worry," she told Aidan. "I will keep eye on our comrade."

Aidan nodded and moved forward, the rest of them following.

Once they cleared the small opening, they stepped out into a large cavern and Gaius took a deep breath. He couldn't believe how relieved he was to be in a larger space where he could straighten to his full height.

Armed dwarves stood in front of an entryway that led to large marble stairs.

Now that they were free of the confines of those tunnels, they walked three to four across and headed up the stairs. As they reached the top, they all stopped, gaping at what they saw.

The inside of the mountain had been carved out and a full city had been built within. A city of molten steel and working machines. A city of industry.

Gaius had never seen such a sight; the dwarves of the Empire were mostly like . . . everyone else in the Empire. Stonemasons, blacksmiths, and farmers. A few members of the Senate. Loyal to their own kind but, at the end of the day, still just . . . Sovereigns, like the rest of them.

If they had a world like this, built inside the Septima Mountains . . . none of the Iron dragons knew about it.

"This is amazing," Brannie said. "I wish Izzy was here. She'd love this."

"Lord Aidan?" a redheaded dwarf asked.

"Yes."

"Yeah. Your father's been waitin' for ya. This way."

Aidan briefly closed his eyes and let out a breath. "Son of a—"

"Let it go for now," Gaius gently reminded him. "We have bigger issues than your father's . . . uniqueness."

The dwarf led them through the big city, passing the stalls of many vendors. Gaius wished he had time to look at everything they had to offer, if just to buy his sister a little something.

Yet they didn't have time for anything and moved through the crowd quickly until they reached a tavern.

The red-haired dwarf led them inside to a dwarf with a shaved head covered in tattoos and a braided black beard that reached the floor. He had one leg up on the table and a pint in his big hands. Also at the table was Lord Jarlath.

"Boy!" Jarlath called out when he saw his son. "So you made it!" It was easy to see the dragon had perhaps had more than his share of dwarven wine. "And you brought your . . . weird friends. Good for you!"

Appearing embarrassed, Aidan glanced at Gaius before walking close to his father.

"Father, the Stone Castle is under attack."

Jarlath smirked, and looked to his tattooed dwarf friend.

"Which one?" he asked his son.

"Which one what?"

"Which of those bastards betrayed me? Their father."

"It was Ainmire, but—"

"Ha!" Lord Jarlath rapped his knuckles against the wood table and pointed at the Dwarf King. "Told ya it'd be that weak boy. You owe me thirty gold, dwarf."

"What the fuck is wrong with you?" Aidan snapped. "Your home is under attack. Our *lands* are under attack."

"The Stone Castle will stand. It will always stand."

"And your family?" Aidan pushed.

"Not to be trusted, are they? Except you, but only because you're loyal to the queen and the Mì-runach scum."

Aidan almost had his hands around his father's throat when Kachka shoved the dragon back.

"You," she said, pointing at the tattooed dwarf. "You are Dwarf King?"

The dwarf coldly eyed her back. "An Outerplains whore in my city. Sometimes you just can't keep the trash out, can you, Jarlath?"

Before Gaius even had a chance to react to that insult, the remaining Daughters of the Steppes had their weapons drawn and were moving forward, but without flinching, Kachka raised her hand, stopping them in their tracks. The group, as a whole, had come a long way since Gaius had met them on his death trek a few months back.

Kachka stepped forward and, hooking her foot under his wooden chair, she rocked it hard, so the back of the dwarf's head slammed against the wall.

The dwarves in the pub stopped speaking, all attention now on Kachka and their king.

If Kachka noticed any of them, Gaius had no idea. Everything about her at that moment was focused on the Dwarf King—and Gaius didn't envy the dwarf one bit.

Pinning the chair against the wall with her foot, Kachka stared down at the defiant royal.

"I am Kachka Shestakova, Scourge of the Gods. Tell me, Dwarf King, did your great sin bring us here to *you*?"

The tattoos on the Dwarf King's head told a story. A story of heroic deeds. So typical of men, to put their rare feats of greatness right on their bodies. As if they constantly had to prove themselves.

"You know why I am here, Dwarf King," Kachka said when he continued to just stare at her. "What I need from you."

"I've been told," he finally said, his voice like rough gravel.

"Then where is it? Tell me and then we can go. And we will never know your great sin."

"Or what?" he shot back. "You Whores of the Steppes will kill us all?"

"No," she told him flatly. "We will just kill you, Dwarf King."

As the pair glared at each other, Gaius suddenly felt the need to step in. It was his way, Kachka now understood, and perhaps she needed that balance. It helped that her cousin Tatyana performed the same task for the team. But with her off with the siblings and Nina Chechneva that left poor Gaius to stick his thick neck out.

"Or perhaps we can come up with another option," Gaius suggested. "One that involves little to no bloodshed."

Now the Dwarf King locked on Gaius. "Who are you?"

"Gaius Domitus of the—"

"Domitus? *An Iron?*" the king suddenly bellowed, jumping to his feet, and the dwarves around them also stood, their weapons now out.

Although these dwarves were small in height, they were wide, strong and, Kachka knew, well trained in warfare. From hand-to-hand combat to full-on assaults.

What the Dwarf King had said to Kachka had been what she'd expected. They heard this from many males outside the Outerplains who had never gone toe-to-toe with the Daughters of the Steppes. They'd all heard of the damage the Riders had done. The cities they'd destroyed. They saw the Daughters as a "challenge." Females to be conquered and possessed before being tossed away for others younger and prettier.

They found out the very hardest way possible, though, that Kachka and her tribal sisters were not to be fucked with lightly. Or at all.

Yet despite all that, she had not expected their reaction to Gaius. The Sovereign Empire's reputation had mellowed over the years under Gaius's rule, but perhaps if Overlord Thracius had come after her people, she'd be less inclined to deal with anyone from his bloodline. Even an enemy of the old guard.

The Dwarf King glowered at Aidan. "You bring an Iron here? *To my kingdom?*"

"I didn't—"

"Do you know what Thracius did to my people?" the king went on. "The lives he destroyed? What he did to our children?"

"He's the Rebel King," Brannie quickly explained. "Overlord Thracius's enemy. He defeated him in battle and took his throne."

"So? Blood is blood."

Gaius took a step toward the Dwarf King, and the other dwarves moved a bit closer to the group, ready to strike should Gaius make the first move.

"When I was young," Gaius said calmly, "Overlord Thracius thought my sister had been rude to his favored daughter. Vateria. But . . . my sister is very pretty and he had plans to mate her off to a friend of his. So he decided to teach her a lesson by using his talon to tear the eye from my head while we both begged him not to." The Rebel King pulled off his eye patch, revealing the brutal scar and the eyelid sewn shut all those years ago to keep dirt and dust out of the now-empty space. "He wanted her to understand, you see, that he was not to be questioned. Not to be challenged in any way by anyone."

"Why didn't you kill your uncle then?"

"My sister and I were twelve winters old. We couldn't even fly, much less take on my uncle. Then he killed our father in front of us and . . ." Gaius let out a breath. Kachka immediately understood this was still hard for him.

"But," he finally went on, "we never forgot. And we never forgave. Not this. Not him."

"So you killed him during the great battle of Euphrasia Valley?"

Gaius laughed. "No, no. That was her," he said, pointing at Brannie.

"It was not me. I just distracted him until Izzy could fuck up his spine enough so he couldn't fly away. My cousin Éibhear did the rest." She looked at the Dwarf King. "And it was *not* pretty. He was in a really bad place then. Éibhear. You see, he blamed himself for the death of—"

"I don't care," the Dwarf King cut in.

Brannie stopped telling her story, but she did mutter, "Rude," under her breath.

"There. Feel better, Dwarf King?" Kachka said. "Now will you help or not?"

"Come," he ordered, walking past Kachka and Gaius to the pub's front door. "I already know what you've come for."

Aidan stared at his father. "Do you care at all about what's happened to your family?"

Lord Jarlath continued to drink his ale, showing no interest in much of anything.

Brannie tapped her friend's arm. "Come on. Let's get this done. So we can get you back to your mates and your sister."

He nodded and walked out, the rest of them following.

The Dwarf King led the way, a few of his warriors bringing up the rear. As they moved, Kachka asked, "How do you know what we are here for?"

He glanced back at her, smirking. "A god told me."

"You know," Brannie explained, "once you've been around Annwyl for a while, you'll realize that information is not as shocking as you'd think it would be."

Chapter Twenty-Nine

Ainmire, eyeless, stared at his old home, but he felt nothing as he watched the True Believers use catapults. They weren't trying to take the castle down. He'd warned them nothing would take it down. But the attack was keeping his father's armed forces quite busy and that's all they wanted.

It had hurt when they'd taken his eyes from his head, but his commitment to his god had given him vision he hadn't had before. Now he could truly *see*.

And hear.

They came in without words or battle cries, but Ainmire heard the flutter of their wings, the tiny clacks of their talons.

A female came down onto the dragon beside Ainmire. That dragon had *not* fully committed to Chramnesind. He still had both his eyes. So he never saw the She-dragon until she'd landed on his back and slammed her broadsword into his spine.

It took a lot to fully commit to their god the way Ainmire had, so many of his brothers and sisters didn't know they were under attack from behind until it was too late.

Moving quickly, Ainmire backed away from the battle, which was now much closer. And, as he did, he prayed to his god. Not for salvation, but for what was happening inside that mountain to be a success. Before he'd walked into his old home earlier that evening, both his eyes still in his head, he hadn't been worried. But then he'd seen Aidan and his Mì-runach chums. And the Cadwaladr bitch.

That's when he'd become worried.

The Dwarf King led them out of his city but deeper still into the Western Mountains until they came down a long passageway to a narrow crevice protected by a small battalion of dwarf warriors.

The king moved them aside with a gesture and pointed. "In there."

"You must be joking," Gaius said to him. "We can't fit through that crevice."

"Neither can we. But what you want is in there, Iron. Placed there by the gods an age ago. How you get it out is your problem."

Gaius shrugged. "Fair enough." He gestured to the crevice. "Zoya."

The dwarves moved farther back as she approached, then faced the crevice. Doubling up her fists, she began to pummel the stone face. They all turned their heads as chunks of rock began to fly.

After about five minutes, Zoya stopped and faced them all, raising her hands with their now bloody knuckles. "Now we can all enter, comrades!" she crowed.

"Thank you, Zoya."

"You are welcome, Rebel King." She slapped her hand against Gaius's spine as she walked past him and Gaius looked to Kachka.

"Owww," he whispered to her.

Then Kachka did something rather remarkable. She

rubbed his back before entering the battered opening. An effort to ease the harshness of Zoya's hearty backslaps.

He doubted that Kachka had any idea what that small move meant to him. More importantly, he doubted she understood what it meant to *her*.

Gaius followed behind Kachka, but she stopped before he could go into the crevice with her.

"Stay here."

"Kachka—"

"I am the one they sent, Gaius. Not you. Me. Stay here. Watch my back."

She disappeared inside and Gaius began to pace back and forth, his gaze constantly straying to the Dwarf King and his soldiers. Finally, he stopped.

"What haven't you told us?"

"You Irons. You don't trust anybody."

"Have you *met* my family? Oh. That's right. They destroyed half your people! So, yeah . . . I don't trust anybody." Gaius stepped closer. "So what haven't you told us?"

"Are you calling me a liar?"

"I don't know. Are you?"

The king studied him a moment. "I'm sorry, Rebel King, but I can never risk what happened under Thracius's rule happening again to my people."

"Why would I attack your people?"

"Not you."

Gaius frowned. "Then what are you talk—"

"Gaius."

Gaius turned toward the voice behind him. Kachka stood in the opening, a small leather bag in her hand. She held it up for him and smiled.

Letting out a breath, Gaius started toward her, but he stopped when something wrapped itself around Kachka's waist. She looked down at what appeared to be something living. By the time she looked back at him, she was yanked out of sight.

"*Kachka!*"

The slimy tentacle dragged Kachka back through the small passage, through the tiny cavern where she'd discovered the eyes of Chramnesind and into a larger cavern filled with a lake.

"Hello, dear," a beautiful woman said to her. She reached down to grab the bag from Kachka's hand, but Kachka yanked her dagger from her belt and stabbed the tentacle around her waist.

The woman roared and the tentacle released Kachka. She rolled backward and got to her feet.

The woman shook off the pain. "Foolish bitch. Now give that to me."

"I give you nothing." Kachka looked down and realized that the woman stood in water that covered her from the knees down. And whatever was going on under that water was . . . unnatural.

There was more than one tentacle down there.

"What are you?" Kachka had to ask. Had to know.

"Blessed," the woman replied. She held out her hand. "Now . . . give it to me."

Kachka didn't reply, she simply crouched down to avoid the arrows shooting past her and into the woman's neck and shoulder. Marina's aim, true as always.

And that's when the woman exploded, her rage shaking the walls of the cavern, the water she stood in bubbling as if it boiled.

Flames suddenly erupted around her and she went from human to She-dragon.

"Vateria," Gaius gasped from behind Kachka. And Brannie ran up, abruptly grabbed Kachka by the back of her neck, and yanked her out of the way just as he shifted into his natural form.

"*Vateriaaaaaa!*" he bellowed.

The She-dragon grinned, showing row after row of fangs. "Cousin." She held open her forearms. "It's been so long. Come! *Greet your kin!*"

Gaius charged across the lake, and Brannie pushed Kachka toward Zoya just as she and Aidan shifted to dragons.

Kachka thought that was so they could all attack Vateria, but the She-dragon wasn't alone. Two more steel-colored dragons ran in from another entrance. One had two axes, the other a sword and shield.

Brannie took on the two interlopers while Aidan rushed to Gaius's aid. Something Kachka was eternally glad to see since Gaius was not just fighting that She-dragon . . . he was also fighting her multiple tentacles, which had only grown larger and more disgusting when she'd shifted.

Zoya helped Kachka to her feet.

Gripping the leather bag in her hand, Kachka pointed to a high spot on the cave wall that was like a small balcony. "Marina! Go!"

She pulled out her own sword and backed up. "Zoya . . . move mountains, comrade."

Zoya grinned and ran to the other side of the cave, where she grabbed large boulders and began flinging them directly at the She-dragon's head.

Kachka stepped back, looking for a way out. She didn't want to leave her friends, fighting to protect her, but her main concern was this thing that Vateria wanted. From the little Kachka knew about the She-dragon, she understood that the last being in the world who should get her claws on anything with this much power was Vateria Domitus.

As she kept backing up, kept searching, Kachka walked into something small. She turned around, expecting to see the currently unhelpful dwarves, but found a little boy standing behind her.

"Hello," he said.

Kachka just stared at him.

"Mommy says a Rider would never hurt a child." He pulled his hand from behind his back, a steel dagger held tightly in his fist. "Let's find out if Mommy's right."

Kachka growled in pain as the child's blade sank into her leg and she stumbled back. The boy raised the weapon again and Kachka made a mad, wounded dash for the entrance she'd come in from.

Gaius heard Kachka's muffled grunt and turned to see her being attacked by a small boy.

Vateria wrapped one of her tentacles around Gaius's throat and squeezed. "Isn't the boy beautiful? Exquisite, really."

She ducked as Zoya threw another boulder at Vateria's head.

"I know what you're thinking," she babbled on as several of her tentacles battered poor Aidan across the chamber. "That what I have done with Duke Salebiri is exactly what my god is fighting against. But you see, I will be what defeats Annwyl the Unholy Whore. Me. And my children. We will defeat her and her Abominations and then, our sweet god will honor us all. How do you feel about that, cousin?"

Gaius, unclear on what Vateria was talking about, closed his eyes, reached out past the cave walls, and called to his sister.

Aggie.

Gaius.

I need you, sister.

It was something they'd only done once before. By accident. When Thracius had torn out Gaius's eye. The pain.
The pain had been so unbearable that Gaius hadn't realized
he'd silently called out to his sister until he *felt* her inside his
head. She removed the pain while, at the same time, giving
him the strength to run as she used her own body to shield
him from their uncle. Preventing Thracius from removing
the other eye as he was about to do.

This time, however, Gaius had no intention of running.

Gaius gripped the thing around his neck and yanked it
off. Squeezing it between his talons, he gazed directly into
Vateria's shocked face as he said, "Cousin . . . my dear sister
sends you greetings," before flinging her and her gods-damn
tentacles across the cavern and into the opposite wall.

Kachka shot through the opening and found the dwarves
standing around, looking incredibly uncomfortable about
what was going on. Uncomfortable and confused. But not
helping without their king's say.

"What did she promise you, Dwarf King?" Kachka asked
while turning and kicking the little boy chasing her back into
the cavern.

"That Duke Salebiri will leave my people alone," he
replied.

Kachka stared at him. "Who do you think that female is?"

"Ageltrude. Wife of Duke Salebiri."

"No, Dwarf King. That is *not* who she is." She kicked the
boy, who charged her again. "She is Vateria. *Daughter* of
Overlord Thracius."

"You're lying."

"I do many things. Lying is not one of them."

The boy burst out of the crevice and charged Kachka again. She wasn't about to start killing children, but she was more than happy to slap one around. But as she pulled her hand back to knock the weapon away from him, the Dwarf King let out a deafening scream and swung his axe.

The boy, quicker than she expected, stumbled back, falling on his ass, and Kachka caught the king's weapon before it split the boy in two.

"What are you doing?" the king demanded.

"Kill his mother if you can. But the boy—you wait until he is old enough to wipe his own ass. That should be the way of things, Dwarf King."

The king yanked his axe back. "Fine."

The boy jumped to his feet, running back the way he'd come, screaming, "*Muuummmm!*"

"What are you waiting for?" Kachka asked him. "Go. Get your revenge on Thracius by killing his daughter."

She watched the dwarves, led by their king, follow after the boy. Once she was sure they were gone, she turned and went the other way.

Gaius had Vateria on the ground and was strangling the life from her, enjoying the way her eyes were bulging from her head, and she was hitting at him, trying to get him off her, when he heard Brannie yell, "Gaius! Behind you!"

Annoyed, he looked over his shoulder. Dragons, former soldiers of Thracius's army he was guessing, poured into the cavern from another entry point.

Brannie batted the She-dragon she'd been fighting out of her way to protect Gaius's back. That's when he realized that the other two dragons Aidan and Brannie had been fighting were also cousins of his.

A claw slapped across his face and he was tossed off when Vateria pressed her back claws against his chest and shoved.

Gaius flew back, watching Vateria get to her feet. She started to come toward him. That god she'd chosen had changed her, but he didn't really have time to be disgusted. Not with the Dwarf King and his soldiers coming in from the other entrance.

Their war cry rang out, and although they were considerably smaller than the dragons, there were suddenly a lot of them . . . and they went for the weakest points on dragons' bodies with the most deadly weapons.

The dwarves climbed over Vateria and her soldiers, chopping at them with their axes and swords.

A small group of Vateria's soldiers attacked Gaius, old Praetorian Guards who recognized him on sight. He blocked several weapons with his sword and shoved them off. He wanted Vateria. He would have Vateria!

But when he turned around . . .

"*Where is she?*" Gaius bellowed at the Dwarf King.

Blood covered half the king's head, face, and shoulder. He pointed with his sword toward the entrance they'd come through. That was also when he realized that Kachka was gone. He knew she was trying to get the eyes away from Vateria, and Vateria had gone after her.

"Marina! Zoya! With me!" he yelled, shifting to human and sprinting after his bitch cousin.

Kachka ran until she reached what she knew every dwarf city had access to . . . a mine.

There were signs that gave directions to each of the mines—gold, steel, iron, silver—but they were written in dwarvish and she had no idea how to read that.

So Kachka headed for the first functioning mine she saw. But someone grabbed her arm and pulled her toward a separate set of stairs.

"Gold is your friend, luv," the woman said, pushing Kachka up the stairs. As Kachka ran, she glanced back at the woman. She wasn't one of the dwarves. She was tall, lean, and brown-skinned. Like Izzy or her mother Talaith. She was also dressed as a warrior or soldier of fortune. She was even more out of place in the dwarf mines than . . . well, than Kachka was.

But without any other options, she had to take her chances this woman wasn't trying to destroy her.

So she took the steps three at a time until she reached the top.

Kachka pulled the leather bag out of the top of her boot where she'd stashed it for her mad dash to the mines and pulled her arm back to toss it into the molten gold. That's when she heard, "Down!"

She did as ordered, dropping down to the ground, and the dragon who had been about to grab her, sailed right over her. The dragon turned in midair, wings out, claws reaching for her.

Two arrows slammed into the dragon's face and neck. A short spear hit it right in the chest, through the heart, killing it as its body fell from sight.

Hands grabbed Kachka again, only this time it was her comrades Zoya and Marina hauling her to her feet.

"Kachka—" Marina began, but then the dragon was back. It hadn't been killed. Nor did its wings seem to work, hanging limply from its back, so that it floated to the ledge instead of flying.

The three of them scrambled back, watching the dragon carefully land. It pulled the arrows from its face and the spear from its chest and that's when Kachka knew it was Vateria.

"Those of us," Vateria said, "who have been truly blessed by our god, need more than these weak weapons to kill us." She held out her claw. "Give it to me, barbarian, before I stomp you into the ground like the worthless trash you are."

Kachka began to tell her to fuck off, but she and her comrades were forced farther back when there was suddenly a large dragon ass landing right in front of them.

Gaius snarled. "Get away from them, cunt."

"Cousin. You should have let my father finish the job," the bitch teased. "My god would like you better with *both* eyes missing."

"You expect me to believe you worship anyone but yourself?"

"Chramnesind understands me as no one else ever has. Accepts me just as I am. The others give up so much . . . and yet I give up nothing but receive so many rewards. He loves me the way my father always did. Unconditionally."

"Gods, you really haven't changed."

"Why should I? I'm so perfect."

"You have *tentacles*."

"And I love them. Just look what they can do."

With that, Vateria sent Gaius, Marina, and Zoya flying, leaving Kachka alone.

"Now . . . give it to me, human."

"I am Daughter of Steppe, She-dragon. I will not yield. To you or anyone."

Vateria smiled. "I've heard of you, actually. My god told me about you. What was that nickname again? Oh, yes. The Scourge of the Gods." She laughed. "What idiot gave you that?"

The brown-skinned warrior suddenly appeared again,

leaning from behind the She-dragon. "This idiot," she said, before she grabbed Vateria's dragon form and tossed her into the molten gold beneath.

"And," she went on, "if I do say so myself, it's a brilliant name for you to have, Kachka Shestakova. One you've rightfully earned."

"Who—?"

"Kachka!"

Marina leaned over the other side of the stairs. She was on her belly, slowly slipping toward the abyss.

"I can't hold her!"

Kachka scrambled to her comrade's side, reaching down to grab Zoya Kolesova's other arm. Together, they hauled the Mountain Mover up. It took all their strength. She was very heavy.

They pulled until they had all of her on the stairs, letting out a breath and collapsing on top of her once they were done.

Beneath them, Zoya snorted. "I knew you heartless bitches loved me. All heartless bitches love Zoya!"

Gaius heard laughter and woke up. He was on the ground by the furnaces where all the different metals for the dwarves' weapons and jewelry were melted in giant crucibles. Yet the laughter wasn't Vateria's so he knew Kachka and her comrades were safe.

Relieved, he sat up, bending and stretching his neck, which now hurt from the impact of the fall.

He had his head down, eye closed, when he heard . . . something.

Gaius lifted his head and saw gold-covered talons easing out of the crucible.

Snarling, he got to his claws just as Vateria launched

herself at him, melted gold covering her from head to back claws.

She tackled Gaius to the ground, the pair rolling across the mine floor, slamming into furnaces and knocking over other crucibles.

They were Iron dragons. Born of fire. They felt nothing as they battled each other through the dwarf mines.

But Vateria was no longer the Vateria Gaius once knew. Emotionally, of course, she was still the same evil bitch she'd always been. Her god had not changed that. Yet he had changed the rest of her, made her stronger. Although she seemed to have no skill with weapons, she had her tentacles and claws, and her talons tore at Gaius, her tentacles wrapped around his throat, choking him.

Gaius, however, still had his rage. He grabbed his cousin by her hair, the gold starting to harden, and yanked her back. Off him. Gaius stood, dragging the bitch with him. Still gripping her by the hair, he turned and flung her into a wall.

He yanked out his blade and started to walk over there, ready to cut her into pieces that he would bring back to his twin.

"No!" the child's voice screamed as he dashed over to Vateria, throwing himself in front of her, arms wide. As if he could protect her with his tiny human body. "You get away from her!"

Gaius studied the boy, then looked at Vateria. It dawned on him, as bright as the two suns now coming up in the skies outside these mountains.

"Your son." It swept through him. Cold. Brutal. The rage that had made his name for him. The rage that allowed him not to care. About anyone. Anything. Growling now, he said again, "Your *son*."

Vateria's forearm wrapped around her offspring's body. For the first time ever, he saw fear in her eyes. True, absolute fear. Because for once, she cared about something other than herself.

"You wouldn't dare," Vateria told him.

But this Gaius would dare. This Gaius, who remembered his sister, trapped with Vateria, *would* dare many things to right that wrong.

Gaius raised his blade over his head, his entire body shaking, his gaze locked with his cousin's, enjoying the pain he knew he'd cause her.

Even knowing this was wrong, nothing would stop him. Nothing.

Gaius yanked his forearms back a bit more to get the most power behind his attack when he heard Kachka scream from above, "*Gaius, no!*"

He fought against her voice. Fought against how right it sounded.

"Do not! He is just child!"

"Vateria's child," he reminded her.

"Would this make your sister proud? Or are you finally becoming Thracius himself? Do not do this."

Gaius's will began to wane. Kachka was right. Harming a child to get at its mother? That's what his uncle not only would do but *had* done.

And now he was about to do the same.

Don't, Gaius.

Aggie—

Please. Don't.

He'd let his sister in and hadn't even realized it. So, if he did this, she would do it too. It would be her memory as well as his.

That he couldn't do. She had enough bad memories to last her a lifetime. He wouldn't add the guilt of this sin.

Gaius lowered his weapon and, gripping her offspring

tight, Vateria reached back and opened a mystical doorway.
She was in it and gone in seconds.

Dropping to his knees, Gaius let the pain of what he'd
almost done flow through him. He needed to feel this so that
he never did it again. So he never came that close to the edge
again.

He didn't know how long he stayed there, kneeling in the
dirt. But he felt Kachka's hand press against his leg.

"It is all right, Dragon King."

"It's not all right. I almost—"

"But you did not. Because if you had, I would have come
for you. For your great sin, I would have been your punishment. For I am the Scourge of the Gods. But I am not here
to punish. Because you made right choice."

Gaius finally found the strength to laugh. "You are really
loving that name."

"I am."

"It fits her," said another voice.

Gaius looked up, rearing back a bit. "You." He watched
the soldier for hire he'd met on the road a few days ago walk
around him.

"Me."

"You sent me to gold mines," Kachka said.

"I did."

"Why?"

"Just being helpful."

"Who are you?" Gaius asked.

"Just call me Eir. Oh! I have something for you." She
removed a sword from the scabbards strapped to her back
and handed it him.

It was a gladius. Rather plain. But a very sweet gesture.

"Thank you, but you don't—"

"Please. Take it. Make good use of it." She walked over
to Kachka, held out her hand. "Give me the eyes."

Kachka stared at the soldier, eyes narrowing. "No."

"It's all right, Kachka," Gaius told her.

"How can it be all right?"

He gave a small smile, now fully understanding who this friendly neighborhood soldier-for-hire truly was. "It just is. Trust me."

"All this trouble . . ." She pulled the leather bag from her boot and handed it over to the woman.

"Thank you," she said. "And good luck to you both."

She walked off and they watched her until Gaius asked Kachka, "How did you get down here so fast?"

Frowning, she shrugged. "I have no idea." Kachka studied the ground at her feet. "And this," she said, gesturing with her hands, "was hot and covered in flame."

"Right. To melt the gold."

"But now it is cool. And eyes are gone with brown woman."

"Yes."

"Because she is a god, is she not?" Kachka finally asked.

"Yes. I believe she is."

"She looks like Izzy and Talaith. Are they gods too?"

"No."

"But she was?"

"Yes."

"I think you are right. There is something about her . . . But why did she give you sword?"

"Because I gave her one when I thought she was a poor soldier for hire."

"You made an offering to a god and she gave you a plain boring sword you could get at any blacksmith?"

Gaius opened his claw and studied the sword. "Apparently."

"That is disappointing."

"It is." Gaius got to his back claws, stretched his sore neck again. "We should get back to Brannie and Aidan."

"Doubt they need us but . . . sure." She gestured to Gaius. "Did you know you were covered in pieces of gold?"

"Oh." He glanced at the gold that had hardened on his scales. "Go over there," he told her, gesturing to a large crucible about fifty feet away.

Kachka did and Gaius dropped to all fours, covered himself in flames, and did a good dog-shake to get all the gold off.

Once done, he lowered himself to the ground. "Get on."

"You will let me ride your back like horse?"

"No. I am not a horse. I am a dragon and king. So shut up and get on my back."

And using his hair to climb onto him, Kachka teased, "And such a moody king."

The battle was still raging in the cavern when Kachka returned with a now-human Gaius, plus Marina and Zoya.

"There," Kachka told Gaius. "Many of your kind to kill with your new gods-given sword."

He lifted the blade, studied it. "Yeah. I guess."

"Maybe it is magickal sword," Marina suggested. "One with great power."

Gaius slashed the blade through the air a few times before shaking his head and admitting, "It's not a magickal sword."

"No," Kachka and her comrades agreed.

Brannie slammed a dragon down on the ground and rammed her sword into his neck. Once he stopped moving, she stood, searching for another victim. But she saw Gaius and Kachka first.

"You made it!" she said.

Gaius nodded at two dragons. "See those two over there?"

Brannie nodded. "Aye."

"They're my cousins and loyal to Vateria. Kill them both."

"Okay," Brannie said, rather happily.

"She likes her job," Marina noted.

Gaius agreed. "She really does."

The suns were high in the sky by the time they made it out of the mountain on the Southland side. Gaius expected a great battle to still be raging. Instead, he found a massacre.

He faced a sheepish Brannie. "They didn't wait twenty-four hours."

"I see that."

"It worked in our favor, though," Aidan pointed out.

"I thought Brannie told you to shut up," Gaius reminded Aidan.

"Yes, sir."

"You see I'm trying to make a point here."

"Which I do understand, King Gaius. But it might be more effective if it wasn't a bunch of Cadwaladrs slaughtering the fanatics that aren't already dead."

"They're not all Cadwaladrs," Brannie noted. "It's my Uncle Rhys's battalion."

Aidan cringed and Gaius gawked.

"Your uncle *Rhys*? Rhys the Hammer?"

She cleared her throat. "Yeah. I see him over there . . . ripping that dragon into two distinct pieces."

"So in future . . ." Gaius prompted.

"I'll think before I contact me mum."

"That's all I ask. This works in our favor today, but next time it could be an entire village of uninvolved humans that your Uncle Rhys goes after. And that would just make us look bad. So . . . keep that in mind. Yes?"

"Yes, sir."

"Thank you."

Brannie and Aidan walked away to help the Dragon Queen's battalion finish off the rest of the fanatics, and Gaius smiled down at Kachka.

"As a king," he explained to her, "you're always teaching the young."

"You are full of much shit, dragon."

Gaius laughed. "I know!"

Chapter Thirty

Queen Annwyl sat beside Queen Rhiannon on the stairs that led to the Great Hall. Together they silently watched the day-to-day goings-on of Garbhán Isle. Annwyl didn't know how long they'd been there.

Finally, Rhiannon said, "So it's begun."

"Yes. They attacked the Stone Castle in the Western Mountains. We'll know more when Gaius gets back with Brannie and the others. They should be here soon."

"I see."

"And, right now, Fearghus is meeting with Bercelak, his generals, and Brastias, of course."

"Good. What about Brigida?"

"Talan will handle the Armies of the Abominations. Which, by the way, is what they named themselves. They think it sounds terrifying."

"Well, it kind of does."

"True."

"And Talwyn?"

"She'll be with me."

"Good. Excellent." Rhiannon brushed her hair from her face. "We have training on our side."

"We do. But they have fanatics willing to die for their

cause. And they have a lot of them. More and more coming every day to join their ranks. We can't underestimate them."

"No. No. We can't."

Taking Rhiannon's hand with both of her own, Annwyl said, "Don't worry, Rhiannon. You just have to remember one important thing."

"And what's that?"

"I am crazier than *any* of them."

Laughing, Rhiannon put her arm around Annwyl's shoulders. "Excellent point, dear Annwyl. Excellent point."

Fearghus stood with Briec and Éibhear. The three brothers were trying to figure out how they were going to handle a dilemma.

"We have to come up with something," Briec finally said, annoyed. "We can't just stand here."

"It'll be ugly," Éibhear reminded them. "Remember last time?"

"Then we should have someone else do it."

"Who?"

Fearghus looked around and immediately saw them. They were perfect.

"Got it."

Dagmar walked quickly down the hall toward her study. She had so much on her mind, she barely noticed the screams.

"No! You can't! Please! No!"

Dagmar froze, her dogs stopping with her. She ran back to the library she'd just passed, and shoved the door open.

They had him pinned to the big table. Two holding him down, another holding the axe.

"Dagmar! Save me!"

They paused, looking at her, waiting for her to stop them.

But . . . she couldn't. Cringing, knowing this was just the beginning of the nightmare, Dagmar . . . nodded.

"Noooooooooooooooooooo!"

The axe fell and the Rider, Nika, grabbed the golden hair she'd just cut from the head of Gwenvael the Handsome.

"See?" she said. "That was not so bad, was it, beautiful dragon?"

"Vipers!" Gwenvael accused the women, yanking his arms free. "Horrible, vicious vipers!"

He stalked to the door, stopping beside Dagmar. "And you!"

"I know you're angry, but Bercelak will never allow you to lead one of his legions with all that hair."

Gwenvael pointed a damning finger. "This betrayal will never be forgotten."

"Gwenvael—"

"*Ever!*"

"So pretty," Nika said to her sisters. "But such a big baby about a little hair."

"Shut *up*," Dagmar snarled, yanking the hair from the Rider's grasp. "And never speak of this again."

"But—"

"Ever!"

Elina watched in fascination as Gwenvael the Handsome sobbed on Talaith's shoulder.

"His hair?" she asked Celyn again.

"He loves his hair."

"Yes, but—"

"You're thinking again. Logically. When it comes to

my royal kin. Why? Really. I mean . . . why? Logic . . . not involved here. Even in a little way."

"Then I shall stop."

"It's for the best. You'll just give yourself a headache."

The sobbing grew louder, and Elina was about to leave just so she wouldn't have to see any more when Kachka walked into the hall, followed by the other Riders who'd accompanied her.

"Sister!" she called out. "You are not dead!"

"Not yet."

Celyn shook his head. "That's a lovely greeting between sisters . . . *and what were you thinking!*" he suddenly bellowed at his younger sister, who'd walked in with Aidan the Divine of the Mì-runach and King Gaius.

"Are you yelling at me?" Brannie demanded. "*At me?*"

"Yes, at you! First off," he said, shooting out of his chair and storming over to his sister, "you don't ask Mum if you can go off with this idiot to fight the battles of Irons!" He glanced at Gaius and muttered, "No offense," before yelling at his sister again. "And second, *I'm* in charge of you! Me! Not him! And not Mum!"

"She's my general! I take orders from her! Not some idiot who used to fly into walls."

"*I was still learning!*"

Unable to stand a second more of this, Elina stood and walked out of the Great Hall, grabbing Kachka's arm as she passed and pulling her along.

"You are part of that now," her sister reminded her.

"I am . . ." Elina's words faded off when she realized that King Gaius had followed them out. If he'd kept walking, she would have assumed he'd used their exit as an excuse to leave such a ridiculous argument between siblings. But he didn't keep walking. He stopped by Kachka's side. Looking as if he rightfully belonged there.

That's when Elina asked, "Have you two been fucking again?"

Before Kachka could reply, Gaius leaned down, smiled, and said, "Yes!"

Kachka rubbed her forehead.

"She won't admit it, Elina, but it's been great."

"Go away."

"To our room?"

"It is not—" Kachka stopped. Took a moment. "Just go," she said finally.

Gaius leaned in and kissed Kachka on the cheek. He started to walk down the stairs, but suddenly turned around and fled back inside. Elina didn't know why until Keita charged up the stairs after him, yelling, "Yoo-hoo! King Gaius! You must see the new colors of patches I have for you and your missing eye!"

"So," Elina said, trying not to smile, "a king husband. That is impressive, sister."

"He is *not* my husband."

"No. But I have seen that look before. Fearghus has it when Annwyl screams at the walls that she will not be forced to hire the stonemason. Briec has it when he argues with Talaith about damaged fruit. Gwenvael has it when he watches that tiny, weak Northlander order big soldiers around and they listen. She cannot even take down an elk, but there you go. And King Gaius . . . he now has that look for you."

"I do not want to have this conversation."

"Because you know I am right."

"Because you need to shut up."

Trying to pretend that she wasn't bonded to that Iron dragon, Kachka motioned to all the activity in the courtyard.

"They're getting ready?" Kachka asked in their native tongue.

"Yes. They will be going to war. As will you, I'm guessing, sister. Now that you are the Scourge of Gods."

Kachka shrugged. "I guess."

"You should. You are very good at it. Even our mother could never deny that."

"And you?"

"Stay here. Like a man, I will guard the children here."

"The children here need no guardian. But protecting the home has no shame either. If they get past us, the tiny Northlander will need someone like you at her side."

A sudden din of loud voices stopped the sisters' conversation and they watched the Kolesova sisters come down the stairs, hugging and greeting each other with loud cheers.

"Elina Shestakova!" Zoya Kolesova greeted. "Are you as happy to see your sister as I am to see mine?"

Staring straight at her, Elina replied flatly, "No."

Kachka snorted and quickly looked off.

"Me, too!" Zoya replied, her arms around two of her sisters, as Nika led the way, most likely to the closest pub.

"What are Zoya's sisters doing here?" Kachka asked when they'd gone around the corner of the house.

"They've come here to seek an honorable death at Annwyl the Bloody's side."

"Oh," Kachka said with a nod. "That makes sense."

Aidan found his sister where he least expected it. On the top of the battlements of Queen Annwyl's home. In her dragon form, staring out over the land that she'd never seen before.

He landed beside her.

"I thought you'd be at Devenallt Mountain."

Eyes closed, letting the wind blow against her face, Orla replied, "Queen Rhiannon sent me here. Don't know why."

"She has a good sense of things, our queen."

"She kept Mother and the others close by, though."

"Of course she did."

"Will they be safe?"

"As long as they're not stupid."

Orla finally looked at him. "So . . . no then?"

Aidan laughed, glad his baby sister's sense of humor hadn't left her completely.

"You'll be safe here, Orla," he promised her.

"But you're not staying. Are you?"

"I can't. Not now."

"And Father?"

Aidan blew out a breath. "With the dwarves. I guess. I don't know if we'll see him again. At the very least, we probably won't see him for a while."

She shrugged. "He never liked me anyway."

"You will stay here, won't you?"

"Where would I go?" she asked forlornly.

Aidan nodded in agreement before noting, "Your darkness is magnificent, by the way."

"It *is* a lost art." She gave what some might call a very small smile. "Cheeky bastard."

Gaius was on his bed, letting his sister know he'd be home soon and to get the vote from the Senate so the legions would be ready to move as soon as he was there, when Kachka walked into the room, slamming the door behind her.

"What is wrong with you?" she demanded.

"So many things, actually. Yet my handsome face and strong nature make it all meaningless."

"My sister thinks we are bonded now."

"We are. Just admit it."

"I will admit nothing. But I will especially not admit *that*."

"So," Gaius said, choosing his words very carefully, "you're saying you're not strong enough to love me?"

Kachka, her hand on the doorknob, froze. "What?"

"Well, to bond yourself with a dragon in a world that looks down on that sort of thing . . . takes a special kind of strength."

She faced him again, shaking her head. "You manipulate like a royal," she accused.

"No, Kachka. I manipulate like a king." Gaius slipped off the bed, eased his way around her. "A *war* king. Imagine that. Imagine what we can do together during this war. The Rebel King and the Scourge of the Gods."

Behind her now, Gaius leaned in, nuzzled her ear, slid his hands around her waist.

"Duke Salebiri and his fanatics will loathe and fear us in equal measure."

"I will take no orders from you. I will let no male rule me. Dragon or otherwise."

"I don't want to rule you. We work together. A team."

"Eh," she grunted, clearly not happy with that description.

"At least try it."

"Fine. As long as we understand each other."

"We understand each other perfectly."

Gaius kissed her neck, stroked her hair. He'd begun

easing her toward the bed when the door opened and Keita swept in, several multicolored eye patches in her hands.

"Look what I have for you, King Gaius!"

Kachka spun out of Gaius's arms and slammed her hands against the She-dragon's chest, shoving her back into the hallway.

"Away with you, female!"

"Rude cow!"

Kachka slammed the door in Keita's face and threw the bolt down.

She then shoved Gaius toward the bed while snarling, "I should have killed that She-dragon the first time she suggested my sister wear a dress."

"See, Kachka Shestakova?" Gaius said, falling back on the bed and happily watching her yank down his leather leggings. "We are *perfect* together."

Epilogue

The arguing had been going on for almost three hours now. A few fights had broken out.

Lætitia had seen this coming. Had warned Aggie to be prepared. She'd been right. Senator Tyrus Gabinius of the House of Gabinius—an important human family—had ranted and raved about sending out their legions. The fight had started on Southland territory—why was that a problem for them?

And, as in all politics, Tyrus had those loyal to him. So the Senate was now divided. Many were for sending out legions before Salebiri became too big to fight. The others disagreed strongly.

Aggie, however, was about at the end of her tether. Her brother might enjoy all this back-and-forth, but she didn't. Not when the stakes were this high.

She glanced to her left. The Mì-runach who protected her stood close to her chair. It wasn't called a throne, but that's what it was. And, like any monarch would be, she was tempted to unleash them on all these idiots.

A bad decision, she knew, but still . . . the temptation was definitely there.

Aggie gave the dispute another thirty minutes before she was utterly and completely done.

"My lords," she said, but the dragons and human ignored her. "Senators, please."

Still they argued on, until Aggie stood. She took in a breath and then unleashed her flame against the thick marble floor. It melted the stone in the middle, a zigzagging line going straight down the aisle separating the arena seating.

The Senators immediately fell silent, and Aggie carefully folded her hands in front of her.

"Senators . . . normally, I would enjoy all of this brilliant and exciting discussion. Debating the pros and cons of the issues of the day. But that is a luxury we no longer have. Not anymore."

"So," Tyrus Gabinius stated loudly, "you're going to force us into a decision. Is that it? Well, the House of Gabinius will not agree to a declaration of war." He stepped down from the seats into the middle of the aisle, arms thrown wide. Like the finest orator in the land.

Aggie walked down the small steps from her chair to the Senate floor. With her hands still clasped in front of her, she made her slow, methodic way to Tyrus. When she was finally in front of him, she said, "The majority of the Senate has made its decision. So, Tyrus Gabinius, deny us this, hold your legions back from what the Empire needs . . . and my brother and I will take *everything* from you and your family. We will leave not enough for even the crows to dine upon."

She gave a small smile. "Do you understand me, Senator?"

He didn't respond, but she didn't need him to. She nodded at the others. "Senators. Always a pleasure."

With her piece said, Aggie made her way out of the Senate,

the Mì-runach right behind her as she walked back to the palace. She was nearly in her throne room when Lætitia suddenly stepped in front of her, blocking her path.

"You have a problem," Lætitia announced.

"And good afternoon to you, Aunt."

"I don't have time for niceties. Not after what your brother's done."

Assuming her aunt had somehow heard about Gaius's clash with Vateria, she replied, "I will *not* discuss my brother's decisions with you. That's between us."

"And that barbarian!"

Confused, Aggie asked, "What barbarian?"

Gripping her arm, Lætitia dragged Aggie down the hall and into the throne room.

"*That* barbarian," she announced, pointing a damning finger at the woman sitting on Aggie and Gaius's throne. She didn't sit there like a queen, but as if she'd just slumped down in the seat because it was available.

"I know her."

"You do?"

"Yes. Back in the Southlands. Gaius helped her sister or something. I don't see what the problem is, though."

"He was kissing her."

Aggie blinked. "Pardon?"

"You heard me."

"Aggie!"

Aggie pulled away from her aunt and ran across the room into her brother's arms. He lifted her up and spun her. She kissed him on both cheeks.

"I'm so glad you're safe," she told him when he finally put her back on the ground. "And that you did the right thing."

He frowned a bit. "You sure?"

"Absolutely." She pressed her hand to his cheek. "My brave brother."

She glanced at the woman still sitting in their throne. "I see you've brought a friend."

"Yes." He led Aggie to the woman's side. "Aggie . . . this is Kachka."

"You will not give her my whole name, dragon?"

"I love her too much to torture her with all that."

"I remember you. You and your sister."

"Elina."

"Do I get an introduction?" Lætitia asked.

"Well—"

"*Gaius*," Aggie cut in before her brother could say something they'd all regret.

He took a breath. "Lætitia Clydia Domitus. This is Kachka Shestakova."

Lætitia suddenly stepped back, eyes wide. "You . . . you brought the Scourge of the Gods here?"

Aggie frowned. "The Scourge of the what?"

Gaius tapped Kachka's shoulder. "Hey, look at that. Your name has made it to the Empire. Look how terrifying you've become."

"How can you joke about this?" Lætitia snapped.

"What do you care, royal, that I am Scourge of Gods?" Kachka flatly asked their aunt. "Have you committed some great sin that will bring me to you as punishment?"

"No."

"Then do not worry." She stood. "While my comrades bathe in your giant tub, I will go out and hunt something down for dinner."

"I'm sure we have enough food in the kitchens for everyone," Aggie offered.

"I do not need your pathetic sheep to feed me."

"Lovely girl," Aggie said to her brother.

"Isn't she great?" he asked, his grin spread across his

entire face. Aggie couldn't remember the last time she'd seen him so happy.

"Are you two kidding?" Lætitia snapped. "I mean, that woman—"

"Could you excuse us, Aunt Lætitia?" Aggie asked.

"I—" she began, but when Aggie snarled a little, the She-dragon threw up her hands. "Fine! But we're not done discussing this!"

They waited until their aunt had stormed off; then they began giggling.

"She is never going to forgive you, brother," Aggie said around her laughter.

"I know. But some things simply can't be helped."

"Is your barbarian worth it?"

"More than you realize."

Happy for her brother, Aggie hugged him just as they heard Aunt Lætitia yelling at Kachka Shestakova's comrades somewhere in the palace, which probably meant they were using her bath.

"I'll deal with it," Gaius said, pulling away from his sister. He got a few steps before he stopped and said, "Oh. I wanted to give you this."

Aggie scrunched up her nose when her brother held out a sword to her.

"What do you want me to do with *that*?"

"I got it from . . . someone. It's not really for me, though. But Kachka suggested that I should probably teach you a few things. It never hurts to be able to defend yourself during a war."

"But I've got the lugheads," she reminded him, gesturing to the Mì-runach who stood on the other side of the throne room door.

"*Aggie.*"

"Oh, all right! Give it to me." She snatched the weapon

from her brother and watched the color drain from his face as he stumbled back a few feet.

"What?" she asked. "What's wrong?"

Gaius suddenly grabbed her arm and dragged her into a small dressing room just off the throne room. There he pulled her in front of a large standing mirror.

"Oh . . . my."

The elaborate silver armor covered Aggie from head to foot. Even the sword was no longer plain.

Aggie shoved the weapon back into her brother's hands and, as soon as she no longer held it, the armor was gone and she was back in the dress of a Sovereigns ruler.

"Put that somewhere . . . away," she told him.

"But—"

"*Away.*"

Gaius took his sister's hand. "I'll get it a sheath. Put it by your bed. If you ever need it, especially while human, it'll be there." He squeezed her hand. "All right?"

"All right." She licked her suddenly dry lips. "Where the hells did you get that thing anyway?"

"From a god. A very helpful god. Who knew exactly what I needed. To keep you safe whether I'm with you or not."

Aggie shook her head. "You do understand that we didn't have these problems until we allied with the Southlanders?"

"Aggie, we can't blame them for everything. Just most things."

Arms around each other's waists, the twins returned to the throne room, where Kachka Shestakova now stood, a dead and extremely large boar with one arrow through its head hanging around her neck.

"It was right outside," she explained. "Where are kitchens? Or should I butcher it here in this giant room?"

Aggie cleared her throat and pointed. "Down that hall and to the left."

Kachka Shestakova walked away, a hearty trail of boar's blood following her.

"Well, brother, I have only one thing to say about that barbarian woman."

"Which is?"

"She is *magnificent*."

Gaius's wide grin returned. "Isn't she? And the best part—"

"—she will irritate poor Aunt Lætitia to within an inch of her life."

"She will," Gaius promised. "And Kachka will enjoy *every* minute of it."

Books by Bestselling Author
Fern Michaels

More from Bestselling Author
JANET DAILEY

Calder Storm	0-8217-7543-X	$7.99US/$10.99CAN
Close to You	1-4201-1714-9	$5.99US/$6.99CAN
Crazy in Love	1-4201-0303-2	$4.99US/$5.99CAN
Dance With Me	1-4201-2213-4	$5.99US/$6.99CAN
Everything	1-4201-2214-2	$5.99US/$6.99CAN
Forever	1-4201-2215-0	$5.99US/$6.99CAN
Green Calder Grass	0-8217-7222-8	$7.99US/$10.99CAN
Heiress	1-4201-0002-5	$6.99US/$7.99CAN
Lone Calder Star	0-8217-7542-1	$7.99US/$10.99CAN
Lover Man	1-4201-0666-X	$4.99US/$5.99CAN
Masquerade	1-4201-0005-X	$6.99US/$8.99CAN
Mistletoe and Molly	1-4201-0041-6	$6.99US/$9.99CAN
Rivals	1-4201-0003-3	$6.99US/$7.99CAN
Santa in a Stetson	1-4201-0664-3	$6.99US/$9.99CAN
Santa in Montana	1-4201-1474-3	$7.99US/$9.99CAN
Searching for Santa	1-4201-0306-7	$6.99US/$9.99CAN
Something More	0-8217-7544-8	$7.99US/$9.99CAN
Stealing Kisses	1-4201-0304-0	$4.99US/$5.99CAN
Tangled Vines	1-4201-0004-1	$6.99US/$8.99CAN
Texas Kiss	1-4201-0665-1	$4.99US/$5.99CAN
That Loving Feeling	1-4201-1713-0	$5.99US/$6.99CAN
To Santa With Love	1-4201-2073-5	$6.99US/$7.99CAN
When You Kiss Me	1-4201-0667-8	$4.99US/$5.99CAN
Yes, I Do	1-4201-0305-9	$4.99US/$5.99CAN

Available Wherever Books Are Sold!

Check out our website at **www.kensingtonbooks.com**.

More by Bestselling Author
Hannah Howell

__Highland Angel	978-1-4201-0864-4	$6.99US/$8.99CAN
__If He's Sinful	978-1-4201-0461-5	$6.99US/$8.99CAN
__Wild Conquest	978-1-4201-0464-6	$6.99US/$8.99CAN
__If He's Wicked	978-1-4201-0460-8	$6.99US/$8.49CAN
__My Lady Captor	978-0-8217-7430-4	$6.99US/$8.49CAN
__Highland Sinner	978-0-8217-8001-5	$6.99US/$8.49CAN
__Highland Captive	978-0-8217-8003-9	$6.99US/$8.49CAN
__Nature of the Beast	978-1-4201-0435-6	$6.99US/$8.49CAN
__Highland Fire	978-0-8217-7429-8	$6.99US/$8.49CAN
__Silver Flame	978-1-4201-0107-2	$6.99US/$8.49CAN
__Highland Wolf	978-0-8217-8000-8	$6.99US/$9.99CAN
__Highland Wedding	978-0-8217-8002-2	$4.99US/$6.99CAN
__Highland Destiny	978-1-4201-0259-8	$4.99US/$6.99CAN
__Only for You	978-0-8217-8151-7	$6.99US/$8.99CAN
__Highland Promise	978-1-4201-0261-1	$4.99US/$6.99CAN
__Highland Vow	978-1-4201-0260-4	$4.99US/$6.99CAN
__Highland Savage	978-0-8217-7999-6	$6.99US/$9.99CAN
__Beauty and the Beast	978-0-8217-8004-6	$4.99US/$6.99CAN
__Unconquered	978-0-8217-8088-6	$4.99US/$6.99CAN
__Highland Barbarian	978-0-8217-7998-9	$6.99US/$9.99CAN
__Highland Conqueror	978-0-8217-8148-7	$6.99US/$9.99CAN
__Conqueror's Kiss	978-0-8217-8005-3	$4.99US/$6.99CAN
__A Stockingful of Joy	978-1-4201-0018-1	$4.99US/$6.99CAN
__Highland Bride	978-0-8217-7995-8	$4.99US/$6.99CAN
__Highland Lover	978-0-8217-7759-6	$6.99US/$9.99CAN

Available Wherever Books Are Sold!

Check out our website at
http://www.kensingtonbooks.com